THE GHOST
RUNNER

THE GHOST RUNNER

A Makana Mystery

PARKER BILAL

B L O O M S B U R Y

NEW YORK · LONDON · NEW DELHI · SYDNEY

Published by Bloomsbury USA, New York

All papers used by Bloomsbury USA are natural, recyclable products made from
wood grown in well-managed forests. The manufacturing processes conform to
the environmental regulations of the country of origin.

LIBRARY OF CONGRESS CATALOGING-IN-PUBLICATION DATA HAS BEEN APPLIED FOR

ISBN: 978-1-62040-340-2

First U.S. Edition 2014

1 3 5 7 9 10 8 6 4 2

Typeset by Hewer Text UK Ltd, Edinburgh
Printed and bound in the U.S.A. by Thomson-Shore Inc., Dexter, Michigan

Prologue

Denmark, February 2002

The wind cutting across the dark, deserted streets was an icy blade that dug deep into his bones. He shivered and, for the millionth time, cursed his luck at having landed in this country. Seven years he'd spent here and not a day went by when he didn't wish himself elsewhere. A warm place at least, if not home. The weather and the constant reminder of his being different. It had strengthened his sense of purpose. That much was true. If he had never known Westerners before coming here, now he felt he knew them well enough to last a lifetime. His features, his skin, his faith, all marked him apart. For seven years he had lived as a shadow. They looked down on him, almost as if they expected him to apologise for his existence.

A gust of icy wind cut short his thoughts. It whipped through any amount of clothing you cared to put on. It made his head ache. It was inhuman to expect anyone to live under these conditions. The rain that poured down day after day, week after week. The locals didn't seem to care. The way it ran off their backs they might have been ducks. Muttering a silent curse under his breath, Musab hugged the cheap jacket to him and carried on walking. Already he was beginning to think he might cut short his evening stroll. The wind that shook the bare trees made him uneasy and he had the sense that something unearthly was about to come down on him. As if summoned from his thoughts, a handful of snowflakes flew out of the darkness to strike his face. He let out a groan of dismay. Underneath the long parka he wore a gelabiya and beneath that a set of thermal underwear he had purchased from a Turk bandit in the market in Aalborg. The kuffar had overcharged him, despite all the *aleikum salaam*s that Muslims used in this forsaken corner of the earth to lull you into a false state of trust.

Pausing for a moment at the corner, Musab turned to gaze back the way he had come. The large black Transit van was still there. Its lights were off, but from time to time he could make out movement inside the darkened cab. He was not unduly worried. He was aware that PET, Politiets Efterretningstjeneste, the Danish intelligence services, were keeping an eye on him. It wasn't surprising. In the last few months everything had changed. Ever since the attacks on the United States last September they had taken a renewed interest in him. The people of this country had taken the attacks personally, as if they had been launched against them, not against the great Satan of the United States. Sentimental. They sucked in all things American unquestioningly, so that their own culture was barely distinguishable. He had watched from his living room, images of the Twin Towers tumbling down. It had dug deeply into him, a sense of pride, yes, not that he had been involved in any way, but at the audacity of it, the nerve to pull off the most spectacular attack in history. Carried out by young brothers, devoted to the jihad. He had watched the images on the news of people weeping in the streets here. They took it personally. They held memorial services, in schools and warehouses. The nation wanted to send a message of sympathy. It made Musab laugh. How stupid. But he felt the change soon after that. Taxi drivers were dragged from their cars and beaten, for wearing a turban. Nobody cared if it wasn't Muslim. Women had their headscarves pulled off in the street. Children were set upon by their classmates. He himself was spat on in a train station. Nobody turned a hair. It was as if 9/11 had released a hatred that had always been there, simmering just below the surface. That was when they had hauled him in. Once, twice, three times. Always the same questions. Did he know of any attacks planned for this country? Did he understand that his permission to stay in this country was conditional on his co-operation? This was a bluff. They were legally bound to defend his right as a political refugee, no matter what his opinions were. That much he knew. The Danes prided themselves on being progressive, on defending the weak and the downtrodden. They couldn't just turn on him now. His lawyer had made this clear. They couldn't touch him. So instead, they kept an eye on him. It wasn't a problem. He had noticed little signs. Phone calls where nobody was there when you lifted the receiver. Amateurs. They left little traces of their presence everywhere they went.

Laughter and music spilled over him as a car rolled by. A young man stuck his head out of the window and yelled something that was snatched away by the wind. A bottle flew by to splinter against the ground as the car accelerated away in a trail of curses and cackling howls. Drunken fools on their way to hell. The music sank into the silence as the car disappeared around the next corner with a screech of rubber. There was a chance they would come back, if it amused them to humiliate him further.

Musab had spent three years in an asylum holding centre, a rusty old passenger ferry docked in Copenhagen harbour, while waiting for his application to be processed, for the various offices to verify his story, to investigate his claim that he was a political dissident. In the end they concluded he was telling the truth, that if he ever went back to Egypt his life would be in danger. They granted him the right to stay in this country, fruit of their noble aspiration to be seen as civilised and humane. It made him laugh. Where else in the world would he be treated like this? They had no idea what things were really like, away from their fairy-tale land. Still, they didn't just set him free. There were conditions. The state declared he was to be sent to a remote town in Jutland. It might as well have been the moon. There was nothing and no one here. The long winter nights were interminable and the wind was cold and merciless. At night the lights on the fishing trawlers in the harbour bobbed on the water, the sea as slick and heavy as diesel oil.

His face was numb with cold, his lungs ached with every breath. In the distance he could make out the hum of cars passing on the motorway. Really he had nothing to complain about. His needs were taken care of. He had a roof over his head and there was no work for him. The state provided him with clothes, furniture, food, spending money. Musab was in no doubt that if he went home he would be arrested, just being abroad under these circumstances would have made him look guilty of something. And if there was one thing in life he didn't want to do it was return to an Egyptian prison. So he bided his time though the idea of returning home was never far away. He longed for the familiar sounds and smells, to be among people like him. Sometimes the loneliness was so bad he wondered if death might not be a better alternative.

Another car raced by, disturbing his thoughts. A halo formed around the street lights, each orange orb glowing like a matchstick.

The snow was now blowing in thick flurries, out of the darkness, across the bare fields beyond the houses. The soft flakes filled the air like weightless insects, glowing like warm silver in the orange glow of the overhead lights.

The Transit van slid up behind him, a smooth, silent shadow that he felt rather than heard. His woollen cap pulled down tightly over his ears. Overhead, the tops of the tall trees stirred in the wind. He had just begun to turn when something hit him from behind, pushing him to the ground. The air was knocked out of his lungs and he lay on the icy ground, stunned, unable to move. A snowflake landed on the pavement in front of his face. He watched it, suspended between the blades of a tuft of grass. For a brief second it remained there. Then it vanished and was gone for ever. It was the last thing he was to remember from this place. A jolt of current went through his body and he blacked out.

When he tried to open his eyes he found that he couldn't. He felt an engine surging beneath him. His body was numb. Through the narrow gaps around the blindfold he caught a fleeting glimpse of light and shadow hurtling past him. Then he passed out again. When he woke up he breathed in the dragon's breath of aviation fuel, heard the screech of jet engines warming up. Now the cold vanished from his bones, replaced by fear. His feet scraped along the tarmac as he was carried between two powerful men, then up a short flight of steps. His wrists were strapped together. He could not feel his legs. A needle went into his arm and the world seemed to float away from him. The engines rising to an insane scream as they hurled along a runway. He lay like a corpse, unable to lift his head.

After that there were confused snippets. Flashes of the world turning around him. A glimpse of unfamiliar stars through a porthole. The jolt of a landing. Voices. Again into the air. The same plane or another? Some part of him was aware that he ought to be taking note of what was happening around him, but the rest of him was so far gone that he didn't care. He was floating in a stream of warm fluid. Even turning his head was a challenge. Night passed into day and then night again. The next time he opened his eyes he was shivering inside a narrow cell so dark he could not see his hand in front of his face. He was naked but for a filthy diaper around his loins. It stank like a cowshed. Where was he? He was hungry and freezing. Most of all he was scared. He seemed to have fallen off the end of the earth. The door was flung open and two men stood there. One of them opened up the jet of a high-pressure hose and he was flung back against the wall by the force of the water. It was so cold he felt his heart stop. He gasped for air, convinced he was going to die, to drown, or have a heart attack. When the water subsided the two men entered. They threw a set of clothes at him. Underwear and a jumpsuit and waited for him to dress. Then they manacled his feet together and tied his wrists with a plastic loop that dug into his skin. Then he was inside another aircraft, only different, bigger this time and more noisy. He was stretched out on his back on a hard floor that vibrated with the hum of powerful engines. His eyes were covered.

'You can forget about the world you know, buddy,' came the voice of a man bending over him to check his bindings, 'you're a ghost now.' Then the rising whine of jet engines and the movement of air around him. He lost track of time and sensed they were approaching their final destination.

He smelt it first. A familiar stirring in his memory. And the warmth of the air. No longer the frozen Nordic climate. No snowflakes and ice. A flutter in his heart told him this was the dust he had known as a child. He began to struggle again, twisting and wrenching himself from side to side, feeling the thin plastic bands digging into his wrists and ankles. The metal floor of the transport plane was hard against his back. He sensed they had stopped moving and lay still. He heard the whirr of a hydraulic system and sensed, rather than saw, the rear cargo door lowering. Then he felt the sun touch his face, and the slow spread of warmth over his body. His limbs seemed to be coming alive. The way a king might stir when the door to his tomb has been broken open after being buried for centuries. Like Ramses, meeting the dawn as the sun crept in along stone passageways.

Instinctively, he tensed as a pair of boots approached. Someone knelt beside him. 'Relax,' a voice confided in Arabic, 'you don't need to fight any more. You're home.'

I

Cairo

April 2002

(4 months later)

Chapter One

A necklace of tail lights arched across the skyline like a twisted rainbow. No two pairs were quite the same. Red was not always red, but perhaps a shade of orange, a garish green or even blue. Here and there the carnival spin of a twirling amusement flashed in a rear window to alleviate the boredom, coloured lights bursting like tiny explosive charges. Many vehicles showed no lights at all, either because they were defective or because their drivers found them an unnecessary expense. Makana had had plenty of time to study the subject. Years in fact, and tonight the Datsun had been stuck in traffic for what felt like hours but was probably only about forty-five minutes. They were now suspended in mid-air on the 6 October flyover in Abbassiya. Like upraised horns, the twinned minarets of the Al Nour Mosque rose up alongside them.

The whirling carnival lights around the rear window of the minibus ahead of them were a distraction that ticked away in the back of Makana's head, as was Sindbad's constant stream of earthy comments and philosophical insights. The real focus of his attention was a black car just ahead of them on the right. It was quite a distinctive-looking vehicle. Old. Makana guessed at

3

least thirty years. The first time he had seen it he had had trouble identifying it.

'What is that?'

'That, ya basha?' Sindbad licked his lips in anticipation, always pleased to show off his knowledge. 'That is Benteley. English car. Very good quality, from the old days of the *Ingleezi*.'

It was a source of wonder to Makana where Sindbad ever came up with such nuggets of information. He never seemed to read anything but the sports pages and yet a layer of information, a seemingly random sample of obscure and unrelated facts, had built up in his head, like a sandbank deposited in the Nile over centuries. It could hardly be said that he was a connoisseur of automobiles, since he was content to drive around in this well-beaten bucket of a Datsun, yet some part of him aspired to the craftsmanship and quality of an entirely different class of car.

The distinctiveness of the Bentley made it a little easier to follow. Tonight the sole occupant of the car was a small, compact man, who wore a set of expensive, ill-fitting and rather worn suits. Short-legged and paunchy, he cut an awkward figure who looked as though he had dressed in a terrible hurry. His shirt collars were never straight, his tie was badly knotted. His name was Magdy Ragab, a wealthy and highly respected lawyer in his late fifties. His dull appearance matched his daily routine. For almost a week now Makana and Sindbad, alone or together, had followed the lawyer as he was chauffeured from his home in Maadi to his office downtown and back again. He visited the legal courts, briefly, ate lunch at his desk and worked long hours, often not finishing until nine or ten at night. It was eight thirty now, which was early for him to be heading home. The cars ahead of them slid forward, bringing them to within two cars of Ragab's Bentley, the right-hand lane having not moved. Sindbad

4

cleared his throat, which suggested he had something on his mind. In anticipation, Makana lit a cigarette.

'How much longer do you think she will need to decide his innocence?'

Sindbad's question implied their subject was innocent. Proof was always hard to find in such matters. According to Islamic jurisprudence three witnesses were required to prove adultery, a demand that had always struck Makana as a neat way of sidestepping the issue. After all, what were the chances of locating three people willing to swear a couple had been engaged in sexual relations? But of course it never went that far. Guilt by association. Two people seen talking together was often all the evidence needed to condemn them. In a society preoccupied with purity, sex became an unhealthy obsession. Displays of physical affection were frowned upon in public, even between married couples, which didn't make Makana's job any easier. How do you prove infidelity? The usual signs were gifts, clothes, a car, an apartment where they could meet in secret. For a man, it was possible to engage another woman in an informal contract of marriage without too much difficulty. It was harder for women and the consequences were harsher. Many husbands didn't care too much about evidence. They were only too happy to apply their own brand of justice, which was often less forgiving than the courts might be. The mere suggestion of infidelity could ruin a woman's reputation. Often such cases ended in an impasse. The person who suspected their spouse of infidelity allowed the investigation to go on until they decided enough was enough. Patience ran out, or money, or nerve. Then it could go either way. Makana had, on occasion, been summoned to bear witness before an impromptu hearing in the presence of a judge, but that was rare, and even then inconclusive. Men responded predictably when confronted with evidence against them. Stringent denials on the heads of their mother and children and anyone else they could think of. Those not prepared to swear their innocence inclined to violence. Grown men hurling themselves across the room to try and strangle their wives for having spied on them, oblivious to the people around them, let alone the judge.

What Sindbad was really asking was how much longer they could expect Mrs Ragab to pay them to follow her husband around. They had seen no evidence of infidelity on his part. In Makana's view, Mrs Ragab would probably never be fully convinced that her husband was not planning to desert her for someone else. She was overbearing and difficult to deal with. Certainly, she did not give the impression of being the kind of woman to turn a blind eye to her husband's errant behaviour. In her imagination perhaps there would always be a younger woman somewhere waiting for Ragab to come to her. All Makana could do was report back that so far Ragab's behaviour was about as normal as you could hope for.

The Datsun had slid forward another few metres to where it was almost parallel with the Bentley, bringing Makana to the point where he was sitting alongside Ragab. Turning his head, he glanced across. The lawyer sat staring ahead at the two rows of cars that rose upwards ahead of them like an illuminated path to the stars. What was going on in his mind? For the first time in a week he had broken with routine. For the first time he was heading in an unexpected direction. And he seemed preoccupied, glancing at his watch and tapping the steering wheel impatiently. The right-hand lane began to move. As it did so, Ragab glanced sideways. His eyes met Makana's. It was only for a fleeting moment, but it was probably enough.

'Better change lanes,' Makana said.

Since he had begun to work for him on an irregular basis a few months ago, Sindbad had learned the futility of objecting to Makana's requests, no matter how unreasonable they appeared. He still had to fight the reflex to protest, but he now knew that trying to convince Makana to see the world the way most people did was like trying to make the Nile flow the other way. Sooner or later you had to accept it wasn't going to happen.

'*Hadir, ya basha*,' he muttered, swinging the wheel to cut into the next lane, causing consternation and some hooting. Makana could see Ragab tilting his head to watch them in the rear-view mirror. If he didn't already realise he was being followed it wouldn't take long at this rate. The switch to the right lane proved to be a wise move. Ahead of them the cars were moving, filing past a stalled minibus whose passengers were standing around. Some admired the view, lighting cigarettes as if they were on an excursion to an exotic planet, oblivious to the discordant serenade from the cars stacked up behind them. Others observed the driver and his young assistant, no more than a boy, as they knelt behind the vehicle and rapped optimistically on the motor with a hammer, as if hoping to scare it back into life.

'Stay close to him,' Makana warned, as his resistance caved in and he reached again for the packet of Cleopatras in his jacket pocket. Something told him they didn't need to be too careful. Ragab had almost looked right through him.

Once off the overpass the traffic resumed its usual insane dance, cars hurling themselves into the fray with reckless abandon. Makana was reminded once more that he was still a stranger here, even after all these years. The Khartoum he had grown up in was really no more than a rural backwater compared to this. Sparsely populated with cars, there always seemed to be enough room to get around at a leisurely pace. The truth was that he preferred Sindbad do the driving, despite the added expense, if only because it left him free to think.

The Bentley slid away from them, passing swiftly through the streets. The dazzle of bright lights reflected in its shiny surface as it sped past the window displays, the flashing neon, and startled mannikins. Bulbs swarmed into arrows, names, invitations: Rahman Fashions, Modern Stylish, Happyness, BabyBoom. A polyglot babel of movie titles, brands, logos, all swimming together in the fluorescent glow like a form of delirium. Then the lights cut away and the Bentley flitted off beneath the trees, slipping into the dark like a moving shadow.

'He's not taking his usual route,' Sindbad announced, speaking Makana's thoughts aloud. They had turned west, towards the river instead of continuing south in the direction of Maadi. A few minutes later they found themselves doubling back, travelling again in the direction of downtown along the Corniche. Ahead of them the big car pulled in to the side of the road.

'Slow down as you go past him and let me out up ahead,' said Makana. When they rolled to a halt under a tree he indicated for Sindbad to stop. 'Wait for me here,' he said. Then he got out and walked back along the busy road.

The Bentley was parked in front of an ugly modern building with a smooth façade that stood out against the lower, more aged apartment blocks on either side. The car was in an area marked off from the road for visitors by an arrangement of chains and metal posts. Makana watched as Ragab ignored a greeting from a uniformed doorman who rushed eagerly about securing the Bentley in place. Makana entered a lobby that ran straight through the building from front to rear. Two lifts stood on either side. When Ragab stepped inside one, Makana followed suit. He could have played safe and waited in the lobby, but by

8

now he was fairly confident that Ragab was preoccupied enough not to notice him. Moving past, Makana stood quietly in the corner behind the other man. Ragab stared at the floor, oblivious of the world around him. On the eighth floor the doors pinged open and Makana hesitated only for a second before following Ragab out. To the left were a set of glass doors on which the words Garnata Health Clinic were painted. The woman on the reception desk glanced up and, when Makana pointed discreetly at the rapidly disappearing Ragab, went back to her work.

The clinic was quiet, modern and empty. At the far end of the corridor lay a waiting area complete with a view over the busy road; beyond that lay the dark gleam of the river and the lights of Dokki on the other side. Ragab had continued down another corridor to the right. Halfway down he entered a room on the left. Makana sat down and picked up a magazine filled with pictures of smiling celebrities he had never set eyes on in his life. The only other person in the waiting area was a man with a mottled head and a tube going into his arm. His nose and mouth were covered by a transparent mask. Beside him stood a tall canister of some kind of gas. Makana flicked through the magazine. After a time a male nurse appeared and wheeled the other man away without a word. When they had gone, Makana got up to stroll over and take a look in the direction of the room into which Ragab had disappeared. The two men almost collided.

Ragab stepped aside without looking up. Makana was fairly certain that he was crying. Tossing the magazine into the heap on the coffee table Makana made his way down the corridor to the room Ragab had emerged from. It was slightly ajar. He could hear nothing from within so he knocked lightly and when there was no reply he pushed the door gently open and stepped inside.

Chapter Two

In the middle of the room was a single bed. The figure lying in it appeared to be covered by a tent of transparent plastic. Makana pushed the door quietly behind him and paused a moment to take stock of the situation. There was no movement from the direction of the bed. No sign that his presence had been detected, only the hum of the machine alongside it which appeared to be some kind of pump. A thick tube fed from this into the side of the plastic tent. Above the machine a screen registered the patient's heartbeat as a series of beeps that drew a green line running from right to left. Makana stepped forward to where he could get a view of the patient and felt his heart momentarily stop pumping the blood in his veins.

At first he thought he was looking at a mummy. It was hard to tell if the figure inside the tent was a man or a woman. Even being certain it was human took some measure of the imagination. Makana had seen corpses smoking in the aftermath of a fire. The skin charred black and the features dissolved in melting fat. In this case, the face looked like a wax mask carved by a sculptor with an unsteady hand. The eyes were thankfully closed.

Most of the hair had been burnt clean off the skull, leaving only the odd tuft of fine blackened wool here and there. An alien from another planet. The blackened hand that rested on the clean sheet was small and crisscrossed with livid scars. Around the tiny wrist a strip of plastic had been fastened with something written on it. Leaning closer, Makana could make out the name, Karima Ragab, and today's date. Who was she? A second wife? The child of another marriage? The fact that Mrs Ragab was not here, nor any other member of the immediate family, suggested this was Ragab's own private matter. So who or what was he looking at? He leaned in for a closer look. It was a young woman, her forehead was broad and her features more rough than delicate. It was the face of a peasant girl, simple and open. What was she to Ragab, and what had happened to her? Before he had much time to think the door opened behind him.

The woman who stood in the doorway was tall, not much shorter than Makana himself. She wore a long coat buttoned up and down. Underneath this she appeared to be wearing dark trousers and a polo-neck jumper. Her head was wrapped in a tightly bound scarf, a dark-blue colour. Her eyes were quick and intelligent.

'Doctor?'

Makana shook his head. Something told him he wouldn't manage to pull that one off with this woman. But she too seemed keen to avoid confrontation. In a matter of seconds she had sized him up and apologised before backing out again. In the time it took for Makana to cross the room and step into the corridor she was already at the far end and turning the corner by the waiting area.

Makana made his way back to the reception desk. The woman sitting behind it looked up at him. She had seen him come in with Ragab and assumed, naturally enough, that they were together.

'There was a woman here a moment ago. You don't happen to know who she is?'

'No, I'm sorry, sir. Is it important?'

'Probably not,' Makana looked concerned. 'It's just that Mr Ragab has asked me to take care of matters and I don't want him to be bothered any more than necessary at this time.'

'Of course,' she nodded, eager to comply. She was young, in her late twenties he guessed, and she was working late which suggested she was not married.

'Were you here when she was brought in?'

'Oh, no. That was this morning. I work the nights.'

'Always? Isn't that difficult for you?'

'No, I prefer it. It is quieter, generally.' She observed him carefully. 'You work for Mr Ragab?'

'Yes.' In a manner of speaking it was true, although Ragab wasn't aware that his wife was using his money to pay Makana. 'For legal reasons, I shall need a copy of the full report from when she was brought in.'

'You mean our register or do you want the police report as well?'

'Both please,' Makana smiled and glanced at his watch. 'So long as it isn't too much trouble?'

'Not at all,' she said, getting to her feet. 'I'll do it straight away.'

It took her five minutes and Makana had a moment to take another look around. It was an expensive private clinic. There were dozens of them around the city, of varying standard, but this was clearly one of the nicer ones. When the report came, Makana took a moment to glance over it. 'What are the chances of her recovering?'

'Perhaps you should talk to one of the doctors.'

She lifted a phone and a moment later a young man in a white coat appeared.

'This gentleman works for Mr Ragab. He wants to know about his daughter.'

The doctor frowned. 'I explained all of this to Mr Ragab earlier.'

'I understand that,' Makana insisted, 'but I will be dealing with the legal side of things, so I need a full briefing. Of course, if you're too busy, Doctor . . . Hamid,' Makana leaned forward to read the name tag on the doctor's coat, 'I can ask Mr Ragab himself. Although obviously, considering the pain he is going through . . .'

'Oh, no, that won't be necessary.' The doctor cleared his throat. Working for a legal company had a certain effect on people. Clearly the doctor knew he was on to a good thing working here. He also knew that Ragab was an important client. He didn't want to upset either.

'Well, obviously, it's a very serious situation, I'm afraid. The chances of her surviving are frankly not good. She has eighty per cent burns as well as extensive lung damage. The skin is a physical organ, just like the heart or liver. The body can only regenerate so much.'

'You've seen cases like this before?'

'You're asking how much experience I have?' The doctor snapped, then he reconsidered. 'I have seen cases like this before. Perhaps not quite so extreme. They occur quite often in the state hospitals. This method of suicide is quite common among the lower classes.'

'Suicide?'

'That would be my conclusion, yes.' The doctor glanced at the receptionist. 'If you need a second opinion . . .'

'I'm sure that won't be necessary. Mr Ragab has full confidence in your work. He knows you are doing your best.'

'That's very generous of you,' the doctor murmured.

Makana sat on the top deck of the *awama* and watched the lights of the traffic on the bridge as it swept by, the gravelly roar of engines broken by the occasional flutter of a musical horn on a microbus or a taxi. It was close to midnight and it showed no signs of relenting. He found it had a hypnotic, almost calming effect on him. At a distance the hectic, nervous energy became a mild distraction, like the stars in the sky. Aside from the traffic, the night was calm and cool. Nearby the faint sound of studio laughter reached him from the little shack on the embankment where Umm Ali and her children were gathered around yet another tireless game show.

On his lap lay the copy of the report prepared for him by the reception at the clinic. The fire in which the girl, Karima, had been so badly burnt had occurred at an address in the old part of the city, close to the Ghuriyya mosque. An area where the heart of the historic city was ground down on a daily basis by modern decay and neglect. Neighbours had alerted the emergency services when smoke and flames were seen coming from the location in the early hours of the morning. The victim was still conscious when she was removed from the wreckage and she was the one who had given the police the name of the lawyer Magdy Ragab. When contacted, Mr Ragab had insisted that the victim be transferred to a private clinic whose services he subscribed to.

What connection was there between this girl and Ragab? The police report was inconclusive. A cheap household kerosene stove was believed to have been the cause of the fire. Whether it had been started deliberately or not, they couldn't say. Nobody else had been in the location, given as a first-floor flat over a shop at number 47, Sharia Helmiya. Not the kind of neighbourhood you would expect to find a man like Ragab.

Makana tossed the report onto the desk and got to his feet. The image of the girl lying in the hospital bed had been seared into his memory. The sight of her ravaged face floated in the air before him. Going over to the railing, Makana lit another cigarette and leaned over to look down into the dark swirl of moving water.

For ten years Makana had been haunted by the memory of his departure from his old life and his entry into this one. Over and over he had run through events in his head, the moment when the car containing his wife Muna and his small daughter Nasra had toppled over the side of the bridge into the river; the same river that ran now beneath his feet, although over a thousand kilometres further upstream in Khartoum. Was that what had drawn him to this precarious houseboat, the need to be near the memory of them, he wondered?

His recollections never produced any astounding insights or revelations, except the obvious one; that he ought to have been able to find another way to escape, particularly from Mek Nimr – the man who had stepped into his shoes, taken over his office and dismantled the criminal investigations department Makana had run. That one moment seemed to define him. Then, eight months ago, out of the blue, came the possibility that Nasra was still alive.

At the time he hadn't known what to make of it. There seemed to be no way of verifying the rumour. Makana realised now that he had never quite believed the story, until this evening. The moment he had stepped up to that bed in the clinic and looked down into the oxygen tent to see the frail, tortured body, he understood that deep down inside of him he knew Nasra was still alive. This evening, as he looked down into the disfigured features of that poor girl in the hospital clinic his mind had fused the two together; his daughter and the girl who lay dying before him.

Chapter Three

Mrs Ragab was waiting for him in Groppi's garden the
following morning. A trio of waiters were fussing around
her table. The place looked forlorn and abandoned. The ground
needed sweeping, the tablecloth had a tear in it. The tea provided
was not of the right sort and the staff lacked the proper training.
Mrs Ragab appeared to have taken it upon herself to correct all
of the obvious defects and was pointing out in no uncertain terms
what needed to be done.

'You can't employ people who look like poor relatives recently
arrived from the *rif*.'

As if summoned to stand as evidence, a young man with a
club foot sidled up with a fresh pot of tea that hung at an angle
so that it dribbled from the spout onto his shoes. Mrs Ragab
pointed.

'Look, just look at him. It's not his fault, but you have stan-
dards to maintain. This place has a reputation, or at least,' she
cast a withering glance over her surroundings, 'it used to.'

The man she was lecturing was a bald, nervous man wearing
a salt and pepper moustache and an oversized waistcoat that
made it look as if he had lost weight overnight. Wringing his

hands he began waving the club-footed waiter away, who started to go and then seemed to lose purpose and so loitered, uncertain what to do with the teapot he was holding.

Mrs Ragab was a formidable woman. She could, Makana was certain, be fairly terrifying under the right circumstances. A large-boned woman with an oversized head and dyed blonde hair that appeared to be clamped in place by an invisible net. There was nothing particularly feminine about her. The heavy make-up she wore rendered her face more grotesque than appealing. She looked as if she might eat the waiters for breakfast if there was nothing better on the menu. The head waiter scowled at Makana as he scurried away, herding his flock of minions before him.

Clutching a perfumed lace handkerchief to her nose, Mrs Ragab ushered Makana to be seated. Leaning towards him, her powdered chin almost brushing the tablecloth, she spoke in a dramatic whisper, despite the fact there was nobody within hearing distance.

'They don't wash their hands after doing their business.'

Unable to come up with a suitable response, Makana opted for silence.

'That's why I insist they boil everything. Never eat anything that isn't boiled.'

'Mrs Ragab, perhaps we could get to the matter of your husband?'

'Yes, of course. I assume that the reason you asked to meet in this place at such short notice is because you have something for me?' She fixed him with a wary eye. Mrs Ragab had come to him by a roundabout route. It seemed she had a cousin who owned a number of hotels and news had reached him of a certain person in the tourist trade whom Makana had helped out with a

18

problem. Even then it had taken some time and not a little effort on Makana's part before she was convinced he would be capable of undertaking the task in hand.

'Such cases are not as rare as one might think,' he had told her.

'Really?' she looked at him disbelievingly. 'I personally have never heard of such a thing.'

Nevertheless, she agreed to hire him for a trial period and so for a week Makana had tailed Ragab back and forth across the city. He had engaged Sindbad's services and they had taken turns sitting outside his office in case he dashed out on foot. But nothing. Until now.

'Mrs Ragab, certain facts have come to light that I think we need to discuss.'

'Facts? What facts?' Mrs Ragab looked taken aback. Gold jangled as she clutched at her throat with a sharp intake of breath, almost as if being strangled by invisible hands. 'If this is some scheme to try and extort more money out of me, I can tell you now that you can save your breath.'

'This is not about more money, though I should point out that so far I have worked for a week and not received any payment.'

'I explained this at the outset. I don't believe in paying in advance for services I have not yet received. Surely you can understand that? Lots of your clients must feel the same.'

Actually, most people understood that Makana began working the moment you engaged him and that everybody needed something to tide them along: a deposit, an advance, call it what you will, but Makana let that one go.

'Tell me what you have learned about that useless husband of mine.'

'It seems that your husband has not been entirely forthright with you, Mrs Ragab.'

'So you have found something!' Her eyes glistened.

'When we first spoke, you told me that you have no children.'

'Must you stick that dagger into my heart yet again?' The painted eyes widened in disbelief. 'We have already established this fact. Do you think I would need your services if Allah had been generous enough to provide us with offspring? A man needs a son. He needs children, if only to prove to the world that he is indeed a man. And what of my feelings? Do you think it is easy for a woman of my age to listen to her friends reporting on the progress of their children? This one to be a doctor, that one an engineer. They try to sympathise by asking why I don't adopt some poor black orphan from Africa, with God knows what diseases. No, Mr Makana, I have no children.'

Makana allowed the tide to wash over him before he put forward his next question. 'Do you know if your husband has any children from a previous marriage?'

'Previous marriage? What are you talking about?'

'So, as far as you know, your husband has no other children?'

'How dare you presume you have the right to ask me such intimate questions?' She frowned at him as if she were addressing a mentally deficient waiter.

'A little before three a.m. yesterday morning, a young woman was admitted to the Garnata Clinic, which I think you know.'

'Of course I know it. We have been members of that clinic for years.'

'Karima Ragab. Does that name mean anything to you?'

Mrs Ragab frowned. 'Are you saying she is a relative of ours?'

'She was admitted as your husband's daughter.'

Mrs Ragab sat in stunned silence. 'That can't be,' she murmured.

'I can assure you, Mrs Ragab, that it is. The girl is seventeen years old and her bills at the clinic are being paid for by your husband.'

'It's a very exclusive clinic, of course,' said Mrs Ragab, examining the backs of her hands, 'not to mention expensive, but I insisted. *I* did. I said, in matters of health there is no point in trying to cut corners.' Mrs Ragab paused, having temporarily lost her way. The head waiter fluttered around the table like a large vulture, a broad smile on his face and a fresh teapot in hand. The smile wilted when Mrs Ragab shooed him away and he beat a hasty retreat.

'Seventeen, you say? The man has no shame!'

'The girl may not survive. In fact, it is probable that she will die.'

'I find all of this very disturbing. I knew nothing of this girl's existence until you told me just now.' Mrs Ragab's mood had changed. The fury had been replaced by confusion and she seemed to see the man sitting opposite her for the first time.

'You have children of your own?' Makana couldn't see the relevance of the question. Mercifully, Mrs Ragab wasn't expecting an answer. She clicked her tongue. 'Men are all the same. Indifferent on the outside but sentimental as an old woman on the inside.'

'How long have you been married, Mrs Ragab?'

'Fifteen years in August.'

'So, it is possible that this girl could be from a previous marriage.'

'I told you. I know nothing of any previous marriage. Believe me, that is not the kind of thing that one can keep secret, not even my husband.' But as she spoke her face grew thoughtful and Mrs Ragab stared into the distance.

'If the girl dies,' Makana went on, 'there is bound to be an investigation. Your husband's name would come out.'

'A scandal, you mean? No, my husband has enough influence to make sure that will never happen.'

'I was thinking that perhaps this is the time for a meeting with your husband.'

'The three of us, you mean? Oh, no, that would never do. I shall take care of this myself.' With that she heaved herself up out of the chair and straightened her skirt. 'I wish they would get some more comfortable chairs. I suppose it comes from employing people more accustomed to squatting on the ground.' She hesitated as she began to move off, and then said, 'You must consider our business terminated. Please send me your bill and you will be paid whatever I owe you. '

'I'll send someone over.'

'Please do that.'

Makana watched her march away. He somehow doubted this was the last time he would see Mrs Ragab. The waiter with the club foot was brushing dead leaves off the next table. He looked across at Makana with a certain degree of empathy.

'Can I get you anything, *ya basha*?'

Amir Medani's office resembled a cave stuffed from floor to ceiling with paper. There were reams of it. Piled high in stacks, along the walls, on shelves, overloaded bookcases, tables. It was tempting to think that nothing ever happened here, but Makana knew from years of friendship with the lawyer that despite the rather humble setting, the rundown building, the cracked windowpanes and the doors that had to be scraped closed, a great deal went on in here. In the outer office, telephones were constantly ringing. At the other end of the line there might be an ambassador or a minister, an assistant to a head of state or official of the United Nations or European Union. Amir Medani knew all of them and his reputation reached far beyond the confines of these noisy, dusty rooms. His assistants all knew Makana and they waved him through to the inner sanctum. Amir Medani had a face that could only be described as lived in. It seemed to carry all the sleepless nights and worries etched into it. His eyes lifted from the paper he was reading, a pair of glasses set up on the crown of his head.

'Don't tell me, I died and you've come to offer your condolences.'

'How have you been?' asked Makana as he crossed the room to the window. As usual it was hard to see anything through the grubby glass and what he did see wasn't encouraging.

'How am I? I'm fine. More to the point, how are you? And where have you been?'

'You know how it is.'

'I'm not sure I do,' said Amir Medani, leaning back and folding his hands. 'Why don't you tell me?'

Makana detected a certain irritation in the other man's voice.

'I see you're busy as usual.'

'We're always busy. The world is in a serious mess right now. Ever since the attacks on America all the rules have been thrown out of the window. People are being arrested all over the place. No procedure.' Amir Medani tossed his paper aside and scrabbled about the table for a lighter and a cigarette.

'Have you heard anything?'

'You can't do this, you know,' Amir Medani exhaled slowly, his face vanishing beneath a wreath of smoke. 'Disappear for months and then just turn up without an explanation.'

'What explanation would you like to hear?'

'What explanation have you got?'

For a while the two men stared at one another, then Makana turned back to the window and Amir Medani sat back in his chair with a long sigh.

'You can't let this business get you down.'

'I think she's alive,' said Makana without looking back.

'You don't know that for certain. Nobody knows.'

'I'm sure of it.'

'Really? How? How can you be sure your daughter is alive? Just because that fool said she was? He was playing you. He was playing all of us, and look where it got him.'

Amir Medani was referring to the one-time artist and entrepreneur Mohammed Damazeen, who had first told Makana that Nasra was still alive in Sudan. Damazeen had been trying to get Makana to help him with some dirty deal he was setting up and which ended up killing him.

'I told you, I made enquiries. Your old sergeant Mek Nimr is now a high-ranking officer inside the National Intelligence and Security Services. He is protected twenty-four hours a day. He lives behind a barrier where nobody can touch him.'

The most shocking part of Damazeen's story was that Nasra had been taken in by Mek Nimr into his own home. Why would he do something like that? He had tried to destroy Makana and indeed had come close to killing him. He might have succeeded if Makana had remained in Khartoum. Instead he managed to escape, though the price he paid had been the life of his wife and daughter, or so he had believed for ten long years. It made no sense for Mek Nimr to take Nasra into his own home, except that in a certain, twisted way, it made perfect sense. If he couldn't get his hands on Makana, then he could make sure he had control over the one thing in this world Makana held dear above all else: his daughter.

'Mek Nimr makes a point of employing only people from his own tribe. His personal servants, cooks, drivers, messengers, all of them are Shaiygia like him,' Amir Medani was saying.

Whenever Makana heard news from home he found himself musing about what it was that was going on there. For the last thirty years the country had buried itself in the fantasy of a religious utopia constructed along the lines of an intolerant brand of Wahhabist Islam, transposed from the Arabian Peninsula and enforced with a level of violence unseen since medieval times. Islam as the solution to all evil. Naturally, this vision excluded vast swathes of the population, whose citizenship was now deemed conditional on their accepting these new rules. Makana was among the last to give up. An old-fashioned idealist in some ways, he had always believed the people would come to their senses and restore the country to one in which diversity was a strength rather than a pest to be extinguished like vermin. A country in which it was not your race or your religion which decided your status, where honesty and right distinguished you, not just professions of piety.

'I thought about going back.'

'That would be the stupidest mistake of your life,' said Amir Medani, stubbing out his cigarette in the overflowing ashtray. It pained him to see his friend in this state. 'Look,' he said. 'I still have a lot of contacts and sooner or later one of them is going to come through. In the meantime I suggest you don't do anything rash. Are you working?'

Makana nodded. The question brought back the image of the girl, Karima, lying on the bed in the clinic.

'Well, that's what you need to focus on.' Amir Medani had got up and come round the table towards his friend. 'Nasra wouldn't want you to waste your life away. She'd want you to go on.'

'You say that as though you agree she's alive,' said Makana. 'Maybe that's what you need to believe.'

By the time Makana arrived back at the riverbank, the sun was setting and the *awama* was bathed in a deep magenta glow. There was a surprise waiting for him. Up on the busy roadside a car was parked under the big eucalyptus tree whose branches hung down over the steep bank like a protective hand. Not just any car. A Bentley. As Makana climbed out of a taxi and made for the path leading down to the houseboat, the car door opened and an awkward-looking figure climbed out. He came towards him and held out his hand.

'Mr Makana,' he said, 'I am Magdy Ragab.'

Chapter Four

Aziza called out a greeting as they descended the winding path, now dissolving into pools of shadow. Umm Ali's youngest daughter was growing up. She was almost fourteen now and as tall as her mother.

'Good evening, Aziza.'

'I see you've met your guest.'

'Yes, thank you.'

'If there is anything you need . . .'

Aziza had recently taken it upon herself to act as a personal secretary to Makana rather than just being the daughter of his landlady. She and her younger brother were all that remained of Umm Ali's little brood, the eldest boy was in the army and Aziza's older sister had vanished and was said to be living with a shoe repairer in Bulaq. Nobody had seen her for months although Umm Ali would regularly inform him that as far as she personally was concerned, the girl was dead to her.

'Shall I bring coffee, *ya basha*?'

'Yes, thank you, Aziza, that would be kind of you.'

Makana gestured for Magdy Ragab to continue along the path that led down the bank, past the rickety shack that was home to Umm Ali and her two children, to the water's edge and the wooden structure that was Makana's home.

The *awama* had recently undergone some much needed repair. When a part of the roof had collapsed during the rainy season, Makana decided it was time to invest some of his own hard-earned cash in the services of a carpenter. If it had been left up to Umm Ali she would have waited to see the whole thing collapse into the river before loosening her purse strings. So the path had been widened and made more manageable in the slippery turns coming down the bank. A friend of a friend recommended a decent carpenter asking reasonable rates and eventually a solid wooden walkway with a handrail had replaced the old plank that bridged the muddy gap between the river bank and the lower deck. Downstairs window shutters were fixed and door handles replaced, and Makana now had what passed for a dining room with a table and chairs which, though rarely used, gave the place a touch of respectability. The carpenter had even thrown in an old wardrobe he had found cluttering up his yard, so now Makana had somewhere to hang his clothes instead of the odd nail hammered into the wall. They climbed to the upper deck where the roof had been fixed and the flimsy walls reinforced and linked together to form a structure that could hold at bay the cold wind that blew off the river in winter. Large double doors now separated the main office area from the open deck at the rear, which remained open most of the time. Cupboards and filing cabinets had taken the place of cardboard boxes for storing his archives and his files. And there was a new set of chairs along with the old one and the battered old sofa pushed against the wall which he often slept on. The window frames had been restored to working order and the glass replaced. The overall effect had a marvellous impact on his humour and the simple act of sitting in his big chair and contemplating the changes tended to improve his mood.

'Mr Ragab,' he ushered his guest, 'please take a seat.'

There was something inherently awkward about Magdy Ragab. A creature of routine, it was possible he was uncomfortable in surroundings that were not familiar. In any case, he seemed not to register Makana's words or perhaps did not feel inclined to sit. Either way, he remained standing in the middle of the room, fidgeting with his hands behind his back, eyes fixed on the distant bridge, where a procession of stick figures, now burnt silhouettes against the light of the setting sun, were making their way home alongside a slow-moving slurry of vehicles of every shape and size.

'You know who I am?'

'Yes, Mr Ragab, I know who you are.'

'Of course you do.' Ragab rolled his shoulders as if trying to shake off his skin. Makana went on. The fact that the man felt ill at ease was perhaps not so surprising seeing as he was talking to someone who had been investigating him for the last week.

'You are a highly respected lawyer. You have your own practice which employs three other lawyers, all junior to yourself, along with about a dozen administrative staff. You started out in criminal cases but now specialise in corporate law. You have a very good list of clients, within some of the top companies in the country. Bankers, industrialists, businessmen of one kind or another. You have contacts in the upper echelons of the military, as well as a good number of politicians and a few television personalities. They trust you because you work hard. You have a reputation for thoroughness and efficiency. You work long hours and you rarely take a full day off. You live alone with your wife Awatif, who is your second cousin on your mother's side.

You have no children . . .'

Ragab nodded his approval. 'I inherited the practice from my uncle, on my mother's side. He was also the one who gave me the Bentley. It's a nineteen seventy-three model and still going strong. They used to make cars to last.'

Makana reached for his Cleopatras. Ragab watched him closely.

'You have done a thorough job,' Ragab went on. 'My wife warned me that you were a rather strange character of dubious background, and that I should have nothing further to do with you, and frankly . . .' He paused to allow his eyes to flicker quickly around his surroundings. 'I have to say this is a rather more unconventional setting than I had expected.'

'It grows on you,' said Makana, blowing out a match.

'I have no intention of letting it do so. I came here because my wife confronted me. She accused me of having deceived her and asked for a divorce. Of course she did not mean this seriously. To a woman of her age and social standing divorce would make no sense. Still, I understand that her pride was hurt. When I asked her how she had learned of these things she told me about you. I came to see where my money had gone.' Ragab allowed himself a smile, presumably because this was the closest he could come to a joke.

'Well, while we're talking about money, I haven't actually—'

Ragab cut him off. 'Please, let me finish. You have been spying on me for over a week now. Spying on me. I think you at least owe me the chance to speak my piece.'

'As you wish,' said Makana, gesturing for him to continue. For his part, Ragab stood apprehensively, hands clasping and unclasping behind his back.

'The truth is, I understand the work you do, perhaps better

than you think. I myself have employed people much like your-self, which perhaps explains why my wife had to reach out beyond the familiar circle of associates to find you.' Ragab stopped himself from going on. Clearly there was some kind of barbed comment on the tip of his tongue which he felt was best left unsaid.

'Mr Ragab, your wife suspected you of infidelity. There's nothing particularly remarkable about that. She wanted to know the truth and she has a right to try and find out. She believed you were keeping another woman, perhaps even another wife, and she worried this would have consequences.'

'That is a very liberal, and if I may say so, convenient explanation.'

'In my experience most cases can be resolved amicably. What I bring to the marriage, if you like, is a degree of openness.'

Ragab smiled again. 'You missed your calling, sir. You would have made a fine lawyer.' Pushing his hands into his pockets, Ragab moved towards the window to look out at the river. 'My wife has a lively imagination. As a young woman she was drawn to a career in the theatre, although I am glad to say that common sense prevailed. Nowadays she is a keen patron of the arts, and knows a good number of artists personally.'

'That must be nice for you both,' said Makana. It wasn't that he had anything against the theatre as such, although he had not visited one since his wife was a university student. 'Frankly, the only thing that interests me at this moment is that girl lying in the clinic and how she got there. I assume that is why you are here.'

'You assume correctly.' Ragab looked momentarily taken aback. He dropped his head for a moment and stared at the floor.

'So let's drop all this business of your social credentials. You don't have to impress me. Why don't you tell me why you are paying for Karima's medical care. Is she your daughter?'

'She isn't, or rather, she wasn't . . . Karima passed away two hours ago.'

The image of the creature in the hospital bed came back to him. It was hard not to feel relief for anyone who had suffered so much and yet Makana felt his heart tighten a notch.

'The doctors did everything they could but they were unable to save her.'

Ragab swayed on his feet and Makana gestured for him to sit. This time Ragab hesitated only for a moment before lowering his frame into the chair. It was a new addition. The carpenter had tried to persuade him to part with the old wicker chair that had been on the *awama* when he first moved in and had been on its last legs. Makana couldn't bring himself to throw it away so instead conceded to the purchase of a Louis XIV wooden chair that resembled a throne. It was more comfortable than it looked and had stout carved legs and heavy arms. The carved back was inlaid with mother of pearl. It had been lovingly restored by the carpenter and seemed more suited to the palace of a khedive of old than to Makana's *awama*. It wasn't a Bentley, but still.

'Why did you register her as your daughter at the clinic?'

There was a long silence. Finally, Ragab stirred. He passed a hand across his face.

'That was necessary for technical reasons. My policy covers members of my family. It is not a big issue, but it avoided certain problems in admitting her. I wanted the best treatment for her and the alternative would have been to leave her to the state medical system, which as I'm sure you know would have been tantamount to a murder sentence.'

'So you lied to get her admitted.'

Ragab blinked. He didn't like being accused of lying. 'The director of the hospital is aware of the details.'

'A theatre lover perhaps? Happy to bend the rules for an old and loyal client?'

'Something like that.' The faint suggestion of a smile flickered around Ragab's lips. Amused perhaps at the ease with which the world arranged itself around his needs. 'You don't like me. I can tell.'

'What difference does it make?'

'None, maybe. Perhaps it could be an advantage.'

'Did Karima kill herself?'

'That's why I wish to employ your services.'

'You want to employ me?'

'You seem surprised. I don't believe in letting sentiment cloud one's decisions. You clearly know your job. For an entire week I was unaware that I was being observed. And your past reputation is well documented.' Ragab nodded beyond Makana at the array of newspaper clippings pinned to the wall above the desk, most of them written by Sami Barakat. 'I checked up on you and made a few calls. Apart from that I consider myself a good judge of men, Mr Makana. I believe you will do your utmost to pursue this matter to a conclusion. Contrary to popular belief, money does not buy commitment. It buys obedience, devotion to the source of the money, but not to the task in hand. Commitment is a commodity one cannot buy for love or money.'

'I'm honoured,' murmured Makana, inhaling smoke deep into his lungs.

'There is another reason, which, once I have explained the outlines of the case to you, I am sure will lead you to the same conclusion.'

'You have my attention.'

Ragab's big hands had stopped gripping the arms of the chair. As he spoke he appeared to be more at ease.

'Most of the people I employ for surveillance or investigative work have a history. That is to say they are usually retired from the police or intelligence services. This has advantages, of course, because they can draw on old contacts for information from within. But in this case, I believe that could be the source of a conflict of interests.'

Makana stubbed out his cigarette. 'Is this connected to your relationship to the girl?'

'Eighteen years ago I was appointed to defend a young man in court. His name was Musab Muhamed Khayr.' Ragab brought his fingertips together in a steeple and lowered his chin in concentration. 'He was a delinquent, a petty criminal charged with selling contraband, mostly cigarettes and alcohol smuggled from Libya. I found him to be not only an unpleasant man to deal with, petty and violent, but also untrustworthy. I hardly believed a word he told me. Still, despite my feelings about him personally, or my disapproval of his actions, I had been entrusted with his defence and this was what I carried out to the best of my abilities.'

Makana noted an air of old-fashioned righteousness about Ragab. A man resigned to the fact that chivalry was dead, that the world was full of people lacking in moral fibre. It was a hard burden to bear, but he was doing his best.

'What happened?' asked Makana.

'Musab was sentenced to five years. It was a harsh sentence, especially for his wife, but he did not help himself by being impertinent towards the judge who naturally took a disliking to him. The smuggling of alcohol is regarded with some severity by many in the judiciary.'

'He was expecting you to get him off the charges?'

'Exactly, he thought he would not go to prison. It astonishes me sometimes how people allow themselves to be deluded in this way.'

'It's an astonishing world.'

'Yes.' Ragab nodded solemnly. 'Anyway, as the case came to a close I discovered that Musab's wife Nagat was living in quite sordid conditions. She occupied a room not fit for a cat, above a garage in Imbaba. I went to visit her in the course of my preparations for the trial. She had just discovered she was pregnant. Her husband didn't even know yet. She had no source of income. I took pity on her.' Ragab faltered. 'I can't explain why. My own father died very young and my mother struggled to bring us up, perhaps the sight of this young woman struck a chord.'

Makana wondered if there was more to it than that, although it seemed to almost go against the grain, a man of Ragab's standing to become involved with the wife of a common criminal, but human nature was nothing if not unpredictable.

'So you helped her,' he said.

Ragab got to his feet and paced around the room as he spoke. 'There were practical matters to do with the case which meant that I saw a good deal of her. She was distraught, as you can imagine. Being pregnant with her husband in prison was not an ideal situation. I did my best to reassure her.'

'How exactly? Did you give her money?'

'Yes, and with little chance of seeing it reimbursed, I might add. I also arranged for her to move into a cleaner, more comfortable place. I even found some work for her in the office of a colleague. It wasn't much, but it provided some income. I used my contacts with a local mosque that provided medical assistance to make sure she received adequate treatment. When she decided to start a business of her own, I also helped her a little with that.'

'You went to a lot of trouble,' said Makana, 'considering how you felt about her husband.'

'That was precisely the reason I felt compelled to help his wife. She struck me as being a victim herself, having been taken in by this man at a young age. She had been blind to his faults, she said, but the pregnancy had opened her eyes. She wanted nothing more to do with him.'

Ragab's large eyes blinked. The way he told it, the story certainly didn't do any damage to his reputation. Benevolence, after all, was a highly valued virtue. Although it seemed like a lot of effort for the wife of a client he didn't even like. Maybe Nagat truly had stirred some measure of compassion from Ragab's childhood memories of his struggling mother. On the other hand, maybe she had stirred something else.

'You can call me a sentimental fool, but the fact is that I felt protective towards her.'

Although in his fifties, Ragab dressed and carried himself like a somewhat older man. Now, silhouetted against the dying light, he appeared younger than his years. Makana wondered how much the domineering Mrs Ragab knew of this story.

'Perhaps I allowed myself to go too far.' Ragab licked his lips. 'When the child came I was seized by feelings I was not familiar with. I wished to protect it, to take care of it in some way.' There was a mournful slant to his eyes as they lifted to find Makana. 'My wife and I did not have the good fortune to be blessed with children of our own, and I suppose all of those pent-up feelings found an outlet in this little girl.'

'Karima.'

'Yes, exactly, Karima.' Ragab turned away and Makana saw

him wiping a hand across his eyes. 'She never had much luck, poor child. Her mother died a couple of years ago, after a long illness. Since then she has run the shop alone. Still a child and yet so grown up.' He turned to face Makana squarely. 'She didn't deserve to die such a horrible death.'

The conversation was interrupted as Aziza appeared carrying a tray on which stood a brass coffee pot and two small cups. Makana noticed that she had exchanged the worn and patched shift she had been wearing earlier for a bright dress covered in red flowers. She even had a glittery gold pin in her hair.

'Anything else I can do, *ya basha*?' she asked as she set down the tray and poured the coffee.

'No, Aziza, that will be fine.'

The girl then managed to withdraw from the room backwards. Something she had picked up from the television no doubt. A documentary about ancient emperors and kings? Perhaps he ought to pay her something? So long as it didn't go through her mother's hands.

'So Karima was born while Musab was in prison,' Makana asked as he spooned sugar into his cup. He left Ragab to help himself.

'That is correct. Nineteen eighty-four, during his first year inside.'

'She was still a small child when he came out.'

'That's right. She was barely five years old.'

'What happened when Musab came out of prison?'

'It appears that Musab underwent something of a transformation while in prison. It happens all too often. Faced with brutality they begin to question their motives. In those dark places of the soul a lot of men find comfort in turning to religion.'

It was a familiar story. Aside from the pressures on inmates to conform, there were plenty of advantages to joining one of the Islamist groups. The prisons were crowded with jihadists of every shape and shade, and many of the guards sympathised. With the right connections many of the hardships could be alleviated.

'By the time he was released in nineteen eighty-nine he had become a member of the Islamic Jihad group.' Ragab returned to his seat and reached for the tin sugar bowl. Perhaps he didn't quite have the qualms his wife did about mixing with the common people. 'Those were difficult times.'

Makana needed no reminding of 1989. It was the year everything changed for him. A new regime came to power and suddenly his position as a police inspector in Khartoum was thrown into doubt. And it wasn't only in Sudan. In Germany, the wall came down between east and west. In China, revolting students had seized Tiananmen Square. In Afghanistan, the final Soviet troops were being withdrawn.

'The world was in turmoil. You know this from your own country. It was a time of great victory for Islam, and many went from here to join the Mujahideen.'

'So Musab joined the holy struggle,' said Makana.

'He joined at the wrong time. The war in Afghanistan had been won. The Egyptians who had fought with the Mujahideen were returning home. Their victory there had led to some euphoria, the sense that the jihad was a global mission to revive Islam. Musab went abroad. Where he went I cannot say. I heard that he had been in your home country, Sudan, but also visited parts of the Soviet Union that were trying to break away: Azerbaijan, Georgia, Kazakhstan. They were trying to ignite a jihad there, to carry on the fight after Afghanistan. He spent nearly five years away. When he returned he associated with the same group of Islamist radicals as before. They had declared war on the

Egyptian state. To cut a long story short, his name emerged in a plot to assassinate the Minister of Justice. Musab claimed it was a set-up. His militant days were over, he said. I managed to pull a few strings. I knew the Danish ambassador personally. We played bridge with him and his wife. I convinced him that Musab was a worthy case for political asylum. It was the only solution.'

'Why go to all that trouble for him? Surely he was no longer your problem?'

'You are right, but I had become close to his wife and daughter. I suppose I was trying to protect them.'

'By sending him away?'

'Nagat had made it clear she wanted nothing to do with him. She had started her own business by then and was doing all right without him.' Ragab set down his coffee cup slowly. 'My first impression of the man has proved to be the most enduring. Dishonest and cowardly, a delinquent and petty thief. When he came out of prison he had taken on a . . . let us say, a more spiritual aspect. He grew a beard, wore traditional clothes, and spoke of piety and conviction, but underneath he was the same.'

'Let me ask you a question.' Makana paced across the room. 'Am I right in thinking that you suspect Musab of having caused the death of his daughter?'

'You are a perceptive man, Mr Makana.' Ragab paused to gather his thoughts. 'I have no proof. I have nothing, just my own instincts, but I am convinced that Musab was behind this.'

'Correct me if I am wrong, but I understand that Musab has been abroad all these years.'

'Seven years to be exact,' Ragab confirmed with a nod.

'Then how?'

'Who knows? Through one of his old contacts, perhaps?

Anything and everything is possible, but that is why I wish to hire your services.'

'Even if he were able to effect something like this, to arrange a fire from abroad, what would his motive be?'

'Jealousy.'

'Jealousy?'

'This is difficult for me to explain, but Musab got it into his head that I was Karima's father.'

'Where would he get an idea like that?'

'Karima was born during Musab's first year in prison, Nagat must have become pregnant just before he was arrested. He might not even have known. Musab was unbalanced, paranoid. It isn't hard to imagine how such ideas entered his head. You touched on it yourself. These people don't understand kindness. I tried to help his wife and therefore he suspected there was an ulterior motive.' Ragab exhaled slowly. 'I don't think he ever quite believed my denials.'

'Assuming you are right, why would Musab wait so long to take his revenge?'

'Who can explain what goes on in the mind of someone like that?'

Makana stepped out onto the stern deck where the sounds of the city filtered across the river. Ragab followed him out. The whirr of bats flitted through the darkness in the trees above them.

'The Musab I knew was a vicious man and a coward. Everyone who knew him testified to that fact. The wife, Nagat, died some years ago of a kidney disease. All that was left was Karima.'

'And you're sure Musab couldn't come back here himself?'

'Oh, no, that is out of the question. The state would arrest him immediately and throw him back into prison where he belongs.'

'What about contacts? Who does he still know?'

'Oh, there are plenty of people who remember him. He has contacts in the underworld. Criminals, murderers. It wouldn't be hard to find someone to do this. I can provide you with a list.' Ragab straightened up. 'All I am asking, Mr Makana, is that you bring me the evidence. Show me who did it and I will take care of the rest. I will make sure they get the justice they deserve.'

In the half-light Ragab's features seemed to dissolve, so that Makana had the impression he was addressing a large, untidy ghost. A spirit from somewhere far back in time.

'How does your wife feel about me working for you?'

'My wife knows nothing about this arrangement between us, and I would prefer to keep it that way.' Ragab reached into his pocket. 'She knows I am here this evening, but she believes it is to settle her account.' He held out an envelope. 'This contains what she owes you for services rendered.' A second envelope joined the first. 'Here I have placed the same amount as a retainer if you should choose to accept the case. We can settle up any outstanding amounts at a later date.'

Makana hesitated only for a moment before taking both envelopes. He had a feeling that Magdy Ragab was the kind of client he could get used to working for.

Chapter Five

Inspector Okasha strode down through the Ghuriyya quarter in his usual manner. As always, his commanding presence had an instant effect. The layabouts who hung around the entrance waiting for opportunity to tap people on the shoulder sidled away without a word. Pedlars shouting out their wares missed a beat, even a woman carrying a basket full of vegetables balanced on her head managed to crane her neck around without spilling a single onion. Okasha carried himself with authority. A big man in a uniform. To many around here his was a familiar face, having worked this part of town for many years, back in the old days.

'Did I tell you about the time I was stabbed?'

'More than once, I'm afraid,' murmured Makana as they descended the steps beneath the high wooden beams, finely carved and painted, that supported the roof linking the sultan's tomb to the mosque.

'My first month on the job and a fool of a man pulled a knife on me. I wasn't expecting it. We only wanted to question him but it seems we hit the target on our first try. Anyway . . .' Okasha paused to exchange a greeting with a gnarled old stick of a man who rose up from where he was squatting against the wall when he recognised the officer.

'You honour us, *ya basha*. Please come and sort out these *harafeesh*. They are only boys but they make our lives hell.'

'Don't worry about it, old man. I shall personally see to the matter.' Okasha closed with a salute to make his vow official before turning back to Makana. 'Now, where was I? So the knife went through my side, narrowly missing any vital organs. Cut straight through the uniform. Of course, that's exactly the kind of thing that makes a man's reputation.'

'And you've never looked back.'

'We caught the culprit in the end. Then he was sorry he had pulled the knife. He kept apologising. Of course, he came to a bad end, they all do.'

They had turned off the main thoroughfare and were cutting through lanes of stalls, tightly packed together, brushing by hanging garments, stacks of aluminium pots and pans of all sizes, towers of shoe boxes and sacks of coffee beans. A handful of armed police officers had been sent ahead and were now clearing the area in front of a narrow shop. The paint around the edges of the wall was burnt and blistered as was a metal sign over the entrance that was sealed by a roll-down shutter. A sergeant stepped up neatly and saluted as they approached. Okasha returned the gesture.

'Has someone sent for the keys?'

'They're just coming now, sir,' the sergeant nodded and Makana turned to see an overweight man wearing a grubby olive-green gelabiya that was open down his chest to reveal an even dirtier vest. Unshaven, his plump face was blurred by a thick moustache that was itself buried within three days' worth of white bristles. He walked with a limp, his right leg moving in a loose circle to catch up with his left. A sandal dangled like a stray leaf of lettuce that had attached itself to his foot unnoticed. As he approached he called ahead.

'*Hadir, effendi.* Here I come.' Onlookers stepped aside, as they might for a leading actor making his entry onstage. A large ring of keys jangled in his hand as he came. It was quite a performance and Makana wondered if Okasha had met his match.

'Nineteen seventy-three,' the man muttered loudly, fixing Makana with one eye. 'I crossed the canal and we taught the Jews a lesson they never forget to this day. Since then I carry an Israeli bullet in my hip, proudly.' The last word was accompanied by a thump of his hand to his chest.

'That's all very well, but can you open this door?' Okasha didn't have much time for other performers.

'*Effendi*, you ask and it shall be done.' With more huffing and puffing the man got down on his knees and began fiddling with the keys. It took longer than expected and Okasha was tapping his feet impatiently until the *bawab* eventually found the right key and the padlock was released. As the shutters rolled up the onlookers crowded round the entrance for a look, and the police officers, distracted, forgot about pushing them back.

The interior of the shop was a charred cavern, the walls and ceiling thick with soot. Mounds of blackened debris had been swept to the sides along with strange contortions of twisted metal, a chair or a shelf. Coiled springs protruded from the remains of what had been a mattress. All was now sodden in water which filled the air with a thick, putrid stench.

'What did they used to sell here?' Makana asked absently, addressing no one in particular. The answer came from an onlooker standing behind him.

'Blankets, pillows, small mattresses. All that kind of stuff.'

'It goes up the moment you bring a match near it,' another concerned shopkeeper added.

'We're only lucky nobody else's shop was affected.'

'What time was this?' Makana asked.

'It's in the report,' said Okasha, but he was cut off by one of the witnesses who elbowed himself forward.

'It was late. Most of us had closed down for the night. We went to the mosque for the isha prayer and we stayed on afterwards, just talking.'

'Then someone came in saying there was a fire down here,' carried on another.

'So, naturally, we ran back to protect our things.'

'Naturally,' agreed Makana. 'And what did you see?'

'The flames were shooting out of here, up past the windows above.'

'Worse than the fire was the smoke,' continued the second man. 'Those things give off fumes that burn the lungs clean out of your chest.'

'What did you do?' Makana asked.

'What could we do? We ran for buckets and filled them and threw them in.'

'Someone called the fire brigade, but by the time they got here it was almost over.'

'And the girl, where was she?' Okasha asked, deciding it was time to get involved.

'Upstairs,' said one of the men. 'She lived there with her mother.'

'What are you saying?' broke in the *bawab*. 'Her mother died last year. Everyone knows that.' This provoked more rumblings, agreements, disagreements.

'That's where the fire started, *effendi*,' offered the sergeant.

45

He turned to lead the way down a narrow gap alongside the entrance. It was so narrow Makana's shoulders brushed against the walls on both sides. At the back a steep, rather unstable staircase rose up the wall. It was made of uneven planks of wood that appeared to have been salvaged from a selection of sources and knocked together by a blind man. The flat was really no more than a single room with a tiny alcove for a bathroom. The floor had been badly weakened by the fire. There were gaps where thin, scarred beams showed through, centuries old. A bed in the corner of the room was covered by a stiff layer of warped black plastic.

'That's where it started,' Okasha pointed as they stepped gingerly around the edges of the room.

'She was lying in the bed?'

'That's where they found her. The mattress was made of some kind of rubber foam. It stuck to her skin. Half of her back came off with it when they tried to get her out.'

Makana looked at the way the middle of the narrow room was charred, almost like a channel leading to the bed.

'I know what you're thinking,' said Okasha, 'but it's more common than you think. People decide to kill themselves, but they can't calculate how much kerosene they need. They tend to use too much rather than too little. The girl lived alone. Her mother died a couple of years ago. We have no idea of the father's whereabouts. Apparently he lives abroad.'

'I was thinking that it looks almost as if the fire began over there, away from the bed.'

'With that kind of material all it takes is a spark,' said Okasha. 'The fire downstairs was blazing so hard they couldn't get near it.'

'So, she poured a trail of kerosene across the room and then lay down in bed and struck a match and threw it away from her?'

Okasha frowned. 'Why do you have to twist things around?'

'I'm just looking at what's in front of me.'

'You're twisting things.'

'Okay, who got the girl out?'

'The men we spoke to down below. Someone spotted the smoke. They rushed up and managed to get her out.'

'And you think they are telling the truth?'

'They have no reason to lie. They have no interest in any of this.' Okasha shot Makana a wary look. 'I understand you've been hired to investigate this for anything suspicious, but I'm telling you there's nothing to find.'

Makana let his gaze wander around the room. It seemed a sad place to end one's life, especially one so young. His eye was drawn to the streak that seemed to stretch across the room.

'You have to ask yourself why anyone would want to harm a girl like that,' Okasha went on.

'Maybe to cover something up? Did you conduct forensic tests?'

Okasha let out a soft laugh. 'Where do you think you are?' He squatted down and indicated the floor with his hand. 'After she struck the match she must have dropped the jerrycan with the fuel in. The floor is uneven. The can would have rolled towards that side, which is exactly where the fire got more intense.' He stood up again and brushed off his hands as he stood. 'Who is it that you're working for again?'

'I told you, it's connected to a client.'

'An ex-client, I thought you said.'

'Not exactly,' said Makana. Ragab had asked that he try to keep his name out of the case so Makana was reluctant to say too

47

much in front of the others who were crowded into the doorway behind them. People talked, and police salaries being what they were it wasn't hard to imagine one of them being tempted to make a little extra cash by passing the information to a journalist.

'Fine, you don't feel like telling me, that's up to you, but there's not much else to see here.'

'What about an autopsy?'

'An autopsy would only tell us what we already know. Why go to all that expense? With the backlog it could take months.'

As they turned to leave Makana noticed a photograph that had been fixed to the wall beside the door. It hung at a lopsided angle but by some miracle part of it had survived. Protected perhaps by the fact that air would have been sucked in through here during the blaze. Nevertheless, inside the frame the fire had eaten its way across from the bottom right-hand side. Protected by the glass, a corner had escaped damage. Makana rubbed away some of the soot from the cracked glass. The frame came apart in his hands. There were a few chuckles from the policemen standing at the top of the stairs, afraid to step into the room in case the floor gave way. Makana knelt and sifted through the debris until he had the blackened part of the photograph. He held it up to the light.

'What is that?' he asked.

Okasha squinted at the picture. 'It looks like a palm tree,' he concluded. 'Nothing too strange about that. There are plenty of them about.'

Makana took a closer look. The picture appeared to be of a flat, open landscape. In the desert somewhere. On one side was what looked like the edge of a big house. An outside staircase. The family home perhaps? It didn't seem to fit in this place.

'Maybe somewhere they visited once. Can't call it evidence.

48

Keep it if you like,' said Okasha, straightening up. 'All this is going to be ripped out when they rebuild the place.'

Makana tucked the picture into his pocket and took one last look around the room before following Okasha out. Back down the stairs in the street they waited while the *bawab* shut up the shop and thanked him for his help. Then, when Okasha had dismissed his men, they went in search of coffee which they found in a small place just outside the old city gates at Bab Zuwayla. Okasha sat with his back to the wall as usual, staring out at the street, eyeing everyone who went by with his usual look of suspicion.

'I was surprised to get your call. Have you been so busy these last few months you haven't had time to see old friends?'

'I've been working. Small cases,' said Makana. It wasn't much of an explanation.

'So tell me how you came to be mixed up in all this?'

'There's not much to tell really. One client led to another. You know how it is.'

Okasha sighed. 'You don't give much away.'

'The point is that my client doesn't believe she took her own life, and frankly neither do I.'

'And this is based on what, your natural intuition? A little bird told you?'

'We both know how often suicide is used to cover up an honour killing.'

'Which in this case is impossible because the girl has no other family here.'

'The father is abroad,' said Makana. 'That doesn't mean he can't arrange things from there.'

Okasha spluttered into his coffee. 'You're not serious, are you?' He mopped his moustache carefully with a pristine white handkerchief he produced from his tunic. 'Why? What motive could he possibly have to kill his daughter?'

'Maybe she wasn't his daughter.'

'This is why you won't tell me the name of your client. Now I get it.' Okasha studied Makana for a moment. 'Do you think perhaps you're taking this thing too personally?'

'How do you mean?'

'Well, it sounds to me like your client has a conflict of interests here. Either he does truly believe the girl's father did it, or . . .'

'Or what?'

'Or he's covering up his own indiscretions. Maybe that's where you should be looking,' said Okasha. 'If you want motives then start with the most obvious. Who would gain from her death? A father who lives in a foreign country, or a wealthy man seeking to protect his reputation? I assume your client is a wealthy man.'

Makana lit a cigarette and stared out at the street. He had difficulty imagining Ragab being capable of murdering anyone. He struck him as the kind who lacked courage in the final instance. Ragab was the kind who was smart enough to always find an easy way out for himself. He didn't like getting his hands dirty. Everything about him, his elevated view of himself, was a strategy to avoid conflict.

'If twenty-two years in this job have taught me anything,' Okasha was saying, 'it is that people never do anything purely for benevolent reasons. Believe me.'

Makana did believe him, everything pointed to it. Yet there was still an element of doubt that he could not cast aside. Perhaps he wanted to believe that Ragab was acting out of selfless reasons.

'In any case,' Okasha went on, 'honour killings,' he pursed his lips in distaste, 'these are not matters to involve yourself in.'

'The girl had eighty per cent burns. Can you imagine how painful that is? Even if she had survived she would never have lived a normal life.'

'I understand.' Okasha ground his teeth together. 'But that doesn't change the facts.'

'You're not saying you condone it?' Makana raised his eyebrows.

'I'm saying this country has some old ways and nothing you and I can do will change that.'

By now they were drawing looks from other people. Okasha glared around the *ahwa* just long enough to make everyone else go back to minding their own business, then he reached for his cup and took a leisurely sip. Holding the cup between thumb and forefinger to sip delicately, managing not to dampen the ends of his moustache. 'There was a woman at the scene yesterday, talking about the same thing.'

'What woman?' Makana recalled the woman who had appeared at the clinic.

'You know, one of those . . . activist types, works for an organisation, no doubt funded by some well-meaning people in Europe who feel they have a duty to enlighten us with their civilisation and whatever else they can think of.' Okasha finished his tea. 'Take the advice of an old friend and walk away from this case. You're taking it too seriously. It's affecting your judgement.'

'There's nothing wrong with my judgement.'

'This is a bad case. It's not for you. Not now, not so soon after all this with your daughter.'

Okasha sat back, having said his piece. Makana stubbed out his cigarette and got to his feet. Suddenly he wanted to be away from here, this place, this coffee shop with its noise and chatter, the street with all the chaos and confusion.

'You know that if there is anything I can do to help, anything at all . . .' Okasha stood and held out his hand. 'And no need to thank me for this morning. It makes a change from all of this hysteria about catching Al Qaida operatives. Now we are all part of the War on Terror. What do they think we were doing before?' Okasha patted Makana on the shoulder as he made to leave. 'Forget about this girl and get yourself a decent case. You need to work. We all do. It's the only thing that makes sense in this crazy world.'

For a long time Makana watched him walk away, then he lit another cigarette and turned on his heels and went the other way.

Chapter Six

Makana spent the next few hours wandering the area talking to everyone and anyone he came across. It's not hard to get people to talk. Give them half a chance and most leap at the opportunity to display the breadth of their knowledge. The real problem was always getting to the little details, the things which stuck out and which, hopefully, would eventually illuminate a way forward. Listening was tricky. It was an acquired skill. You had to give people space and time, you had to sift out what was useful from the flood of irrelevant information. You had to sniff out what was true from what was embellishment, exaggeration, fabrication, fantasy, pure lies. In other words, everything had to be tempered by a good pinch of scepticism.

Mother and daughter had set up the shop some twelve years ago, which would have meant around the time Musab came out of prison and went abroad. There was some confusion about where they came from originally. Some said Siwa, others Alexandria. There was nothing unusual about people arriving in the city from one corner of the country or another. Details grew even more sketchy when it came to why Musab went to prison, but what was clear was that he never came back here after that.

The stallholders and merchants, the porters and tea boys, all grew vague on the matter. Some said they had heard he had gone abroad, others that he was dead. Nagat had carried on. It was the girl who made the difference, explained one woman: 'That was the best thing that useless man ever did. He gave her a child and then took himself away. What more could anyone ask for?' Everyone remembered the girl, from when she was little. They wiped away tears as they recalled how she would run through the streets on errands, never too busy to talk. 'Everyone loved her.' When Nagat fell ill everyone rallied around to help out. They had nobody else to depend on. The two women were alone. 'Around here it's like one big family. Anyone who has something will give to those who don't.'

The sun was beginning to wane and people began to drift away. Makana decided it was time to pack it in for the day. He made his way back in the direction of the main road and Attaba Square, hoping to find a taxi quickly that would take him home before the rush. He had his hand in the air when a voice behind him said:

'Mr Makana?'

Turning, Makana found himself looking straight into the eyes of a young woman. The first thing that struck him were the eyes themselves. He couldn't quite work out their colour. The light from the setting sun was refracted over the rooftops of the buildings behind him, which had the strange effect of making them appear to change colour, going from brown to green, turning through a spectrum of shades in between. The second thing that struck him was that he had seen this particular set of eyes before. They darkened as he watched her.

'Yes?'

'Excuse me for bothering you. I was wondering, are you a lawyer?'

Makana shook his head stupidly. Not a lawyer.

'Only the people in the clinic told me that you were working for Doctor Ragab?'

He remembered her now. Then she had been wearing a midnight-blue headscarf. Now she wore something that was more like a turban that left her face free. She used the word doctor as a form of respect, for someone with an education. A professional. She frowned as if confused. He noticed that she was observant, taking stock of his clothes and general appearance. Makana felt somewhat like a rabbit on a dissection table.

'That is correct.' Which it was, now.

'I happened to be passing. I understand you are asking questions about Karima?'

'Did you know her?'

The woman folded her arms, determined to hold her ground.

'Might I enquire as to the nature of your business with Doctor Ragab?'

They were beginning to draw a crowd. People were stopping to see what was going on. Two fat ladies carrying boxes of cakes tied with string were nodding in their direction.

'You were at the clinic. You knew Karima.'

'Why do you use the past tense?' Her expression froze.

'She didn't make it.' Makana gestured. The fat ladies had engaged the interest of a bored traffic policeman. 'Perhaps we should walk.'

Reluctantly, she stumbled along beside him. 'Are you a journalist?'

'Doctor Ragab has asked me to make some enquiries.'

'Enquiries, into the death of Karima? You mean you don't believe it was suicide?'

'He doesn't. I am open-minded on the subject. Now it's your turn. How did you know her?'

The woman produced a card from somewhere in the folds of her outfit and handed it over.

Makana examined the card. It read: The Association for the Protection of Egyptian Women's Rights. The name printed underneath read: Zahra Sharif.

'You were trying to protect her? From what?'

'Nothing specific. I became involved with Karima some years ago. When her mother was still alive.'

'And what exactly do you do for these women?' Makana took a moment to examine her. She was slim and fairly tall. Her clothes were dark and heavy. A long coat reached down to her ankles. He recalled now that he had spotted her in the crowd, standing off to one side, when he and Okasha had emerged from the burnt-out building. Had she been following him around all day, he wondered?

'Our concern is the condition of women in general. We offer certain services, advice, the little help we can provide. That kind of thing.'

'And your interest in Karima? Did she give any indication of suicidal tendencies?'

'Not at all. Suicide is usually a cry for help.'

Makana was intrigued. What exactly was her connection to Karima? She seemed to comprise a combination of unrelenting ferocity and emotional instability. Clearly she cared. A glance up the road told Makana that the traffic policeman had lost all interest in them and was now flirting with the fat ladies who were laughing so hard they had to clutch their sides.

'Do you think she killed herself?'

'I . . . don't know.' The woman's eyes darted away, and he

noticed a tremor in her lower lip. 'Which direction are you going in?' she asked as a taxi pulled to a halt alongside them.

'Towards the river. Imbaba.'

'Can I ride over with you? We can talk on the way.'

There was no reason for him to feel that he ought to trust this woman and yet Makana felt that he could. As the last rays of the sun's light dwindled to a crimson sliver in her eye, he had the feeling that she had been crying. Her eyes were swollen and the tip of her nose was slightly red.

So he opened the car door and gestured for her to enter. Instead, she walked around to the other side and got in there. As a matter of courtesy, Makana sat in front beside the driver. The traffic through the centre of town was fast-moving most of the way. The lights were coming on, bringing with them that twilight sense of uncertainty as people emerged from the shadows of their daily routines into a new nighttime existence. The sky swirled with inky patterns as the last of the daylight was quenched by darkness. Makana recalled following the sleek Bentley through these same streets a couple of days ago. The lights flowing over the car's smooth surface as though it were tarry oil.

'Tell me about Karima?' he asked, turning to look over his shoulder at the woman who sat pressed up against the opposite door.

'I met her a few years ago. I had several cases in the area. Women who were abused, or afraid. My job basically involves counselling, talking to women, advising them of their rights, or lack of them, and offering them the resources we have available, which isn't much.'

'So did either Karima or her mother ask for your help?'

'I spoke to Nagat a couple of times. She had joined a support group for women whose husbands were in prison.'

'She had decided she wanted nothing more to do with him.'

'I got the impression he had done something very bad, a long time ago. She was very young when they married. They ran away together but over the years she realised she had made a mistake. It often happens. She wanted a divorce, but he wouldn't agree. Then he went abroad.'

The passing light swept over her face, so that he caught brief flashes of her features, like fragments of a puzzle that refused to come together to form a whole.

'How did you know where to find Karima?' Makana asked.

'I have my sources. People call me when there is something they think could be of interest.'

'Women suicides, you mean?'

'It's not always what it appears.'

Makana noticed the driver giving her odd looks in the mirror. Zahra had also noticed.

'What's that smell?' she asked suddenly.

'What smell?' sniffed the driver.

'It smells like burnt plastic.'

'La, *ya sitti*, this is an air freshener.' He pointed at a plastic pine tree bobbing from the rear-view mirror. 'It makes the air better.'

'It's making me ill.'

Makana managed to wind down the window a couple of centimetres before it jammed. The driver fiddled with the air freshener, still watching Zahra and narrowly avoiding several collisions.

'Ask him to pull over please,' said Zahra.

When they came to a halt, Zahra got out without a word. The driver began apologising again. 'It's just a piece of plastic that smells. I swear. I can throw it out. *Wallahi.*' He reached for the offending object and was holding it out of the window when Makana stuffed some notes into his hand. They were alongside the river now on the eastern side of Zamalek. A nursery under a bridge. Plants were laid out in buckets and old gallon tins that had once held olive oil. A man in wellington boots and ragged clothes wandered up and down with a watering can.

When he reached her she was standing by the metal railings. Her body was shaking and he waited at a distance as she sobbed quietly to herself. Lighting a cigarette, Makana exhaled and watched the slow-motion fireworks exploding across the river. Lights of every colour and shape, arching out of the ground on roads and flyovers, outlining the towers of the hotels and the squat insurmountable wall of the National Democratic Party. Alongside it the glow coming from the National Museum. The whole city seemed alive with ghosts that floated on electric currents. The air off the water cleared the warm petrol fug of the traffic.

'Thank you. I really think I might have fainted or something in that car.' When Makana shrugged, she gave a little laugh. 'I'm sorry, I must seem a little unbalanced to you.' A few strands of dark hair had escaped from the headscarf. Tucking them out of sight she smiled wistfully. 'It must seem very unprofessional of me to react like this.'

'You became friends with Karima.'

'It's not so strange. Some women seek legal advice, others are looking for a place to hide, but most of them just want someone who will listen, someone who cares about their problems.'

They had reached a bench that was more or less intact. It resembled a museum piece, weary from all the memories it had to bear. A long procession of lovers' names. Where were all these people now, Makana wondered? Overweight and middle-aged?

Married to other people and not knowing why? With children of their own who had no idea that here lay the evidence of the passion their parents might have once felt for a stranger?

'When I first met Karima her mother was ill. She was dying, in fact. I felt sorry for her at first and later I felt admiration. She was very brave.'

'You must feel strongly about women to get involved in this kind of work.'

'Women?' He was surprised at the vehemence in her. 'Why is it always assumed that this is a matter which concerns women alone? Don't you think men need to take some responsibility?'

Makana stopped in his tracks. 'I've never really thought about it.'

'Well, at least you are honest about it.' She turned to walk on and then stopped. 'I'm sorry,' she sighed. 'I have difficulty separating my emotions from my work. Most of the time it isn't a problem. I mean,' she laughed, 'I'm not like this every day.'

'You see a lot of cases like this?'

'Like this? No. This was special.' The breeze from the river stirred the palms overhead.

'Special in what way?'

'I'm not sure how to explain it.' She avoided his gaze, turning towards the river. 'When you have been involved in this kind of work for as long as I have you get a sense for cases.' She gave a laugh, self-conscious this time. 'I don't know why I am telling you all this. I barely know you.'

'Sometimes that makes it easier to talk.' They strolled on for a time. 'How would you describe Karima's state of mind?'

'If you're asking whether she killed herself, the answer is no.'

'What makes you so sure?'

'She wasn't the type. I mean she was angry, not depressed.'

'What was she angry about?'

'I don't know.' Zahra shook her head helplessly. 'All too often what is called suicide is simply a polite excuse for not wanting to face the truth.'

'What truth are we talking about?'

'That family honour is more important sometimes than the life of a loved one.'

'Who would kill Karima for family honour?'

'Somebody who believes his honour has been offended.'

'Musab?'

Zahra picked at a thread on her sleeve. 'All I know is that I don't believe this was suicide and I'd like to know who killed her and why.'

Musab had been out of the country for the last seven years. Why would he decide it was time to avenge the family honour?

'You don't have much faith in the justice system?'

'I would be a fool if I did.'

'Ragab hired me because he believes Karima did not take her own life. If I find evidence of a cover-up then the police will have to open an investigation.'

She looked him in the eye. 'Maybe you'd like to believe that, or maybe that's what Mr Ragab would like you to believe.'

'Now, wait a second.'

'No, I've done enough waiting.' She was furious, not so much against him as what he stood for. And what was that exactly? The legal system? The police? The male of the species in general?

'I've seen plenty of cases where nothing was ever done,' Zahra continued. 'A father smashes his daughter's head in with a stone because she was seen speaking to a boy. A brother drowns his sister in a canal because he suspects her of talking to the wrong person. Why do you think it goes on and on? Because nobody ever has the courage to stand up and change it.'

Her words hinted at a hidden menace that lurked beneath the familiar and the mundane.

'All over this city there are families so poor they only have one room. Maybe they have to share the same bed. If a father gets his daughter pregnant, is it so surprising? What is surprising is the degree to which society will go to deny it ever happened. Most people would rather not know. Far easier to simply kill the girl.'

'The police let it go.'

'Even if they didn't, the judges are always men. They understand the temptation the perpetrator was facing.' She got to her feet and Makana followed suit. The promenade along the riverbank was deserted now but for a couple holding hands.

'Ragab doesn't strike me as the type.'

'They never do. They all seem like nice, decent people.' Zahra came to a halt. 'Thank you for this, for listening. Most of the time I manage fine, but once in a while I lose my balance.'

'You don't have to apologise.'

'I wouldn't if I didn't feel I wanted to.'

With that she walked away without another word. As he watched her go, Makana realised that she had somehow raised more questions than she had answered.

Chapter Seven

Musab Khayr was the missing piece in the puzzle. According to Magdy Ragab, he was still in Denmark, the country which had granted him political asylum. Ragab claimed to have lost contact with him over the years and indeed had no way to inform him that his daughter had died, assuming he even cared about a child he had made no effort to see for so many years. Then again, Makana thought to himself, perhaps there was a perfectly reasonable explanation for that. Did he ever stop caring about his own daughter? Wasn't that what she would have concluded after all these years? Why hasn't my father tried to find me? It was an uncomfortable thought and one which dislodged Makana's mind from the track it had been on.

As he crossed the square in front of the Husseini mosque the following morning, Makana wondered if Musab could be as hard hearted as Ragab made out? Had something turned him against his wife and child? Perhaps he had changed. Who doesn't? Could he really claim he was the same person he had been when he first arrived in this city, lost and bewildered, trying to find a foothold to restart his life when the last thing he felt he deserved was to go on living? Musab had been in prison, and a lot of things could happen to a man in prison. The brief time Makana had been incarcerated all those years ago remained with him as a vivid memory. It crept up on him in unsuspecting moments. Enclosed spaces. The sound of a door closing. He avoided using lifts whenever possible. It woke him in the middle of the night leaving him drenched in sweat and kicking out, convinced that darkness was closing over him like a grave.

Aswani's was almost deserted save for the flies that buzzed furiously inside the glass-fronted cabinets, dizzy over the feast of raw meat on display. Aswani's face was the usual rumpled map, puffed up and sprinkled with a generous handful of grey bristles.

'Are you paying for him?'

'Where is he?'

Aswani nodded across the room. 'He's already eaten two bowls of humous.'

Sami was seated half concealed behind one of the ugly red pillars that jutted out like unwanted furniture at various points around the room.

'Ah, there you are.' Sami licked his fingers before extending a hand which Makana managed to avoid taking as he pulled out a chair and sat down. Unperturbed, Sami made some pretence of tidying up the debris strewn across the table: napkins, empty plates, scraps of bread. 'I ordered lamb. He has some chops which look excellent, worth waiting for.'

'Are you sure you'll have any appetite left?'

'I'm sorry, I missed breakfast this morning.' Sami grinned, restoring a certain boyishness to his face. 'You know how married life can be.'

Sami Barakat was the source of most of Makana's information

when he needed research doing. As a journalist, he had access to more archives and resources than Makana could ever reach. In addition, he had the private numbers of high-ranking army officials, ministerial assistants, press officers at a dozen embassies, as well as a field of colleagues who had their own networks. Sami's help had often proved invaluable.

'How is Rania?'

'She's fine, spends all her time on the internet. I tease her that she has more friends in New York and LA these days than in Cairo.'

Makana leaned back against the wall and lit a cigarette. The smoke wafted upwards to be gently swept in circles by the overhead fan. A gnarled old man, all bones and missing teeth, paused in the doorway and clicked a set of castanets together, improvised from a couple of shoe-polish tins. It was a half-hearted effort. He looked like he had barely the strength to stand, let alone get on his knees and shine a pair of shoes. He stared at the interior for a while, as if imagining another life for himself, or perhaps remembering a previous one, before wandering off.

'What have you got for me?'

Sami reached into his satchel and produced an untidy folder. As he spread out his papers, Makana felt a twinge of guilt at seeing the vivid scars on the backs of both of Sami's hands, the result of having four-inch nails driven through them a few months ago, while helping on another case. He had regained most of the mobility in his fingers but, as his awkward movements showed, not all.

'Let's see. Okay, Magdy Ragab. Interesting case this. Parents were educated, but not particularly wealthy. Father died young. He was a lawyer, as was his uncle Fahmy, who seems to have taken a hand in rearing the boy after his brother died. Uncle

Fahmy smoothed the path for young Magdy, who did about average at Cairo University's Faculty of Law. He graduated but wouldn't have got far without help.' Sami looked up and shrugged his shoulders. 'So far so normal.'

Aswani swaggered over, his wide hips waddling from side to side like heavy sacks on the back of a donkey. Depositing a mound of green salad on a steel platter he mopped the sweat from his brow.

'I should charge you for holding meetings in here.'

'What for?' Makana asked.

'You're taking up valuable space,' he called over his shoulder as he walked away.

'The man is losing his mind,' Sami declared.

'You were telling me about Ragab,' said Makana, picking at the arugula leaves still dripping beads of water.

'Okay.' Sami ruffled through his notes. 'Ah, yes, here is where it gets interesting. While at university he appears to have become involved with Islamist movements. He attended a number of meetings although it never really went beyond that. He stayed away from the real radicals. Tanzim al-Jihad, and so on.'

'The ones who assassinated Sadat in eighty-one?'

'Exactly. Ragab's sentiments appear to be quite mainstream. Like a lot of people he became more religious as the threat became more serious. He even joined the Muslim Brotherhood for a time and then dropped out. It wasn't helping his career. In the 1990s, however, he was close to Imam Waheed.'

'Sheikh Waheed?'

'The very same,' smiled Sami. 'He wasn't so high profile in those days but he was on his way up, already championing the line that those in government were as good Muslims as anyone.'

Waheed, a popular television preacher, was generally regarded as a government stooge, part of the campaign to try and outflank the Islamist radicals by painting the state as being more Islamic than anyone could wish for.

'Are you going to tell me what this is all about?' Sami asked, as the lamb, fresh from the grill, arrived on a metal platter. Makana explained the events of the last couple of days as they ate. Sami chuckled, 'I'm impressed. Now you are working for the person you were investigating? Chapeau, as the French say. Isn't there a moral clause against that?'

'Perhaps there ought to be,' Makana wondered aloud.

For the next few minutes the case was forgotten as they chewed through the succulent roast meat, stripping the bones with their teeth. Utensils were something of a rarity at Aswani's place.

'Ragab is convinced that Karima's death was not suicide, and I tend to agree.'

'You have anything to support that?'

'Not really.'

'Who would want her dead?'

'It's hard to say. A question mark hangs over the father, a man named Musab Khayr.'

'So we're talking about some kind of honour slaying?'

Makana glanced up. 'Do you know much about that?'

'Just what I hear. We tend to associate it with backward-thinking people who live in the sticks of Upper Egypt, but the truth is it's much more widespread.'

'Musab appears to be some sort of hothead. In prison he had a change of heart and turned to religion. According to Ragab he became involved with the jihadist movement.'

'So he is known to State Security? I'll get onto it.' Sami licked the taste of Aswani's special spices off his fingers – a tangy mix of

67

cumin, chilli, fenugreek and half a dozen other things whose identity he guarded with his life.

'When he came out he was tied to a plot to kill a government minister. Ragab argued his innocence and managed to get him out of the country. Twelve years ago he was granted political asylum in Europe, which is where he's been ever since.'

'And how is he meant to have done this, honour killing by remote?'

'Maybe he got some of his old cellmates to do him a favour?'

'It's all possible.' Sami leaned back in his chair and reached for a cigarette.

'Ragab's involvement in the whole business is a little suspect,' said Makana. 'He appears to have been close to the family, and to Karima.'

'Too close?' Sami raised his eyebrows.

'Perhaps. The truth is, I don't know.'

'If Ragab was involved with the girl in some way, and Musab heard about it . . .' Sami shrugged. 'That could be motive enough for him to get some of his mates to burn her house down.'

The word 'burn' brought back a vivid memory of the tortured creature on the hospital bed.

'Possibly, only by all accounts Musab wasn't close to his daughter. He wasn't even sure she was his.'

'Don't tell me, our helpful lawyer?'

'Ragab denies it. He says Musab's wife was pregnant before he went to prison.'

'But you don't really trust him.'

'Not entirely.' Makana called for tea and reached for Sami's cigarettes that lay on the table. 'There is another thing you could do for me. A woman named Zahra Sharif. She works for some kind of women's group, The Association for the Protection of Egyptian Women's Rights.'

'You want to know about her or the organisation?'

'Both.'

'Is this business or personal?'

'Does it make a difference?'

Sami grinned. 'To me? None at all. I was just thinking it might make a difference to you.'

After lunch Makana walked back over the square and used the footbridge to cross the busy Al Azhar road to reach the imposing high walls of the Ghuriyya complex. Built as a lavish burial place for the sultan, it bore the distinctive striped layers of stone that characterised architecture under the rule of the Mamluks. The sultan had passed through here in a cloud of incense, on his way to meet his fate. Accompanied by an elaborate procession of drummers and horsemen, camels laden with gold, silken banners that fluttered in the wind and elephants which ambled along silently on padded feet, it was a lavish affair. Naturally, someone had to pay for all this entertainment. As they watched him go by, the crowds, discontent and frustrated at the levies being forced on them, would have been muttering rumours of betrayal and treachery. Their wish was granted. The sultan's army was soundly defeated by the Ottomans in northern Syria. His body was not recovered from the battlefield and so never arrived back at this grand resting place he had so fondly built for himself. And so it stood, as empty as a promise, home for centuries to itinerant traders and wanderers of every kind.

This time Makana threw his net wider, moving through the side streets around the burnt-out shell of the shop. It was a sad sight. The windows of the room upstairs were narrow slits ringed with soot that resembled eyes painted with kohl.

'Who knows what they were up to, but no one deserves to die like that.'

An old woman with gnarled feet clutching a bunch of turnips paused in front of him and spoke without lifting her head. He watched her shuffle away. A man from another stall offered him a handful of pistachios. 'There were rumours that the woman had the *'ain*.' The evil eye. 'People gave her a wide berth, especially men. You never know what a witch like that can do to a man.' His eyes skittered away, never meeting Makana's gaze as he swept at the flies with a sheet of cardboard. In a hot little crease of an alleyway a small man was frying kidneys over a gas flame. 'They worked hard,' he said. Beads of sweat fell from his brow into the pan where they hissed against the hot metal. 'They ran a clean shop, mother and daughter. There wasn't a word you could say against them. But people like to talk, especially when they think others are doing better than them.'

The sun beat down through gaps in the roofing. It burned the back of Makana's neck. As he turned his head he caught a glimpse of two men flitting through the bands of shadow and light further down the market. Was it his imagination, or were they following him?

'Her husband lived abroad. She was well rid of him. He was a real piece of work. Trouble followed him like a rabid dog.' A man with hennaed whiskers and a grey eye that wandered of its own accord.

'You knew him?' Makana asked, intrigued.

'Musab, oh yes. When they first arrived here, before they had the shop.'

'Why did they come here?'

'They said they had family here. I never saw anyone. Personally, I think it wasn't so much why they came here as what they were running away from. Like I said, trouble stuck to him like shit.'

'They never talked about that?'

'Oh, no.'

'How would you describe him? What kind of man was he?'

'Oh, that one could take care of himself. It wasn't long before he was mixed up with all sorts. He had business with a carpet merchant down by the furniture store in the next street. The girl was no more than a child.'

'You mean his wife. Nagat?'

'Yes, that's the one. She was very young.' The dyed beard flapped up and down agitatedly. 'Maybe that's why they ran away from wherever it was they came from.'

'Siwa.'

'Siwa, yes, that's right, the oasis.' He scratched his armpit. 'He was one of those types, you know? The kind of man who's going to end up badly, no matter what. You avoid people like that.'

'He went to prison for a time.'

'I don't know anything about that.' The man's wayward eye fixed itself on Makana. 'I don't like to mix myself up in other people's business.' And with that he hurried away.

The furniture store was closed and shuttered and looked as if it had been that way for years. The only hint being a pile of rugs laid out to catch any passing business. A sullen young man in jeans toyed with a string of prayer beads. He pushed his glasses up his nose and stared down the street. He wore a T-shirt stamped with the words: Happy Dreaming. When Makana asked him if he remembered Musab, he shrugged and looked away.

'It was a long time ago. You're probably too young to remember,' Makana said, hoping to jog some kind of response from him. The notion that he was too young for anything stung the boy. He flipped the string of beads over quickly and glared at Makana.

'You'd have to talk to my uncle. He used to run the place in the old days.'

'How do I find him?' Makana asked.

'In the cemetery. He passed away three years ago.' The smile of satisfaction on the young man's face was compounded by the arrival of another man who came up to shake his hand. The two men fell into conversation, ignoring Makana who took the opportunity to sift idly through the carpets, which seemed to be Persian.

'You're interested in a carpet?' the young man snapped. He was in the process of lighting his friend's cigarette.

'I'm curious to know where they come from.'

'They are all genuine.' The man blew smoke into Makana's face as he smoothed the rugs back into order. 'They have a certificate on them,' he said, indicating a label.

'No, I mean, how do they get here?'

'What kind of a question is that?' the man frowned.

'It's just a question.'

'Who are you to be asking such questions?'

Makana looked at the two men and shrugged. 'I might be interested in buying a carpet.'

'You don't look the type to be interested in carpets.'

'Is there a certain type that buys carpets? What type might that be exactly?'

'A moment ago you were asking questions.'

'What kind of questions?' The new arrival had now taken an interest. His eyes ran over Makana as if measuring him for a suit.

'Musab Khayr. Remember him?' Makana asked. The second

man muttered something and tilted his head fractionally in the direction of down the street. Makana followed his lead and saw the two men he had spotted earlier. They were standing by a stall selling women's garments, trying to look interested.

'Why don't you take your friends and go ask your questions somewhere else,' the first young man said, turning away.

When Makana looked again, the two men had disappeared. In their place stood Zahra Sharif.

Chapter Eight

At first Makana thought it was just his eyes playing tricks, that she was summoned from some part of his subconcious that he was not fully in command of. Between the constant movement of people she was there and then she was not. Then the crowd parted once more and he saw her striding towards him. This time her headscarf was white. It hung in a loose loop under her chin and made her skin look darker and her eyes seem larger. Makana had the odd sensation that his heart had tripped a beat when he realised the smile she was wearing was meant for him.

'I thought I might find you here,' she said.

'You have been following me.'

'No, not at all.' She pointed back the way she had come. 'I had to visit some ladies who are running a collective. It's very interesting. Would you like to see?'

Makana was thinking that the smile was definitely an improvement. He checked over her shoulder one more time for any trace of the two men, but they had disappeared. 'Actually, I was going to call you.'

'There, you see, I did better than that,' Zahra said. 'I did call you. There was no reply the first time, and the second time your secretary said she would take a message. She sounds very young.'

'That would be Aziza.' Makana smiled. He really ought to start paying her something as a regular salary, just for answering the phone.

They were standing in the middle of the street, having to dodge from side to side as porters went jogging by, backs bent under huge cartons stamped in Mandarin, boys dragging trolleys loaded with bales of cloth, women carrying baskets bulging with indigo aubergines, bottles of olive oil and armfuls of small children.

Turning to walk on by mutual consent they passed Bab Zuwayla, where Tumanbey, the last of the Mamluks, was hanged in 1517. Across the other side they reached the Tentmakers Bazaar where they strolled through rays of dappled light in the cool, dark space beneath the high roof.

'Let's see, a friend of mine is usually here,' Zahra said. They came to a little opening that was tended by a young woman in her twenties. Her eyes lit up when she saw Zahra and the two greeted each other warmly.

When the introductions were taken care of the girl turned to Zahra. 'I need to ask you a favour. Can you look after the place for half an hour? Only I need to take my son to the doctor and I know my father would hate it if I closed.'

Half an hour for a visit to a doctor sounded optimistic, but Makana said nothing.

'Make yourselves comfortable. Tell the boy to bring you whatever you want.'

When the girl had gone they sat inside the open-fronted shop that was really no more than a large cubicle. The walls were covered in colourful printed cloth used for fencing off

75

streets for weddings and funerals. There were handsewn
appliqué covers. It added up to a vivid collision of colour and
geometry. Makana took the only narrow chair in the place
while Zahra settled herself cross-legged on a heap of cushions,
untied her headscarf and removed it, shaking her long black
hair free so that it fell down over her shoulder. Her eyes glittered with mischief.

'I shock you.'

'No,' he said, although it wasn't quite true.

'You don't look like the kind of person who shocks easily,
nor the kind of stuffed shirt who disapproves of women who
don't cover their hair. No,' she surmised, 'on the whole you
seem like a fairly modern man, which is saying something in
this day and age.'

'You always cover your hair?'

'For work, I have to. A woman who wants to be taken seriously? If I worked in more enlightened circles then perhaps not.
But I have to speak to families, most of which are poor and
simple. I would never be allowed in if I didn't look like a respectable girl.'

'Which you are, of course.'

'Whether I cover my hair or not.' She nodded.

A boy of about twelve peered inside and they ordered coffee.
He blinked twice at Zahra's hair and then bounced away. She
gave a long sigh.

'What are we going to do with this country?'

'I thought we were already doing as much as we could,'
Makana said, reaching for his cigarettes. She held out a hand for
one and he lit it for her. She inhaled deeply and blew the smoke
into the air above her head.

'It's silly, this whole place would go up in a second with just a

76

tiny spark and yet here we are puffing away like idiots.' She giggled. 'I feel like a naughty schoolgirl.'

'Did you grow up around here?'

'Me?' She laughed. 'No. I grew up far, far away in a land of make believe.' She gave him a stern look. 'You are asking questions as if this was an interrogation.'

'I'm sorry.'

'Don't apologise. What progress have you made?'

'Very little, I'm afraid. Karima seems to have led a simple life. Nobody has a bad word to say about her. Assuming it was not a random attack the only person with a possible motive has been living abroad for years. Why would he decide to kill his daughter now?'

'There's something you should know,' Zahra said quietly. 'Musab is no longer abroad. He's here in Egypt.'

'You know this for a fact?'

Zahra nodded her head, looking down. 'I suppose I should have told you before, but I wasn't sure I could trust you.'

'Karima told you?'

'She called me. She was very scared. She barely remembered who he was.'

'What did he want from her?'

'Money, and a place to hide. He was on the run.' Zahra puffed nervously at her cigarette. 'He turned up out of the blue with some wild story about being brought back by force and escaping.'

'That makes no sense,' said Makana. 'Did you tell this to the police?'

'The police?' Zahra snorted and regarded him coolly from under her eyelashes. 'And get myself into a thousand different kinds of trouble?'

They fell silent as the boy set down the coffee on a small round table in the front of the shop, intended to put potential buyers at their ease. The boy tapped his empty tray like a drum as he walked away. Zahra leaned forward.

'Nobody is going to believe me when I tell them a man who is living in political exile in Europe turned up in the middle of the night to set fire to his daughter's home with her in it.' Zahra was still for a moment. 'It seems so unfair. Why her? She never hurt anyone in the world.' Her voice cracked and she buried her head in her hands. Makana sat in silence until she had finished crying. He waited as she dried her eyes.

'Perhaps we should leave this to another time.'

'No.' She sniffed loudly and blew her nose on a tissue she produced from her bag. 'There is no time. If you intend to catch him, you have to be quick.'

'If what you are saying is true then we need to tell the police. They have the resources to find him.'

'Don't you see?' Zahra stared at him. 'How could someone like that, a man who is declared an enemy of the state, who lives abroad for years, involved in Allah knows what kind of activity, suddenly turn up in this country?' She shook her head. 'They know. They must do.'

'You mean State Security?'

'That's why it is hopeless. The police are calling it suicide. Nothing will happen. You are wasting your time.'

She had a point. There was no denying the fact that if it was true, if Musab had returned to the country, and for the moment he only had her word for it, then it had to be with the co-operation of the State Security and Investigations Service of the Ministry of the Interior. The question was why? Why would Musab come back to a country where he was still an undesirable? Why would they want him back? He recalled the two men he had seen in the market. They had the look of State Security written all over them. Were they watching him already? Shrugging off the temptation to sink into paranoia, Makana addressed Zahra.

'You said Musab had escaped. He needed help. He was on the run. Did Karima mention where he might be going?'

'No.' Zahra studied the tip of her cigarette as she flicked ash into the beaten copper bowl that served as an ashtray and then looked up at him. 'How did you wind up doing this kind of work?'

The abrupt shift surprised him. 'I was in the police. One thing led to another.'

'You must have done other things,' she laughed. 'You were a child once, somebody's son.'

And a husband and a father. Makana wasn't used to talking about himself. It wasn't something he felt comfortable with and he wasn't good at hiding the fact. Also, they seemed to be veering away from the matter in hand.

'You're not going to find the answers you're looking for here,' she said, studying the coffee grounds in her cup.

'What makes you say that?'

Zahra went on as if she hadn't heard the question. She spoke in a vague tone, as if thinking to herself out loud. 'These cases get all twisted up in time.'

'Are you talking about something in the family's past?' Makana wasn't sure he was following her. He shook another Cleopatra out of the pack.

'There are things you can't repair, no matter how hard you try.' She looked up. 'Why do I have the feeling you are driven by guilt?'

'Guilt?' asked Makana, lowering the unlit cigarette.

79

'I'm sorry.' She waved it aside. 'Sometimes I speak out of turn.' She reached for her coffee. 'Anyway, I thought we were talking about you?'

'There's not much to talk about,' he said, but then, for some inexplicable reason, he found himself talking. It felt as though a knot that was tied up inside him was becoming unravelled.

'A long time ago I made a mistake. It cost the lives of the two people who were dearest to me in the world.'

'I understand,' she said. 'You wish you could go back and change things, put them back how they were before.'

'Yes.'

She fixed him with a firm look. 'But you can't. The past can't be undone. It took me a long time to learn that no matter how hard we try there are things we cannot put right.'

Meeting her gaze had the disturbing effect of distracting his thoughts to such a degree that he seemed to have trouble following the conversation.

'Is that what this is all about?' he asked finally. 'Something that cannot be undone?'

Zahra held his gaze for a moment and then she shrugged and reached for her headscarf which she began tying in place. 'Isn't it always like that? Trying to put right the past?'

Just then her friend returned, full of noise and energy. Makana had the feeling the whole meeting had been stage-managed with meticulous timing.

'What will you do next?' Zahra asked as they said their goodbyes.

'The family are originally from Siwa. Did you think he would head there?'

'Who knows what goes through the mind of a man like that?' Then, putting a hand out, she rested it lightly on his arm and they stood that way for a moment, neither of them moving. 'You must be careful,' she said. 'The past is not something to be tampered with easily.'

Makana felt the imprint of her touch on him all the way home.

Chapter Nine

It was around five when Makana arrived back at the *awama*, his mind in a state of unfamiliar turmoil, to find the telephone ringing. It was Sami Barakat.

'When do you think you might decide to join the rest of us in the twenty-first century and get yourself a mobile telephone?'

'I told you, I'm thinking about it.'

'By the time you get around to it the world will have moved on. I've been trying to reach you all afternoon.' He sounded as though he was calling from the bottom of a well. The screech of brakes and a voice over a tannoy told Makana he had to be in one of the city's Metro stations.

'Look, a contact inside the Interior Ministry called me.' There was a long break and Makana thought he had lost the signal. It returned with the soft tooting of car horns announcing that Sami had emerged onto the street. 'It seems there is suddenly a lot of interest in your friend Musab Khayr.'

'What kind of interest?'

'The war on terror. As President Bush put it, either you are with us or against us.' Sami paused. Makana could hear him breathing. 'I'm not sure how wise it is to be having a conversation like this on a mobile.'

'I warned you about those things.'

'Too late now, I suppose. The point is this. The CIA are running a program whereby they are picking up possible suspects and shipping them to secret locations for interrogation.'

Makana picked up the telephone and trailed the long cable behind him as he stepped out onto the rear deck and stared across the river.

'You're saying he's in this country.'

'I hadn't actually come to that bit,' said Sami slowly. 'But yes, it appears Musab was picked up four months ago and somehow he ended up here. How did you know he was here?'

'He visited his daughter. Can they do that?'

'Legally, this has no basis whatsoever, but this is war, Makana, there are no rules.'

'So what is the purpose of this exercise?'

'It means the gloves are off. It means torture in the name of freedom and democracy. We do the torture and they get the results without getting their hands dirty.'

'What do they want from Musab?'

'That I don't know. But you said he had been involved with jihadist movements. Clearly they suspect him of some kind of terrorist-type activity.'

'Have you been able to confirm this?'

'Beyond my source at the ministry? No. Though there is a lot of traffic on the internet. Human Rights Watch and some of the other organisations are reporting that Musab was kidnapped and smuggled out of the country. Although he is actually in Egypt, he won't appear on any records. Legally he has vanished without trace.'

'Why did your friend at the ministry tell you all this?'

'He's scared, and with good reason. He thinks that eventually, when all this comes to light, someone is going to pay for breaking the law. The Americans will wash their hands of the whole business, but of course our noble leaders are happy to do their bidding no matter what the cost. Human rights groups are already lining up to make cases on this issue.'

Makana thought for a time. He lit a cigarette and looked out at the river, smoking in silence. Someone was having a party in one of the clubs on the Zamalek side. In the thickening dusk neon strips blinked as they struggled to come awake. The music was like a piercing electronic shriek. A tortured cry of pain from an obsolete piece of industrial machinery. The air juddered with the sound of amplifiers grinding out yet another crooner moaning about lost love. The instruments changed, but the sentiments remained the same.

'Are you still there?' Sami asked.

'Even if what you say is true,' Makana said, 'how does that explain him being able to visit his daughter?'

'I don't know,' said Sami. 'Look, as you said, I'm not sure about the wisdom of discussing this on an open line. Maybe I can come over and show you some stories.'

'Fine. I'm going out for an hour or so, but just wait for me.'

Night had fallen as Makana caught a taxi up on the main road which swung round and delivered him to the rather elegant old building by Heliopolis station where Ragab had his offices. Makana and Sindbad had followed Ragab to and from the place numerous times the previous week. Now it felt strange to be walking through the door. On the ninth floor a broad window revealed the city laid out below as a dark, glittering map. Ragab was expecting him. He came round the large desk to shake his hand. 'I have informed my staff that you are working for me on a private matter, beyond that they know nothing. I would like to keep it that way.'

Makana nodded his agreement and Ragab indicated a plush leather chair for Makana to take as he went back to his own place behind the desk. The comfort made him feel like a lamb being pampered and fed, all in anticipation of the slaughter that was to come.

'It seems that Musab may be back in the country.'

'What?' Ragab looked stunned. 'But that's impossible. You know this for certain?'

'Somebody who talked to Karima before the fire said she had seen her father.'

Ragab slumped back in his big chair. 'Well, I must say, that would explain a lot.'

'Tell me a little more about Musab. You said he had become a devout Muslim in prison, that he had joined a certain jihadist group, and that it was his involvement with this group which led to his seeking asylum abroad.'

'That is correct.'

'You also described Musab as a delinquent, someone who was always looking for the easy way out. So which is it? The devoted fanatic, hell-bent on bringing down this regime, or the small-time criminal?'

'Musab is the type of fellow who doesn't really have much in the way of a conscience. As a young man he was involved in criminal activities. He associated with people who encouraged him that it was possible to get what you want in this world without too much hard work. He followed that line until it landed him in prison. I'm not even certain his conversion to Islam was sincere. He saw it as giving him a chance, and maybe I am reading too much into it, but I think he saw himself as a bit of a hero, a martyr even.'

'Was he actually involved in activities against the government?'

'Oh, yes. Nagat came to me shortly after he was released. She was worried about his behaviour. He made no attempt to find work, but spent all his time at the mosque or attending secret meetings about which she knew nothing. She was afraid. Remember, this was nineteen eighty-nine, at the height of the troubles in this country with militants. The police could knock down the door in the middle of the night and shoot everyone, justifying it with the claim that armed radicals were hiding there.'

Makana remembered the time in question as being a difficult one. When he first arrived in this country, two years later, he had found himself in the curious position of being suspected of harbouring sympathies for the radicals. The irony being that he had fled to this country to escape precisely the same thing: militant Islamism.

'Can you be more specific about what he was actually doing?'

Ragab spoke with the confident air of a man who was comfortable with his position. He regarded Makana with an amused, somewhat condescending look. He cast around the room as if looking for something that wasn't there. 'The usual. Circulating leaflets, recruiting new members, attending meetings, that kind of thing. Then he went away, as I told you.'

'You said you weren't sure where he went exactly.'

'No. But I believe it must have been some kind of training camp, with the idea of returning here to fight against the government.'

'But you must have believed he was innocent of being involved in that assassination plot?'

Ragab lifted his chin. 'Musab is a country boy at heart and in that sense rather naive. I believe someone took advantage of his credulity. He was asked to hold certain documents for safe keeping. I argued that he was unaware of their content and that his life was in danger.' The lawyer allowed himself a smile of satisfaction. 'It took some doing, but in the end I managed to convince him that it was best for everybody, that this way he had a chance to start a new life.' Ragab folded his hands together on top of the desk. 'In the beginning he made only the slightest effort to stay in touch, but eventually even that died away.'

'And you've had no contact with him since?'

'No.' Ragab frowned. 'I don't understand how he could be back in the country. It makes no sense.'

'How much do you know of Musab's activities after he left here?'

'Nothing really. He was thousands of kilometres away. I have no idea of his new life. What will you do next?'

'If Musab is looking for somewhere quiet to lay low then it would make sense to get out of Cairo. I think I might go to Siwa and talk to some of his old contacts.'

'But why not take this to the police? Surely if someone like that is on the run State Security will be involved?'

'If I am right about this, I don't think they will even admit he is in the country.'

'Very well, do it your way. Go to Siwa, take your time, do whatever you have to do. I want to know who killed Karima and why. And Makana, let me know how you are progressing.'

Makana promised he would do his best.

Sami was busy installing himself at the desk on the top deck when Makana arrived back at the *awama*. He had unplugged the telephone and connected the slim portable computer he had brought to the wall socket.

'What am I looking at?' Makana asked, leaning over his shoulder.

'These are reports I came across online, all of them talking about the same thing. Extraordinary Rendition. That's what they call it when the state kidnaps people in broad daylight and spirits them away, no one knows where. There are logs of unregistered flights being given clearance through third countries, such as Spain.'

'What is the purpose of all this?'

'Some of them are being held at secret locations, so-called Black Sites. No one knows exactly where. Effectively they just vanish off the map.'

Makana stared at the list of names being scrolled down the page.

'Who are these people?'

'Suspects. Usually Arabs, Muslims. People they think might have some connection to a terrorist organisation, which nowadays includes just about anyone with a funny name. It also means they have no concrete evidence, certainly nothing that could be held up in court.'

'So these people are kidnapped and tortured in the hope they will confess all?'

'Exactly. I don't think we have fully grasped the degree of paranoia that followed the 9/11 attacks. What they are doing is creating a whole series of laws that deprive normal citizens of their basic human rights, and no one is protesting.'

'You're wasted here,' Makana said. 'You ought to be lecturing the Americans.'

'It would take a decade and by then,' Sami shrugged, 'who knows where we'll be?'

'So why is Musab in this group?'

'Well, it could all be coincidence. Something as simple as sharing the name of someone who is or was involved in terrorist activity. Or he could have donated money to a particular charity that has links to a terror cell. It could be any number of things.'

'So these people haven't necessarily done anything wrong?'

'Most of them haven't done anything. The net is being thrown wide with little regard for the law or consequences. Effectively, what this is saying is if you are a Muslim you have to prove your innocence. There is an assumption of guilt.'

'Why have I not heard anything about this?'

A smile broadened on Sami's face. 'Finally, you are beginning to see the light. This is the future of journalism. There is very little in the mainstream media on this.'

'But these aren't newspapers, or agencies.'

'These are what you call weblogs. Anyone can go online and set one up. It's a new form of journalism. Basically people gather information and post it for the world to see.'

'What's the difference between that and making it up?'

Sami gave Makana an exasperated look. 'This is about consensus. If enough people report something then it will eventually be corroborated. The big agencies feed people what they think they want to hear. Right now, nobody is interested in this stuff. Ten years from now we'll see. People want to tell their own stories. The media is all about protecting corporate interests.'

'I thought that was the state.'

'In this country they protect the state, but out there in the great democracies of the world they protect corporate power. Government is subordinate to those interests, so it's much the same thing under a different name.'

'Did you find anything out about the other thing I asked you for?'

89

'The woman you mentioned? Yes.' Sami flipped through a spiral notebook, pages flying back and forth until he found what he was looking for. 'Here it is. The organisation exists. Rania even said she had heard they do good work. They get money from Holland and a couple of Nordic countries. They defend women. What are you looking for?'

'I'm not sure. Nothing in particular, really,' Makana said. 'I just wanted to be sure.'

'I couldn't really find much on this Zahra Sharif. She is a bit of a mystery, but then,' Sami shrugged, 'we all are, aren't we?'

'Forget it,' said Makana. 'It was just a thought. How about something to eat?'

'I thought you'd never ask.' Sami reached for his telephone and began calling a take-out place that delivered. Makana walked out into the open air and lit a cigarette. The lights across the river glittered in the water below him. What was it that made him feel so uneasy? Makana had the sense that he was on the trail of something much bigger than he had bargained for. He wasn't sure he could see where the edges were and he didn't like that.

II

Siwa Oasis

Chapter Ten

At eight the next morning Makana boarded a West Delta bus in Abdelmoneim Riyad Square. He found a seat which he reserved with his holdall and then waited in the road, smoking, for the moment of departure. His fellow passengers appeared to have come bearing all their worldly possessions. Television sets the size of dining tables, shapeless nylon bags that could have concealed a small camel, carton boxes strung together with complex Chinese knots, along with sacks and plastic suitcases bound with tied leather belts with broken buckles. There was something touching and medieval about it. Less of an excursion than an exodus, as if passengers were trying to squeeze the entire city into the luggage hold beneath the bus. Makana had come prepared for any eventuality which meant that he was quite surprised when the driver got in behind the wheel and the bus left on time. There were no delays either. They stopped just once along the way and for five minutes only to allow people to use the restrooms and for the smokers to alleviate their suffering. Smoking was not permitted on board.

The trip gave Makana plenty of time to think about the case. He stared out of the window at the stark emptiness of the landscape, the desolate struggle against oblivion. The image of the badly burnt body inside the oxygen tent still haunted him. It had tapped straight into his concerns about his own daughter and his imaginings of what kind of a vulnerable situation Nasra might be in. The truth was, he concluded, as the lush turquoise of the Mediterranean flooded into view, that he would not rest until he found his daughter, now that he was convinced she was alive.

They turned west along the coast and the road ran past the high walls of compounds that contained blocks of holiday apartments. Like onshore reefs left high and dry in a sea of white sand, they varied in quality and age; some were decaying comfortably into middle age while others stood out in their bright decadence, shining symbols of rising inequality in the country. Beyond lay the sea, a miracle after the dun-coloured landscape, or so it seemed.

Evening was falling as they arrived in Mersah Matruh and Makana found a room overlooking a deserted square through which lone taxi cabs roamed hopelessly seeking fares. In the summer this place was teeming with holidaymakers, but at this time of year it was deserted. From the window of his room he saw lights which turned out to be a restaurant, although he was the only one interested in eating. A handful of solitary men were following a football match on a television set perched on top of a refrigerator. El Ahly and Assiut were playing, the middle-aged waiter informed him, a gold tooth winking in the neon light. He seemed to think this might be of interest. When Makana asked him about buses to Siwa he said there was one every two hours. Or maybe some of them weren't buses but shared taxis. 'What can you do?' He shrugged, as if the world had a habit of delivering disappointments. Even with the match on, the place seemed barely alive. The food was a disappointment but Makana was too hungry to care. After that he walked a bit to stretch his legs. Taxis juddered alongside him and the drivers peered up at him, imploring him to take them somewhere.

At the bus station the next morning Makana's curiosity was drawn by a couple dressed in modern city clothes. The woman disappeared behind the shelter of a shack offering snacks and soft drinks. The man held a bag from which he produced a garment that he passed round the side to the woman. When she eventually emerged the colourful clothes she had been wearing had vanished from sight. Even her face was hidden. Covered from head to toe in black she picked her way through the debris of discarded bottles and strips of plastic bags, the broken rubble and patches of black where engine oil had seeped into the sand. She walked with remarkable grace, he thought, like a peacock strolling through the grounds of a marble palace, to take her place among the people waiting for the bus.

Alexander the Great was said to have travelled this same route, following a flock of birds that led him to the oasis. The desert had once swallowed Cambyses and his entire army whole. The road followed the old caravan tracks. Nowadays it took four hours. By camel the journey would have taken nine days. Several of Makana's fellow passengers were Bedouins on their way out to work on the oil and gas rigs. They asked the driver to pull over before stepping down. Then, looking round them to get their bearings – there was nothing to see – they covered their faces from the wind and sand with their scarves and set off towards the empty horizon.

Hot air blew in through the windows and rest was made impossible by a non-stop sequence of videos playing on the over-head monitor. A talk show in which a smooth, well-dressed man counselled the young audience in the delicate matter of love in an Islamic climate. Men and women sat on opposite sides of the studio. They were dressed in jeans and T-shirts advertising rock bands. Some of the women had their hair uncovered but most didn't. The host consulted a laptop which provided handy statistics about happiness. It was a combination of a game show and a lecture. Young women listened raptly as he told them that they had three important duties in life: loving their husbands, raising children and improving themselves.

The bus rattled its way up a low ridge, with a painful grating of gears being ground down as they swayed through a narrow, rocky pass. For a moment or two, as the driver wrestled the gearstick into place, they were afforded a view of what lay beyond. Behind them the desert stretched out in unbroken dull monotony, flat brown and devoid of anything to distract the eye. Ahead the road sank gently down into the bowl of the oasis where a rich green sea of palm fronds bobbed in the warm air, fringed by the blue-grey pool of the lakes that kept the desert at bay.

As Makana stepped down from the bus and dug his way through the crowd of travellers, excited relatives and hills of luggage, a plump boy, his trouser cuffs dragging in the dust, sauntered up. From his right hand dangled a knotted length of frayed rope attached to a metal tube.

'Hotel, *effendi?*' A knock-kneed bag of skin and bones nuzzled the ground beside him. It seemed as good a place to start as any. The buggy creaked and the wheels were lopsided, but the boy grabbed his holdall enthusiastically, fending off the competition with a deft crack of the whip. The donkey had grey scabs on its back where sores had healed over. It hardly looked strong enough to stand, let alone pull two grown men. Bulbul, as he said people called him, was not actually a man, of course, but a boy of around fifteen. Physically, however, he was heavier than a lot of men. He wasn't fat so much as well padded. His body seemed to be held together in a rough kind of way by his clothes. A striped polo shirt with a rip under one arm and trousers that were coming apart at the seams. The hems dragged behind him in the dirt like reversed duck feet.

'Here for tourism, *effendi? Ahlan wasahlan.* People come from all over the world and I show them around. No one knows Siwa like Bulbul.'

The sides of the little two-wheeled trap were plastered with stickers donated by grateful visitors: Boston Red Sox – Orlando FL, the Sunshine State – Cleveland Cavaliers. Others spoke of Milano, Barcelona and Zamalek. Football the language of international understanding.

'Visit Cleopatra's Eye, Jebel Mawtah, the mountain of death, ruins, Alexander's tomb?'

'Perhaps a hotel to begin with.'

'High, low, medium? You look like a well-travelled man, sir. I know just the place for you.'

The exhausted donkey looked as though it might collapse at any moment, but he whipped it into a tired frenzy and they clip-clopped along the road. Sitting beside the boy, Makana was regretting his choice. Heads turned as if he were on public display. The hotel was a stone's throw from the bus station but the enterprising Bulbul had taken him by the scenic route. They turned and rode up and down and round for what seemed like ages but could only have been about ten minutes. The donkey was also clearly accustomed to this tour and after a promising beginning slowed his pace to almost a halt, head nodding up and down. Perhaps he was aware that once he started talking Bulbul's attention lapsed.

'The brother has come from far away? *Ma'sha Allah*, welcome, sir. Food, lodging, sightseeing, all of these things. Bulbul knows best.'

On the main square stood a large house with high walls over which luxuriant fig trees and regal palms poked up. The boy reached underneath his seat for a small stone which he tossed casually at the green gate. It struck the metal with a resounding clang. Bulbul gave no explanation, simply clicked his tongue and flicked the reins as they trotted on.

A painting of Field Marshal Rommel hung in the gloomy lobby of The Desert Fox Hotel. Makana wondered if anyone knew who he actually was, or if the identity of the Afrikakorps leader had simply become mislaid in the corridors of time. An idle foreign curiosity. The man who appeared behind the reception desk was a sad figure in need of a haircut and a shave. His shirt was buttoned wrongly, leaving a string of uneven gaps down his chest. He eyed Makana warily, as if he could pick and choose his customers.

'The brother is here on business?'

'Family. I'm looking for relatives on my wife's side. It's a matter of inheritance. Does the name Musab Khayr mean anything?'

'No.' The man scratched his chest through a gap in his shirt. 'You should try the police.'

'I'll do that.'

The green walls of the room were speckled with red flecks which, on closer inspection, turned out to be squashed flies and mosquitos. They were spread across every available surface, walls, grimy window, wardrobe and bathroom mirror. Even the light switch had a couple. Makana lay down and shut his eyes to be woken instantly by a spine-twisting shriek as the muezzin in the mosque next door called people to evening prayer. The amplification distorted the sound to the point where it was just an electronic wail, impossible to comprehend.

As he made his way downstairs, Makana scratched the back of his hands where the mosquitos had already struck. In the lobby a girl of about sixteen stood behind the desk. Down the street he found a brightly lit place cluttered with computers and telephone booths. The man who owned it was clad in a skull cap and gellabiya. Long-winded recitations from the Quran droned on over the sound system.

'I need to use a telephone,' said Makana. Listlessly, the man indicated one of the booths that had been clumsily assembled on the opposite wall. They were very basic structures that looked as though they had been hammered together by an enthusiastic chimpanzee. With no ceilings and no attempt to insulate them for soundproofing, which meant that the voices of every caller rose up into a cacophony, competing with one another in the narrow space. The man in the next booth was actually yelling. Maybe they had a bad line, or else the person he was talking to was far away. People often had the impression they had to shout to make themselves heard over great distances. There were burn marks on the shelf on which the telephone stood where previous callers had rested their cigarettes. Names and numbers were scribbled on the wall in what resembled a logbook of longing and despair. Makana tried the number Zahra gave him and felt relieved when there was no answer. He had no idea what he would have said if she had picked up the phone and so declined to leave a message.

In a café down the road, he waited for what felt like hours before a simple omelette arrived swimming in so much oil that he had trouble swallowing it. The night air was clear and cool.

The stars hung in the sky, but the silence was unnerving. The town seemed deserted after dark. Eventually he made his way back. In his room he fell asleep to the sound of a donkey wheezing over and over again in a wretched, strangled groan.

Chapter Eleven

Nagy, the hotel manager, was talking to a stuffed sack of a man in a police uniform when Makana came downstairs the next morning. They broke off when they caught sight of him. On closer inspection the policeman had the broad chest of a former weightlifter gone to seed, though his grip was still firm.

'Mr Makana, welcome to Siwa. I am Sergeant Hamama, acting police chief for the town. Mr Nagy here tells me you are looking for someone.'

'A relative on my wife's side of the family.' Makana wondered how long this story would hold. 'Actually, I was planning to visit you first thing today.'

'So, I have saved you the trouble.'

The sergeant was overweight and out of breath. He was also in bad need of a haircut. His grin revealed a missing eye tooth. The leather holster on his hip had been repaired by some local artesan. The wide stitching made it look like a traditional tribal garment of some kind.

'We are famous for our hospitality,' said the sergeant, hitching up his trousers that were in constant danger of falling down. 'Perhaps I can help you with your enquiries.'

'That would be very kind,' said Makana, wondering where all this was leading.

Nagy followed them with a cold eye from behind the front desk as they walked out of the hotel and climbed into a battered dark-blue Chevrolet pickup with 'Police' in faded white letters on the side. The windscreen was divided by a forked crack and the doors screeched in protest at being opened and closed. As they rolled off down the street Makana was aware of the attention they drew. He wondered at the wisdom of being seen with the local police sergeant.

'We are a very small town,' Hamama began. 'A very close community. Which means that people are protective. To someone from the outside that can seem a little daunting.'

Makana pulled out his cigarettes and offered them. Hamama clicked his tongue.

'Thank you, but no thanks. We have clean air out here, I always say, why soil it?'

The pickup clattered along the stony road, past the pock-marked building that was the police station and along out through rows of palm trees. Hamama was chuckling to himself.

'I'm sure that in the big city you have all kinds of marvellous systems to record births and deaths and all the rest of it. Out here we have our own ways. Out beyond those trees is the desert and there are no rules out there. No government. A lot of people have no idea what year they were born, or what day of the month. How do you fit them into your system?'

They passed a cemetery. Uneven mounds of bare earth. Here and there a simple piece of wood or metal bearing the name of the deceased. Three women draped from head to foot in black walked by in the opposite direction. Their faces were covered by a sheet of cloth so you couldn't even see their eyes.

'Are you from here originally?'

'Born and raised. Spent all of my life here, apart from the years I was in Mersa Matruh training to be a policeman.'

'So, in a small town like this you must have a pretty good grasp of everybody.'

'Well, pretty good, but this man is the next best thing to a computer. Amm Ahmed.'

'Amm Ahmed?'

'He's lived longer than anyone and he remembers everything. You'll see,' Hamama smiled. The car rocked from side to side as they edged off the road onto a narrow track of deep ruts cutting through the dry mud. The house was so well hidden between the thick palm trees that Makana didn't see it until they were almost touching it. The adobe walls were cracked and dried with age. They blended in perfectly with the trees that surrounded it.

It was hard to say how old Amm Ahmed actually was. Frail, with a tiny head covered in white bristles, he stood half in shadow just back from the doorway, as motionless as a tree himself.

'We've come to consult you, Amm Ahmed,' said Sergeant Hamama by way of an introduction. He stood bow-legged in front of his car and simply raised his voice. 'This man is looking for people from his wife's family.' He looked Makana over.

'What family is that?' The old man seemed to be a little hard of hearing. Makana raised his voice. There were turtle doves cooing nearby, and somewhere in the distance he thought he could hear a man singing.

'The husband's name is Musab Khayr.'

'I haven't heard that name around here for a long time. I think he left.'

'He was married to a woman named Nagat Abubakr, maybe you remember them?'

The old man stepped forward out of the shadow. When he spoke, his adam's apple jumped up and down and his voice was as high pitched and jittery as a bird's.

'Everyone used to know the Abubakr family. But they are gone now. None of them are left.' He was dark and bony, and knotted like a withered palm that had lost its luxuriant crown. One eye was blue and sightless while the other fixed you like a pin.

'Are you sure?' Makana asked.

'They were one of the richest families around here. Owned a lot of land. But they're all gone now. You must remember that, Sergeant?'

Hamama gave a laugh. 'If I could remember as much as you, uncle, I'd be the one living out here with the birds.'

Amm Ahmed muttered something that Makana couldn't catch. He heard the sergeant hack loudly and spit into the soft earth.

'What was that?' Makana asked.

'Squandered their wealth. Married badly.' Amm Ahmed chewed on his toothless gums.

'Is there anybody left who might have known them?'

But Amm Ahmed's attention appeared to have wandered. He turned away.

'I'm sorry that wasn't more helpful,' Sergeant Hamama sighed when they were back in the car. They watched the spindly figure disappear inside the mud house. 'His family came here as slaves years ago. Brought up from the south, your part of the world, on a caravan.'

'Is that singing?'

'The men working the palm trees sing and others working nearby reply. It's a tradition.'

The Chevrolet creaked and groaned as they bumped their way through the ruts. Hamama drove with one hand on the wheel, the other bunched into a fist on his thigh. He threw a long sideways glance at his passenger. The engine wheezed as they climbed the incline onto the metalled road and shuddered back in the direction of civilisation.

'Are you going to tell me what this is really about? Why are you asking about Musab Khayr? And I don't mean that nonsense about your wife's family.'

'A young woman died,' Makana began, considering the wisdom of lighting a cigarette. Hamama seemed to be trying to make up his mind whether to trust him or not. 'Karima was their daughter. I was hired to find out who killed her.'

'Why not leave all that to the police?'

'The police aren't interested. They are dismissing it as suicide.'

'Oh, now I see.' Hamama chuckled to himself. 'You're one of those people who think they know better than the police, eh? Sounds like you've done this kind of thing before.'

'A long time ago.'

'Very good.' Hamama seemed amused. 'You were a policeman once yourself. How would you have felt if civilians started interfering in your work back then?'

'I'm not interfering. Like I said, the police aren't interested.' Makana looked at the sergeant. 'It's a girl from a poor family. Nobody cares.'

'But you obviously do. I'm guessing somebody is paying you for this.'

'Right, somebody who cared about the girl enough to want to know why she died.'

Sergeant Hamama shifted his bulk as if making himself

comfortable. 'So you tell him the girl was murdered and he pays you to come here on holiday. Not a bad game you're in.'

'Almost as good as this folklore trip you're taking me on,' said Makana. 'You have records of births and deaths like anywhere else in the country. I'm not here as a tourist.'

The pickup rolled to a halt. Hamama took a long time to regard Makana.

'All right, we'll make a deal. There's nothing for you here, but I can show you around. You can take in the sights and go home to your master happy.'

'What did you have in mind?'

Hamama scratched his nose. 'This person who hired you, what do you call it, your client?'

'He's a lawyer.'

'Okay, so the man is paying you, right? And I'm guessing he's not short of money. So, we come to some kind of arrangement that is mutually beneficial.'

'I can't see how that is of any advantage to me.'

'This is a small town. You won't get anywhere without help. If I put the word out nobody will say a word to you, and besides, you heard the old man. That family died out years ago. There's nothing here for you to find.'

'Amm Ahmed said the Abubakr family were once big land-owners. Do you know where they used to live?'

'Does this mean we're partners?'

'It means, I'm thinking about it.'

'All right,' said Hamama. 'I can work with that. But don't wait too long. I'm not known for my patience.' He pushed the car into gear and they rolled along. They drove in silence through the town and out through more trees into an area where the road became dusty and bare as it curved around a small hill. The house, or what was left of it, was on the edge of a dry, neglected field.

'There it is,' said Hamama, climbing out and leaning against the front of the pickup.

Makana walked over to take a look. It was clear that no one had lived here for years although it must once have been quite a splendid place. Stepping up onto what might have been a front veranda, Makana wandered through into the rubble-strewn remains of a large courtyard.

'How long has it been like this?' he called over his shoulder.

Sergeant Hamama, who was busy tucking a pinch of snuff inside his lower lip, glanced up. 'Oh, years,' he said, dusting off his hands. 'The family owned all of this, as far as the eye can see.' He ejected a long stream of tobacco-coloured spit.

'What happened?'

'The usual.' The sergeant waved vaguely. 'They died out, I suppose.' He went back to staring off into the distance.

Makana finished his walk around the perimeter of the ruined house. It was probably built in the 1920s or 1930s. The Abubakrs would have been landowners back in the days of King Farouk before Nasser came to power and seized the land to give back to the people. When he arrived back at the car, Sergeant Hamama was still leaning on the front of it, watching him with folded arms. There didn't seem to be much to occupy the local police around here.

From the pocket of his jacket Makana produced the fragment of the photograph he had found in Karima's flat in Cairo. He moved around, holding it up until he found a position where he thought it might fit. The photograph was several decades old, but the line of the horizon was largely unchanged.

'What is that?' Sergeant Hamama craned his neck to look over Makana's shoulder.

'I think it's a memory they took with them when they left here,' said Makana.

'You say this girl died in a fire?' Hamama asked. Makana nodded. 'And you think the reason has something to do with this place?'

'I think it has something to do with Musab Khayr. Do you remember him?'

'It rings a bell. Very faint and far away.' Sergeant Hamama leaned over to eject another jet of tobacco into the dirt. 'If he's the one I'm thinking of he had a reputation as a trouble maker, always getting into fights.'

'Do you remember what happened to him?'

'I think he left and no one heard anything more about him.'

'That sounds like the man I am looking for. This would have been when?'

'Around the time Sadat was killed.'

'Nineteen eighty-one. Twenty one years ago.'

'Like I said, a long time.'

'Who owns this land now?'

'*This* land?' The sergeant turned to survey the plot stretching away behind the house as if he had never seen it before. 'I don't know. I can check. It might still belong to the family.'

'The house must have been something. Shame it fell into ruin.'

'It's hard land to work. It's the salt, you know, in the soil.'

'Right.' Makana returned the singed picture to his pocket and pulled out his cigarettes. 'Who is the senior officer in charge here?'

'Well, right now that would be me.' Hamama scratched his belly.

'Who was in charge before?'

'Captain Mustafa.'

'Do you think I could speak to him?'

'You could,' grinned Sergeant Hamama, 'but you'd have to go to heaven first.'

A squawk from the interior of the pick-up alerted Hamama to a radio call. He was still smiling at his own humour as he reached in through the window on the driver's side. Makana sighed and surveyed the ruin. This was Karima's family home, but she'd never seen it. The photograph would have been her mother's. She kept it as a memory, or did it signify more than that? It wasn't a lot to go on. A fallen-down house full of birds' nests.

Hamama straightened up, tossing the radio handset in through the window onto the seat. He raised one hand to shield his eyes from the sun.

'I knew you were trouble when I first set eyes on you,' Hamama grunted as he wrenched open the door of the car. 'Get in.' Makana climbed in as Hamama started the engine. They pulled onto the road and started back towards town at what seemed like recklessly high speed.

'What's going on?' Makana asked.

'They've found a body in the lake.'

Chapter Twelve

Birket Siwa was a long flat sliver of water that lapped gently at the soft white sand now tinged with red. The air was oppressive and there was barely a ripple on the lake's placid surface. Seagulls flapped impatiently at a distance. The fish had also already had their fill. The face was ravaged where between them they had torn away strips. Both eyes were now empty pools half filled with grey matter and brakish water. The dead man lay on his side in the sun. His knees were folded up and he looked as if he had been tipped over as he lay kneeling. His belly had been split open and a slithery mass of intestines and vital organs had spilled out. Coated with sand they resembled fat worms coming out of the earth. The stench was suffocating, trapped within a wave of heat. Not a breath of air stirred the water and a strange, almost supernatural stillness hung over the scene. A policeman with a caved-in face and the frame of a scrawny dog stood watching as they arrived, holding a small group of onlookers at a distance.

'Stay here.'

The springs gave a squeak of relief as Hamama climbed laboriously out of the Chevrolet and balanced his cap on his head. Hitching up his trousers he made his way over. The onlookers consisted of a man and a donkey, on the back of which was perched the impassive figure of a woman, or a girl, perhaps. Impossible to say when she was completely dressed in black and her face was covered. The donkey's ears twitched. Makana climbed out of the car and immediately felt his feet sinking into the damp sand. As he straightened up the skinny policeman gave a groan and bent over to start retching all over his boots. Sergeant Hamama gave a sigh of disgust, whether at the body or this sign of weakness wasn't clear. The cause of the officer's nausea became apparent as Makana drew near. The dead man's intestines appeared to be alive, wriggling and twisting as handfuls of grey salt eels squirmed and plopped into the sand out of the cavity in the man's belly. A stench like rotting fish broke over them, a suffocating, sulphorous reek that seemed to stick in the throat. Makana lit a cigarette and at the sound of the lighter Hamama glanced sharply back at him. Then he spat on the ground and hoisted his baggy trousers back up.

'Who found him?'

Wordless, the skinny police officer gestured in the direction of the couple with the donkey before being overcome by another wave of nausea and he bent over and vomited again.

Sergeant Hamama muttered something to himself and then approached the couple. The donkey shied away and the old man tugged it back into place. The woman sitting side-saddle on the back didn't move a muscle.

'Well, what have you got to say for yourselves?'

'I don't usually come this way,' the man began. 'As Allah is my witness I don't know what made me do so today. I just saw him there.'

'All right, okay,' Hamama was impatient. 'Did you see anything, anyone at all?'

The man shook his head. The woman remained motionless and silent.

'Did you touch anything?'

'No, of course not. I could see he was dead.' He turned to point over his shoulder to a finger of land that jutted out into the water. 'I went to the hut over there, to use the telephone. I called my nephew Abdelrahman who sells chickens in the market and told him to go to the police station.'

'Why didn't you call the police directly?'

'I didn't know the number.'

'You didn't know the number?' Sergeant Hamama repeated incredulously. 'Okay, does she have anything to say?'

The man turned to the woman and murmured something to her, leaning close to receive her answer. Then he turned to the sergeant.

'She has nothing to add to what I have just said.'

'*Al hamdulillah.* Now you get along, but I don't want you telling everyone in town what you've seen here. Is that understood? I don't want people coming out here and trampling over everything, you understand?'

'Yes, *effendim.* We won't say anything.'

'And don't forget to give your details to the officer there, just as soon as he's finished wiping off his face.'

The skinny officer was trying to rub the vomit off his boots by scuffing them into the sand. He sauntered over finally. Hamama rolled his eyes at Makana, then he nodded his head in the direction of the body.

'Where you were before, as a policeman, did you ever see anything like this?'

'Some,' said Makana.

'You were a detective? You dealt with homicides?'

'It was a long time ago.'

'Do you believe in fate?' Hamama regarded Makana carefully.

'Fate?'

'I don't think your turning up here was coincidence. I believe you are here to help me solve this thing.'

'Is this part of our deal? I mean, if I help you I suppose that cuts down what I owe you for helping me?'

'This man who has been butchered is not just anybody. He's our Qadi, or he was.' Hamama glanced at the remains of the judge. 'I think that trumps any missing persons case you have.'

'So we're even?'

'Yes, all right, we're even. Now what can you tell me?'

'Do you have a forensic team?'

'Yes, along with our helicopter and specially trained dogs. I imagine they'll be along in a minute.' Hamama produced a packet of gum and stuck a piece in his mouth and began chewing.

'A doctor, at least?' Makana asked.

'I suppose it'll have to be Doctor Medina.' Hamama tilted his hat onto the back of his head and stared at the ground beneath his feet. 'It couldn't have been an accident, could it?' It wasn't so much a question as a drowning man clutching at straws. 'It wasn't suicide either.' Hamama rested his hands on his ample hips and stared at the sky. 'We don't get many murders here. It's a peaceful place. People settle their differences quietly.'

They both turned as another car came rattling fast up the stony track. A similar pickup to the sergeant's, except the bonnet on this police car had been repaced by an olive-green one, from a military vehicle no doubt. The man who climbed out was a rangy, hard figure of a man in his thirties. He reached into the back, lifted out an old canvas stretcher and carried it over.

'Sadig, this is Mr Makana.'

The new arrival's face remained impassive. He had one stripe on his arm. Glancing briefly at Makana he nodded in the direction of the body.

'It's true then, someone cut the Qadi to pieces? I thought he was making it up when I heard.' 'A lot of people are going to be upset about this,' muttered Hamama. Sadig just grinned.

'And a few people will be celebrating tonight, that's for sure.'

Sergeant Hamama sniffed. 'I didn't explain. This is Mr Makana.'

'So you said.' Sadig took another sideways look at him.

'He's come all the way from Cairo to ask some questions about the Abubakr family.'

'The who?'

'You know, the big old house out there by the Dakrur road.'

Sadig took a longer look at Makana, in case there was anything he might have missed. 'I haven't heard anything about them in years. Didn't they all leave?'

'Yes.' Sergeant Hamama nodded. 'The place has been abandoned.'

'Can't see why anyone would be interested in that.' Sadig set down the stretcher alongside the dead man. 'My, my, the Qadi. Who would want to do a thing like that?'

'You knew him?' Makana asked.

'Everyone knew him,' replied Sadig, without looking up.

'Let's try and get him on here,' said Hamama. 'Call that idiot over to give us a hand.'

'You think we should move him?' Makana asked. Both Sergeant Hamama and Sadig turned to stare at him. 'Aren't you going to at least take photographs of the crime scene?'

'We don't have time for that. If we leave him out here much

longer there won't be anything left to photograph.' Hamama nodded upwards where vultures were circling. Already crows were hopping closer.

'What about the doctor? Shouldn't we wait for him?'

Sadig chuckled. 'Doctor Medina? We could be here a week. We'll be lucky if he's capable of standing on his own two feet without support.'

'We need to move him,' Sergeant Hamama concluded for Makana's benefit.

It took all four of them, including the skinny policeman. The Qadi was a heavy man and would have been hard enough to handle while still in one piece. The guts spilled out behind them as they wrestled with the slippery body, coated with a layer of brine that gave it a white sheen. By the time they had finished there was blood, guts and sand everywhere including all over their clothes. A yellow plastic sheet was fetched from the coffee shop out on the point and draped over the body to stave off the flies that were closing in despite the afternoon heat beginning to fade. The red globe of the sun flattened itself against the horizon like a balloon from which the air was slowly escaping.

'This is a small town,' Hamama said as they drove back into town. 'Everyone goes to the same school. They all marry one another's cousins. We have small-town problems and we take care of them ourselves. But something like this . . .' He shook his head. 'This is the kind of thing that brings people running and sticking their noses into our business.' He glanced over at Makana. 'We have to find out who did this as soon as possible. And you're going to help me.'

It was still light when they arrived at Doctor Medina's house on the outskirts of town. A large villa sinking into the shadows, set back in a garden thick with tamarind bushes and fig trees. Old palm trees bowed gracefully over a sandy drive that ended below a staircase on the left-hand side of the building. Wooden shutters on the upper floor were all closed. To the right of the stairs was a large screen door hanging from one hinge that led into the cool, dark interior of a waiting room. A fan turned lazily overhead but the benches were deserted. Sadig and the skinny officer carried the stretcher through another set of doors into the interior.

A tall, dishevelled man appeared. There was a distracted air about him. His shirt collar was askew, the tails hung out of the front of his trousers. His white coat was torn and stained and had what appeared to be burn marks on the sleeve. He stood swaying in the doorway as if unable to make up his mind which way to go, running a big hand alternately over his unshaven chin and through his hair which was thick and greying, pushed back from his forehead in a messy ruffle. There was something boyish and lost about his features and Makana caught the sharp reek of alcohol on his breath as he squeezed past into the examination room, doing his best to hold up his arm of the stretcher before the ungainly Qadi slipped to the floor. Sergeant Hamama stopped off in the reception room to use the telephone on the counter. A worried man. The two policemen placed the stretcher on the wooden table that served as the doctor's operating table, then retired outside to smoke. Makana and the doctor looked at one another over the Qadi's corpse splayed out on the table between them. The plastic tablecloth had slipped and the raw guts were exposed. The raucous buzz of excited flies filled the air and the doctor went over and flicked on a blue UV light set high on the wall that hissed every time one of them was drawn in and fried on the electric grille.

Doctor Medina leaned against the row of cabinets behind him and lit a cigarette.

'And you are?'

'I'm Makana.'

'Of course you are.' Doctor Medina's eyes narrowed as he inhaled deeply. 'I see you've met our dear Qadi, our little community's judge and spiritual guide.'

'I happened to be with the sergeant when the call came in.'

'A bad time to arrive.' The doctor's eyes were deep-set and dark. They examined Makana more carefully now. 'A visitor? Sightseeing?'

'He's an investigator from Cairo,' said Sergeant Hamama as he stamped into the room, 'and he's helping me with this.' He stuffed pieces of gum into his mouth, his jaws chomping up and down between words. 'Now, tell me what we have here.'

'We have one dead Qadi,' said Doctor Medina. 'Other than that your guess is as good as mine.'

'That's all you can say? Why do you think we brought him to you?'

'You brought him here because you have no choice.'

Doctor Medina turned and stubbed out his cigarette deliberately in a steel kidney dish that was piled high with butts and ash.

'It goes without saying that your services are invaluable. Is that what you want to hear? Good, now that you've made your point perhaps you wouldn't mind telling me what killed our illustrious friend?'

'Perhaps I should be more cautious?' Doctor Medina mused as he removed the tablecloth and leaned over the corpse. 'I could get myself into a lot of trouble.'

'You'll be in more trouble if you don't co-operate. That much I can tell you.' Sergeant Hamama thrust his hands into his pockets and glanced mournfully across at Makana. 'If I go through official channels this could take weeks, and by then I'd be up to here with officials and red tape. They'd drum me back to directing traffic while they took all the glory.'

'That is the closest I am going to get to thanks.' Doctor Medina pulled up a surgical mask and peered down the dead man's throat. He paused, then reached over to the set of instruments laid out on a tray and selected a set of long forceps. A harsh whiff of ammonia was beginning to come off the corpse. The set of forceps came alive, little arms flailing from side to side beneath the doctor's broad grin. 'Salt-water crabs,' he said, dropping the creature into the sink where it could be heard scrabbling about trying to climb up the porcelain sides.

'Can you tell if he was drowned first or cut open?' Makana asked. The doctor glanced at him over his surgical mask.

'What did you say he is here for?' he asked Hamama.

'He's looking for someone.'

'Who exactly?'

'It doesn't matter. Someone from a long time ago.'

'Musab Khayr,' said Makana.

'That *is* a long time ago,' said Doctor Medina, looking over at Makana.

'Do you remember him?' asked Makana.

'This is a small town. Everyone knows everyone.'

'Doctor, I hate to remind you, but we have a dead Qadi on our hands,' grumbled the sergeant.

'As you say, and since he's dead he's not going anywhere.' Doctor Medina turned back to Makana. 'Why are you interested in Musab Khayr?'

Before Makana had a chance to speak the sergeant answered

for him. 'A girl killed herself and he's being paid to think of it as murder. Now can you get on with this?'

'They must be paying you well for you to come all this way,' said the doctor.

'Forget about it,' Sergeant Hamama said in an exasperated tone. 'His expenses don't run to financing the medical profession.'

'Sounds as if you have already enquired,' said Doctor Medina.

'Please, just get on with the job.'

'Very well.' The doctor turned his attention back to the dead man on the table. 'In answer to your question, it is relatively simple to conduct a rudimentary examination.' Another fly sputtered against the electric grille leaving a charred smell in the air. 'How was this girl related to Musab?'

'She was his daughter,' Makana said.

'He was a nasty character. I remember that much. He ran away with Tewfiq Abubakr's daughter.'

'Unlucky man.' Hamama, still chewing fiercely, took over. 'Had three daughters, and they all ended up badly.' His memory seemed to be miraculously restored.

'One of them went abroad. They had a big house on the Dakrur road,' said the doctor.

'We went out to look at the place,' Sergeant Hamama went on. 'Not a lot of it left. Now, why don't you do something useful and tell me how the Qadi died?'

Doctor Medina stepped away from the body and leaned against the counter that ran along the wall. He pulled down his mask and reached for another cigarette which he had trouble lighting until Makana stepped in with his lighter.

'Watch out he doesn't go up in flames,' muttered Sergeant Hamama.

The doctor ignored the comment and focussed on his

cigarette. 'He's been in the water for more than twelve hours. My guess would be around twice that.'

'How can you tell?' asked the sergeant.

'Rigor mortis,' said Makana.

'Very good,' said the doctor, his eyes on Makana. 'Maybe you don't need me, Sergeant.'

'Twenty-four hours, so that would make it around sunset yesterday evening.' Hamama was moving around the table, hands thrust into his trouser pockets. He stabbed a finger at the corpse. 'Doctor, do you have any idea what kind of instrument could do something like that?'

Cigarette ash spilled down the front of Doctor Medina's white coat as he leaned forward to examine the edges of the wound.

'Something sharp.'

'Very good.' Hamama stared at the ceiling. 'I really couldn't ask for a better team.'

'A good, clean blade, I would say. Not very long.' The doctor began digging away with his fingers at the flap of skin. 'Nice, clean slice. No signs of struggle.'

'It looks almost surgical, wouldn't you say?' Makana suggested.

'Yes,' Doctor Medina mused. 'It does look almost too clean, except where the fish have got at it.' He glanced at the sergeant. 'I'm going to need some time. I have to do blood tests and so on.' He took hold of the head and twisted it from side to side, lifted up the hands, pressed his thumbs into the arms. 'Salt has a preserving effect. It slows the process of decay,' he said.

'Why don't you have the air conditioner on?' Hamama grumbled.

'It's broken.'

'You should talk to Wad Nubawi.'

'I will,' sighed the doctor, closing his eyes momentarily.

'Musab left here with Abubakr's daughter, neither of them has been seen since.'

'Not that again.' The sergeant was looking back and forth between them as though he couldn't decide which one of them to hit first.

'Who would he go to if he did come back?'

'He wouldn't dare,' said Doctor Medina.

'Can you tell if he drowned?' Sergeant Hamama asked. The others looked over as though they had forgotten he was there.

'I'll have to check the lungs to see if there's any water in there. But already I wonder about the amount of blood.'

'Blood?' echoed the sergeant.

'An incision of this size would produce a sudden release of blood. The blood vessels would show signs of rupture.'

'And that is not the case?' asked Makana.

'Look, I'm not a pathologist. It's a while since I've done anything like this.'

'I'll say one thing.' Hamama strolled to the head of the examination table and peered down into the bloated face. 'He wasn't much loved but I can't say he deserved this.'

'If I do this I'm going to need a formal request in writing.'

'You don't need to worry about that.' Sergeant Hamama scowled. 'All you need is to do it quickly. There's no time to waste. As soon as the papers get hold of this story I'll be up to my ears in protocol.'

'I don't want to go to prison.' The doctor moved to the sink and ripped off his gloves to begin washing his hands.

'I told you, don't worry about it. You'll have everything you need.'

'What do we do with him when I've finished? We can't keep him here,' Doctor Medina went on. 'The other patients might complain about the smell. And we can't bury him until we hand him over. So we need storage.'

'What kind of storage?' Sergeant Hamama frowned.

'Ideally, a freezer of some kind.'

'You don't have one?'

'An ice box. I don't think he'd fit. I deal with the living, Sergeant, not the dead.'

'Don't worry about it,' said Hamama. 'I'll think of something.'

'How important was he?' Makana asked.

Hamama straightened up, one hand to his aching back. 'The Qadi has been the judge of this town for years. Everyone knows him. He runs the courts. Not criminal courts, you understand. For serious offences we send people to Mersa Matruh. This is more land disputes, divorces, debts that were unresolved. He represented the state, and around here no one likes being told what to do. This is a very traditional place, Makana. People like the old ways.' He broke off to address the doctor. 'I've solved your problem. Wad Nubawi has a big freezer in his shop. I'll send a couple of the boys over to fetch it.'

'You want to keep him in a supermarket freezer?' Doctor Medina stared at the sergeant.

'Why not?' Sergeant Hamama shrugged. 'Makes no difference to him.' With that he picked up his hat and headed for the door. 'You can keep him out in the garage. We don't have a choice. Until I receive word that we're getting extra resources we're stuck with the man.' With one hand on the handle he paused and looked at Makana. 'I'll run you back to your hotel.'

'If it's all right with you, I'd rather walk. I'd like some fresh air.'

'Well, take as much as you want. It's the one thing we have plenty of out here, along with sand, of course.'

The door slammed behind him. Doctor Medina took his Rothmans out of his breast pocket. He regarded Makana curiously as he lit one.

'Our sergeant seems to have taken a liking to you.'

'He wants to keep an eye on me.'

'He seems to think you can help him with the case.'

'He's desperate.'

'Well, just be careful not to step on too many toes. People around here are sensitive about outsiders nosing around in their private affairs.'

'I take it you're not from here originally.'

'Is it that obvious?' Doctor Medina smiled. 'The answer is no. But I settled here so long ago that most people will grudgingly accept me as a local.'

'I'll drop by to see how you're getting on.'

'Do that,' said the doctor.

On the short walk back to the hotel Makana noticed how astonishingly peaceful it was. He had forgotten how quiet the world could be. The road was dark and there were very few lights, but the stars were out and he was guided back to town by the ruins of the old town of Shali which rose up on a little hill. The walls were illuminated by bright floodlights. There was a ghostly aspect to the collapsed, abandoned houses, as if the spirits of that other time were still holding vigil over the present.

The lights and sounds of Cairo seemed as far away as another galaxy. As he reached the main square a flaring match drew Makana's attention to the second floor of a building with a long open veranda. A man was leaning on the brick parapet smoking, watching Makana go by. Above and behind him a halo of coloured lights rotated slowly under the ceiling, like a celestial chart of the heavens seen through a kaleidescope. A constellation of the insane.

In the telephone shop on the far side of the main square, the Quran recitations still groaned through the squeaky loudspeakers. A lopsided picture of the Kaaba that hung on the wall behind the counter was the only decoration on display. The man behind the counter wore thick spectacles and a bushy beard covered his face. He looked up as though annoyed at having to break away from whatever meaningful task he was engaged in on his computer screen. Behind the thin circles of glass there lurked that familiar combination of disdain and righteousness. Makana called Ragab. There wasn't much to report, but Makana felt obliged to let him know that his money was being put to constructive use.

'I've located Karima's family home. It looks like nobody has lived there for a long time.'

'Do what you have to do,' said Ragab. 'But don't feel obliged to stay there if it is leading nowhere. No harm in changing course.'

When he stepped back out, the silence felt like a relief from the droning voice imploring piety. The streets were deserted, but arriving back at the hotel Makana found the lobby crowded with people. At first he thought it must be another football match, but Nagy, the manager, was sitting with a group of men watching the news on television. There were demonstrations in Cairo.

'The Palestinians,' Nagy said, glancing up from his chair. His eyes were sunken in the glow from the television set. Smoke curled from his hand as he covered his mouth to smoke. 'May Allah destroy the homes of all the Jews.'

Somebody laughed over in the corner and Makana made out a large, clumsy figure whom he had seen earlier in the day sweeping the floor.

124

'Don't laugh, Ayman, this is serious.'

The big man fell silent and stared gloomily at the floor. He seemed to have the role of the lame dog everyone enjoyed kicking. Makana turned back to the images on the screen. Things had been escalating since the end of March when the Israelis had invaded the West Bank in retaliation for a suicide bombing at a hotel in which thirty people were killed. Now tanks bearing the blue star of David were rolling through Ramallah. There were reports of a fierce battle in the town of Jenin. Yasser Arafat, chairman of the PLO, was under siege in his headquarters and protests had broken out all over the region. The excited news commentator showed demonstrators marching in Damascus, Khartoum, Rabat, as well as Cairo.

'Mubarak is frightened,' murmured one of the figures sitting in the dark, as images from the solidarity protests in Cairo returned. 'Students are chanting, Mubarak, you coward, you're a client of the Americans.' He waved his phone in the air so that people could see his sources were authentic. It wasn't the kind of detail you were likely to hear on the state-run media. Perhaps Sami had a point about new kinds of journalism; people wanted to tell their own stories.

'It's all being run by the Ikhwan,' suggested another figure, only to be shouted down by the one with the mobile telephone.

'The Brotherhood doesn't want trouble with the government. This is the work of communists, believe you me.'

'Nasserists, as well,' offered Nagy from the back, which brought general approval. He went further. 'Who knows, maybe they will bring down the government,' he said, apparently in all sincerity. The notion was dismissed with hoots of laughter as the image of a Kentucky Fried Chicken restaurant that had been smashed up was displayed on screen as an example of the 'vandalism' that was taking place. Makana left them to it and retired upstairs. As he walked down the corridor towards his room a shadow emerged from his room.

'Hey!' he called. 'What do you think you're doing?'

The man turned to reveal himself as Sadig, the hard-faced police corporal. Head shaven like an escapee from a lunatic asylum, tunic unbuttoned. He shut the door calmly and walked towards Makana nonchalantly.

'That's my room. What are you up to?' Makana demanded.

'Me?' Sadig shrugged with an insolent sneer, 'who knows? I could ask you the same question.'

'Am I supposed to understand what that means?'

'It means you may be able to fool the sergeant, but I know what you're up to.' He leaned closer. 'I don't think it's a coincidence that you turn up just when we find the Qadi cut to pieces.'

He brushed past Makana, making sure his shoulder bumped into him hard. Makana heard him chuckling to himself as he descended the stairs. Makana wondered if Hamama had planned the whole thing. He knew he was staying behind at the doctor's place. It would have provided them with a perfect opportunity if they wanted to know more about him. And Sadig's lingering was not by coincidence. It was a reminder that while he was here he was under their control. They wanted him to know they could search his room any time they wanted to.

It wasn't that the room contained anything of value. An old holdall, a few clothes, a couple of books. Nothing appeared to have been touched. Makana stood in the middle of the room and then decided to search the place thoroughly. He pulled the wardrobe away from the wall, tipped it on its side, removed all the shelves. Nothing. Then he did the same with the bed, stripping it, taking the mattress off, turning it over to discover a brown stain the size of a body which only made him wonder what had happened here. He lifted up the frame and examined the underneath. Cobwebs and dust, the evidence of woodworm activity, a wrapper from a condom with words in German. There wasn't much more to go through. A chair, a small mirror which he lifted off the wall. The bathroom was the same, nowhere to hide anything. So they weren't planning to plant evidence on him or set him up that way. So what had Sadig been doing? Checking up on him, or just trying to scare him? Perhaps both.

'What's all the noise for?' Nagy appeared in the doorway. He surveyed the chaos.

'Unwanted visitors,' said Makana.

'I'll tell Ayman to spray again in the morning.'

'No, I need another room.'

Nagy looked at Makana, sizing him up, trying to decide whether he could afford to lose a client and deciding he would be able to live with the inconvenience.

'Take the one next door. It's already made up. I'll get the key. And leave this now, we're trying to watch the football. I'll get it fixed tomorrow.'

So much for politics and the plight of the Palestinians. Makana's new room, whose collection of squashed mosquito corpses stuck to the walls was marginally smaller, afforded him a view of the conical minaret he had only heard previously. Now he could stare at the battered metal loudspeaker that seemed to have been pinned as an afterthought onto the side of the stubby, uneven brown pillar of clay and bricks. Once installed, Makana sat on the bed and reached for the telephone to call Zahra. She took a long time to answer. He was about to hang up when she said hello.

'I thought you must be out.'

'Don't be silly,' she laughed lightly. 'It's a mobile. You are never out with a mobile.'

'No, of course not,' he said, feeling a little foolish.

'I was hoping you would call.'

'Really?' That his heart was capable of somersaults startled him.

'I was wondering how you were getting on?'

'It's hard to say.' Makana settled himself back against the wall with his feet on the bed, and went on to explain about the Qadi's untimely death.

'But why have they involved you in that? Surely that will just delay you?'

'I think it's their way of keeping an eye on me. It's all right. If it means they will help me I'm happy to co-operate.'

'So, you're helping the police?'

'In a way, although that doesn't seem to deter them from searching my room.'

He heard her sharp intake of breath. 'I don't think you should stay there, really. It sounds dangerous. Can't you just come back and tell Ragab that you found nothing?'

'The truth is there is little sign of Musab here. Nobody has seen him for years.'

'It just seems so remote and . . .' Zahra hesitated. 'Isn't it possible the answer lies here in Cairo?'

'This is the perfect place for him. It's quiet and isolated and there is only a small police presence.' Makana felt like a fanatic insisting on his version of the truth. His enthusiasm faded as no response was forthcoming. 'He must still have friends here. I just haven't found them yet.'

'It sounds like you are settling in there.'

Makana laughed like a teenager. 'Don't worry, I already miss Cairo.'

'Is that true?'

'Sure,' he said. 'Certain aspects of it.'

'Such as what?' she asked.

'Well, I don't know. It's very quiet here,' he said, realising his mistake only after he had spoken.

'Ah,' said Zahra. 'I thought you meant you missed the people here.'

'That too.'

After that they both seemed stuck for something to say and Makana found himself on the one hand wishing the call over, and on the other not wanting to put down the receiver.

'Well, I wish you luck with your investigating.' There was a long silence. So long that Makana began to think the line had been cut. 'Is it okay for me to call you on this number?'

'Yes, of course,' he said. 'I imagine I will be here most evenings.'

'Because it's so quiet, yes, I know,' she said. He heard her laughter ringing long after he had hung up the phone.

Chapter Thirteen

Nagy was slouched over the reception desk when Makana came down the next day. He folded the newspaper he was reading and straightened up. There was something about his manner which seemed different to the previous day. An odd combination of fear and respect. Makana realised that word had already spread of the Qadi's death and his own involvement in the investigation.

'How do you find the new room, *effendi?*'

'It's fine, thank you.'

'If there's anything you need, all you have to do is ask.'

'I'll bear that in mind. I need some cigarettes. Where is the nearest shop?'

'Don't worry about that. I'll send the boy.' Nagy stepped to the doorway behind him and called through it. 'Walad! Where is that idiot boy? Ayman!'

'Never mind. I can walk.'

Makana exited the hotel before Nagy could stop him, though his voice echoed down the street still yelling for the porter. Makana walked in the direction of the bus station where he was sure he had seen a shop. It was closer than he imagined. The whole town could be circled in twenty minutes. The sign outside the shop read Wad Nubawi's Supermarket. A shop with aspirations. It was remarkably well stocked, and crowded. A table by the entrance was stacked with plastic bags of melting frozen beans, okra, falafel, all on offer. They were sprinkled with frost that slid away to join the swelling pool of water forming beneath the table. A dusty rectangle marked where a freezer had once stood. A man in his fifties with the sharp cheekbones and a Bedouin scarf wrapped around his neck was counting up items at the register. Three women in black were demanding answers. It took Makana a few minutes to realise that the women were speaking a language he did not recognise. When he spoke, the Bedouin addressed them in Arabic, probably for Makana's benefit.

'What could I do? They said they needed it for something. It's not my business what they do with it. The police have authority. We're all under their command. Now these beans will last a week in your refrigerator at home, but you'd better take them now because they'll be gone by midday, as Allah is my witness.'

The women bustled out of the shop, cawing to one another in excitement. The Bedouin straightened up and narrowed his eyes at Makana.

'What service can I offer you?'

'You seem to be busy.'

'Never too busy for new customers,' the Bedouin smiled. 'You're the one from Cairo everyone is talking about.'

'Everyone?'

'I heard you're here to find the man who cut the Qadi up from one end to the other.'

'You must hear a lot of interesting things,' said Makana. 'I'll take two packets of Cleopatra.'

A bony hand set the cigarettes on the counter. As Makana went to take them the man swiftly withdrew them. He was grinning now, revealing a gold tooth.

'Maybe you can tell me what's going on?' It was only half playful. Underneath the smile was a hint of menace.

'It's police business. You should ask Sergeant Hamama.'

'Ah,' he waved dismissively. 'He never tells me anything. They took my freezer.'

'I can see that,' nodded Makana. 'It can't be easy.'

'I think I have a right to know. I have a delivery in three days. What am I supposed to do?'

'I suppose you'll have to cancel it.'

'Naturally. And how am I supposed to make a living like that? I have a family to feed.' He reached into a plastic bag alongside the cash register and selected a dried date which he bit into, spitting the stone out through the doorway with practised skill. There was an aspect of quaint theatricality about him and a certain bitterness.

'Are you going to sell those to me or what?'

The man looked down as if asking how the cigarettes had got there, then he pushed them across the counter and took Makana's money.

'I don't really see why they need outside help. We take care of things our own way around here.'

'Maybe that's exactly why,' said Makana.

Outside, the karetta hurtled by and wheeled in a tight circle, the skinny donkey scuttling to stay upright, hooves skidding on the tarmac as Bulbul mercilessly flogged its raw hind quarters with his whip.

'My Sudanese brother! Have you seen Jebel Mawta yet? How about the tomb of Ar-Simun? And Cleopatra's Eye?' The plump

132

boy brought the cart to walking pace and leaned down to whisper. 'Perhaps the brother would like something more interesting? Hashish, very good quality. Johnnie Walker black label?'

'Where would you find such items in a place like this?'

It was the opening he had been waiting for. The boy's face lit up like a stage performer feeling the warmth of the spotlight. 'Bulbul can find anything you want, even women. You want to go to Abu Sharaf?'

'What is there at Abu Sharaf?'

Bulbul stamped a sliver of blue plastic that passed for a flip-flop and cackled. 'You really don't know anything, do you?' Eyes darting around he leaned down from his perch once more. 'Don't you know why there are no female donkeys in this town?'

'I hadn't noticed,' admitted Makana.

'Well, it's true. People are very religious here. They would be offended if they saw donkeys mating in the street. So they banished all female donkeys to Abu Sharaf. So when someone asks you if you're going to Abu Sharaf, they are really asking if you are looking for a woman.' And with a final flourish of laughter he skidded away, whipping the poor donkey while standing up like a Roman emperor in his chariot. As he veered around the edge of the square he leaned out of the cart and spat deliberately on the road, right in front of the big house on the corner.

The local girls' school comprised a dull, single-storey building surrounded by a high wall, all of which was constructed of the same grey breeze blocks. It was hard to imagine a less inspiring sight. The sound of children reciting multipication tables trailed behind him as Makana walked along the veranda that connected the classrooms, aware of the attention he was attracting. Small faces turned towards him, distracted by the appearance of a stranger in their midst. Finally, a teacher stepped out to ask what he wanted, children crowding into the doorway behind her. Before Makana could speak another woman appeared at the far end. She made a signal with her hand and the teacher gestured for him to proceed.

'Madame Fawzia will speak to you.'

Madame Fawzia, when he finally reached her, was a stout woman with a set expression on her face. The emotionless look and presence of an official who knows their own importance. With a nod she gestured for him to follow and they turned along the L-shaped arm of the veranda which appeared to be the administrative wing.

'How can I help you?'

'No doubt you have heard the terrible news about the honourable Qadi? Well, I am here to help the local police with their enquiries.'

'Ah,' the warden's headscarf bobbed. 'You're the one who came from Cairo.'

'That's correct.' It seemed there were certain advantages to working in a small town. News travelled fast, so fast indeed that she didn't even question his authority. He had been seen in the company of Sergeant Hamama. That was commendation enough.

'*Ahlan wasahlan*. You are very welcome here.' She almost managed to squeeze a smile out of her constricted features. 'Thank you for coming to aid us in our time of trouble.' There was something flat about her performance, as if she were merely going through the routine of what was expected of her. Sighing heavily and using a series of keys attached to a long chain that she drew from somewhere inside her clothes, she unlocked the door to her office, which was stale and gloomy, with only one window high up in the opposite wall providing any glimpse of the outside world. She went round behind the desk, saying, 'I don't really see why you have come to me. One of our students is not involved in anything wrong, I hope?' Gesturing wearily for him to take a seat, the warden sat down, rested her elbows on the table and waited.

'Nothing like that,' Makana smiled to put her at ease, although the stern frown showed no signs of fading. Smoking, he decided, was out of the question. 'Actually, I am conducting an enquiry in parallel to the investigation into the Qadi's death.'

'I don't understand. Are the two investigations related?'

'They may be.' Makana changed his tack and stopped smiling as it seemed to be having a contrary effect, making Madame Fawzia more nervous rather than less. A woman who admired authority expected someone working with the police to reflect the sobriety of the office. 'Such enquiries are complicated and may not make sense to untrained persons. The key to any investigation may lie in an entirely unexpected direction. We would be failing in our duty if we did not explore every possible aspect of a case.'

'Of course. Then how can I help, Mr . . .'

'Makana,' he said tersely. 'A woman who I believe used to attend this school, Nagat Abubakr, she married a man named Musab Khayr.'

'That is correct.' Madame Fawzia twisted the engagement ring on her finger. 'Though it was a long time ago. I don't see—'

'You knew her?'

'I know Nagat. I attended this very school with her, many years ago.' The memory temporarily eased the fierce look on the woman's face, which was round and hard. 'Why are you asking about her? Has something happened?'

'I'm afraid Nagat passed away a couple of years ago.'

'I'm sorry to hear that.' Madame Fawzia lowered her eyes to stare at her hands, clasped together in front of her on the chipped surface of the desk. The ring was tarnished and around her high neck a simple pendant hung on a thin chain.

'I am here in connection with her daughter, Karima, who died in a fire.'

'Her daughter?' Madame Fawzia's eyes floated towards a curling, desiccated map of the world that hung on the wall to her right. The colours were faded to soft browns and khakis, as if the world were a forgotten kingdom. 'This is all very sad news, but we lost contact when she moved to Cairo.'

'That would have been in nineteen eighty-one.'

'Yes, exactly. The year the president was shot.' Madame Fawzia fiddled with her ring. 'It must be sad to lose a child.'

'You have children yourself.'

'No, I never had any of my own. I console myself with the thought that most of the wives of the prophet, may peace be upon him, never bore him children either.'

'Nagat's family was once quite wealthy. I understand the family used to own a lot of land?'

'They had a few fields, but Nagat's father was a lazy man. He didn't do much with it, even the house was in ruins. He carried himself grandly, but they couldn't afford to fix it up.'

'Musab Khayr. What can you tell me about him?'

'Musab? Well, they left together. Everyone knew they wouldn't be back.'

'What made people think that?'

Madame Fawzia shrugged her shoulders. 'We just knew.'

'What can you tell me about Nagat's sisters?'

'Her sisters?' Madame Fawzia seemed momentarily confused. 'Her sister. She only has the one, Butheyna.'

'I thought there was a third sister?'

'Oh, there was Safira, but she ran away.'

'Ran away?'

'Disappeared. She was strange that one. People said she spent more time in the company of jinn and afreet than with real people.' Madame Fawzia regarded him carefully as she spoke, as if conscious of not wanting to sound too far-fetched.

'What about Butheyna. Where can I find her?'

'Oh, she left. Her husband got a job in the Gulf somewhere. Kuwait, Qatar, one of those. I can find a telephone number for you.'

'That would be helpful. And Musab Khayr, what kind of man was he?'

'I didn't really know him.' Madame Fawzia's eyes were fixed on the light coming through the high window. 'We were at school together, you know. Me and Nagat. In the same class. I think we even shared the same desk one year.'

'Did she ever come back here to visit, with her daughter?'

'She never came back.' Madame Fawzia grew still, her eyes narrowing as they came back to find Makana. 'The truth is she wasn't welcome here. That man was trouble and nobody ever understood why she ran away with him. I still don't see how this relates to the Qadi's death.'

'Like I said, these are two parallel investigations. It's purely routine.'

'I see.'

Getting to her feet, she came round from behind her desk and peered at the framed class photographs that covered one wall of the office. 'She must be here somewhere. Let me see.' She traced her way back along the years until she came to the right collection of students. Leaning closer she frowned. Finally, she stabbed a stubby finger at the glass. 'There.'

It was difficult to gain much from the annual school photograph, hard enough to pick out the girl from within the rows of faces. She would have been around fifteen, Makana guessed as he came nearer. He had the impression of a slim figure, her eyes looking away, off to one side. There was something furtive about her, as if she was uncomfortable with having her picture taken. Other girls grinned broadly, or tried to look sincere, or serious, or pretty. Nagat looked unhappy.

'How long after this did she leave?'

Madame Fawzia fiddled with her ring. 'Oh, quite soon afterwards. A year perhaps, maybe less.'

'She was very young. It must have been quite a scandal.'

'Oh, she was used to creating scandal.' For the first time Madame Fawzia smiled, her eyes still absorbed with the old school photograph. 'We all look so young,' she murmured to herself.

'You knew her quite well.'

Madame Fawzia turned back to him. 'We were friends. I sometimes think she liked to have me around because I did what she asked. Nagat liked to be in charge. She wasn't like Safira.'

'What exactly happened to Safira?'

'Nobody knows. She wandered off into the desert. It's easy to get lost, and if you do no one will ever find you. It was an unlucky family.'

'Do you know who owns the family land now?'

Madame Fawzia shook her head.

'You've been very helpful,' Makana said. 'I shall make a note of it in my report.'

'That's very kind of you,' she murmured.

'I only have one last request. I need a copy of that photograph.'

'A copy?' Her brows furrowed. Finally, she reached for the frame on the wall and removed the picture from inside before handing it over.

'Your need is greater than mine. I can have an extra copy made up to replace it.'

'That's very good of you,' Makana said.

As he made his way back through the streets Makana spotted a messy, fugitive figure stepping out of the post office.

'Doctor Medina?' Makana hailed. The deep-set eyes, red from lack of sleep or something else, momentarily sought escape and then resigned themselves. The two men shook hands. As they fell into step Makana spied the Bedouin in the supermarket. He was leaning forward, his forehead almost touching the glass, chewing slowly. The gaunt face was framed by posters advertising washing powder and chocolate eggs.

'I caught one of Hamama's men searching my room last night,' said Makana.

'Really? Did they find anything?'

'I don't know what he was looking for.'

'Money, probably. They are all disreputable.' Doctor Medina paused to find his Rothmans. He nodded at the *'ahwa* they were passing. 'Why don't we drink a coffee?' he suggested.

They sat on the terrace that was about a metre wide around a metal table that sat awkwardly on broken paving stones. The doctor nodded greetings to what seemed like a continuous stream of people wandering by.

'You seem to know everybody,' observed Makana.

'In America, everyone has a therapist to talk to. In Italy, the Catholics have their priests. Well here, all we have is our doctor.

So I know all their intimate secrets. I know about the kidney stones, the constipation, the impotence. They would like to hate me and some no doubt would like to kill me but they know they would not survive for long without my help.'

'How long have you been here?'

'It feels like a lifetime,' sighed Doctor Medina. 'I love the open air, the land. When I first came here I would go out into the desert for days. So much space, and the stars! Instead we crowd together like sheep. What does that tell you about human nature?'

As the doctor puffed away on his cigarette, Makana wondered if his buoyant mood was due to a lack of alcohol or the anticipation of what was to come. The fact that the doctor was able to function more or less normally suggested that he had some control over his drinking but Makana had met alcoholics before. The smart ones were clever at concealing it.

'You should be careful of Sergeant Hamama.'

'Why do you say that?' asked Makana.

'Simply a friendly warning. You can be sure that he wants something from you in return.'

'Like what?'

'Who knows? Hamama may not look ambitious, but he is. Ever since he took over as police chief when Captain Mustafa died.'

'When was that exactly?'

'Only about a month ago, maybe less. Captain Mustafa was an outsider, like me. He'd been here for years but was never really accepted. Hamama is a local boy. There's a lot of support for him but he doesn't have the rank. There are rumours that the high command in Mersa Matruh have their doubts about him. That's why he's so keen to clear this case up as fast as possible. It's his chance to prove himself. The longer it drags on the more likely it is they will send an outsider in.'

'What happened to the captain?'

'A car accident.'

'Where was this?'

'Out on the old desert road west of the town.'

'Where does that road lead?'

'Oh, it'll take you anywhere you want to,' the doctor smiled. 'The desert routes take you west into the Libyan desert and beyond, to Niger, Mali, or south to Chad and Sudan, but it's dangerous.'

'In what way?'

'It's easy to hide in such a vast open space. There are a lot of bad people out there. The type you don't want to meet. Smugglers, armed men of one faction or another.'

A movement drew Makana's eye to the upper floor of a building on the far side of the square. The previous evening he had noticed a young man there. He appeared to be back again, yawning, leaning on the parapet blowing smoke into the air.

They finished their coffees and got to their feet. Doctor Medina insisted on paying. 'How are you getting around?' he asked as they stepped back into the road.

'On foot, most of the time, unless Sergeant Hamama happens to be around.'

'I have an idea,' said the doctor. 'Follow me.'

They crossed the square to the narrow street that ran behind the hotel, past the mosque Makana could see from his hotel window and which appeared to be inhabited only by stray cats. At the corner was a small restaurant and beyond that a shop that rented out bicycles to tourists. Doctor Medina hailed a young man of about twenty with long hair who emerged from the shadows, his hands black with engine oil.

'Kamal, this is Mr Makana. He needs some means of transport while he is staying here. I thought of the Norton.' Kamal scratched the back of his neck. 'It is working, isn't it?'

'Of course, *ya doktor.*' With a gesture of apology, Kamal ducked away to attend to a couple of blonde girls in search of bicycles.

'He keeps telling me he's fixed it,' Doctor Medina said to Makana, 'but it's never ready. This is a good opportunity to sort this out once and for all. It's a good machine,' he beamed. 'You'll like it.' With that Medina turned and began walking away. He had only taken three paces before he stopped. 'Why don't you come over later?' he called. 'I may have something to show you.'

Makana promised he would look in. As the doctor left, Kamal came back over.

'Would you like to see it?' he asked before leading the way through to the back of the workshop. The Norton looked like it belonged in a museum.

'How old is that thing?' Makana asked sceptically.

Kamal grinned, rubbing his hands with a dirty rag. 'It's from when the British were here, during the world war.'

'And it still works?'

'Oh, these machines just need a little care and attention. They last for ever.'

It was a spirited defence, but Makana was not entirely convinced about the wisdom of getting on a death machine like this.

'How long has it been sitting here?'

'Well, it had a few problems. Some spare parts are difficult to get hold of, but the doctor loves this thing. It's just that, well, he had a couple of accidents.' Kamal glanced at Makana to see if he understood that he was referring to the doctor's drinking habits.

'You know him pretty well.'

'The doctor? Sure, everyone knows him. He's a good man, he just has his moments.' Kamal ran the rag over the wide leather seat. Makana could see cobwebs between the spokes. 'You're the one who came here to help the police, right?'

'Something like that.'

'They need all the help they can get.' Kamal grinned. 'You should see the sights. Iskander the Great came here, you know, famous Roman general?'

'I think Iskander was Greek.'

Kamal frowned. 'Greek, Roman, what difference does it make? In the end they left. Just like the British. Everyone leaves in the end. Except us.' As he talked, Kamal was nervously going over the motorcycle, twisting the throttle, tugging the gear cable, stamping on the footbrake.

'You want to leave?'

'Me?' The young man sniffed. 'I would leave tomorrow if I could.'

'Where would you go?'

'Cairo, of course. I've never been. What's it like?'

Makana considered how on earth to begin explaining a city like Cairo. It would be like the story of the blind men and the elephant. Each one touches a different part of it and imagines an entirely different creature. But Kamal wasn't expecting an answer. He already knew.

'I imagine it shines. There are a million lights, and beautiful girls, like the ones you see in Amr Diab's videos. And no one ever sleeps.'

It would have been cruel to puncture the boy's illusion, to remind him of those who lived in obscurity, hidden from view in the dark corners of the metropolis, the abject poverty, and the millions just like him who had watched their dreams crumble to dust. As they came back out into the sunshine a horn sounded as the battered police pick-up rattled and screeched its way to a halt and Sergeant Hamama leaned out of the window.

'Get in,' he called to Makana.

Chapter Fourteen

A half-eaten *ful* sandwich wrapped in newspaper occupied the passenger seat. Hamama tossed it quickly up onto the dashboard as Makana climbed in. The car took off before he had even managed to pull the door closed.

'People are not happy. I've been on the phone all morning. Everyone wants to know what happened. Naturally, they all seem to blame me.' Hamama steered carefully around a family of goats that had taken up residence in the middle of the road. 'The Qadi was a highly respected figure. Of course, everyone around here hated him, but what can you do?'

'He must have made a few enemies over the years.'

'A man in his position? Naturally.' Hamama glanced over at Makana. 'This case is important to me. I talked to Mersa Matruh this morning and I get the feeling my promotion depends on me catching this killer. Doesn't make it any easier.'

'It shouldn't be that difficult, for a man of your experience.'

Sergeant Hamama narrowly avoided running over a donkey and several pedestrians.

'You wouldn't be laughing at me now, would you?'

'I was trying to be encouraging.'

'Well, keep it to yourself next time.'

'What I really meant was that whoever did this had a motive. And that motive may lie in the Qadi's old cases. The sentences he has handed down over the years.'

'It's a possibility. Still, it's not going to be easy. What kind of a man can cut another up like so much basturma?' The sergeant drew a hand across his substantial belly and shivered. He threw Makana an odd sideways glance. 'You're not here to keep an eye on me, are you?'

'What do you mean?'

'I mean,' the sergeant hesitated, apparently not sure what he meant. 'State Security, the Ministry of Justice?'

'I'm not here to spy on you,' Makana said. 'So you don't need to send your men snooping around in my room.'

'You mean Sadig?' Sergeant Hamama sniffed. 'He gets carried away. He thinks I'm too trusting and that it's a little suspicious you turning up just when the Qadi gets butchered.'

'And what do you think?'

'I think good police work is about eliminating possibilities. That means everyone is a suspect until proven otherwise. You'd do the same, right?'

'I suppose so.'

'Now listen,' Hamama went on, 'I think Sadig gets overexcited. He doesn't mean any harm, so there's no need for this to go any further. The point is, if you help me to find out who butchered the Qadi I will be very grateful.' He saw the scepticism on Makana's face. 'I mean it. Whatever you need is yours.'

'So I shouldn't expect him in my room again?'

'You have my word on it.' Sergeant Hamama settled himself back in his seat and stared ahead as the lake came into view, shimmering softly in the sun.

'Where are we going by the way?'

'The scene of the crime. Where else?'

They slowed and Sergeant Hamama pulled off the road. The two men sat for a time in silence with only the sound of the wind whistling by. It should have been peaceful, but Makana felt uneasy. He cracked open the door and stepped out. The salt in the sand formed a hard crust that cracked under his shoes. The spot where the Qadi had been found was marked out with a couple of poles from which plastic tape flapped in the breeze.

'Any idea what he was doing out here?' Makana turned towards Hamama who was leaning on the front of the car. 'Perhaps we should talk to his office.'

'Lucky for us you're here, or I would never have thought of that.'

'You've already done it?'

Hamama tried not to look pleased with himself and failed. He reached into his pocket for a packet of gum to celebrate and chewed away gleefully. Perhaps what he needed was less an expert to help him in his investigation as a witness to his own brilliance.

'Some kind of business delegation was on the way out here to meet him.'

'What kind of delegation?' asked Makana, turning his back to the wind to light a cigarette.

'The assistant I spoke to thought it was something to do with a tourist venture.' Sergeant Hamama squinted at the lake. 'They come here and smell money. They want to build fancy hotels and open up the airport, bring people in from all over the world.'

'The town benefits, doesn't it?'

'Does it?' Sergeant Hamama studied his scuffed boots. 'We have a limited supply of fresh water and these tourists come from places where it rains for months. They still want their pools filled and three showers a day, and I don't know what else. And besides, the big money goes right by us and into the pockets of the big fish.'

'And the Qadi was involved in the sector?'

'He was the Qadi, he took care of all the legal matters.' Which was Hamama's way of saying he really had no idea.

Makana looked out over the thin sliver of water that seemed to almost float on top of the sand. Beyond it the desert unfurled like a silken carpet. Where it ended was another story. You could literally drive for days and still not find the end to it. The desert made him think of home, and the long journey that had brought him here.

'How did he get into the water?' Makana wondered aloud as they walked back along the edge of the lake towards the car.

'How?' Sergeant Hamama straightened up and focussed all his powers. 'His killer must have rolled him in, I suppose.'

'It's hardly deep enough here, and he was completely immersed.'

'Well, maybe he walked further out.'

Makana pointed at the shack out on the point. 'That's where the farmer made the phone call, isn't it?'

'That's Luqman's place,' said Hamama. 'He sells snacks and things to the tourists. He's all right. We questioned him but he saw nothing.'

'Maybe we should try again,' suggested Makana. 'Sometimes things come back to people.'

Hamama planted his hands on his ample hips. 'I told you, my men already talked to him. He didn't see anything. It's a waste of time.'

'We won't know that until we speak to him, will we?'

Hamama stared at Makana for a moment and then spat out his gum on the sand. 'I'll bet they really hated you,' he said.

'Who did?' Makana was mystified.

'The people who used to work with you,' said Hamama over his shoulder as he climbed into the police car.

Makana was silent as they drove back a short distance before turning to follow a short track onto the point that jutted out from the shore. The sergeant had no idea how right he was. He thought of his former adjutant, Mek Nimr, and the lengths he had gone to to get Makana expelled, first from the police force and then the country.

Khalid Luqman was in his mid-thirties, a slim man with a pleasant face and an air of calm about him. His hair was shaved close to his head. There was an air of scruffy abandonment about the coffee shop. Two makeshift structures were built on the sandy patch of scrub. One of them appeared to be a storage room and the other was a shack open on three sides by means of panels that were lifted up and held in place by strands of frayed nylon rope. A warm but not unpleasant breeze blew in from the water. The area in front of the shack afforded an unimpeded panorama of the lake and beyond. In the distance a strange escarpment of striated rock rose like a whale against the horizon while further to the right a fringe of palm trees indicated the direction of the town. The water, pale with salt, lapped at the edge of the promontory where deckchairs and tables made of old cable reels had been spread out. Two of these chairs were occupied by a European couple wearing sunglasses. They stared out at the water and passed a cigarette between them. The sweet smell of hashish drifted in with the breeze. Nails held between his lips, Luqman was trying to repair a chair that looked beyond salvation. The plasters on his fingers suggested he was not the most skilled of handymen. Seeing them he put down the hammer and got to his feet, spitting the nails into his palm.

'Ah, Sergeant, let me just . . .' He started off towards the couple. Hamama waved him down.

'Leave them in peace. I'm not here for that.'

Luqman blinked at them both as he was expecting bad news. He had a bright, alert look about him, which somehow didn't belong in this place.

'How can I help?' he asked, ducking under the counter to get into the shack. Tacked to the wall behind him was a reproduction of an old painting that showed a man in a turban playing a flute to a collection of tortoises gathered at his feet.

'This is Makana,' Sergeant Hamama indicated. 'He's . . . uh, helping us.'

'Yes, I heard, from Cairo.' Luqman allowed himself a moment to examine Makana before turning away and pouring two cups of tea. Makana wondered if there was anyone in this town who had not heard of his arrival. 'I already spoke to Sadig and the thin one, I don't remember his name. I told them everything I know.'

Hamama reached into a pocket for a tin and extracted a pinch of snuff that he tucked inside his lower lip. 'We just need to go over it once more,' he said.

'How deep is the water off here?' Makana asked.

'It's not too deep,' replied Luqman. 'We used to have a boat for people to go out on.' He jerked a thumb over his shoulder where a small rowing boat lay overturned on the ground. 'But it needs fixing.' The wooden hull was a patchwork of repairs. It would have taken a miracle for it to float, and another one to get a sane person to climb inside. The sound of high-pitched laughter drifted back from the couple out by the water. Perhaps in a certain state of mind safety was not of primary concern. Hamama muttered something and ejected a long brown stream of tobacco and spit into the dirt at his feet.

'Like I said, I told them everything I know,' said Luqman.

'Yes, yes. Look, we need to establish his exact movements prior to . . . being killed. You have nothing to worry about, this is standard procedure.'

'I thought he was found over there.' Luqman pointed.

'The body had been immersed in water for many hours,' said Makana. Luqman studied him while he produced a packet of Marlboro from under the counter and lit one.

'The Qadi was a respectable man, hard to know why anyone would want to kill him.'

'Did you see him that afternoon?' the sergeant asked.

'No.' Luqman smiled at the sergeant. 'You're doing real good with this detective stuff.'

'Just answer the question,' Sergeant Hamama snapped.

'Sorry.'

'Yoo hoo!'

All three of them turned to look at the two tourists sitting out on the water's edge. The woman was smiling and waving her hand in the air. Luqman excused himself.

'It must make him feel like he's better than the rest of us somehow, the fact that he's always dealing with rich Americans or wherever they're from.'

'They're French,' said Makana.

Hamama frowned. 'Now how would you know a thing like that?'

'I recognise the language.'

'French,' muttered Sergeant Hamama regarding Makana from beneath sunken eyelids. 'Of course they are.'

Luqman returned, ducked under the counter and then ducked out again with two cans of beer and a couple of plastic cups in his hand.

'I'll bet he makes a good living out here,' said Sergeant Hamama. 'And I wouldn't be surprised if there are a few perks in dealing with all those foreign women,' he added, spitting more tobacco and hitching up his trousers. '*Haram*. A young man can easily be led astray.'

'I don't imagine the Qadi approved of all of this,' Makana indicated the tourists sunning themselves. 'Drinking, smoking, associating with the opposite sex.'

'No,' mused Hamama. 'I don't suppose he would. Listen, Luqman,' he said as the other man rejoined them, 'did he come by here two nights ago?'

'The Qadi?' Luqman laughed. 'Never. You would have to tie him up and drag him.'

'And no wonder,' muttered Hamama, as the sound of giggling came from the couple out by the water. Smoke circled over their heads. '*Astaghfirullah*.'

'What time did you leave that night?' Makana asked.

Luqman studied the tip of his cigarette. 'It was quiet,' he said. 'I think I must have left around eight. Maybe eight fifteen.'

'After the isha prayer?' asked Hamama.

'Oh yes, I said my prayers and when I came back my last guest had gone. Most of them don't like to be out here much after dark.'

'You didn't see anyone else?' Hamama asked.

'No. I locked up, switched off the lights and cycled back to town.'

'How long have you had this place?' Makana asked.

Luqman's gaze rolled wearily over his surroundings. 'This

place? It must be about ten years now. Before that we used to work the land.' He shrugged and dropped his cigarette into the earth. 'But there's no future in that nowadays. More money in tourism.'

His tone suggested a mixture of regret and self-pity. There was also the matter of pride. Tourism brought with it a level of subservience that Makana had witnessed elsewhere.

'He seems harmless enough, don't you think?' Hamama said on the drive back.

'He runs the place on his own?'

'He's a bit of a loner. He never married and keeps to himself mostly. His uncle helps him out sometimes.'

'And the tourists?'

'What about them?' Hamama spat out of the window, carelessly splattering a good amount of brown liquid on the side of the door.

'Have you questioned any of them?'

'Well, I sent Sadig round the hotels but he doesn't seem to have turned up anything yet. Unlike you, he doesn't have a facility with foreign languages.'

'You sent Sadig because he has a fondness for breaking into people's rooms?'

Sergeant Hamama pulled a face. 'You're taking it personally. I told you that was a misunderstanding. He's a good man. He just gets carried away.'

At the Qadi's office they were met by Mutawali, the Qadi's deputy, a small, neat man with a trim beard. He was dressed in grey and held his hands folded across his chest as though, for the entirety of the meeting, he was about to begin praying.

'It is a terrible, terrible business,' he fretted. His whiskers and prominent front teeth made him resemble a large rodent. 'The

Qadi was a pillar of this society. *Allah yerhamu.* We are all lost without his guidance.'

'Yes, quite,' nodded Hamama, impatient to get on.

'I don't need to remind you, Sergeant, that we are relying on you to see his killer is brought to justice. At no time before have we been in such urgent need of leadership.'

Reminded of the responsibilities that went with his office, the sergeant scratched his ear. The deputy went on: 'This is a difficult time for all of us, but in an investigation like this it's important to move quickly.'

'Of course,' nodded Hamama. 'That's actually why we're here. We think it might help to take a look at the Qadi's case files.'

'Quite out of the question,' said Mutawali. 'I'm sorry, Sergeant, but I really don't see the relevance of this line of investigation.' The room they were in was bare. Makana had been expecting a library of books. Works of religious exegesis, jurisprudence, Islamic history, poetry, as well as the Hadith, accounts of the life of the prophet Muhammed. Here there was nothing. Bare walls. Spartan, uncomfortable furniture. It spelled humility. A man who had no use for worldly goods. 'The Qadi was a good man, beloved by everyone in the community.'

'Not quite everyone,' said Makana quietly. The assistant turned his gaze to him.

'I'm sorry, I'm not clear what your role in this is.'

Sergeant Hamama cleared his throat. 'Mr Makana is something of a specialist. He has come from Cairo to lend his expertise to our enquiries.'

A look of unease came over the deputy, as if he suspected there was something else going on here. He tried to rally himself.

'I commend you on your initiative, Sergeant. This is

unexpected. But I still insist; our records contain confidential information. I cannot simply throw open our files to yourself and your assistants. I would be failing in my duties.'

'Nobody is asking you to do anything wrong. This is a murder investigation,' Makana reminded him. 'Whoever did this is capable of great violence. Until we know who they are and why they did it, other people might be in danger.'

'I understand, really, I do. And believe me, no one is more wounded by this terrible crime. But I have my duties and our dear, departed Qadi would not be happy to know that the moment he was gone from this world I began flaunting all the regulations he taught me to respect.' Mutawali shook his head solemnly.

'Even if it is to find his own killer?' Sergeant Hamama raised his eyebrows in disbelief.

'The Qadi did not believe in favouritism, in making exceptions for personal reasons. I do not believe he would find it appropriate now.'

'Well, then our business here is concluded. Thank you. You have been a great help,' Sergeant Hamama got to his feet and turned towards the door.

Makana remained seated. He cleared his throat. 'You told the sergeant that the Qadi was out at the lake for a business meeting with potential investors. Was it normal for him to go out alone?'

'I think there is some confusion here. It is true I believed that the Qadi had gone to meet with investors, but I have since checked his calendar and can find no such appointment.'

'Then he went out there for personal reasons?'

Mutawali spread his hands wide. 'The Qadi sacrificed his personal life for the community. He worked tirelessly for the benefit of all of us.'

'I'm sure,' said Makana. 'But basically you have no idea what he was doing out there.'

'If you put it like that, no. Did you come here specifically for this case?' The Qadi's deputy seemed suspicious of Makana's motives.

'I came for a different case actually. A young woman was killed in Cairo. Her parents came from here. It's possible she was murdered, burnt alive and made to appear as a suicide.'

'Alas, such cases are not uncommon.'

'You mean young women taking their own lives, or honour killings?'

'Honour killings are an expression of utter desperation. Imagine the agony of a father who decides to sacrifice his daughter for the sake of the family name? It is the ultimate sacrifice.'

'I thought Islam had brought an end to the sacrifice of girl children?' said Makana.

'Without traditions we are nothing. We have no place in this world without the rules laid down by our forefathers.'

'Even if that entails murder?'

Mutawali gave Makana a withering look. 'You are a city person. People abandon who they are when they move to the city. They are lost in a trance of bright lights and noise. Here we remember where we come from.'

It was difficult to argue with the description of Cairo.

'He's a strange one,' said Hamama as he dropped Makana off in the town square. 'If I have to go through official channels to see those records it could take months.'

'If the Qadi was out there for personal reasons then the explanation might be closer to home.'

'Sure, but let's get one thing straight. I'm still in charge here. Next time you get a bright idea, it would be better if it came from me. I don't want you making me look foolish again, you understand?'

With that he stamped his foot down and the car surged forward before the passenger door was closed. Makana stood on the corner and watched the pickup pulling away, a jet of tobacco-coloured spit flying out of the side window as it flew away trailing a cloud of dust.

Chapter Fifteen

It was quite a walk to Doctor Medina's house and Makana concluded that a bicycle might be a useful asset and perhaps a safer bet than an ancient motorcycle.

By day, the house resembled something from a fairy tale. The kind of place that could have been built by mischievous jinns. A path paved with grey stones curved to the front of the two-storey villa. By the door was a faded metal sign that announced it as a clinic. Makana tried the door and found it locked. Moving around the side of the house he looked up the outside staircase. At the top of this was another door, this time standing open.

Makana climbed the stairs and stepped inside to find himself in a large open living area. A fan turned gently overhead. The blades gently stroking the sheets of paper that lay on the desk by the window. A set of shelves took up the far wall. To the left of this, opposite the front door, a corridor led to the interior of the flat which appeared to extend the length of the building and ended in another staircase which must have led down to the clinic. Left of the front door was a dining area with a long table discoloured by water stains. Vertical ornamental bars provided a barrier between this and the living room. A modern touch.

The building was from the 1960s, Makana guessed. A big rear window offered a view of a sea of bobbing palm-tree crowns. A large rounded Westinghouse refrigerator hummed like a tractor at the far end of the dining room. Beside it was a door leading into a kitchen.

The flat had the familiar, lived-in feel of a single man's home. Two identically battered sofas faced one another across the middle of the living room. Simple constructions of wooden spars and cushions that looked at least forty years old. The books and papers scattered about the room seemed to have been abandoned in mid-thought months ago. Makana felt sand grating against his fingertips as he brushed a hand over the papers on the desk.

'Oh, I didn't hear you come in.'

Doctor Medina stood in the entrance to the corridor. His shirt and trousers looked as though he had slept in them for a week. In one hand he held a glass tumbler decorated with yellow and red flowers. The white coat had been replaced by a dressing gown. His flies were undone and his hair was all over the place.

'The door was open,' Makana explained.

'You're an investigator.' Doctor Medina straightened his glasses. 'You're doing what you do, investigating.'

'You asked me to drop by, remember? This morning in town?'

'Did I? Yes, yes, of course I did.' The doctor began fussing about the room as if attempting to restore some sense of order. Scooping up an armful of newspapers from one sofa he looked around for somewhere to put them before finally dumping them over the far side between the sofa and the wall, where there was already a pile mounting like a shifting dune of sand.

'How long have you been here, Doctor?'

'Oh, twenty-five years. No, it must be more.' He paused, frowned, gulped from his glass. 'Could it be thirty?'

'I suppose there is a lot to keep you busy.' Makana drifted around the room aimlessly.

'Busy? Oh yes, I suppose there is.' The deep-set eyes had a mocking air to them, as if the world was beyond taking seriously. 'But enough about me, how about you? Have you made any progress?'

'Not that you would notice.'

Doctor Medina nodded as if he understood. With his dishevelled hair and rumpled appearance he resembled a disgraced academic. The room seemed to match that confusion. Medical books lay open on sideboards, pharmaceutical reports were piled on chairs. A human hand, the delicate bones curled as if in beckoning, rested on a stand. The doctor walked backwards, waving his glass in the air. 'Can I tempt you?' A stack of papers collapsed, spilling across the floor like an avalanche.

'No, thank you.' Makana was drawn to a photograph that was at least thirty years old. A younger version of the doctor dressed in a shiny tuxedo with a bow tie and longer hair. Beside him a woman wearing a wedding gown. The room seemed to be swamped with stories. Case studies, medical reports, scientific discoveries, and buried somewhere within all that was the doctor's own life. A collection of stories that had all had their day. They had been told and discarded, or lost in the oblivion of time and, of course, drink.

'You disappoint me. I was hoping you would turn out to be an ally. Willing accomplices are so hard to find in these pious days.' The doctor carried on talking until his back hit the side of the Westinghouse. Wrenching open the refrigerator he reached inside for a large demijohn of clear liquid. Ice cubes rattled into the glass. 'I make it myself, with locally produced dates of course, under the most stringently controlled scientific conditions, naturally. I add a touch of lime for flavour.' Grinning, he took a sip from his fresh drink as to confirm this fact. 'If there was a way of assessing these things,' he said, holding the glass up to the light, 'this would be up there with the best of them, Courvoisier, Chivas Regal . . .'

'I'll take your word for it,' said Makana. He was fairly certain the invitation was mere formality. A seasoned alcoholic, while eager to give the impression of sociability, was not really interested in sharing his supply of illicit booze with others. 'Have you made any progress on the Qadi?'

'Ah, yes, our glorious house guest.' The doctor's hand rose in a toast and then stopped himself. 'Perhaps you would like to see him?'

They trooped downstairs by the inside staircase. Doctor Medina led the way through the clinic to the storage room that had once been a garage. It smelled of damp. In the middle of the room stood a long low display cabinet for frozen goods. It was somewhat battered. The top was covered by styrofoam panels. The upper sides were made of glass. The contents were illuminated by a row of strip lighting that ran along the inside and gave the interior a blue glow. The Qadi lay in state like Lenin, or some modern-day Tutankhamun in a space-age chariot. He did not look much improved by time. His bloodless features were now encrusted with ice. He was wrapped in a white sheet over which a long transparent plastic bag had been drawn. The bag was emblazoned with a red logo and letters in English that read – *AGI LandTech*. Not the most glorious epitaph one could have hoped for. Neon lights overhead stuttered into life as the doctor began to remove the styrofoam. It wasn't a particularly dignified casket. In the overhead light the lower half of the drop freezer appeared to be decorated with a series of stickers, logos and advertising posters including a ripped one that revealed half of a smiling woman's face as she sank a row of perfect white teeth into an ice-cream cone.

'Not exactly halal,' observed Makana.

'No,' agreed Doctor Medina. 'Do you think he minds? I doubt it. He was a pompous old fool anyway. So full of himself and his authority.'

'Respect for the dead is not part of your medical duties, I take it.'

'On the contrary, I have great respect for the dead, especially what they can teach us about helping the living. I'm not a religious man, Mr Makana. What do I call you by the way, do you have a first name?'

'Makana is fine.'

As the doctor lifted his glass in salute Makana half expected the Qadi to sit up in protest. Of all the indignities a pious man could suffer, surely being gloated over by a drunk waving a glass full of illicit alcohol would have to rank close to the worst.

'What did you find?'

Doctor Medina wiped a hand over his face and set his glass down on the edge of the freezer. He peered at Makana over the rim of his spectacles.

'You understand that I am not a trained forensic pathologist. I don't do autopsies. This whole thing is ridiculous. I risk losing my licence.'

'You had no choice. This is an emergency and your help was requested by the police.'

'That makes me feel a lot better,' muttered the doctor. He nodded down at the body. 'Water in the lungs.'

'So he was drowned?' Makana looked down at the gash

running across the Qadi's body almost from one side to the other. 'And the cut happened before or after he was dead?'

'After. And not only that, I found something strange. I ran a blood test and found traces of secobarbital.'

'A sedative?' asked Makana.

Doctor Medina nodded. 'It would knock you out. Remember this is at least twenty-four hours after his death, so the quantity ingested must have been fairly substantial.'

'You're suggesting somebody poisoned him.'

'I need to do some more tests, but my hypothesis looks like this: the killer overpowered the Qadi with the sedative, then he drowned him, then he disembowelled him.'

'That makes no sense. Why cut open the body of a dead man?'

'Who knows? Perhaps it has some ritual signficance. There is nothing rational about murder. You ought to know that.' The doctor reached for his glass. 'I can only tell you what I know. It is up to you to draw your own conclusions.'

It struck Makana that in this case the exact opposite was true. Someone had gone to a lot of trouble. If they just wanted to get rid of him then a stone to the back of the head would usually do the trick.

'Why the abdomen?'

'You mean symbolically?' Doctor Medina's eyebrows rose. 'Well, the belly is traditionally where life is thought to reside. The centre of the body. In women it is where the womb is found, of course. The very cradle of life itself.'

'And since the Qadi very clearly wasn't a woman?'

'It's true. He was many things, but that he wasn't.' The doctor sighed. 'I can't tell you why it was done but I can tell you how. It was performed with a very sharp instrument, and it was done cleanly. The edges show there was little or no hesitation in the

163

movement of the blade. It was one neat cut. Almost surgical.' He glanced up as the implications of his words struck home.

'You mean someone with medical training did this, like . . . a doctor.'

'Exactly like a doctor.' Swaying on his feet Doctor Medina peered into the bottom of his glass before lifting it and draining it in one. 'Let's go upstairs, it's cold down here.'

He switched off the overhead lights leaving only the glow from inside the refrigerator cabinet, illuminating the Qadi's chilled remains.

'Why cut him open at all then, if not to kill him?'

'To help sink the body in the water?'

Makana dismissed the suggestion. 'He was found in shallow water. He couldn't possibly have disappeared from sight. Unless the killer didn't know that.'

'You mean the killer might not be local?'

'It's a possibility,' said Makana.

'What other explanation is there?'

'That it means something.'

'You mean like a message?'

'To be honest, I have no idea.'

Upstairs, Makana sat down while the doctor poured himself another drink. As he was slicing a lime to drop into his glass he said over his shoulder, 'So tell me, why all the interest in Musab Khayr?'

Makana told him about the fire and Karima's death. The doctor pulled a face. 'I've seen some bad cases but it is always one of the worst things you can see.'

'I think someone tried to make it look like suicide.'

'It happens,' the doctor shrugged. 'You think Musab is behind it?'

'You must have been here back then, around the time he left.'

'I might have been. Just because you live here doesn't mean you know everyone.'

'No, of course not. But you knew of him.'

'Only in passing,' said Doctor Medina. 'He was involved in the smuggling gangs. But almost every family has someone who is involved.' The doctor sipped his drink and pronounced it too weak. 'Sure you won't join me?' he asked before spilling another jolt of the clear spirit into his glass.

Makana leaned back in the sofa and blew smoke at the ceiling. 'Musab went to prison. While inside he renounced his former life and turned to Allah.'

The doctor giggled into his ice. 'They all do it.' He pushed a hand through his unruly hair and managed to light a cigarette without setting fire to himself, but only just. 'Religion is a fraud. No,' he wagged a finger unsteadily. 'It's a disease. It allows people to look down on their fellow man while extolling the virtues of brotherly love. They withdraw from the world and prepare for paradise and the hereafter where they are assured of a good seat to watch the rest of us burn. A pest, a plague. Religion is a parasite that feeds on us all.'

'Musab married Nagat Abubakr. You mentioned her father last time I was here.'

'I did?' Doctor Medina's face screwed up in concentration. 'Well, her father, Tewfiq Abubakr, was descended from a very big family in the old days. Wealthy landowners.'

'Do you know what happened?'

'What always happens. They fell on hard times. The sons were less gifted than the fathers. Isn't that always the case? I know it was in mine. My father was . . . well. Anyway, they sold off the land gradually to pay off their debts. The house fell into ruin, and by the time Tewfiq came along they were pretty much finished.'

'Does the family still own any land?'

'Not as far as I know.'

Makana wondered about the picture hanging on the wall of Karima's flat in Cairo. What had it meant to her? A photograph of the old family home that she had never seen. Was it a promise of a brighter future? Many people dreamed of returning home to collect their just reward. Was that what Karima had been taught to believe by her mother?

'What about his family?'

'I don't know. I have a feeling they also left soon after he did.' Doctor Medina was staring deep into his glass. 'He went to prison for something related to smuggling, didn't he? What was it?'

'Cigarettes and alcohol, as far as I know. There may have been carpets involved.'

'Carpets?' The doctor's eyes widened and he rolled his head back. 'Ah, now you see, carpets is another matter. You should speak to Wad Nubawi.'

'The one with the supermarket?'

'The very same.' The doctor jabbed a finger at the floor below. 'Wad Nubawi can get you anything you need, including refrigeration for any corpses you might happen to have about the house.'

'I didn't see any carpets.'

'Oh, they don't keep them there next to the frozen bamia,' the doctor chuckled. 'You have to ask. Carpets, refrigerators, televisions, air conditioning, even whisky, if you ask him kindly.' Doctor Medina pointed vaguely in the direction of south. 'There is a place out there. Kalonsha. People talk of it almost as if it was one of those fabled cities. You know, like in *The Thousand and One Nights?'*

'Kalonsha?'

'It's an old well on the desert routes. There are roads leading across the continent and nothing to stop you out there. The borders are impossible to police. Too big, too remote.'

As he was seeing him out, Doctor Medina asked Makana about the motorcycle.

'Kamal says he wants to just give it another look over before he lets me have it.'

'That boy is bone lazy, everyone around here is. But you won't regret it. The Norton is a fine machine. One of the few good things the British left out here. They also left us about twenty-two million landmines. Every now and then some poor child runs off to chase a stray sheep and gets blown to shreds. So just remember, never go off the tracks.'

'I'll bear that in mind,' said Makana.

By the time he arrived back in town night was falling and the muezzin was chanting the call to the sunset prayer. The distant clip-clopping of a donkey announced a karetta on the far side of the square. Makana watched Bulbul throw a stone at the door of the big house on the corner. Turning back, his eye was caught by the flutter of colour overhead and the lights turning on the ceiling. The entrance to the coffee shop was partially concealed behind a wall and a heap of building sand that someone had forgotten. The only announcement was the English word *Internet* scratched on the wall with a piece of charcoal. A barrage of plastic crates forced any potential visitor to slip sideways through the doorway where a bare set of concrete steps led upwards. The veranda was deserted but for a small group of young men who lounged on big cushions in the far corner. It was dimly lit. A silence fell over the group as Makana appeared. Eventually, one of them got to his feet, slipped on a pair of sandals and wandered over. A short man in his late twenties with a thickening waist who had already lost most of his hair. He smiled as he approached.

'Welcome. How can I be of service?'

'Is this some sort of private club?'

'Oh, no,' the man dismissed the thought with a laugh. 'Anyone is welcome here. We have coffee, tea, soft drinks.'

'Tea is fine,' said Makana.

With a slight bow, the young man withdrew, disappearing through a set of louvered swing doors into what was presumably the kitchen. The white neon light from within seemed stark in contrast to the gloomy veranda. There was a strange feel to the place and Makana was aware of being watched by the men in the corner as he crossed over to a table by the wall where he could lean on the parapet and look down over the square. He lit a cigarette and found himself thinking of Zahra Sharif. Why did he feel she seemed to hold out some kind of promise?

'Are you here on business?'

The man set down the tea on the table. He had a round face, soft features and large, thick eyelashes that batted nervously.

'I'm looking for someone,' said Makana.

'Aren't we all?' The young man smiled blandly, glancing over at his group of friends, clearly eager to get back to them. 'I was just thinking I hadn't seen you around here before.' His eyes widened in invitation. 'It's always nice to see new faces.'

Makana sipped his tea and smoked his Cleopatra, wondering how he could possibly be of interest to this man in that way. 'Nice place you have here.'

'The breeze makes a difference,' said the man. 'It comes from the desert. I'm Hamza by the way.' He held out a hand which felt like a damp rag.

'Makana. I had an old friend from here, years ago.'

Hamza bit his lip with concern, as if there was nothing more he would like to do than help. His talents as an actor were going to waste in this oasis.

'I'd like to help, but I'm not very good with names.'

'No, of course. I understand. His name is Musab Khayr.'

The name demarcated the limits to Hamza's thespian talents. The wagging of the head continued, only now he was just going through the motions.

'Like I said, I'm not good with names. I'll ask around.'

'That would be kind of you.'

As he made to go Hamza's eyes narrowed as two areas of his brain connected. 'One second. You're the one from Cairo, aren't you? The one everyone is talking about?' Without being invited, Hamza sat down. He glanced around him and lowered his voice. 'You're here to investigate the death of the Qadi.'

'Where did you hear that?' Makana asked.

Hamza dismissed the question with a wave of his hand. 'I hear things all the time. Is it true what they say, that he was cut from his throat to his manhood?'

In a small town, information would have spread from any number of sources. The policemen on the scene, Sadig and the skinny officer whose name no one could remember, or even more likely from the man on the donkey who first found him, along with his faceless wife.

'What did you think of him?'

'Of the Qadi?' Hamza sat back, a touch warily. Now he wasn't sure who he was talking to.

'It's all right,' Makana assured him. 'I'm just trying to form a picture of the man. I need to understand why he was killed.'

'Right, so I am helping you in your investigation?'

'You could say that.'

Hamza relaxed a little. 'Well,' he began, warming to the task as if being interviewed by a magazine. 'Nobody liked him. An old man who wanted everything to stay the same. We have plenty of those.'

'He represented the law.'

'Oh, he made sure the law suited him. That's the other thing.' With another glance over his shoulder, as if any number of eavesdroppers might have sneaked up on tiptoe. 'He ran everything. Building permits, planning permission. All of that had to go past him and you can be sure he took his share. They all do. Between him and that sergeant there isn't much left for the rest of us.' The sorrowful look suggested his life was one of eternal suffering.

'Sergeant Hamama?'

Hamza went on, ignoring the query. 'I don't envy you trying to find who killed him. Throw a stone off this balcony on market day and see who it strikes. Nobody liked him, not even that fool Mutawali, even though he is no doubt crying even as we speak. But . . .' Hamza thrust a forefinger into the air, 'there's a difference between not liking the man, hating him even, for what he represents, and cutting him up like a kharouf.' Hamza sat back and rested for a moment, breathing heavily. Then he got abruptly to his feet to return to his friends in the corner. He paused as he went by. 'I wish you luck with your work, but whoever did this does not deserve to be punished.'

Makana sipped his tea. It wasn't particularly good tea. The young men who frequented the place clearly preferred

Coca-Cola and the like. It was a kind of haven for those who liked to think of themselves as belonging elsewhere. Somewhere more modern perhaps. A certain kind of male. When he arrived back at the hotel, he found Nagy standing in the doorway. He thrust his hands into his pockets and didn't return Makana's greeting, though he muttered under his breath as he went by, 'I wouldn't spend too much time in that place. People might get the wrong idea.'

In the lobby the television played to an empty room. Central Security Forces in full riot gear trying to control the crowds. Palestinian flags waved in the air like angry palm trees. A shot of the Mukataa in Ramallah showed a besieged Yasser Arafat waving from a window. He looked like a man who knew his time had run out. Israeli tanks rumbled through the streets. Women picked up their children and ran.

Chapter Sixteen

The phone rang the moment he stepped into his room, almost as if Zahra knew where he was and what he was doing.

'How are you finding Siwa?'

Makana took comfort in her voice as he sat in the dark room. It was hard to believe that just over a week ago he had not known of her existence and now it almost felt as though he had come to depend on her presence, distant as it was.

'It's not all that unfamiliar actually,' he said. 'In a strange way I feel more at home here than in Cairo. It reminds me of Sudan.'

The sound of her laughter lifted his heart. 'I'll bet you're the kind of man who can feel at home anywhere in the world.'

Through the window the lights on the mosque illuminated the muddy finger of the old minaret, carving soft shadows out of the ancient darkness. Down below a solitary figure walked along the narrow alley behind the hotel.

'There's something about this place which is different,' he heard himself say.

'It's a strange place.'

'I didn't know you'd been here.'

'A long time ago.' There was a long pause. Then she said, 'Last night I dreamed about Karima. I dreamed she was alive and dancing. Isn't that funny?'

'Why was she dancing?'

'I don't know. It was a celebration of some kind. Perhaps a wedding. Actually, I think it was my wedding. Isn't that strange?'

'What happened then?'

'Oh, then I woke up,' she said. 'And it made me feel sad all over again.'

They talked about this and that, about the demonstrations and what was going on in the world and injustice in general. For a time Makana imagined having this kind of conversation every evening, of sharing his life. Millions of people did it. He had done it once, hadn't he?

'I sort of feel I'm being sidetracked by this business with the Qadi. As far as Musab is concerned, I don't seem to be making progress.'

'You're still getting a feel for the place.'

'By now I thought I would at least have found his family, but no one seems to know them.'

'People move. It's not so strange,' she whispered.

'I don't know. It almost feels as if something happened back then. Something that changed everything.'

'Something like what?'

'I don't know. I'm just speculating.'

How long they talked he couldn't say, but it must have been close to an hour. It felt good to be able to share his thoughts with someone. Despite this, Makana slept uneasily, waking in the early hours, disorientated, listening to the sound of a lone dog barking in the distance. What was he doing here? For a moment he was puzzled. He tried to imagine Nasra's life. The image to which he found himself returning was of her face, the last time he saw her alive, through the window of the car as it plunged through the rails and down into the river below. Could she really have survived?

The following morning the lean, hard Sadig was waiting in one of the armchairs in the lobby, eying Nagy's daughter, who was serving him coffee in a cup with a saucer, the way they did for the tourists. The porter, Ayman, an oddly misplaced giant with a perplexed expression, was also watching the girl, although slyly, out of the corner of his eye from across the room where he was mopping the floor in his bare feet. Sadig whispered something to the girl, grinning like a cat. Catching sight of Makana wiped the smile off his face. He came to his feet and rushed over to block his exit.

'Where do you think you're going?'

'Why, am I under arrest?'

Sadig hooked his thumbs into his belt and stretched himself to his full height. 'The sergeant sends his compliments. He asks if you will assist with interviewing foreign visitors in the hotels.'

'Why? You need more time to search my room?'

The corporal nodded towards the street. 'The sergeant is waiting.'

Hamama rolled up as they emerged from the hotel.

'There's no time to waste. You have to interview them all before they have breakfast and disappear. I'm counting on you.' He pointed at Makana as he rolled off.

The exercise proved a waste of time. They drove round half a dozen hotels and attempted to interview a selection of tourists, most of whom were either half asleep, or trying to eat their breakfast in peace. It became obvious that a number of them suspected the appearance of Sadig and Makana as the prelude to some kind of a scam designed to relieve them of their holiday savings. Some did not speak English – or if they did it was not a form of the language known to Makana. Others claimed to understand it but clearly did not. Throughout all of this Makana had to contend with Sadig's sarcastic comments about how shameless these people were, how they had no respect for the customs of the country they were in, which of course did not prevent him from leering at the women, which in turn did nothing to decrease the tension and caused a good degree of bad feeling in some cases. It made Makana wonder all over again at Sergeant Hamama's wisdom in sending this man along.

'It's a waste of time,' Sadig announced as they emerged onto the street for the tenth time. 'I knew it would be.' The tall officer climbed back into the police car and started the engine. Makana leaned down to the window on the passenger side.

'You talk as if it doesn't matter who killed the Qadi.'

Sadig leaned back and stared at Makana. 'Everyone says you're so smart, well, let me tell you something, in case you haven't worked it out for yourself already. Nobody is ever going to come to trial for this murder.'

'What makes you so sure?'

'Because it's the way things work around here. People protect their own. And besides,' grunted Sadig. 'The old fool had it coming if you ask me.'

With that he slammed his foot down and the battered car veered away, very nearly taking Makana's arm with it. Across the street, he saw Wad Nubawi leaning in the doorway of his supermarket. When he noticed Makana watching him he disappeared inside. Makana crossed the street.

When Makana came in Wad Nubawi was staring at a shelf of

tins and marking something on a sheet with a pencil stub as if it was of immense importance.

'I see you're making friends,' he murmured, without turning his head.

'A man was killed. They asked for my help. I can't really say no.'

'Everyone knows you're here to help the police. No secrets around here.'

Makana stared at a packet of biscuits level with his eyes. On the shiny label a long-haired blonde prince waved a sword. He couldn't quite work out the connection between contents and image.

'I get the impression he was an unpopular man.'

'Who, the Qadi?' Wad Nubawi stopped his counting and went back to the start of the row to begin again. 'He interferred in people's business. Around here people don't like that.'

'It's a Qadi's job to interfere, isn't it?'

'I wouldn't know about that.' Wad Nubawi grunted. He sighed and started on the same row for the third time.

'Did you know him?' Makana moved along the shelves, following a trail of images. A giant tuna fish leaping from a foaming sea. A chestnut tree covered in red blossom on a hillside. A beaming wife holding up a bowl heaped high with steaming okra to cheer a weary husband. Each item seemed to contain its own built-in plot, bringing adventure and good fortune to your dining table. Happiness and well-being in return for the consumption of their contents.

'Everyone did. Look,' Wad Nubawi gave up all pretence of trying to work. He tossed the pencil and paper onto the counter alongside the cash register and helped himself to a date. 'I don't know what you are getting at. There was no fight between me and the Qadi, understood? He did his job and I did mine. That's my freezer the old fool is lying in even as we speak. How do you think people are going to feel next time they come to put their hand in there for a bag of falafel?'

The image of the dead Qadi lying frozen in Doctor Medina's garage was still fresh in Makana's mind. He could see how it might not sit well with customers and keeping the news quiet around here was probably not an option.

'Did you ever come across a man named Musab Khayr?'

'Musab Khayr? Let me see . . .' Wad Nubawi sucked his teeth and stared at the ceiling for a moment. 'No, I can't say that I recall that name.' He fished for a cigarette under the counter and lit one in a single move. The smoke seemed to change the colour of his eyes, making them even more grey and evasive than they had been before. He was lean and efficient in his movements, with no excess use of energy.

'I thought everyone around here knew everyone else.'

'We know how to mind our own business. It's not like in the big city.' Wad Nubawi watched Makana as he smoked. 'What has any of this got to do with the Qadi's death?'

'Nothing. Everything. You know how it is with this kind of investigation. It's almost impossible to say how things are connected.'

'They say you're an expert.'

'I'm not here to find out who killed the Qadi.'

'But you're helping Hamama.'

'As long as the sergeant feels I can be useful then I am happy to assist.'

'But you're really here about this other man?'

'Musab Khayr was married to a girl from here. Nagat. They ran away together.'

'It happens.' The grey stubble on Wad Nubawi's lean face vanished in a cloud of smoke. His eyes turned the soft colour of honey as he looked off through the window at the sky. 'People think life will be easier for them out there. They have no idea. Usually, it's worse.'

Maybe anything was better than being trapped in a place like this, thought Makana, but he didn't say it. He was staring out of the window at the square, trying to imagine a young couple planning to run away to a new life. Or were they running away from something?

'You think this Musab fellow is mixed up in what happened to the Qadi?'

'It's probably just coincidence,' said Makana, turning back to him. 'But I'd like to talk to someone from his family.'

'I don't see how that might help.'

'It's the way this kind of thing works. You never know what you've got until you pull it out of the water.'

'Not much fishing goes on around here,' said Wad Nubawi, exhaling through his nostrils. He flicked the cigarette butt out into the street. 'We prefer meat that is so fresh you can still feel the animal's heart beating.' He grinned, showing off his gold tooth.

As he approached his hotel, Makana spotted Hamama's pickup parked outside with the second of the sergeant's adjutants, the skinny police officer without a name, leaning on it smoking and staring forlornly at the ground. In the doorway stood Ayman, the hotel porter, looking as if he'd been left behind by life. He grinned when Makana held a finger to his lips and watched as he slipped around the corner, down the narrow side street which took him behind the hotel. Looking up Makana saw the window of his room was open. The corner of a cloth flew out, slapping against the shutter to produce a tiny explosion of dust. Cleaning his room sounded like an historic event, although probably it was simply an excuse for Nagy to go through his things in case there was anything of value that Sadig had overlooked.

A few minutes later he turned a corner and saw the row of bicycles lined up outside the rental shop. A figure emerged and he recognised Nagy's daughter, Rashida. She stopped and looked back to exchange a smile with Kamal, before moving on.

When Makana walked in Kamal waved him through to the rear of the shop. A small door led out of the back where the motorcycle stood. He had done a lot of work on it clearly, but it still looked as though it ought to be in a museum.

'What's this?' Makana pointed to an axle sticking out at right angles from the rear wheel.

'It used to have a sidecar. They used them to carry guns and attack the Germans.' Kamal shrugged as if all of that made as much sense as anything.

'Will it run?'

'Oh, yeah.' There was something slow and patient about the boy that Makana liked. 'I took it to pieces. It's as good as new. Better even.' He grinned.

'Better? Where did you get spare parts?'

'Sometimes you find them, others you have to improvise,' shrugged Kamal, rubbing a rag over the dial of the speedometer.

'How much do I owe you?'

'You don't have to pay anything. The doctor has been paying me for years to fix it.'

'Take this anyway.' Makana thrust a handful of notes into his hand. 'You might not get the chance again.'

Starting the machine up brought all of Makana's doubts back. The thing was unwieldy and heavy, but when Kamal showed him how to turn the throttle up the engine seemed to settle into a steady, reassuring thump, and once on the road it felt solid beneath him. By the time he had got out to the lake he was beginning to enjoy himself. He hadn't ridden a motorcycle since he was in the army signals corps and then too, by some strange quirk of fate, it had been another English machine. A Triumph.

Luqman was sitting out by the water's edge when Makana got there. He smiled when he saw the Norton.

'It takes a brave man to trust his life to a machine like that.'

'Either brave or stupid, I'm not sure which,' agreed Makana as he managed to haul it up onto its stand.

The lake was serene. Still and calm. Far off in the distance two dark rags flapped low across the water. Impossible to say what kind of birds they were.

'No customers today?'

'Not yet,' Luqman glanced around the collection of junk that passed for furniture and turned back again. 'They tend to do their sightseeing in the morning. Sunset. That's the time for them to come out here. You know, relax after a hard day.'

'It must be exhausting.'

'There's a lot to see. The oracle of Amun, where Alexander came to ask his fate.'

'Sounds like you know a lot about it.'

The narrow shoulders lifted and dropped. 'People expect me to know everything. A Coke and a smile, isn't that what they say?'

'I'm the wrong person to ask,' said Makana. 'What is that?'

Luqman turned to look at the faded poster of the flute player and the tortoises. He smiled.

'Topkapi in Istanbul. Have you ever been?' Makana shook his head. 'Well, in the seventeenth century they would have very elaborate parties in the palace gardens. These creatures would wander around with lamps on their backs. It must have been magical.' Luqman shrugged. 'I just like the idea of the tortoise keeper with his flute. Why are you here anyway? More questions?'

'Not really. I just thought I'd come out here and look around.'

'Is this really what you do for a living?'

'It's not much, but it's what I've always done.'

Luqman offered his American cigarettes. 'This land,' he began, gesturing around them with his lighter before holding the flame for Makana, 'it has been in my family for centuries. There's something honest about working the land, you know.'

'You mean, in contrast to running a tourist café?'

'For example. In the old days it felt like clean money. I grew up with that. My whole family working the land. We weren't rich, but we survived.'

'Times change.'

'It's human nature. Someone sees an opportunity to make some money and work a little less, so they sell it off piece by piece. But the money doesn't last for ever and one day it runs out and there's no land to work and the hotels close down, or they only employ people who are young and have a certain training.' Luqman stared off into the distance. 'People don't think ahead.'

'But you're still here.'

'I tried living abroad, but I came back.' Luqman gestured at the lake and the desert beyond. 'I never get tired of looking at it.'

A chattering of voices brought their attention to the road where a group of three tourists appeared, with sunglasses and hats, the boys in shorts, the girl sensibly dressed in long trousers.

'I'm sorry, business calls.'

'Looks like you have enough to keep you busy.'

'It's peanuts.' Luqman shook his head. 'Don't take this the wrong way, but it was the Qadi and his friends who make the big money. We eat the crumbs that fall from their table. And now, with all this in Palestine . . .' Luqman clicked his tongue. 'People in America think that it's all one place and after the 9/11 attacks the only people who dare to come here are the brave ones, or the crazy ones who don't care.'

Makana watched him transform himself as he walked away, smiling and greeting the newcomers, helping them to decide where they wanted to sit. It was easy to see why they trusted him. He had a charm and worldliness about him that set him apart from the other people Makana had met so far, all of whom could lightly be characterised as provincials. Luqman had travelled, certainly to the big cities of Alexandria and Cairo, and further afield. It seemed like a pleasant existence, just sitting by the lake waiting for people to come by and give you their money, but Makana knew it wasn't quite as idyllic as it looked. He sensed a bitterness about Luqman that suggested an underlying resentment. He wondered how deep it ran. There was no doubt that Luqman was smart, but was he capable of violence? Aren't we all, Makana thought, given the right circumstances?

The tourists had stopped to examine the Norton. Luqman pointed and Makana felt obliged to wander over.

'Is it yours?' one of the men asked in accented English. He was tall and broad-shouldered, with the healthy look of one who drank a litre of fresh milk every morning. The three were chattering amongst themselves in their own language. The one who had asked the question was clearly an aficionado.

'It's not mine,' Makana admitted. 'I just borrowed it.'

'Ah.' They were German and seemed to appreciate machines.

'Have you been here long?' Makana thought that he hadn't seen them on the hotel round he had done with Sadig that morning.

'This is our last day. Tomorrow we take the bus back to Cairo.' This time it was the girl who spoke. She had an alert expression. She wasn't interested in motorcycles. The two boys were still walking around the machine, commenting on this or that, as if they had come across a living specimen of an extinct life form.

'You didn't happen to be out here the other evening?'

Her eyes narrowed. 'You mean when there was that accident?'

'Yes, a man was killed.' Makana could see her expression change. She called to the others, but they waved her off, too busy fussing over the Norton.

'We heard it was an accident. He drowned, no?'

'It is still under investigation.'

The woman examined him with a wary eye and glanced over at the boys, who were completely engrossed in the matter of the motorcycle. She had the manner of the well-seasoned traveller. Short hair and practical clothes. She had also clearly learned to be wary of local men trying to impress her and regarded Makana with some caution.

'We're trying to gather all the information we can get.'

'You are with the police?'

Makana skipped over the question. 'We visited all the hotels this morning, I didn't see you.'

'We left early. We wanted to see the sunrise from above the Temple of the Oracle.'

'The temple, of course.'

He was about to turn away when she said, 'We cycled past here the other evening.' She hesitated, calling more insistently to the boys. A conversation ensued between the three of them. The girl grew visibly more agitated. Makana glanced at Luqman who shrugged his shoulders.

'He was already dead,' the girl blurted out. The boys let out cries of dismay.

'They don't want me to speak. They think it will complicate things for us. We don't want to get involved.'

'It's all right,' said Makana. 'There's no need to worry,' he said to the boys who were becoming more aggressive now, trying to draw the girl away. She fended off their hands, starting to cry now.

'The man was already dead. We didn't do anything wrong!' The two young men turned their backs on her. She faced Makana. 'There was . . . a woman.'

Makana examined the German girl. In these climes she was an exotic creature, with her fair hair and blue eyes. He wondered which of the two men she was involved with? Neither one, or perhaps both? Who could say what their habits were? They were on holiday, they should be allowed to do what they liked. When their time was up they could go home to their regular, ordered lives, and all of this would slowly fade. He recalled the Qadi. A short, squat, middle-aged man wearing robes. Grey beard that was trimmed along the line of his jaw. A touch of vanity.

'A woman? Are you sure?'

'Yes. We saw a woman. Alone. You understand? You never see them alone. Always two or three.'

'Yes. What time was this, can you remember?'

'Around three. It was hot.'

So, some hours before the body was discovered by the farmer and his wife. When he asked if she could describe the woman, the German girl shook her head.

'But they all look the same, no?'

'Yes, of course they do. They all look the same.'

She gave Makana a long look, as if she had entrusted him with something valuable and then she turned away, hesitated, as if she had some last comment to add, and then left, jogging back to where the two men waited close to the road. The three of them got on their bicycles and started back to town.

Makana watched them go. Luqman was standing behind him.

'Sorry, it looks like I lost you some business there.'

'Maalish,' said Luqman philosophically. 'But don't pay too much attention. She sounded confused. You know what it's like. She probably wants to appear more interesting than she is.'

'I don't know,' said Makana.

'Strange though. You see a dead person and don't report it?'

'They don't trust the police. They didn't want to get mixed up.'

'Yes, but still,' Luqman muttered. Makana went back to the Norton. He had anticipated problems starting it again. His natural lack of faith in the durability of things. But to his surprise it took just two kicks of the starter and the engine was purring nicely. The German boys gave a roar of encouragement as he passed them on the road. Perhaps there was a living to be made in this, Makana thought to himself. He ought to begin charging.

Chapter Seventeen

The road between the lakes was long and straight as an arrow. The grey colour of the water and the distant outcrops gave the landscape a sense of having been drained of all living matter. Even the sky had the same ghostly, half-dead appearance. At the end of the lake he kicked the gear into neutral and coasted to a halt. The road turned back towards town, but the other way snaked off into nowhere. From here, running in any direction you cared to choose, there was nothing but sand and dry outcrops of rock that stuck up like bony knuckles. To the south the camel routes led through a string of oases down to the corner where the borderlines of Sudan, Egypt and Libya met. An arbitrary point in the ground, the intersection of a cartographer's ruler when the continent was being sliced up by the European powers. To the west and north was the Libyan Desert, which would deliver you through the distant ridge to the coast, or deeper into the Sahara. There wasn't much else between here and the Atlantic Ocean, three thousand kilometres away.

Instead of stopping in town, Makana went straight through, managing to find the road he had taken with Sergeant Hamama out towards Jebel Mawtah, The Mountain of Death. There was no traffic. High bands of reeds sheltered the road on one side, a grove of palm trees on the other. This gave way to a view of the rounded, low hill on top of which the square shape of the temple was visible. The ruins of the Abubakrs' old house somehow looked even more forlorn, perched on the edge of the field. Makana wasn't sure what he hoped to find here, but he parked the Norton on its stand and wandered through the remains of the building. What was it like growing up out here, he wondered, so far from town? Nagat would have had to walk to school every morning, which would have meant almost an hour each way. The rest of the time was no doubt spent working around the house and in the fields.

A spindly figure was making its way towards him, balancing easily as he walked steadily along the uneven ridges of earth that divided the flooded fields. Makana smoked a cigarette as he waited for the man to reach him. A man in peasant clothes, baggy cotton breeches and a long shirt that might once upon a time have been white. Over his shoulder was hooked a short hoe with a rough wooden handle. White stubble covered his face and head and Makana estimated him to be in his fifties. They met beside the crumbled mud walls of what might have been a store-house or barn behind the main house.

'You won't find anyone here, you know,' he said as he drew nearer. 'They left long ago.'

'Did you know the family?' Makana offered his Cleopatras but the man declined with a tilt of his head. He had the slow measured pace of a man who has learned patience from the land.

'Well, you could say that.' The man raised a hand and pointed. 'I live over there. I've lived and worked this land all my life.'

'What is it you grow here?'

'Dates, lemons, figs, beans, anything really. It's hard land. There's a lot of salt in it.' He reached up to the wall beside him to break off a piece with his fingers. 'We call it Kharshif. The salt makes it good for walls. They are strong.' A grin crossed his face. 'But when it rains, it dissolves and the walls just disappear. Luckily it doesn't rain too much around here.'

'What about the Abubakr family, did you know them?'

'My grandfather used to work for his grandfather. The entire family worked for him.' A hand swept outwards. 'All of this land belonged to them.'

'They sold it off.'

'People make choices.' The man shrugged. 'Sometimes they are unlucky.'

'Unlucky?'

The man glanced over at the ruins. 'People said the family was cursed. Others said they brought it on themselves. Allah knows.' His eyes were narrow and steady. 'What is it to you anyway?'

'I'm doing a favour for a friend of the family.'

'You're not a policeman?'

'Do I look like one?'

The man looked him up and down warily. 'You ask questions like one.'

'Well, I'm not. One of the girls was named Nagat. She died a few years ago. I was looking for her husband.'

'A lot of bad luck here. Three girls. One after the other. The mother died in childbirth. They say she would have given him a son.'

'You knew the father? Tawfiq Abubakr?'

'I knew him. Everyone around here did. He owned the land we worked. Nobody shed a tear for him when he died.'

'Who owns the land now?'

'That's not my business.' The man shrugged and squinted into the distance. 'We work it just as we always have. Nobody says anything.'

'None of the girls remained here. One went abroad, the other to Cairo and the third disappeared.'

'She ran into the desert. Never came back.' He shifted the weight of the hoe on his shoulder, impatient to move on. 'People say they ran to save themselves.'

'What else do they say?'

The man's narrow gaze returned to find Makana's. 'They say that the eldest daughter took the place of the wife.'

'Is that what you say?'

'I say that what happens under a man's roof is nobody's business but his own.'

'The middle girl, Nagat, married a man named Musab Khayr. Do you know where the family lived?'

'Of course.' The bony arm lifted and pointed. 'Just along there. But you won't find anything. They left too. Everyone's gone. I'm the only one left.' And with that he walked off.

Makana headed over to the house the Khayr family had lived in, surprised at how easy it was to suddenly have a lead on him. This was a much more humble building. A simple farmhouse. It had collapsed long ago. The walls were worn down to a shapeless heap. All that remained of the roof was a few roughly hewn, uneven palm trunks, slumped this way and that. As he approached, a couple of weaver birds darted out from underneath the rubble. Makana watched them fly away over the fields.

When he arrived back in town, Makana parked the motorcycle in the alleyway behind the hotel, in a spot where he would be able to see it from the window of his room. He was beginning to develop a fondness for the machine. It was already growing dark. The street lights were coming on, pinpricks of shiny glass against the falling night. As he straightened up he caught a glimpse of a solitary woman passing the end of the street. Reminded of the German girl's story, Makana was curious. Hurrying along, he reached the corner to see the figure disappearing into the next street. Makana walked quickly, passing the rather grand house that Bulbul insisted on throwing stones at every time he went by. A lone cat sat astride the wall. One paw extended, it paused in giving itself a bath to watch him go past. The street narrowed into an alleyway that wound upwards. A brief flutter of black cloth told him she was just ahead of him. The street led towards the ruins of old Shali that dominated the hill. The remaining houses were no more than solitary walls, jagged edges where the rest of the structure had vanished, or, as he now knew, dissolved in the annual rains. The bright walls contrasted with the dark spaces in between. Windows and doorways through which people had once walked.

A group of small boys sidled up alongside Makana to ask for change. Three, four, five of them, like stray cats. Did they live here, in these ruins? Their clothes were ragged and their feet mostly bare. Makana tried to brush them off, but they were insistent.

'Where you from, mister?'

'Cairo.'

'No, you're not. You're not from there.'

Makana reached the corner and looked left and right. Nothing. The road tapered away in both directions, twisting out of sight around a bend both ways.

'Give us a cigarette, mister.'

The eldest of them wasn't more than ten years old. Makana started to go left. The boy pointed right.

'Do you know where she went?'

'You want to go to Abu Sharaf, mister? You want a woman?'

Makana didn't know what he wanted. Why was it so important for him to catch up with her? He couldn't explain. In a gesture of defeat he turned to begin going back downhill. The walls behind him seemed to rise up, closing in on their secrets.

The boys' laughter trailed him down the incline back to the street. This time as he went past the big house he paused to take a closer look. It belonged to another age. He would have guessed the style was Ottoman. The upper floor appeared to be made of wood. It had a gabled roof and elaborate carvings in the balustrade that ran along the balcony. The only thing it had in common with the houses up on the hill was that it too looked as if it might be about to fall down. Over the high walls the thick fronds of regal old palm trees swelled majestically on the current of warm evening air. The wooden shutters on the windows were cracked, the slats hanging down at an angle. There were no lights visible. He ran a hand over the high metal door feeling the dents where rocks of various sizes had struck home.

The square was deserted. At Hamza's coffee shop the coloured lights turned their strange orbit on the ceiling of the veranda and the sound of laughter trickled down over the quiet streets. The lobby and reception area of The Desert Fox Hotel were empty. He heard a telephone ringing when he was halfway up the stairs and knew it had to be coming from his room. He rushed up and along the corridor but by the time he had opened the door it had stopped. He threw open the window and looked down to check the Norton was still there. It was. Then he lifted up the holdall and went through his things. Whoever had been through them had been careful not to be too disruptive. He was now convinced that Sadig had gone through his room to check for proof that he was with State Security. As he sifted through his clothes he recalled how Muna used to admonish him for not taking more care of his appearance. She would throw shirts out when she had had enough of them, just to make him buy something new. He crushed the shirt in his hands. Why had this feeling of loss become so acute? He had managed for years, or so he had thought, and now suddenly it felt unbearable. The telephone began to ring.

'Zahra?'

'Sorry, it's just me,' Sami's voice crackled down the line. 'Is this the same Zahra you asked me about? Okay, none of my business. So tell me, how is life in the wilderness treating you?'

'I feel as though I'm on the edge of the known world. Beyond this there is literally nothing.'

'I can't tell. Is that good or bad?'

Makana felt a sudden longing to be back in Cairo. He could hear noise in the background, people calling out and the crashing of plates.

'Where are you?'

'Aswani's,' said Sami, with his mouth full. 'You have no idea what you are missing. He got hold of a couple of lambs cheaply and he's roasted them whole. Amazing. Wait, let me step outside.' There was a pause and then relative peace with the familiar sound of cars nudging one another along with their horns in the distance. Music playing somewhere. 'How are you getting on?'

'They have their own problems to deal with here.'

'Any connection to why you're there?'

'I'm not sure,' sighed Makana, reaching for his lighter, 'but it certainly complicates matters. I'm now helping the local police.'

'Isn't that going to delay you?'

'I don't really have much choice.' Makana paused, convinced that he could hear breathing on the line from somewhere close by. Sami said something that he didn't catch. 'What did you say?'

'I said at least you've had a break from the city. Things are bad here. What's happening in Palestine is getting worse. People are very angry. The Israelis have gone into Jenin. They are flattening the town. There are reports of a massacre. No journalists can get in.'

'Did you find out anything more about Musab?'

'That's the reason I'm calling. Your source appears to be right. He could have visited Karima before she died.'

'What are you saying?'

'He appears to have gone missing.'

'I thought he was in detention?'

'Exactly. They appear to have lost him.' They being State Security.

'How could that happen?' asked Makana, thinking aloud. Was it possible he was imagining that someone was listening in? Perhaps we give them too much credit, he thought. Sometimes it was good to be optimistic.

'The answer is, it can't, not without help from inside. My source inside the ministry tells me they are desperate to find him before news gets—' The line went dead. Makana remained sitting there with the receiver to his ear listening to the hum of the dialling tone, waiting for the call to restore itself. He tapped the lever cautiously a couple of times, but Sami was gone. When he finally replaced the receiver on the hook it began ringing. He lifted it again expecting to hear Sami's voice but there was silence. After a time he heard someone clear their throat.

'Yes?' Nagy from downstairs.

'Yes, what?' asked Makana.

'You called reception.'

'No, I didn't.'

'Oh, yes, that's why I lifted the phone. What can I get you?'

Makana hung up without saying another word.

In his sleep, Makana mistook the knocking at the door for a clock ticking. Time running out. When he opened his eyes he heard Sadig calling his name.

'Open the door, Makana, before we break it down.' Nothing would have given him greater pleasure, he might have added. Makana pulled on his trousers and reached for a shirt. Breaking down the door suggested they were getting desperate in their efforts to impress him. Nagy was probably standing behind him with the pass key in his hand. Makana pulled the chair away from the door and unlocked it. Sadig stepped in with a disappointed look on his face, as if he had been hoping to catch Makana in the middle of some obscene act. He stuck his head around the bathroom door for good measure and when he came back the scowl on his face had deepened.

'Get dressed. I have orders to arrest you.'

'On what charges?' asked Makana.

'The sergeant will explain.'

It wasn't Nagy, but his daughter Rashida who was hovering by the door. She was shaking, he noticed, her hands trembled as she took the key from him. Her father was waiting at the foot of the stairs.

'What do I do now? How do I know I'm going to get paid? I have a business to run here.'

His malevolent look suggested he had known all along that it would end like this. Nobody paid him any attention except the girl, who implored her father to be quiet.

Sadig straightened his beret and produced a set of handcuffs.

'Is this really necessary?' asked Makana.

'It's nothing personal. I'm just following orders.' A claim that was flatly contradicted by the thin, sadistic smile that crossed Sadig's face as he tightened the cuffs around Makana's wrists before leading him out into the street.

'Where are we going?'

'You'll see.'

Despite the early hour a crowd had gathered. Makana recognised a few faces. Wad Nubawi stood in his doorway with folded arms. Bulbul's sad donkey staggered up alongside.

'Ha, *ya basha*, have these pigs started with their usual tricks on you too?'

'Get away from here, boy. *Yallah!*' Sadig thumped the side of the karetta and Bulbul took the hint, skidding away on unsteady wheels.

'Just say the word and I'll get you out,' Bulbul called over his shoulder. Makana watched him go. He was in no doubt that the boy probably could manage such a feat. Nothing about this place surprised him any more.

Chapter Eighteen

They walked up the hill into the ruins of Shali, along almost the exact same route Makana had taken the previous evening. No sign of the young boys this time, nor of the lone woman. The crowd tagged along behind them, perhaps hoping for a lynching. More people were waiting further up the narrow street as they turned a corner. Boys clambered onto unstable walls. Women rocked toddlers on their hips. Where had they all suddenly appeared from? Sadig had to thrust people aside, which he did with some relish, enjoying exercising his powers. And people obviously knew him. When they saw who it was they moved aside swiftly enough. Beyond the rubberneckers was a police cordon made up of a couple of uniformed men. In the distance Makana could make out the skinny, nameless officer alongside the stout figure of Sergeant Hamama. In the background, leaning on a wall was the rumpled shape of Doctor Medina. They were staring intently at something that was hidden from view. It was only when he reached them that he saw what it was.

'Why is he handcuffed?' Hamama rolled his eyes.

Sadig shuffled his feet. 'I thought you told me to seize him, sir.'

'I told you to bring him here, not arrest him,' grunted

Hamama. He chewed his gum fiercely while the sullen Sadig stared at the ground. Then he barked, 'Take those things off him. I can't apologise enough,' he said to Makana. 'This is an embarrassment to all of us.'

It still took Sadig time to find the key on the ring he carried on a chain attached to his belt. Makana wasn't paying much notice, his attention was elsewhere.

The man was sitting upright against the crumbled remains of a wall. There was a good deal of blood on his head and down his face. It soaked into his clothes, which were cheap, ragged and worn. Grey trousers and a brown shirt with a faint pattern of dots and dashes. Makana wasn't the only person in town with an exhausted wardrobe. In this case, cast-offs handed down to him by his employer no doubt. The blood had formed a darker stain in the shirt, running down in an irregular shape that pooled in his lap. His hands lay in the dust on either side of him. Some kind of creature, a dog perhaps, had chewed at his fingers which were raw and exposed. The whiteness of bone protruded on which black and blue flies glistened in frenzied movement. It took a moment to recognise Ayman, the hotel porter. His head was tilted to one side and one might have concluded from his appearance that he had simply sunk down to the ground exhausted and fallen asleep. If not for the blood, that had congealed into a stiff sheet on his chest and on his head, where more flies glistened and buzzed furiously. They grew more intense the further down the body they moved. Makana followed the trail downwards. The man's trousers had been pulled down and the genital area mutilated savagely.

'Was it the dogs that got to him?'

'I thought that at first,' Doctor Medina said with a heavy sigh.

He had designated himself official crime-scene photographer, the murders having stirred a professional streak in him that had not been seen in years. 'Some pieces are undoubtedly missing,' he said as he snapped a couple more shots of the lower body.

A shudder went through Sergeant Hamama as he met Makana's eye. Then he turned to his men. 'We have to keep this quiet. Do you hear what I say? Not a word of this outside this circle.'

Doctor Medina tutted and rolled his head. 'How long do you think that's going to last?'

'It'll last until I say so.' Sergeant Hamama stared at his men. There were grunts of obedience. 'Poor kid, he wasn't right in the head, you know?'

Makana massaged his wrists as he took a closer look. He hadn't paid much attention to the stooped figure who shuffled around in the gloom behind the reception counter, or along the dark corridor beneath the stairs. Ayman was usually to be seen carrying crates in and out of the storeroom at the back, or dragging a dirty rag over the floor.

'Trying to pretend you don't know your own victim?' Sadig grunted impatiently.

Makana stared at the corporal and wondered what the source of this hatred was. Had he done something to offend him, or was there something here that he wasn't seeing? He turned to Hamama.

'Am I being accused of something?'

The sergeant shifted his weight, hands on his ample hips. 'There are witnesses who say they saw you near here last night. Someone give me a cigarette.'

'I thought you'd given up, Captain,' said the weedy officer, producing a packet from his tunic.

'That'll have to wait, and don't call me that.' His eyes flickered towards Makana as he spat out his gum. 'I'm not captain.'

'Not yet,' grinned the toothy officer as he struck a match. Sergeant Hamama drew the smoke into his lungs and exhaled slowly.

'What witnesses?' Makana asked.

'Some local boys who were playing up here.' Sergeant Hamama studied the tip of his cigarette. 'These things taste worse than ever. I must be getting old.'

'And that makes me the murderer?'

'Are you going to try and deny it?' Sadig demanded.

Makana turned to face him. 'Don't you ever get tired of being wrong?'

Sadig went for him then but somehow the skinny officer managed to get in the way and the blow hit him in the side of the head, sending him reeling. Sergeant Hamama then grabbed Sadig by the scruff of his neck and threw him backwards with remarkable ease. Underneath the thick layer of padding there was still a good deal of muscle.

'What kind of fools do I have working for me?' Hamama yelled, snapping his lighted cigarette at the man. Embers popped off Sadig's tunic. 'Why am I surrounded by idiots?'

'Captain,' the skinny officer murmured. 'Ya Captain.'

'What is it?' Hamama snapped.

The skinny officer nodded down the hill to where the crowd was watching the show with their mouths hanging open. Hamama turned on him.

'I told you to get those people back!'

The sergeant turned to Makana. 'I don't know how much longer I can keep this thing under control. This is the second murder in a week. We've never seen anything like this.'

199

'It's the same killer.'

'And you're going to help me catch him.' Hamama brought his face close. 'I don't want you going anywhere. I want you to remain right where I can see you.' With that he took a step backwards and tried to compose himself. 'Doctor,' he said quietly over his shoulder, 'what can you tell me?'

'It's hard to say anything at this point,' began Doctor Medina.

'I don't want to hear that!' Sergeant Hamama yelled. 'You understand me? I need you to help me here. Give me something.'

Doctor Medina pushed his glasses back up his nose. His eyes darted from side to side. 'Whatever your men have not managed to contaminate has been disturbed by animals and the kids who found the body. I mean, in terms of forensic evidence, I don't know.'

'It's not the evidence,' said Makana. Everyone turned towards him. 'Forensic evidence can only tell us so much. We don't have anything to compare it to. We don't have the resources or the time. The killer has struck twice within three days.'

'What are you saying?' Sergeant Hamama held up a hand for silence. All attention was focussed on Makana now.

Makana took a deep breath. 'I'm saying we need to ask ourselves why – why was he killed this way?'

Sergeant Hamama lowered his head and stared at the ground. 'Why? What does that tell us?'

'He means we need to pay attention to the method used,' said Doctor Medina. 'I agree with him. This looks like a similar type of mutilation as we saw on the Qadi.'

'I don't understand,' said Hamama. 'What is this person doing?'

Makana looked down at the sad figure on the ground. There

was something pathetic about the exposed feet, gnarled and callused from years of going barefoot. It didn't seem like much of a death. Makana turned to Sergeant Hamama.

'Most murders are committed in a domestic setting. In the home. The husband hits his wife too hard, or the wife gets tired of her husband's bullying. It takes place in a heated moment, with no thought or calculation. The killer loses control. There is no thought of how to cover it up, how to hide, that comes later if it comes at all. Most murders are solved, as you know, Sergeant, by the murderer walking into a police station and confessing. What we have here is different.'

'Thank you, but I think I can see that,' snapped Hamama.

Makana went on. 'Both here and in the case of the Qadi, the body has been left out in a public place. That tells us the killer wants the bodies to be found. He wants them to be seen.'

'You mean like a public execution?'

'Something like that.'

'Maybe they were surprised?' suggested Doctor Medina.

'No. The bodies were arranged. The Qadi was bowed over in a position of prayer.'

'The hypocrisy of religion,' said Doctor Medina.

'Perhaps,' conceded Makana. 'And here we have Ayman exposing himself to the world.'

'Someone set them up on display,' said Doctor Medina.

'But why?' Sergeant Hamama looked back and forth between the two men. 'Why go to all that trouble?'

'Perhaps because there is some kind of message in all of this staging,' said Makana.

'Message?' cackled Sadig, thrusting himself forward. 'What kind of message do you think there is in cutting a man's balls off?'

'That's enough insolence!' Hamama stood between them. 'Get down there and keep those people back. And stay down there.'

As Sadig marched off down the hill, knocking aside anyone who got in his way, Doctor Medina spoke.

'It could almost be some kind of sacrifice.'

'We don't live in the dark ages any more, Doctor.'

Doctor Medina ignored Hamama. He turned his back to the body and faced down the hill at the crowd. 'He wanted everyone to see.' He glanced over at Makana. 'He's trying to scare us all.'

'The whole town?' Hamama was incredulous. 'What about the Qadi? He was out by the lake where no one was going to see him.'

'Except the tourists who ride out there,' said Makana.

'None of the tourists saw anything,' protested the sergeant.

'They were afraid of coming forward, afraid of getting involved,' said Makana. 'But that road is usually busy. People go out to Luqman's place all the time. It could have sent them fleeing from town.'

'Which would be bad for business,' concluded Doctor Medina.

'There must be something that ties the two victims together,' said Makana, lighting a cigarette. Sergeant Hamama put out a hand for one. Makana lit it for him.

'We've been over this,' Hamama said. 'I've put in a request to see the Qadi's records.'

Doctor Medina was thinking aloud. 'One is a powerful and wealthy man, well respected and educated, while the other is a nobody. A poor, uneducated man with the mind of a child.'

'So what do they have in common?' repeated Sergeant Hamama.

202

'Between them they cover the entire span of society,' said Makana.

Sergeant Hamama looked at a loss. 'How does that make any sense?'

'The killer is accusing the whole town,' said Doctor Medina.

'The whole town? What does that mean?' asked Hamama.

'The only person who can tell you that is the killer,' said Makana.

'Aren't you jumping to conclusions? We don't know how many there are, and the moment we start making assumptions is the moment we start making mistakes.' Sergeant Hamama was clearly struggling. He threw his cigarette down and spat on the ground. 'How you smoke these things, I do not know. Now listen. We have to get the body out of the sun,' he said, tilting back his hat to look at the sky. Makana could make out ragged scraps turning in the air. 'It's going to start getting warm soon and then this is going to stink. Find out where that stretcher is.'

The shout went down, with the skinny officer yelling at everyone. With Sadig out of the way he seemed to relish his new-found authority. Eventually two ambulance men made their way up through the crowd. When they arrived there was some discussion about how best to transfer the body. By the time they had finished the stench and the buzz of the flies in the dry heat was beginning to give Makana a headache. He stepped aside to make way for the circus. Everyone had a view and each time something had to be done everyone chipped in with their opinions. How best to cover the body. How to get it onto the stretcher. Sergeant Hamama was giving orders left and right, directing people like a traffic policeman. He alone seemed to command enough authority to cut through all of this. Long bloody tendrils of flesh dragged in the dust, hanging down from between the man's legs as they lifted him onto the stretcher. Makana caught a final glimpse of the cracked flesh on the bare feet and felt a twinge of regret. Ayman had been a simple fellow. It was hard to imagine what he had done to deserve this fate. Rigor Mortis had set in and they struggled to get the stiff body strapped to the stretcher. In the rising heat tempers began to fray.

Doctor Medina mopped at his brow with a damp handkerchief. 'At this rate there's not going to be much room left in that freezer. You'll have to requisition another one.'

'Is there an alternative?' Sergeant Hamama asked.

'Formaldehyde. But I would need a lot.'

'I'll look into it,' said Hamama. He stabbed a finger at Makana. 'I want to know where you are at all times, is that understood? I want to know your every thought the minute you have an idea.'

'You're not taking me in?'

'It's for your own safety. This is the second murder in a week. I can't guarantee how people are going to react.'

'Perhaps you should have thought about that before you sent Sadig down to arrest me.'

'It's like I told you, he gets carried away.' Sergeant Hamama rubbed a finger across his brow and shook the sweat off onto the floor with a flick of his hand. 'He's not a bad person.'

'Does this man have a criminal record?'

'Ayman? No.' Hamama snorted dismissively. 'He was a simpleton, that's all. Now, I'm going down there to talk to that crowd and then we are going back to the station. Doctor, I want you to start working on this body right away. Do whatever you can and give me the results as you go along.'

'I don't suppose there's any chance of being paid for my services?' asked Doctor Medina, his voice wavering so that

Sergeant Hamama didn't even have to say a word before he'd managed to talk himself out of his own proposition. 'No, I thought that might be too much to ask.' The doctor picked up his bag and vanished down the hill in pursuit of the stretcher. Makana turned to the skinny officer whose name he still hadn't learned.

'Did you know him well?' Makana asked.

'Ayman? Of course, everyone knew him.'

'Did he have a wife, a family?'

'No, of course not.' The man chuckled. 'He knew nothing about any of that.'

'Any of what?'

'Women, marriage. That sort of stuff. He was like a child, you know? His mind never grew like most people's.'

'Was he violent?'

The skinny policeman rocked his head from side to side. 'He was strong. When we were kids he could wrestle four or five boys at the same time, easily. But he wouldn't hurt anyone, unless he was provoked, and then, ha, you'd better watch out.' He laughed to himself, shaking his head at the memory. On the ground flies buzzed angrily over the clot of blood baking in the dust.

A small crowd was gathered around the entrance to the police station. Sadig, who had joined them on the way back, now moved forward and thrust them aside, trying to make amends it seemed.

'Come on, don't you have work to do?' he berated the crowd.

'Tell us what is happening,' implored a man with sad, drooping eyes.

'It's police business, that's what, now clear off.'

'That's not right. People are being murdered,' shouted an indignant older man.

'Who's to say that we won't be next?' added another.

'You will be if you carry on getting in my way,' Sadig yelled back.

'If there is a lunatic among us, we have a right to know.'

'The sergeant will make a statement when he is ready,' offered Sadig.

There were more cries and protests as Sergeant Hamama steered Makana up the stairs and through the front door of the old building. The crumbling pillars around the entrance provided a hint of what lay in store inside. The front hall was deserted but for a battered wooden table and a tangle of broken metal chairs in one corner that, in another time and place, might have been considered a modern sculpture of some kind. The walls were pockmarked with what might have been some kind of rot, or perhaps bullet holes. Over the high doors leading to the interior hung an enormous photograph of al-Raïs, the president, gazing down on them. A stern and officious portrait. Although they always looked the same, each of these portraits was unique in its own way, selected for some particular aspect of his character. Makana recalled the picture that hung over Madame Fawzia's desk at the girls' school in which Mubarak had almost an expression of benevolence; the father of the nation. But obviously that wouldn't do in a police station where a more commanding presence was called for.

Passing beneath the honourable Raïs brought them through to the main waiting area. Benches ran along one wall, paralleled by an uneven brown smudge at head height testifying to the number of hours people had spent sitting on them. There was a high counter opposite and a sour acrid tang came from a hall that led down towards a toilet at the back of the building. Hamama led the way behind the counter and into a third room, the inner sanctum, where tables and piles of paper abounded.

A larger portrait of the president, this time over a rather faded flag, covered one wall. As he swept in, the bulky sergeant waved him inside his office.

'Shut the door and sit down,' said Hamama, throwing his hat onto the table. He went over and twisted the switch on the wall back and forth a few times, muttered and gave it a thump with the heel of his hand. Finally, the overhead fan consented to begin rotating slowly.

The name on the door, hand painted white letters on a small brass panel, made it clear this was Captain Mustafa's office. Nobody had taken the trouble to remove it yet, possibly out of respect for the former commander of this post, but Hamama clearly had the place marked out as his own.

'How did he die?'

'Who?' Sergeant Hamama looked up irritated from a drawer he was rifling through.

'The captain.'

'There was some defect with his car, as I understand it. Bad luck. Could happen to anyone.' Hamama slammed the drawer shut and looked around him. 'Ali! Ali!' he yelled. The door opened and the skinny officer appeared. 'Go and fetch me some gum.' He pulled a grubby banknote out of his pocket and held it in the air. Ali stepped across the room and plucked it from his hand and disappeared out of the door again without a word.

'The captain was a good man,' said Sergeant Hamama settling himself back into the big chair behind the desk. 'Old-fashioned, but good at heart.'

Over his head a smaller portrait of the president appeared on the wall, in full military regalia, his chest covered in medals. The neatness of the room, everything about it in fact seemed to spell the exact opposite of the man now sitting behind the desk.

'Now, I want you to tell me again that you did not kill that man.'

'You don't seriously consider me a suspect?'

'Please, no questions. Just tell me,' the sergeant stared intently at him. 'A simple yes or no will do. Did you kill him?'

'No.'

'Good.' The sergeant thumped his hands down flat on the desk. 'Now, that wasn't so difficult, was it? You understand, I never suspected you of doing it. For what it's worth you seem like a well meaning sort of fellow, it's just that you are a stranger in town and people around here have a habit of mistrusting people they don't know.'

'And now that you've asked me you think they will be satisfied?'

'Between you and me I don't care, but I can always say I have questioned you and found you innocent of all charges. Nobody can accuse me of not following up.'

Along the wall to Makana's left stood a row of grey metal filing cabinets. Over them hung a yellowed map of the area. The kind of map you might see in a classroom, with a wooden bar running along the top and bottom to hold it straight. The paper was dry and cracked, torn along the edges. The colour and detail had faded to such a degree it might have been a pirate's map of where treasure lay buried.

'What about Ayman, you said he had no record?'

'I don't need to check any records. I know everything there is to know about everybody, and a good deal more than that too.'

The door opened and Ali came in carrying a pink packet of chewing gum which he handed to the sergeant.

'What's that?'

'Strawberry. It's all they had.'

'All they had? How can that be?' Hamama didn't give the other man a chance to reply. 'Never mind, just bring us some tea.' He ripped open the packet and crammed several pieces into his mouth and grimaced, but kept on chewing as he stared at Makana. 'Okay,' he conceded finally, 'Ayman didn't have a record, not really, but he was this close.' Hamama reclined in his chair and lifted one boot to the edge of the table to rock himself further backwards. 'Ayman had a certain fondness for little girls. A few years ago a complaint was made. Nothing came of it because, well, everyone knows he was not right in the head. And his uncle, whose hotel you are staying in, promised to keep a tight control on the boy. He was a boy, really, body like a man, but mind like a child.' Rubbing his chin, Hamama leaned forward and rested his elbows on the table. 'You seriously think this is some kind of message to the whole town?'

'I don't know what the killer has in mind, but I believe there is more to this than merely the murder of these two people.'

Sergeant Hamama chewed in silence. 'I don't see that. I really don't.'

'Did you question the Qadi's wife?'

'No, no.' The sergeant straightened up a pile of papers on his desk. 'I couldn't do that. The man is barely dead and this business of the burial is a little awkward. I can't tell the woman that her husband is being held in a common supermarket freezer.'

'You don't think she has heard by now?'

'It doesn't matter. I'm not risking it.'

'More than your job's worth?' Makana asked.

'Look, I don't know how you do things in the big city, but here you have to tread carefully. It's a small community and we all depend on one another. We live together.'

Makana was staring at the wall map. 'Where exactly did he die? Can you show me?'

'Who?'

'Your predecessor, Captain Mustafa?'

'Why is this of interest to you?'

'I'm just curious by nature.'

'But this has nothing to do with these murders. Don't you think you ought to be focussing your mind on the killings?'

'I am, I just need to know certain things.'

After a moment the sergeant stood up. He stared at Makana as if still unsure what to make of him. Finally, he leaned over and tapped a finger on the map.

'He was out here, just west of the oasis.'

'What's out there?' asked Makana, lighting a cigarette.

'Not much really. Would you mind not smoking in here? I'm trying to stop.'

Makana dutifully stubbed out the cigarette as carefully as he could before returning it to the packet. He got to his feet and went over to study the map.

'There's an old storage depot built by the company that constructed the road, but it has been empty for years.'

'And these are tracks?'

Sergeant Hamama squinted. 'The old camel routes through the desert.'

'They're not marked, I assume.'

'No, nothing out there is marked. You have to know your way.'

'So who would know these routes apart from Bedouins and camel herders?'

'People guard the knowledge well. You can lose your way easily and never come back.'

'Who else would know how to use these routes?'

Sergeant Hamama looked at Makana. 'What are you getting at?'

'Nothing, I'm just curious. Musab Khayr, would he have known?'

'Maybe.'

'He was involved in smuggling so I suppose he did.'

'There are all kinds out there. Smugglers, rebels from some conflict somewhere, common bandits. Not much difference between them if you ask me. Groups of armed men. That's what it boils down to. You can't keep track of them and you can't control them. The truth is you don't know who you might run into out there.'

'Why was he out there alone?' Makana asked as Ali appeared balancing a small tray which he set down on the desk.

'Who?'

'Captain Mustafa.'

'I've wondered about that quite a bit.' Hamama said, settling himself back down in his chair to begin spooning sugar into his cup of tea until there was a layer two fingers thick in the bottom of the glass. He stirred it thoughtfully. 'The truth is that I don't really know. Captain Mustafa had his own ways and he didn't confide in me all the time.'

'Maybe there just wasn't anyone around that he trusted,' Makana said quietly.

'That's what I like about you,' smiled Hamama over the top of his glass. 'You don't beat about the bush. Captain Mustafa and I were not the closest friends in the world. We disagreed on a lot of matters, but he didn't deserve to die like that.'

'How exactly did he die?'

'You're really not going to leave this subject alone, are you?'

'Once I know all the details I'll drop it.'

'Okay. Well, there was an electrical fault. A spark ignited the fuel in the tank. The car exploded.'

'Isn't that rare?'

'What do I know? I'm not an expert. People die in different ways.' His jaws worked up and down on the gum. 'Satisfied now? Do you mind if we move on? I mean, you do want to solve this case, don't you? Because I have a duty to protect the people of this town. I don't want a mad man wandering around cutting people up.' Sergeant Hamama set down his glass. He drew a circle with his forefinger on the desk and spoke without looking up. 'I'll tell you something, Makana. I don't know you. I don't know where you come from, or how you ended up in this place, but I believe in fate. Call me an old woman, but I believe you were sent here for a reason.' He tapped his knuckles on the desk. 'I believe that is so, and I think maybe that reason is to find this killer.'

Chapter Nineteen

Ayman's room was not actually a room at all, but a space fenced off from the rest of the storeroom at the back of the hotel by a stack of plastic crates full of empty bottles that once upon a time contained some kind of soft drink. Crates and bottles alike were draped in layers of dust and spun together with cobwebs. The bed was strung with palm-fibre rope that had stretched with time to resemble a hammock more than a bed. His belongings were in a cardboard box. A meagre collection of clothes and shoes, all of which appeared to be in tatters. Torn shirts and ripped trousers, just like the clothes he'd died in. Shoes that were split along the seams or had lost a heel. It wasn't much of an existence.

'His parents died years ago. He had no brothers and sisters.' Nagy remained by the door, his ususal bad temper softened by compassion. 'Ayman's parents were distant cousins.'

Makana rifled through a tattered primary school book. Apparently Ayman had been trying to teach himself to read. The stub of a pencil had been used to underline words. Boy. Camel. Bird. Nobody really knew how old he was exactly, but around forty was the general consensus, although his mind had not advanced much beyond that of a ten-year-old child.

'They left him with us when he was still small.'

For safekeeping no doubt. The family wanted him kept at a distance, in the care of a relative say. A shelf held up by string and nails contained an oil lamp and some old glass jars filled with pebbles.

'He collected them,' Nagy explained, shaking his head in wonder, 'like a kid collects marbles. He was fascinated by the colours and shapes.'

At the centre of the shelf was a small, chipped coffee cup. Inside it was a slip of blue ribbon. Nagy was busy pushing things aside, sliding crates against the wall, thinking about all the possibilities this space offered. Makana slipped the ribbon into his shirt pocket.

Nagy winced as he straightened up, one hand to his back. 'All these years I looked after the boy and this is how I get repaid.'

'The world is filled with injustice,' commented Makana.

Mutawali, the Qadi's assistant, scurried along the arcade rather than walked. He seemed flustered and when he caught sight of Makana waiting for him on the veranda outside his office he threw up his hands with a groan.

'I heard you'd been arrested!'

'A misunderstanding,' explained Makana as the little man fiddled with his keys to open the door.

'A misunderstanding, you say? Frankly I don't understand anything of what is happening in this world today.'

The room was dark and musty, the windows covered by shutters that had not been opened for years. A flat metal bar held down a row of stacked papers, some in folders. Makana stood in the middle of the room as Mutawali moved around as feverish as a mouse. Setting the pile of papers he had been carrying under his arms on the desk, he opened a second set of French windows that opened onto the veranda and the courtyard beyond.

'As you can imagine, with the Qadi's sudden death we are left with a great amount of work that needs to be dealt with.'

'I'm sure,' said Makana. 'And I won't take up any more of your time than is necessary.'

'This whole business has been a terrible shock for us. This is a small community. For the life of me I cannot understand why anyone would want to kill the Qadi in such a brutal way, or this boy from the hotel.' Mutawali settled himself behind the desk with a heavy sigh and ran a hand over his face as though trying to restore some element of vigour to the slumped features. 'Very well, then, get on with it.'

'The two victims appear to have nothing to do with one another. No relationship at all. It would be helpful to know if there had been any contact between them, to establish a motive, you understand.'

'I'm not sure to what extent I should co-operate with you.'

'Why not?'

'Well, the fact that you were a suspect, no matter how briefly, does cast a certain shadow on you, you must admit.'

'It was a case of one police officer being overzealous. It was personal.'

Mutawali fretted with his fingers, tapping the edge of the desk. 'People don't like you, I can understand that. You're an outsider. You make them nervous with your questions. I think it's the way you ask that makes everyone cautious, even me. We wonder if we are walking blindly into a trap.'

Makana was looking out of the window which afforded a pleasant view over the town. The deep green of the palm trees contrasting with the stark walls of the ruins and beyond that the world seemed to dissolve into shades of grey. A faint heat haze could be glimpsed hovering over the lake.

'Sergeant Hamama has put in a request for permission to see the Qadi's records, but you know how these things are. We might have another victim on our hands before the paperwork goes through.'

'Yes, I understand.' Mutawali clutched his hands together on the desktop. 'I'm sorry, I wish there was more I could do, but my hands are tied.'

'Well, perhaps you could tell me a little about the Qadi's business dealings, informally, I mean.'

'Well, I'm not sure that I can.'

'Let's start by distinguishing between his official duties and his private interests. Perhaps that way we can figure out who the Qadi was due to meet that afternoon.'

'I . . . well, it's highly irregular.'

'So is murder.'

'Yes, yes, very well. Where to begin? The Qadi had a wide range of interests.'

'Was it just tourist companies?'

'No, not really.' Mutawali fell silent.

'I think I understand your problem,' said Makana.

'You do?' The deputy's eyebrows shot up.

'Of course. Murder is a messy business. It opens up a lot of doors that sometimes it would be better to leave closed. Do you follow me?'

'I . . . I think so.'

'This kind of case brings a lot of outside interest. Specialists.'

'Such as yourself,' said Mutawali, shifting in his seat.

Makana was silent for a moment, letting the deputy squirm. 'Do you want to know what I think? I think you are a man who likes things to be in their place. The Qadi was your superior so you were bound to obey him. That doesn't mean you approved of his methods. Sometimes he did things that you knew were not quite right, but you went along anyway because you were obliged to, but now that he's gone you are left holding the baby, as it were.'

'That is one way of putting it.'

'If the Qadi crossed the line between his official responsibilities and his personal interests that needn't reflect badly on you.'

'Naturally. I mean, I would hope not.'

'So, in this particular instance. If you were to hazard a guess as to who the Qadi might have gone out to the lake alone to meet, what would you say?'

Mutawali cleared his throat. 'It was nothing to do with tourism. It was a survey company. *AGI LandTech.*'

'They are conducting a mining survey in the area?'

'Gas deposits.' The slim man blinked his eyes nervously. 'It's not the first time. They come around every now and then, but they never find anything substantial enough for anyone to take a real interest.'

'Why was he out there alone?'

'Sometimes he preferred to do things that way.' Mutawali examined the tabletop. 'I always assumed it was not my business to know.'

'Is it possible to talk to them?'

'Oh, no, I think they went back to Alexandria, where they are based. I can give you a number. They are rather odd types these survey companies. It's a touchy subject and they don't want to step on any toes.'

'Whose toes were they worried about?'

'There are those who think that exploitation of the region's natural resources would be bad for us, for tourism, for the region in general.'

'But the Qadi wasn't one of them.'

'No, he wasn't. Do you have to report all of this?'

'I don't think you have anything to worry about,' said Makana. 'Can you think of any possible connection between this man Ayman, and the Qadi?'

'The Qadi was not in the habit of associating with hotel porters.' Mutawali smacked his lips as if the thought gave him a bad taste in his mouth. 'He had no business in that hotel. If he had guests they usually stayed somewhere with a little more class shall we say.'

'And is it possible that Ayman might have turned up in the courts at some stage?'

'Yes,' said Mutawali slowly. 'Naturally, that is the most likely possibility. But even then I don't see how that would explain why their deaths should be linked. If this man appeared in court, then presumably he and the Qadi were on opposite sides of the law?'

'At this point it is dangerous to make any kind of assumption.'

'I understand. Look, I would appreciate it if you put in a good word for me.'

'I can see that you were put in a difficult position, but everything now depends on your full co-operation.'

'Naturally. I'm sorry if I appeared to be un-cooperative. It wasn't that I was trying to hide anything. I just thought you were here for another investigation.'

'I came here looking for a man named Musab Khayr. Does that name ring a bell?'

Mutawali rubbed his chin. 'It does actually. It's a long time ago, I was just a junior clerk, but I recall he was a criminal, mixed up with the smuggling bands. I think he worked for Wad

Nubawi, who is an old reprobate. Apparently he's changed his ways, but in the old days . . . Well, they ran this town in a climate of fear. This Khayr man was one of their thugs.' The Qadi's deputy folded his arms. 'I think there was a terrible scandal and he left, fled for his life.' He shook his head. 'You're wasting your time looking for him here. He would never come back.'

A crowd of men had gathered outside the police station. Their anger rumbled over them. At the top of the steps stood a nervous-looking Sadig. His eyes followed Makana as he drifted along the edge of the crowd and turned the corner onto the square. There a group of boys was kicking around a decapitated head. On closer inspection it turned out to be an old football. An old leather ball, now shredded by constant use. It no longer contained air, but had instead been stuffed with old rags and flapped around. One of the boys broke away and ran over to fall in beside Makana. It was Bulbul, still wearing the worn plastic slippers held together with bent nails.

'Is it true there is a crazy man killing people who are not good Muslims?' he asked.

'Where did you hear that?' asked Makana.

'People say all kinds of things,' shrugged the boy.

'Tell me about that house over there. The one on the corner.'

'The old house?' Bulbul spat on the ground. 'It's haunted by jinns.'

'Nobody lives there?'

'Not any more. There used to be an old Turkish lady, but she died. People say she was actually a jinn.' The boy stared morosely at the old house on the other side of the square. 'They say that she's still in there. At night sometimes you can hear her moving around.'

'That's why you throw stones at the gate when you go by?'

'It's just a habit,' the boy shrugged again. 'It stops the jinns from coming out. So how about it, you want to see the Mountain of the Dead? What about the Temple of the Oracle, have you been there yet? I'll give you a special price.'

'Some other time,' said Makana reaching for a cigarette. The boy held out his hand for one which Makana ignored. 'Who was she?' he nodded at the old house.

'I don't know. Some crazy old Turk,' said the boy, losing interest. No business to be done and no free cigarettes made for dull conversation. The ball rolled ahead of them and he bounced off to retrieve it, cutting a surprisingly unathletic figure for such a young person.

Doctor Medina was in his clinic poring over Ayman's remains. The white coat he wore had, unbelievably, acquired more stains, which didn't seem possible. There was also blood on the surgical gloves he wore. Ayman's naked corpse was laid out on plastic sheeting that was stretched over the examination table. For once the doctor appeared to be enjoying himself. He also, surprisingly, appeared to be sober.

Makana stayed close to the open doorway where the heady stench of rotting flesh and formaldehyde was less overpowering. He lit a Cleopatra to cover the smell.

'Thank god, another smoker,' said the doctor, who was puffing energetically at the cigarette which hung from the corner of his mouth.

'You seem to be enjoying yourself.'

'I haven't had this much fun since medical school,' the flabby features tightened to accommodate the grin, revealing a trace of a much younger man. 'You're earlier than I expected. The sergeant hasn't arrived yet.' The deep-set eyes widened. 'Or perhaps that was intentional?'

'What have you got so far?'

'As I suspected, he was killed by a blow to the rear of the cranium. A blunt instrument. I've managed to extract wood splinters and some paint.'

'What colour paint?'

'Hard to tell at the moment. Everything is red.' Doctor Medina flashed a broad grin at his own witticism. Makana leaned his head out of the doorway to exhale. It wasn't so much to prevent the contamination of the examination room as to breathe something that wasn't chemical. The doctor was carrying something on a spatula towards the spotlight over the big stainless-steel sink in the work surface that ran along the wall. He placed the matter into a small sieve and poked a gloved finger through the contents. 'Possibly green.'

'A green wooden post.'

'Something like that,' nodded the doctor absently. 'As for the rest, well, maybe you should take a look at this yourself.' He came back over to the body and pointed out the terrible wound between the man's legs. Makana stepped closer. He had attended autopsies before. In his previous life, as he liked to think of it nowadays, when he had been a police inspector in Khartoum, it had been a regular occurrence. And while he had never particularly enjoyed them, the discomfort they provoked was often softened by the wonder he experienced at witnessing the delight doctors took in disassembling a human being.

'What am I looking at?' Makana stared into the dead man's eyes. The lids were half shut which gave the impression that Ayman was observing them, waiting for his moment to jump up and take his revenge.

'Here,' the doctor indicated. 'He was castrated, obviously, the testicles removed and the penis sliced away. Somebody clearly didn't like our friend.'

'Or they didn't like him the way he was.'

'It looks pretty brutal, doesn't it?' Doctor Medina was either grimacing or smiling, Makana couldn't tell. 'There's no bruising, so at least he was dead when this was done.'

The man's skin was covered by a waxy, grey sheen. It was hard to tell what colour he had once been, or even that this had been a man at all. In either case it made for uncomfortable viewing.

'Was he sedated? Like the Qadi?'

'Yes, I still haven't identified the drug yet.'

'Same killer.' Makana regarded the corpse. This at least was something, a common thread tying the two victims together. 'Do you know how it was administered?'

The doctor held up a finger and drew Makana's attention to a small puncture mark on Ayman's neck. A whiff of something indescribable rose from the body and Makana instinctively took a step back. He lit another cigarette unable to decide if the nausea he felt was from an excess of tobacco or from the body lying in front of him.

'This tells us that whoever did this knows what they are doing,' said Doctor Medina.

'How much training would they need?'

'Not much actually. It could be a trained nurse, or an ambulance orderly. Anyone with a basic knowledge of medicine. Or a doctor, of course.' He held up his hands. 'There's always that.'

'Could you make a list of qualified people in town?'

'I could, but it wouldn't in any way be complete. We have no idea of people who come and go. A doctor or orderly, say, who is no longer in the profession.'

'It would be a start,' said Makana.

'What would be a start?' demanded Sergeant Hamama as he lumbered into the room. 'I thought I told you not to begin this without me?'

He seemed more stressed than he had been when Makana had seen him in his office. Now he resembled a drowning man, floundering against the rising tide. He threw a glance at Makana. 'Things seem to be taking their own pace and I'm beginning to wonder at the wisdom of including you in this investigation,' he snapped before turning to the doctor. 'So, what have you got?'

'I was explaining to Makana that the sedative used might indicate someone with medical training.'

'You mean, like a doctor?' Sergeant Hamama's beleaguered gaze flitted back and forth between the other two. He saw conspiracy everywhere he looked.

'Not necessarily.'

'Just as well for you,' said Hamama, 'because there aren't many of your profession around these parts.'

'It doesn't have to be a doctor,' Makana pointed out. 'A nurse, a medical orderly . . .'

'Not many of those around either.' Hamama rubbed his chin. 'Can you draw up a list?'

'Makana just asked me for exactly that.'

'Oh, he did, did he?' Hamama studiously ignored Makana.

'And as I was telling him, such a list could never be anything but approximate.'

'Approximate is good enough to start with. I need something to go on, and be sure to put yourself at the top of it,' grunted Hamama. 'Now what can you tell me about this poor idiot?'

'The mutilation took place after he was killed.'

'Is that good or bad?'

'Perhaps it means the killer has some compassion after all,' said Makana.

'What else have you got?'

'The victim was hit with a heavy wooden object. No sharp edges, probably rounded.'

'That's not bad. So they hit him first and then what?'

'The signs are that a sedative was administered to make sure he didn't wake up in the middle of the operation,' sighed Doctor Medina. 'Then he bled to death.'

'Could the blow have been delivered by a woman?' Makana asked. Both men turned to stare at him.

'A woman?' scoffed Sergeant Hamama. 'Why should a woman do something like this?'

'Oh, you mean, considering the size of the victim, a small person might have been intimidated. The use of a sedative . . .' Doctor Medina was cut off by the sergeant.

'I still don't see why you think it might be a woman?' said Sergeant Hamama.

'I wasn't the only person up there last night,' said Makana. 'I was following a woman, or someone dressed as a woman.'

'Why didn't you tell us?' demanded Sergeant Hamama. 'So is it a man or a woman we are looking for?'

'Either, I suppose. The German girl I spoke to also saw a woman out by the lake the evening the Qadi was murdered.'

'Is that possible?' Hamama turned to the doctor who shrugged and straightened his glasses.

'Well, in theory, yes, I suppose. If the angle was right. Ayman was quite tall, as you can see. The fatal blow was delivered from behind.'

'So a very tall woman,' said Hamama, giving Makana a wary look.

'The attack happened on a hillside. The killer could have been higher up than the victim, at an angle.'

'Or standing on some ruins,' offered Doctor Medina. 'And the Qadi was fairly short.'

'It makes no sense. None of it,' Hamama shook his head at both of them. 'A man dressed as a woman, maybe.' He snapped his fingers at Makana. 'Don't you have a cigarette for me?' Makana held out the packet and his lighter. Sergeant Hamama bent his head over the flame until smoke was coming out of his nostrils. 'After you left I had a phone call. It seems that news of this case has filtered upwards. The newspapers in Cairo are writing about it. They are threatening to send a team out to clear it up, not that that is going to happen right away, but you know what it means, a whole load of bright, clean policemen sticking their noses into our business. Time is running out.'

'Did you find anything in the files on Ayman?'

'I told you, I don't need to look at the files. He had no file. He was just a poor fool who liked looking at girls. That doesn't mean he deserves to be chopped up like a piece of liver.' Hamama peered at the corpse. 'Why are his eyes like that? Looks like he's staring at me.'

'It's just the body settling. After death the body tends to lose liquid and so it shrinks.'

'I skipped lunch today. I couldn't face it. At this rate I'll be a mere shadow of myself.'

'Perhaps it's time to talk to the Qadi's widow,' said Makana quietly.

Sergeant Hamama winced and hung his head. 'You don't understand. The Qadi was a powerful man with powerful friends. It's no coincidence I'm getting these phone calls from government people, from high-ranking officers. State Security.

All those people are now her friends. We can't afford to go stepping on her toes.'

'Perhaps you should stop worrying about your promotion and start thinking about solving this case.'

'He's right,' said Doctor Medina.

'And if I need your advice I'll ask for it.' Sergeant Hamama raised a finger. 'I'm warning you to go carefully. I'll drive. You can follow me on that infernal machine.'

'It's a classic,' offered Doctor Medina. 'One of the all-time greats.'

'Now, I wonder why that makes not the slightest difference to me?' Sergeant Hamama grunted.

The Qadi's house was a fine new villa on the southernmost outskirts of the town. Bright magenta bougainvillea leaves climbed over the high walls. The gate gave onto a sumptuous garden with more flowers and a pergola covered in vines that fluttered briskly in the desert breeze. The driveway was grand. It needed to be to accommodate the Qadi's two cars, both of them Mercedes. One of them, blue, had official number plates, for trips to the office or around town, while the second one was a sleek, ivory-coloured vehicle with private plates. It seemed almost too new for this dusty climate. Makana and Sergeant Hamama were met by a young maid in a smart outfit who ushered them into a reception room. Stepping inside the interior felt as if they were entering another dimension. Somewhere far away from the dusty village which lay on the other side of those walls. The floors were covered with grey marble that shone with a well-polished lustre. Persian rugs were laid out, along with plush sofas and chairs, all in elaborate Louis XIV style with carved arms and striped upholstery. The maid reappeared bearing a brass tray of cold drinks followed by tea, along with a plate of delicate biscuits which Sergeant Hamama tucked into with gusto, apparently oblivious to the amount of time that was being wasted. Makana was on his third cigarette before the double doors opposite them opened and a handsome woman entered. Dressed elegantly in a black abaya that swept to the floor, Makana noted that she also wore make-up and lipstick on her uncovered face. A sign of modernity in the late Qadi's favour. Sergeant Hamama, cap in hand, somehow looking more of a mess than usual in these surroundings, whispered his way through a lengthy series of condolences on the part of the department and himself personally, before going on to include the entire town. To listen to him you might be forgiven for believing that the country was in mourning.

'When will the body be released?' she pleaded as she crossed the room. She wore, Makana noted, open shoes through which painted toenails were visible with every step.

'Soon, madame, very soon.'

'It has been a week now. You cannot imagine the suffering it causes me not to be able to give him a proper burial.'

'This is an unusual case and requires certain scientific procedures to be completed.' Sergeant Hamama did his best to dig himself out of the hole he found himself in.

'What scientific procedures?' Her eyes widened.

'I can assure you, it is all standard procedure.'

'But who is performing this? And where is he being kept?'

'Doctor Medina's services have been engaged and—'

She didn't allow him to finish. 'But that man is a scandal! He's a drunk. My husband would never have approved.'

'Unfortunately, Doctor Medina is our best consultant on this matter until further resources are allocated.'

227

'You must press them. Insist. Tell them how urgent this matter is to the people here.'

'I can assure you, madame, I am doing my utmost.' Hamama bowed his head. 'Nothing I say can convey the sorrow that has fallen over our town.'

The Qadi's wife didn't blink. 'I was hoping you had come to tell me that you had found the man who murdered my husband,' she said in a cold voice.

Sergeant Hamama glanced over at Makana, suddenly at a loss, a dusting of powdered sugar clinging to his chin.

'No effort is being spared. We have brought all our resources to bear on the case, including the service of experts from outside.' He gestured at Makana who found himself under the penetrating gaze.

'An expert in murder?' She sounded sceptical as she looked Makana up and down before turning back to the sergeant.

'Oh yes, he has many years of experience and a strong record of helping the police in Cairo with some of their most difficult cases.'

'We are honoured indeed,' said the Qadi's wife with only the slightest dip of her powdered and stiffly wrapped chin. Her expression said she was not convinced. 'Of course, I shall do whatever I can to help you in your endeavours.'

'We hate to trouble you at this time, madame,' Hamama was wringing his cap as if he was strangling a cat, crushing it into a shapeless mass with his big hands. Makana felt a compulsion to put an end to the man's suffering. He cleared his throat.

'To understand the killer's motives we need to get a picture of your husband's activities.'

The widow turned her eyes on him. 'Naturally, but this is easy. My husband, may Allah show him mercy, was a public figure. Everyone knew him.' She bowed her head and pulled a handkerchief from her sleeve to press to her nose. There was a moment's respectful silence during which Makana ignored the hard stare he was getting from Sergeant Hamama. They hadn't come here to be gentle to the good widow, but to solve a murder. When she had recovered herself the Qadi's wife continued. 'He served this country for nearly thirty years. The Minister of Justice called me personally. They were friends you know.'

'I'm sure he was most respected in the highest offices of this country,' said Hamama.

'I appreciate this is a very difficult time for you,' Makana continued, 'but we need to act quickly if the killer is to be apprehended.'

'Yes, yes of course.'

'Let me assure you, madame, the vile creature who did this will pay for his deeds,' Sergeant Hamama shook his fist for emphasis.

Makana waited a moment before going on. 'Your husband, the departed, would undoubtedly have upset a few people in the course of despatching his duties as an official of the law.'

'He had great faith in the people of this community. He used to say that the rotten fruits were few and far between. He always prayed to Allah to guide him and make him a better judge.'

'May Allah have mercy on him,' murmured Sergeant Hamama, and the wife echoed this sentiment. Makana was beginning to grow weary of this charade.

'Might I ask, and I apologise if this seems indelicate,' Makana said. 'But how did your husband pay for all this on the salary of a lowly government functionary?' He gestured at their surroundings. 'Did he have private investments of some kind?'

'If this is your expert line of questioning,' the Qadi's wife shot at Hamama, 'I see no improvement from the usual incompetence.'

'I assure you, madame,' Makana appeared to try and make amends, 'I had no intention of casting doubts on your husband's integrity.'

'What is this?' she snapped. 'I will not have the good name of my husband sullied by a nobody whom I have never set eyes on in my life before this day.'

'It seems like a reasonable question,' said Makana. 'But perhaps you were not involved in your husband's business dealings. Is there someone else we can approach with these questions?'

'You will not approach anyone with these questions.' She glared at the sergeant who coughed to cover his embarrassment and then, realising she could expect no help from that quarter, she turned on Makana. 'My husband was an honest man. It is true that he found his official salary somewhat limited when it came to providing for his family the quality of life he wished them to have. He supplemented his income with consultancy work.'

'Consultancy?' Makana's eyebrows rose slightly. 'Legal counselling. Who for?'

'There is nothing unusual about this. Strictly speaking, my husband's private matters are not something I feel I can discuss with someone who has just walked in from the street.'

'I can assure you, madame, that Mr Makana meant no offence,' Sergeant Hamama sniffed. 'Forgive me if we have strayed over the line of good taste.'

'Not at all,' said the Qadi's wife, with downturned eyes.

'As Sergeant Hamama says,' Makana went on, 'no stone shall be left unturned. There is one obvious matter we have not entered into . . .' Sergeant Hamama frowned at him in warning, but Makana proceeded as if he did not grasp the meaning of this expression. 'As you are no doubt aware, there has been a second victim. A man named Ayman, a porter in a hotel.'

'I heard something about it,' she murmured.

'Do you know of any relationship between this man and your husband?'

'Relationship?' Her eyes darkened again.

'I mean, is it possible the Qadi knew this man? Did Ayman ever come to the house?'

'A hotel porter? Why would he come here?' She looked genuinely appalled at the idea.

'Ayman took an interest in young girls,' Makana went on.

'Makana!'

'You're not suggesting that my husband and this porter shared such a common interest?' Her eyes widened as her jaw dropped. She turned to the sergeant, but he too seemed at a loss. 'I must say that I had my doubts when I heard that you were being considered to step into the shoes of Captain Mustafa. On the basis of what I have seen today, I would hasten to remind you that the rank of captain of police carries a great deal of responsibility. If this is the kind of expert you bring to the investigation of such a grave matter, I wonder whether you have the necessary qualifications.' When she had finished with Hamama she turned to Makana. 'If the man was a delinquent who preyed on young girls then he would have crossed my husband's path as a felon and no doubt was convicted as such.'

'Well, that's the thing, there is no record of Ayman having been charged or convicted.' Makana paused. 'Is it possible that they knew each other at school? Could they have been friends?'

'My husband was raised in Alexandria where he was educated

231

at one of the finest schools in the country. He did not associate with hotel porters.' Pressing the handkerchief to her upper lip to dab at a drop of perspiration, she addressed Sergeant Hamama. 'I think I have provided enough entertainment for one morning. If you have any further questions please go through my husband's assistant. I am sure he can answer far better than I, and Sergeant . . . a nasty rumour reached me that my husband's mortal remains are being stored alongside frozen vegetables. I put this down to the work of malicious tongues, but having witnessed your performance today I wish to convey to you personally that I want to bury my husband before the week is out. I would appreciate it if you would order the doctor to release his body as soon as possible.'

'As soon as it is at all possible, madame.' Hamama bowed low.

'Good day, gentlemen.'

She glared at Makana as she swept from the room.

Outside they stood on either side of the Chevrolet pickup, Hamama trying to reconstruct his cap.

'You're a liability, Makana. I thought you were going to solve this case for me in record time, but all you are doing is digging my grave.'

'I didn't come here to solve your case for you. I came to find someone.'

'Yes, I know, a man no one has seen for decades. Why don't you just admit you're barking up the wrong tree. Go home, Makana, and leave us in peace.'

Chapter Twenty

The bearded man behind the counter at the telephone exchange was engaged in a discussion with two earnest young men who wore neatly trimmed beards and carried brief-cases. At first Makana thought they were debating some detail of religious praxis, but it emerged their complaint was of a more technical than theological nature. They wanted to know why his computers ran such an outdated system. The bearded man's eyes blinked in the cold neon light.

'You have no right to talk to me that way,' he said. He gave a nod to Makana as he came in, complicity emerging in the face of hostility. Makana chose a booth at the end and dialled Sami's number. No Quranic recitations over the sound system today. Since his last experience Makana had been wary of using the telephone in his room. He didn't want his conversations to be reported to the whole town every time he put down the receiver. The connection was marginally better.

'I was wondering when you would get back to me,' said Sami. He sounded as though he had been asleep.

'The line went. You were telling me about our friend and his troubles with State Security.'

'They've lost him for sure. Right now they are trying desperately to get him back before the news gets out.'

'It must be embarrassing.'

'Well, as I understand it,' Sami yawned, 'there's so much internal competition between one agency and another they say it might have been arranged between them.'

'You mean one arm of the system trying to outmanoeuvre another?'

'It's impossible for him to have escaped without some kind of inside help. So either a sympathiser or something else.'

Behind him Makana could hear the argument rolling on between the three men at the counter. There was a certain absurdity to it, almost as if the two younger men simply wanted to prove their superior knowledge.

'They locked down the city but there's still no sign of him,' Sami was saying. 'So, either he is lying low, which means someone is giving him shelter, or he's already out of town.'

Lying low would involve contacts. But Musab hadn't been back for years. He would have been out of touch, plus he never planned to come back, he was brought against his will, which meant that he wouldn't have had time to prepare. He might have been lucky and found somebody to help him, or he could have done what came most naturally, and run for it. Sami seemed to be reading his thoughts.

'I'm beginning to come round to the idea that you might not be wrong going all the way out there,' said Sami. 'But you need to be careful.'

After he hung up, Makana remained seated in the little booth. Everyone said Musab would never come back here, but didn't that make it the obvious place to go? And besides, what choice did he have? Musab knew the old desert routes. It would be the best way of getting out of the country. He would need a car. Railway and bus stations would be watched carefully. To get hold of a car probably meant stealing it. Nothing too flashy. Something inconspicuous. Something that could manage the desert roads. A pickup perhaps? A jeep if he was lucky.

When he came out he found the two men had vanished and the bearded man was behind the counter staring at his computer again.

'You're the one who came from Cairo, aren't you?' he said as he took Makana's money. 'You're looking for Musab Khayr.'

'You know him?'

'I know of him.' The bearded man grinned, a rare expression in a face that could only be described as wooden. 'He went abroad to fight the jihad. We need more people like him.'

The square was dimly lit by scarce lights. A single donkey karetta was making its way along, stacked high with butagaz bottles.

The hotel lobby was dark. Makana retrieved his own key from the hook behind the deserted reception desk and climbed the stairs. The lights on the upstairs corridor had all gone, save for one weak bulb at the head of the staircase. If you didn't break a leg on the stairs you risked thumping your knee into the walls. Makana stiffened as he felt rather than saw a shadow move ahead of him. It turned out to be the girl, Nagy's daughter Rashida, who was crouched in front of the door to his room. She rose slowly as he approached. There was a bruise high up on her left cheek and her eyes had a wild, frightened look about them.

'What happened?' Makana asked.

She swallowed, touched a hand to her face. A tear welled out of her eye, glistening briefly in the weak light as it trickled down over her fingers. She mumbled something that he didn't catch.

'What is it?'

'Rashida!' Nagy's head appeared at the top of the stairs. 'Stay away from her!'

Makana ignored him. 'What is it?' he asked the girl. 'What do you want to tell me?'

There wasn't time for more as Nagy rushed over and pushed him roughly aside, grabbing his daughter by the arm.

'You stay away from my daughter!' he yelled, wagging a finger in front of Makana's face. 'You hear me?' Then he turned and dragged her away down the hall. He caught a final glimpse of her as she glanced imploringly over her shoulder, her eyes floating liquid and dark as they were swallowed up by the gloom.

Makana unlocked the door to his room. He sat down on the side of the bed and reached for the telephone. He dialled Zahra's number and let it ring. After four times it passed him on to a message service. Three times he listened to the recording of her voice but couldn't bring himself to say anything. Finally, he hung up and lay back in the darkness, trying to think. Reaching for his cigarettes, he switched on the bedside lamp. On the table beside the bed lay the picture Madame Fawzia had given him. The class photo he now carried around with him everywhere he went. He brought the photograph close to the light and studied the rows of faces. There was something about that picture of those little girls which was important. He felt sure of it, he just couldn't see it. As he fished his cigarettes out of his shirt pocket, something else fell out into his lap. The blue ribbon he had found in Ayman's room. He held it closer to the weak light from the bedside lamp. Each of the girls was wearing one identical to it. He stared at the photograph for a long time. Who was he really looking for, he wondered. He was no longer sure.

* * *

236

Breakfast in the Desert Fox Hotel had proved such a dreary disappointment that after the first day Makana had sought out an alternative, which had led him to a place on the corner of the narrow street behind the hotel. It wasn't particularly fancy. On the contrary, the arrangements could only be described as rudimentary at best. It was off the tourist track and so had a neglected air about it. White plastic tables and chairs sank like forgotten monuments into a sand-covered floor. The kitchen was a sophisticated version of a desert camp. A narrow, uneven brick counter built by someone clearly unfamiliar with the concept of walls, fenced off an area dominated by a large clay funnel out of which spewed a fierce gas jet. The small, energetic couple who ran the place juggled pots and pans over this single flame with amazing dexterity. Nobody ever seemed to complain about having to wait. Indeed the place was generally so busy it was hard to find a seat, which Makana took as a good sign. In any case, the food was far better than the stale bread and tinned jam provided by Nagy at the hotel. Makana collected a newspaper lying on the counter and found himself a seat. It wasn't long before the woman, who was so short he didn't even have to tilt his head to look into her face, was standing beside him. She came up to somewhere around his chest height when he was on his feet. Umm Hamida. What she lacked in stature she more than made up for in spirit. She flew around like an impetuous jinn, carrying on a non-stop conversation with her husband, who seemed to have been consigned to a silent existence in another, parallel universe in which everything moved much more slowly.

'You're still walking around, so that must mean you're a free man,' Umm Hamida offered as she went by his table. Tea arrived before he had time to open his mouth. 'We have liver today. You can't resist it. We do it the Alexandrian way, with hot pepper.' Makana was allowed time to nod his agreement before she was gone. He read through the newspaper. The Palestinian intifada went on. The front pages were dominated by a picture of an Israeli Defence Force Caterpillar bulldozing houses in Jenin. US Secretary of State, Colin Powell, had delayed a meeting with Yasser Arafat, until he condemned a suicide bombing in Jerusalem in which six Israelis had been killed. The violence seemed to be spreading. A bomb had exploded outside a synagogue in Tunisia, killing twenty-one people, fourteen of them tourists. Elsewhere Lloyds of London had raised estimates of their losses incurred by the attacks on the World Trade Center to almost 2 billion pounds sterling. Worldwide it was believed insurance costs would reach some 50 billion US dollars. And British Prime Minister Tony Blair had told Parliament that the time for military action against Iraq over weapons of mass destruction had not yet arisen.

'If it was any fresher it would have legs on it,' said Umm Hamida as she set the plate of fried liver in front of him. Plates of eggs and white cheese also arrived along with warm flat bread and a bowl of mashed fava beans on which a shield of golden olive oil floated. Pushing aside the paper, Makana began to eat, suddenly aware that he had not eaten since lunch-time the previous day.

'Are you going to find the animal who did it?'

A man loomed over him. He had a large, oddly shaped nose with some kind of growth on it that resembled a cauliflower.

'What did you say?'

'The Qadi. Are you going to find the one who killed him before he gets the rest of us?'

'We have families to think of,' another chimed in. Makana slowly became aware that everyone in the place was looking at him.

'I'm sure Sergeant Hamama is doing his best.'

'Hamama,' muttered the first. 'He's only interested in helping himself.'

'We heard you were sent from Cairo to help us,' another man sitting in the corner said.

Before Makana had a chance to answer this, the first one broke in again, berating his friend. 'What are you talking about, Cairo? You can see he's one of us. He's from the south. Am I right?'

Makana didn't have to speak, they seemed to have him all figured out for themselves.

'I don't have time for those fancy types from Cairo. They understand nothing about us. They just have their bits of paper.' Dramatically, the man with the large nose pointed into the distance. 'We know nothing of that. We live by our own rules. You know why? Because out there the only borderline is between you and the Lord.'

'Let the man eat in peace,' Umm Hamida shooed them out of her way, cutting between them like a stubborn ewe.

'Let me ask you,' Makana ventured before they moved on. 'Does anyone remember the Abubakr family? They used to live on land over beyond the mountain.' He noticed a look pass between them. The second man spoke up.

'Is this something to do with the Qadi?'

'One of the daughters married a man named Musab Khayr. Another went abroad. The third girl disappeared. Does anybody remember that time?'

The man with the bulbous nose spat in the sand. 'I remember the father. People said bad things about him, but I thought them unfair.'

'What do you know?' another interrupted.

239

'They used to have lots of land,' said a third man. The first man concurred.

'It's true. In the old days they owned most of the land on that side of town. The grandfather, or some such, maybe the great grandfather. He was a rich man. Everyone worked for him.'

'He was an idiot. Nobody missed him when he went. The daughter died. Remember that?'

'Yes, now that you mention it, I do remember. It was an accident.'

'The eldest sister killed herself. I remember that. She drowned in the lake.'

'No, she went away.' The man rubbed his large nose. 'One of them did, anyway. And one of them died. That I remember.' A look passed between the two men. 'It was all a long time ago.'

'You think Musab killed the Qadi like that?' asked the second.

'Can you think of any reason why he would want to kill the Qadi?'

'Musab never needed a reason to kill anyone. He did it for fun.'

After that they seemed to lose interest in the subject. They busied themselves with paying and getting ready to leave.

'You don't want to pay any attention to what that lot say,' said Umm Hamida. 'They have no idea what day of the week it is. Ask them the same thing tomorrow and you'll get a different answer.'

When he had finished eating Makana decided to stretch his legs. He walked to the end of the narrow road thinking he might speak to Kamal at the bicycle shop, but the place was closed. Two tourists stood outside staring at the shuttered door.

So Makana turned and made his way up the winding road that led into the ruins of the old town. What had lured poor

Ayman to lumber up this hill that evening? Had he been on his way to meet someone? At the scene of the crime the ground was still stained with dried blood. A handful of flies buzzed lazily in the warm air. Over the houses Makana could see the blue-grey sliver of the lake in the distance and the distant hump of the hillside. Beyond that the desert stretched away into infinite nothingness. Lighting a cigarette, Makana turned his attention back to survey the town behind him. Just below him the uneven pillar of the mosque rose up. A strange clicking sound of electrical static was coming from the speakers as if someone had left a switch on. Why would Ayman come up here in the middle of the night? There was nothing to show that he had been dragged up here, or forced against his will. Such a place, remote and yet central. A meeting, an assignation? With a woman?

As he stubbed out his cigarette, Makana stepped closer to the low wall. A small bird was worrying at a scrap of silver paper jammed under a fallen stone. It took to the air as he reached down. He sniffed it. A sweet wrapper. Tucking it carefully into his pocket, Makana spotted the nose of a car jutting out of the wall below him. Makana began descending the hillside by a series of winding paths that wound between the walls. The dried mud was flaked with flecks of light from the salt crystals it contained. They gleamed like gems hidden in the dull earth. He became lost, turning left and right. Finding his way blocked he scrambled up onto a wall to get his bearings. When he finally reached the bottom he discovered there wasn't a road there at all. The way had been obstructed by a mound of crumbled earth that might once have been a wall. The nose of the car, a Lada Niva, was buried in the sand. The car's paintwork was worn by sunlight and age to an uneven brown colour. Makana looked around him.

The Lada might have been an old army jeep. Hidden out of the way here, out of sight. Cairo plates. Shielding his eyes with his hands, Makana peered through the dusty rear window of the car. The interior was empty save for a plastic crate in which stood rows of what looked like withered plants. Their roots were wrapped in black plastic. The rest was wilted stems and dried leaves as if someone had forgotten them in there a long time ago. A stray dog began barking and when he turned it loped mournfully by to nose through a patch of wasteland, covered in broken bricks, pieces of tin, plastic bags – blue, white, striped, all the colours of a faded rainbow.

He was on the other side of the hill now and it took him fifteen minutes to find his way back around.

Makana was sweating by the time he reached the Norton. The machine was already hot enough to make him swear and pull back his hand when he touched the bare metal. Climbing into the saddle he turned the ignition switch and stamped on the starter a couple of times before being rewarded with the throaty grumble of the engine coming to life. He was aware of people watching him as he went by, no doubt wondering what evil this eccentric stranger had brought with him. Makana was beginning to get the feeling that the answers he was seeking were common knowledge, to everyone but himself. They all knew Musab and they knew what had taken him away from here. Some of them no doubt knew what might bring him back. They let him walk around and ask his foolish questions though none of them had the slightest intention of telling him what he needed to know.

Picking up the road west Makana rode out of town. The air cooled him down. Dust blew sideways across his path, at times gusting so hard that he felt the Norton wobble beneath him. The depot was about five kilometres outside of town; it wasn't hard to find. It stood alone in the middle of nothing. A simple rectangular structure set back from the road. The walls were not the usual mud adobe but fired brick, though now faded almost to the same colour by sun and wind. Sergeant Hamama had said the place was abandoned, but it didn't look that way. The doors were made of sheets of corrugated iron held together by a brace of crossed metal struts. They were locked with a heavy chain and padlock. Makana parked by the side and switched off the Norton. Without the engine chugging away he was suddenly plunged into silence, broken only by the gentle whistle of the wind. Looking south he saw the dust whipping itself up into a cone that rose high into the air, and twirled around. A desert jinn.

Traffic on the road was limited to the occasional vehicle going by. Makana peered through the corroded gaps in the corrugated steel gates. Inside he glimpsed a yard with a shelter along one wall. It had metal supports and roofing sheets. Underneath were parked three large Magirus-Deutz trucks. Covered in dust but serviceable by the looks of them. At the far end he could see what looked like storerooms. Makana circled the entire perimeter of the compound and then returned to the part just behind where the lorries were parked. It took him ten minutes to gather up enough broken bricks to pile into a rather unstable tower. It took several attempts before he was able to balance himself on this wobbly perch and reach the top of the wall. Heaving himself upwards, Makana managed, not without difficulty, to get onto the wall, catching his clothes in the strands of barbed wire that had been strung along the top of it. Once on the wall he could hold on to one of the supports to step over the wire and climb down onto the back of one of the trucks.

It was a bit of a disappointment. He didn't find much more

than he had already seen through the gate. The storerooms at the back were empty but for a heap of old tyres and didn't look as if they had been used for anything in a long time. He returned to the trucks and discovered that the cabs on two of them had been locked. On the third one there was a hole you could stick your finger into where the lock ought to have been. The interior didn't reveal much. A sun-bleached Quran lay face up on the dashboard to provide divine protection against mishaps. Apart from that there was nothing. He lifted the seats, looked through the tool locker, but came up with nothing more interesting than a broken lighter. He climbed down again and walked around the yard some more. There was a large blackened area in one corner where something had recently been burned. Makana sifted through the ashes with a stick and came up with a blackened tin can and a few strips of torn cardboard. Someone went to a lot of trouble to keep the place clean. As he straightened up and looked around him one last time he caught, out of the corner of his eye, something fluttering in the warm breeze. It was a torn piece of string or rather tape, that had been tied to one of the iron supports holding up the roof of the shelter. Makana went back over and climbed up into the back of one of the trucks. He had to step up onto the side of the flatbed and then, with a bit of fiddling, he managed to free it. It was a strip of white plastic which someone had knotted over the metal bar to use for something else perhaps and then forgotten. He turned it over. There were words printed on it, formed into a shape. A company logo. Something he had seen before, *AGI LandTech*. He rolled it up carefully and tucked it into his trouser pocket. Then he climbed up onto the wall and dropped down on the other side. Two minutes later he was back on the road with the noise of the machine and the wind whistling in his ears. He didn't have any goggles, which meant that he had to squint against the wind and still the sand made his eyes water.

Far off in the distance the escarpment rose up like a crater on a distant planet, tapering down to meet the road that was nothing but a thin, dark thread that lost itself in the horizon. This was the old road along which Alexander had once led his trusted army through the desert in search of the blessing of the oracle. This was also the road Captain Mustafa took when he was killed. It took him less than ten minutes to reach the spot.

The remains of the pickup lay in the sand by the side of the road. From a distance it resembled the blackened, ugly carcass of a crow. Burnt and twisted. Setting the Norton on its stand Makana walked around the wreck. The road vanished into a point whichever way you cared to look. This was the kind of place it was easy to lose one's sense of purpose. What had Captain Mustafa been after out here? Turning the other way he looked south and west towards the magnificent nothingness that was out there. Was it an accident or had the captain been surprised by a convoy of smugglers, old Wad Nubawi and his boys coming in from Libya with a fresh cargo of cigarettes and video players? Or was there something more?

'Are you lost?'

An old Bedford lorry, the bonnet held down by a strand of electrical flex that trembled like a divining rod, rolled to a halt beside him. An old man, his face the same colour as the grubby white cloth wrapped around his head, leaned out of the window. Where he had come from wasn't clear. He seemed to have materialised out of thin air like a mirage.

'This road,' Makana pointed south-west, 'where does it lead to?'

'The desert.' The old man peered over his shoulder as if to make sure they were talking about the same track.

'It doesn't look like there's much out there.'

'Don't you believe it,' the old man laughed. 'There's plenty. There's a whole city of wonders. All you can dream of and more. Have you never heard of Kalonsha?' The old man chuckled to himself as he wrestled the lorry into gear and trundled off in a cloud of black exhaust. Kalonsha. Makana recalled that Doctor Medina had mentioned the name. The word echoed round in Makana's head like a mystical incantation, the way the sufi devotees turn in circles repeating the name of the Almighty in order to rise up and attain a transendental state, a trance that would take them on high.

Chapter Twenty-one

Patience appeared to have run thin. When Makana arrived outside the police station a spectacle awaited him. The crowd from the previous day had swelled both in size and, it appeared, outrage.

'Deliver him to us and we will show him our own justice!'

'Typical police corruption, arresting an innocent man!'

It seemed they were not all in agreement with one another. At the top of the steps Sadig was grinning with delight. Nothing he enjoyed more than the sight of people at each other's throats.

'What's all this about?' asked Makana.

'We've got him.'

'You've got who?'

'The killer. The one who cut up the Qadi.' Sadig rearraranged his beret on his head. 'So lucky for you we won't be arresting you, and we won't be needing your help any more,' he said with undisguised satisfaction. 'Not that you've actually done anything for us.'

Inside, Makana found further pandemonium. What was going on exactly wasn't clear. The families of the two victims had been let inside and were now busy harassing the officers whose job it was to hold them back. Makana eventually managed to get through. Sergeant Hamama was strutting through the crowd with a grin on his face. He waved magnanimously, trying not to show his delight, but he was clearly a proud man.

'Who is it?' Makana asked.

'Our friend Khalid Luqman. You remember him?' Hamama ushered Makana into his office and gestured for him to take a seat before sinking down behind his desk with a sigh.

'I can't tell you how relieved I feel. I was getting pretty worried there for a time.'

'You're sure that he's the one?'

'I can smell it on him.' Sergeant Hamama smiled, and ticked off his fingers. 'He has motive and there's no denying he had opportunity. He was perfectly placed.'

'What is the motive?'

'He had a grudge against the Qadi.' Hamama leaned back in his chair. 'Listen to this. It turns out that Luqman's great grandfather was a Turkish official back in the days of King Farouk. He was awarded the land. Luqman was short of cash and keen to sell it off, but the Qadi ruled that the land belonged to the government. Luqman was furious, of course, but there was nothing he could do. The law is the law.'

'What happened to the land?' Makana asked.

'It was eventually sold by the state to a private developer. I have the details here, but it was all official and above board.' He ruffled through the papers on his desk before giving up, eager to get on with the telling of his story. 'The point is, he thought the land was his on account of some old papers of his great grandfather's, but he was wrong. Anyway, apparently it hit him hard. Old family fallen on hard times. I mean, there he is selling

Coca-Cola to the tourists and him a big landowner. Hah, he never forgave the Qadi. He threatened to kill him only two months ago. We have witnesses.'

'Witnesses who heard him threaten the Qadi?' Makana went through his pockets for his Cleopatras and came up with an almost empty packet. 'Who were they?'

'There were eight of them. It was outside the Qadi's office. Luqman didn't care who heard him.'

Having debated whether to wait, Makana lit his penultimate cigarette and smoked quietly for a time. Sergeant Hamama sniffed but watched without comment.

'So this means your promotion will go through.'

'Yes.' A broad smile arranged itself across the sergeant's face. 'I imagine they will be satisfied with this outcome.'

'So what was his motive for killing Ayman?'

'Ayman?' Hamama rocked back and forth a few times in his chair. He didn't like the question. 'What about him?'

'Well, I thought we were agreed that the same person killed both men. So why did Luqman kill Ayman?'

'That was your theory, Makana. I was never fully convinced of the two being linked.'

'Then you're saying that we still have a killer out there?'

Hamama sat forward and his chair came down to earth with a bump. 'Why do you have to start twisting things around? We don't know the two deaths are connected. Even if they are, you can't prove that he didn't kill both men.'

'Why?'

'Why what?' Sergeant Hamama pulled a face.

'What is his motive? Why would Luqman kill Ayman?'

'I told you, I don't know. We've only just started our interrogation.'

'Did he explain the mutilation?'

'He will, don't you worry. Right now we're leaving him to think things over. They're sending a superindendent from Mersa Matruh to confirm.' Sergeant Hamama allowed himself a smile. 'I think this could be the moment to officially announce my promotion.'

'*Mabrouk*,' Makana congratulated him. 'Will you let me talk to him?'

'You don't understand. The case has been closed. We have a suspect and a motive. It's only a question of time before that becomes a full confession.' The sergeant pointed a finger. 'You know what that means? It means thank you very much for your help, and goodbye. I'll get one of the boys to drive you to the bus station.'

'I'm not sure my business here is finished,' said Makana, although from Sergeant Hamama's tone he suspected that maybe it was, whether he liked it or not. He wouldn't want any credit for solving the case going to a stranger. If a delegation was on its way from Mersa Matruh, Hamama wouldn't want anyone else around who might throw a shadow on his moment of glory.

'I'll give you twenty-four hours, but then I want you gone.' Hamama got to his feet and went over to the door. 'I'm grateful for your help and everything. Don't take it badly. I know you had your theories, but sometimes these things just don't work out.'

'Doctor Medina said that both the Qadi and Ayman were drugged. Luqman has no medical training, does he?'

'You don't know that for sure.' Hamama shook his head in disbelief. 'And even if that was true, he has motive and opportunity. Don't forget the body was found out in the lake, just by that coffee shop where he provides tourists with illicit substances for smoking.'

'Let me talk to him. You've got nothing to lose. If I'm wrong you already have someone locked up. Those people out there don't really care who goes to prison for this. All they want is for someone to be punished.'

Hamama swung the door back and forth, undecided. 'You're taking this very personally. What does it matter to you?'

'It matters because it matters, and you understand that. That's why they are going to make you captain.'

The sergeant's eyes were dark, wet stones set in the fleshy mass of his face. He had the bewildered look of a dog faced with a particularly devious cat but Makana had appealed to his vanity. With a curse he threw the door open so hard it slammed into the wall behind it.

The holding cells were below ground. A grubby doorway bore the imprint of countless hands steadying themselves as they stepped through into a stairwell that led downwards. At the bottom another doorway gave onto a short corridor. Here the mantle was low and dotted with brown stains where countless prisoners had not been quick enough to duck their heads. The latest addition to this cartography of pain was fresh and matched a corresponding open wound on Luqman's forehead. He was clearly in a bad way, eyes wired with fear and already bearing the signs of a man whose mental balance has been shattered. He scuttled away from the door as it swung open and crouched down in the far corner with his hands over his head when they came in.

Luqman raised his arms higher to shield himself as Makana approached. He squatted down in front of him. Several of Luqman's fingers had been broken. They jutted out like broken twigs, at odds with one another. Makana shook his last cigarette out of the packet and held it up to him. Luqman gave a whimper as Makana placed the cigarette between his lips and lit it for him. The blood from his head wound had run down and congealed around his eyes. He stared at Makana as though he had never seen him before.

'You remember me?' Makana asked.

'Sure,' Luqman nodded, before spitting blood on the ground. 'You're with them.'

Makana glanced over at Hamama who was hovering in the doorway.

'What happened to him?'

Hamama stared at the ceiling. 'Regretfully, some of the mob out there managed to get hold of him before we could stop them.'

'They threw me to them!' Luqman whispered to Makana. 'You should get out now, before they do the same to you.'

'I will,' said Makana. 'But first I need you to answer a few questions.'

Luqman stared at the ground, the cigarette smoking between his lips. He seemed to have forgotten it was even there.

'The only reason I didn't kill that old fool is that I didn't have the courage to do so.' He stared at Makana. 'I should have done it years ago.'

Behind him, Makana heard a grunt of satisfaction from Sergeant Hamama.

'Why did you want to kill him?'

'Why?' Luqman's face broke into a garish grin. His teeth painted with blood. 'How many reasons do you need? I wasn't the only one either. Go out and ask the crowd.'

'The same crowd that wants your neck?' asked Hamama.

'They are hypocrites, all of them! If they had the courage they could tell you. Everyone hated him.'

'But you're the one who killed him,' said Hamama.

Luqman sucked in the smoke, his eyes on the ground, like a hunted dog.

'What difference does it make what I say?'

'Stop these games.' Hamama stepped forward and Luqman reared back, pulling himself into the corner as the sergeant loomed over him. 'You had a reason to kill him.'

Luqman's eyes found Makana. 'Lots of people had reasons. You think I'm the only person he swindled? That man used his authority to line his own pockets. From the moment he arrived in this town that was all he cared about.'

'Here he goes,' muttered Hamama.

'I know what I am talking about. He cheated people out of their land, sold off the rights to hotel chains and survey companies, some of which don't even exist. I'm not the only one. The money went straight into his pocket.' Luqman nodded in the direction of the sergeant. 'Ask him, if you don't believe me. Ask him what happened to Captain Mustafa.'

Makana glanced over his shoulder at Hamama. The sergeant shrugged.

'I told you this was a waste of time. Listen, boy, I tried to help you, but the fact of the matter is that you're going to have to start helping yourself, and that means telling the truth.'

'I am telling the truth. Why don't you tell him? Tell him!'

'Okay,' sighed Sergeant Hamama, straightening up. 'We're going to leave it there. Now, I want you to be clear about this. I need a full confession from you by morning, and I'm going to get it, one way or another.'

Luqman's head sank and his body was wracked with sobs.

'You're not helping yourself,' Makana said softly. 'You need to tell us everything you know.'

'What's the point?'

'Listen to me,' said Makana. 'I can't help you if you don't tell me everything. You know something, don't you?'

One of Luqman's eyes was swollen into a red ruby egg. The other one swivelled away from Makana.

'What is it you're not telling me?'

Luqman glanced over at Hamama, who was standing by the door.

'Who are you trying to protect?' Makana asked. 'The German girl said she saw a woman out there by the lake. You saw her too, didn't you?' Luqman's eyes lifted and Makana saw something there. 'You knew her. Who was she?'

'Nobody.' Luqman stared at the floor between his feet. 'I didn't see anybody.'

'I don't see what any of this proves,' said the sergeant from the doorway. 'He saw a woman, or he didn't. What difference does it make?'

Makana ignored him.

'Okay, I only have one more question. What did you use to drug the Qadi?'

'Drug?' Luqman frowned.

'Before he was cut up, the Qadi was administered a drug. Doctor Medina found traces in his blood. I'd like you to tell me what the name of that drug was.'

'I don't know anything about any drugs!' Luqman pressed his hands to his ears and began to sob, rocking from side to side against the wall.

'What did you expect?' Sergeant Hamama asked as he slammed the door to the cell shut behind them and the guard shot the bolt across. 'That the great Makana would succeed where the Egyptian police had failed? Do you have such a high opinion of yourself?'

'Luqman didn't do it.' Makana headed for the door.

'What makes you so special?' Hamama called after him. He seemed offended.

'The murderer is still out there,' said Makana. 'The longer you waste with Luqman the more chance they have of getting away.'

'You really think a woman could have cut the Qadi up like that?'

'Maybe. A woman, or a man covered from head to foot in black.'

'Here we go again.'

'Whatever you decide about Luqman, don't let him out of here.'

'Why not?'

'In the first place, because someone is likely to take justice into their own hands, but also because I think he knows who the real killer is.'

'A man dressed as a woman,' Sergeant Hamama muttered, as he stood aside and held the door open for Makana. 'The team from Mersa Matruh will be here in twenty-four hours. You'd better have something better than that by then.'

Chapter Twenty-two

The light was draining from the sky as Makana emerged from the police station. Street lights like glassy gems twinkled over the town. The crowd of protesters had diminished as people headed home for the evening.

At the internet and telephone exchange on the square, Makana tried the number Mutawali had given him for *AGI LandTech*, the survey company in Alexandria that was interested in the gas reserves. It took him a while to locate someone who knew about the Siwa project. Finally, a young man came on the line. He explained that so far as his records showed there had been no meeting planned with the Qadi on the day in question.

'Are you sure about that?'

'Yes. It's true we had an interest in the area but the whole project was suspended.'

'Do you know why?' asked Makana.

'It wasn't from our end. We were ready to go with the drilling. I understood it was something to do with land permits.'

'Can you tell me when that was?'

'A couple of months ago, give or take.'

Makana thanked him and rang off. Outside the supermarket a pickup was unloading blue butagaz bottles. Wad Nubawi leaned in his doorway supervising. Inside the supermarket the space left by the freezer had now been filled by sacks of rice with Chinese lettering on them. At the back a row of shiny new standing freezers hummed happily away.

'You solved your problem,' observed Makana.

'It was either that or go out of business.' Wad Nubawi had shrewd, lively eyes that radiated mischief. Being out of business was not something he would ever have contemplated quietly. Also, Makana thought, the choice of replacement was interesting. It was more difficult to store a corpse in an upright freezer cabinet. Was Wad Nubawi expecting more deaths, he wondered. Makana replenished his stock of cigarettes and then remained where he was.

'Was there something else?' The older man reached for a date from the bag beside the cash register. For the first time, Makana noticed the left hand was missing the first and second fingers.

'Where did you get them from?' Makana nodded at the freezers.

Wad Nubawi stiffened. 'All the paperwork is in order.'

'Relax, I'm only interested in Musab Khayr. You knew him when he was here. In the old days.'

'In the old days?' repeated Wad Nubawi. The eyes had a hollow space in them where he seemed to retreat. Makana had the sense that he was trying to coax a reluctant spider out of a hole. Wad Nubawi was silent for a long time, then he said, 'Are you still helping Hamama?'

'I don't work for him, if that's what you mean.'

'Well, that's what it looks like from where I'm standing.'

'Why did Musab leave? What happened all those years ago?'

'Shouldn't you be asking him these questions?'

'I would if I could find him. Do you know where he is?'

Wad Nubawi struck a match that roared as it flared. 'The last I heard he was on his way abroad. Germany, or somewhere.'

'I heard he came back.'

'Now where would you hear a thing like that?' The flame flickered softly in a corner of the grey eyes.

'If he was trying to get out of this country, this would be the way for him to go, wouldn't it?'

'Why would he be trying to leave if he just came back? That makes no sense.'

'You didn't answer my question. He knows the way across the desert, doesn't he?'

'If you say so.'

'You would know if he came back here.'

'Why are you asking me about him?'

'You used to know each other. He used to work for you.'

Wad Nubawi blew out the match in his hand that had burned down to his fingertips. 'If he came back he would be making a mistake.'

'He has enemies here?'

'I said it would be a mistake. I didn't say anything about enemies.' The lean head tilted to one side. 'Now, if you don't mind, I have work to do.' Wad Nubawi made to move away.

'He's in a lot of trouble. He wouldn't want to be seen.'

'This is a small place. Nothing stays secret for long.'

'Could he make it across the desert by himself?'

'Why not?' Wad Nubawi shrugged. 'He's driven these roads since he was a boy.'

'So, he could make it to Kalonsha without help?'

Wad Nubawi allowed himself a smile. 'Kalonsha is a dream. You don't know what you're talking about.'

'People talk about it as if it were real,' said Makana.

'People talk about a lot of things they've never seen in their lives. Like Allah and paradise. Where would we be without that?' Wad Nubawi's eyes were flat and emotionless. 'I can't see him coming back here, not for anything in the world.'

An old melodrama played on the television in the lobby. Jerky black and white images of a couple walking along a beach. Any minute now one of them would burst into song, thought Makana as he went behind the desk to retrieve his key from the hook. He made his way upstairs. A cat wandered along the first-floor corridor and rubbed itself against his leg. If left to their own devices these creatures would overrun the entire town. Downstairs a woman launched into a plaintive song about impossible love as Makana unlocked his door and stepped into his room. As he did so he heard a soft movement somewhere to his left. Another cat was his first thought, only this was somewhat bigger. He clicked on the light to see Rashida, Nagy's daughter, hiding between the bed and the wardrobe.

'Put off the light,' she whispered urgently.

'If I put it off it'll look suspicious.'

'He'll think you're asleep.'

Makana couldn't think of a counter argument. He reached for the switch and the room was plunged into darkness. After a moment or two he could make out the shape of the girl as she stood up. There was enough light coming in from outside to make it possible to see. Makana moved towards her and she pulled back.

'Please,' she said, 'sit down. There is something I have to tell you.'

The bed creaked long and loudly as Makana sat down on the

bed. Both of them froze, listening for any sound. In the distance a car engine rolled away. An owl sounded from the direction of the mosque. The girl crept back into the little niche beside the wardrobe and sank back down to the floor.

'My father must not know that I have spoken to you. He would kill me.'

It was always possible that a nightly diet of televised melodrama had begun to have an effect on the girl's mind. On the other hand, Makana had seen the bruises.

'Is this about Ayman?'

There was a murmur that he took for a yes.

'You were close to him?'

'I knew him since I was a child. All my life he has been there. My father took him in when he was small.'

'He was part of the family.'

'His father was my father's cousin.'

'Why was he living with you?'

'I don't know. His parents moved away and he came to live here.'

The girl's answers seemed to only lead to more questions, but Makana decided it was best to let her tell it in her own time. Rashida had fallen silent.

'It all happened a long time ago. I was very small. Ayman's parents left. He came to live with us. Then my mother left.'

'Your mother left you and your father?'

'She just left.' In the gloom, Makana could make out the girl crouched against the wall. She was fiddling with her fingers.

'When was this exactly?'

'Like I said, I was very small. I barely remember her.'

'Why did she leave?'

'I don't know, but I think something bad happened.'

'What exactly happened?'

'I don't know. Nobody ever talks about it.'

'You mean everybody knows?'

'Sure, people who were around at the time.'

'And this had something to do with Ayman?'

'That's the feeling I have.' Rashida hesitated. Makana produced the piece of blue ribbon from his pocket.

'I found this in Ayman's room.'

Rashida turned it over in her hands. 'It's a school ribbon. All the girls used to wear them.'

'Ayman used to like watching the girls, didn't he?'

'He didn't mean anything by it. He was just simple that way. I don't think he would ever do anyone any harm. He never hurt me.' She handed back the ribbon.

'Is that why your father took him in?'

'His family left. They didn't want him with them. Isn't that terrible?' Rashida said. 'My father's not a bad man. I believe that, really. I think he did something once and it was wrong and since then he has never . . . well, you've seen him.'

'You mean he's never forgiven himself.'

'Yes, yes, that's it.' She gave a long drawn-out sigh of frustration. 'I've had enough of this place. Kamal thinks we should run away together and get married.'

'Kamal from the bicycle shop?'

'That's the one,' Rashida nodded in the gloom. 'He really wants to go, and I really love him. But this is all I know. All I've ever known. What could there be out there that is so interesting?'

Makana, suddenly tired, stretched out on the bed and leaned against the wall. The weariness of a man caught up in a web of his own making.

'It's true that it's not all good out there. Things are not so bad here, are they?'

'A little quiet perhaps, but I like that.'

It sounded like she wanted him to talk her out of it. If somebody didn't then it was likely she would do it anyway. What was there to keep her here? Rashida fell silent. Someone was coming up the stairs. It had to be her father. If Nagy found him in his room in the dark with his daughter they would be in a difficult situation and he had no doubt that the girl's fears were well founded. The footsteps approached until a shadow crossed the narrow slit of light under the door. The shadow stopped moving. Nagy was listening at the door. All three of them, it seemed to Makana, were holding their breath. Then the moment passed and the footsteps resumed their way down the hall.

'Do you have children?' Rashida whispered.

'A daughter,' Makana heard himself say. 'She must be about your age.'

'And where is she?'

'I don't know. I'm not even sure she's still alive to tell the truth.'

Speaking these words aloud, in the dark, seemed to bring their own comfort.

'Before he died, Ayman told me he had seen a ghost.'

'A ghost?'

Rashida fiddled with the sleeve of her dress. 'A ghost that had been haunting him for years.'

'Ayman was a big boy. Why would he have been scared of a ghost?'

'I don't know. I think because of something he did a long time ago.'

262

Makana was having trouble trying to work out if she was being serious or just spinning out a yarn to pass the time.

'You think this ghost killed Ayman?'

'If you do something bad it will always come back to find you. I think this ghost came back from the grave and did those terrible things to him.'

'And now you're afraid it's going to hurt you?'

'Not me,' said Rashida. 'My father.' Then she stopped talking and got to her feet. He watched as she padded silently across the room to press her ear to the door.

'What is it?'

'I have to go,' she said.

Makana sat up. 'Listen to me, Rashida. There are no ghosts. They don't exist. Whoever killed Ayman is still out there and we need to find them. If you're really worried about your father you must help me.'

'I can't stay,' Rashida hissed. 'If he finds me here he will kill me.'

There was no doubt that she was right. The girl opened the door slightly, allowing a crack of light to enter the room. 'If I go now, perhaps we can meet later.'

'Where?'

'Cleopatra's Eye. At midnight. I'll tell you what you want to know.'

The door opened just wide enough for her to slip out and she was gone. Makana sat there for a long time. He wondered if perhaps he had imagined the whole thing.

He lay back on the bed and closed his eyes, trying to make sense of what she had just told him. The door flew open and Nagy stood there silhouetted against the watery light in the hall.

'What are you doing, hiding in the dark?'

Makana sat up as the light came on.

'You son of a bitch, I know your kind.'

'What are you talking about?'

Nagy made no attempt to approach Makana. He remained in the doorway and pointed an accusatory finger.

'She was in here, wasn't she?' When Makana said nothing, he went on. 'Well, you'll pay for this, just you wait and see.'

'Don't hurt her, Nagy. She hasn't done anything wrong.' Makana called after him, but Nagy was already gone.

After that he must have fallen asleep for a time because it seemed to take an age for him to realise that the telephone was ringing.

'Hello?'

'I'm worried about you,' said Zahra. She was whispering, her voice so low he could almost imagine her in the room with him. He rolled onto his back and watched a spider crawl across the light shade over the bed.

'There's nothing to worry about.'

'I think you might be in danger.'

'Well, my time here seems to be coming to an end. Hamama wants me out of here. He thinks he's solved the case.' He explained about Luqman's arrest.

'If they've got their man there's not much more for you there.'

'True, but unless someone does something he is going to be held responsible for two murders he didn't commit.'

'And that someone has to be you?'

'There doesn't seem to be anyone else around.' Makana got up and walked over to the window. Through the broken slats of the shutters he could see the stubby finger of the minaret across the narrow street.

'These killings seem to be connected to something that happened here a long time ago.'

'What kind of thing?'

'I don't know, but it's as if everyone knows, except me.' Makana leaned against the window. 'Both men were killed in a very public way, almost as if they were intended to be a statement.'

'You're beginning to worry me again. I really think you should leave straight away.'

'I'll be leaving in the next day or so. Like I said, there's not much more for me to do here.'

'And no sign of Musab?'

'None. The family is gone and nobody will talk about him. If he's here, he's lying low.'

The loudspeakers crackled into life and the drone of the recorded azzan started up, adding to the cacophony of the other muezzins all over the town calling people to prayer. It was the only sign of life. Otherwise the mosque appeared to be unused. It would be a good place to hide. Undisturbed by anything but a few pigeons unless something went wrong with the loudspeaker system.

'I look forward to seeing you,' she said.

'Me too.'

Makana heard his own words repeated in his head long after he had hung up the telephone. Me too? What was he thinking? He gazed down at the empty side street and considered his feelings for Zahra. Did this mean he was finally putting the past behind him? Over the years he had grown used to the familiar heartache that had lodged inside him since losing Muna. It was a part of him now. He wasn't quite sure he was prepared to let go just yet. Then what? How long would he carry this weight around with him? A year? Ten years? Already it felt like a betrayal, but how can you betray someone who is dead? Perhaps it was time to let go and trust himself to fate? A brief glint of light drew his attention to the dark shadow of the minaret opposite. Had he imagined it? How many times had he constructed an elaborate alternative to that long-ago night in his mind? He imagined them setting out on a different route, leaving the city in disguise, travelling east or south. So many choices and he had made the wrong one. Or had he? Makana refused to believe it was fate that had decided the outcome. He had made the decision to run, no one else. And here he was, ten years on, still running. Perhaps Zahra offered him the chance to move on. Start afresh. Maybe if he repeated that to himself enough times he might one day start to believe it.

Chapter Twenty-three

The Norton puttered happily along the soft ruts that passed for roads in these parts, rising and sinking, bobbing gently over the bumps as if they were waves on a calm sea. The main bulb of the headlight was playing up and provided only an intermittent beam that danced over the soft sand ahead of him like a wavering finger. Occasionally it vanished without warning, plunging him into soft darkness that closed around him like a fist. Overhead, the moon was a silver scimitar slicing over the crowns of the palm trees. It too provided only fragments of light. He leaned forward to tap the headlight and the beam stretched out and then vanished again. As the Norton rose and fell on the uneven track the light stuttered on and off as if to the beat of a strange drum.

Makana was not entirely convinced this was not a waste of time. Assuming the girl managed to get past her father, what could she tell him? She had seemed genuinely scared and so long as there was a slim chance she might shed some light on what happened here all those years ago then he was obliged to meet her. Still, Makana couldn't help feeling he was losing track, not so much of this as the course of his own life. Riding through the trees in the dead of night to meet an excitable young woman? Maybe it was part of this strange environment in which nothing ever seemed to lead where it was meant to. What connection could there be between the brutal murder of a retarded hotel porter without even a decent set of shoes to his name, and the slaying of a conceited and quite probably corrupt old Qadi? And as for Musab, he might just as well be chasing a phantom.

In the medieval age, Arab geographers had reported that Siwa contained a thousand fresh-water springs. In all likelihood, this was romantic embellishment which helped to conceal a lack of research. Geographers used to work by gathering second- and third-hand reports of places. By the end of it there was no guarantee that the places they described existed anywhere but in their imagination.

During the day, Cleopatra's Eye was a pool of brilliant sapphire-blue, pure and clean. At night it was a dark, gleaming disk from which there emanated a certain mineral glow. It was surrounded by a fence of high canes and papyrus reeds that swayed over his head. It was also deserted. A low brick parapet circled the water. The tall reeds rustled noisily in a brisk night breeze. Trails of air bubbles gently rose through the water.

Makana paced the small clearing. The road into town disappeared into the palm trees, dissolving in the shadows. In contrast the sandy slopes of the hill to the north were silvery and bare in the moonlight. Makana stopped dead in his tracks as the faint sound of someone singing in the distance reached him. Musical instruments. Strings, keyboard and voices. Was his mind playing tricks on him? He smoked another cigarette. It was already past 1 a.m. and something told him that Rashida wasn't going to show.

The sound of the music, he decided, was not in his head, although so soft that it might have been. It rose and fell with the wind as Makana found himself moving towards the source. He slipped through the thin band of reeds that lined the northern side of the road and crossed a ditch to find himself on open ground. He paused for a moment to take his bearings and focus again on the direction the sound was coming from. Above him the flanks of a hill rose gently towards a flat-topped summit. In the dark it resembled a sleeping monster. The music was coming not from the top of the hill but from further over towards the east. Makana moved slowly, his feet slipping in the loose sand. He was curious to know where the noise was coming from.

To the east of the hill was a depression that ran past the old burial chambers that skirted Jebel Mawtah and gave the hill its name, the Mountain of the Dead. At the far end of this elongated gully three vehicles were parked under a grove of trees, all of them identical. Black Cherokee Jeeps. The music filtered out into the night air through the open doors. A group of men wandered about a small camp fire. Tourists, was Makana's first thought. They preferred camping out in the wild rather than trusting the town's hotels. They were dressed in casual outfits, baggy trousers with lots of pockets on them and T-shirts. He spotted a woman among them. Makana was about to turn around and go back to the pool but something kept him hanging on. The woman and one of the men were foreigners. If he had to guess he would have said Americans. Something about their manner. The others were Egyptians, although they dressed in similar fashion. Wealthy locals taking some friends for an excursion into the desert? Guides often dressed more like their clients than like other locals. But that didn't seem right either. Makana moved closer, staying low. The more he looked at them the more they resembled military personnel. The way they stood. Their clothes. These weren't tourists.

As if in answer to the question forming inside Makana's mind a tall, shaven-headed officer appeared, coming back towards the fire while buttoning up his trousers. There was laughter and chatter between the men. Lieutenant Sharqi. Makana rolled onto his back. He lay in the cool sand and stared at the stars high above him. What was Sharqi doing out here, he wondered, hiding in plain sight? He lay there for a while, listening to the music and the idle chatter. Makana had run into Sharqi before and he knew that he commanded a special anti-terrorist unit, part of an elite military intelligence corps somewhere inside the complex workings of State Security. It could be a coincidence, of course. The Americans could have been here on a courtesy visit and they decided to take a bit of a tour, off the beaten track. It could have been a coincidence but something inside him told Makana that it wasn't. They were here for a reason, and the most likely reason was Musab Khayr. He lay there for a while trying to make sense of what he had just seen, and then he crawled back slowly away from the lip of the gully until it was safe enough to stand. He walked quickly down the shallow incline, his feet sinking into the cool sand with every step.

He had almost forgotten about Rashida when he got back. The pool was still deserted. The water gleamed in the moonlight like a solitary eye aimed at the heavens. The reeds sawed back and forth in the cool breeze. Makana crossed the clearing and lifted one foot to rest it on the low wall. He undid the laces and shook out the sand from one shoe. It was as he was replacing it that the shadow rose up through the water towards him. A cold tremor went through him. He could wait until Judgement Day and Rashida would never turn up, because she was already there.

The shadow that floated just below the surface of the water seemed alive. It expanded and contracted like a gigantic black jellyfish. The abaya she was wearing fluttered about her in the water like wings. Was it possible she had been there earlier and he hadn't noticed? After trying in vain to haul her in, Makana took of his shoes and slipped over the side into the water. It was cold enough to make him worry he was having a heart attack. A couple of strokes brought him alongside the body which rolled when he touched it, the long folds of cloth wrapping themselves around his legs. He wrestled to try and get a grip on her. He felt the cloth tearing, stitches ripping. The body turned and he found himself looking into Rashida's face. Her eyes were closed and her face looked so calm she might have been sleeping. The body was slack and clammy to the touch as it nudged up against him, almost as if she was trying to say something, to whisper in his ear. Then it rolled again and the clothing seemed to enshroud him. Fighting panic, Makana kicked with his feet while straining to keep a grip on the body as he dragged it to the edge of the pool. He hauled himself up onto the wall with difficulty, feet scrabbling to find some purchase on the rock. Still holding on to one arm, Makana slumped exhausted. Rashida floated below him. Her face turned towards his. He felt another tremor of emotion go through him. She was so young. She didn't deserve to die, not like this. Eventually he managed to drag her up onto the wall, his muscles aching. He wiped the hair away from her face. Who had she told that she was meeting him tonight?

Makana straightened up and looked around. The wind was picking up. The canes were whipping back and forth, their tips bending until they were almost brushing the ground. The palm trees were rustling wildly overhead. A handful of dust whipped up from the ground and blinded him for an instant. Someone had followed her, or him, to this place. And that someone had killed Rashida. He listened carefully for a time, for the sound of sirens, or engines approaching, but there was nothing. Yet. But something told him they would be coming soon.

Makana slid the body back into the water as gently as he could. It would keep her safe from wild dogs and birds, for a time at least. Then he pushed the Norton towards the trees, turned on the ignition. He felt a surge of gratitude when the engine came to life. Then he was riding back along the road, feeling the soft sand sliding underneath the wheels. Distracted, he realised he was going faster than he should and eased back on the throttle. The headlight was still not working properly. It went dark for long periods. He trusted to his sense of where the road was, without actually seeing it. As he came around a bend the beam flickered on briefly then went out again. Makana was not aware of making a decision. Something inside made a subconscious connection. A faint glint from ahead of him where there should have been darkness. He lifted a hand instinctively to protect himself and ducked in the same instant. Pain sliced into the side of his hand, and his head was thrust backwards. Kicking down on the footbrake Makana felt the rear wheel slide out from under him as the Norton went down, spinning sideways. He skidded off the bike, the soft ground cushioning his fall. The air was knocked from his lungs and he lay there winded. The engine had stalled. There was no sound but the surge of the trees overhead which sounded as regular as a tide rising and falling. His hand hurt and when he touched his fingers to his head he could feel blood. Slowly, he got to his feet and looked back the way he had come. Moonlight broke through a gap in the trees and he saw something. Moving forward slowly, one step at a time, hands out in front of him, he didn't see it until he walked into it. Something so thin and sharp as to remain invisible in the dark. A steel wire. Stretched taut across the road. Fixed between two trees. It would have taken off his head if he had ridden straight into it. A nasty way to die. He dismantled the cable and threw it aside. Then he hobbled over to the Norton and wrestled it upright. His knee and shoulder hurt, aside from the pain in his hand and the blood from his ear. None of that affected him as he bounced on the kick-start. He felt angry. Somebody had used Rashida to get at him. They had set her up and then killed her. The engine burst into life and he climbed back into the seat. High above, the silver moon was trapped in the madly waving fronds.

Chapter Twenty-four

As he turned into the main square and puttered along through the town Makana spotted a light burning out off to his left through the trees. Doctor Medina was working late. He had also, as it turned out, been drinking. He stood swaying in the doorway just long enough for Makana to confirm the fact.

'You've had an accident? How is the Norton? Don't tell me you've damaged her?'

'Don't worry about it. Your precious machine is fine.'

There were candles burning in the window sills and an old jazz record was playing on the ancient gramophone set on a table in the corner. The scratchy record made it sound as though the clarinet was being played in the middle of a rainstorm. Doctor Medina stared bleary-eyed at Makana. He looked haggard and exhausted.

'Don't you ever sleep, Doctor?'

'I should try it some time. I hear it works wonders. What happened to you anyway?' Doctor Medina waved his glass in the general direction of Makana's injuries.

'I must be making progress. Somebody grew tired of my

questions it seems,' said Makana, lifting a hand gingerly to touch his ear. 'Would you mind taking a look?'

'Not at all. Come right in.'

'I need to make a phone call first.' The telephone was on the window sill. Makana walked over and lifted the receiver to dial Sergeant Hamama's number. It took a while for him to answer and when he came on he was clearly half asleep. Makana told him quickly about Rashida. The sergeant said he would get out there straight away. Makana hung up. When he turned around he found Doctor Medina staring at him.

'Sounds like you had a lucky escape,' he said. 'Sure you don't want a drink to steady your nerves?'

'Maybe later.'

'Rashida. I can't believe it. That poor girl! What could she possibly have done to deserve such a fate? Sit down,' he said. Makana reeled from the whiff of alcohol as the doctor leaned over him. Still, it seemed that when called upon to perform a professional service, Doctor Medina was capable of sobering up in an instant. He set his glass down on the table and went to fetch his bag. While he was rummaging around, Makana told him about the trap that had awaited him on the road.

'It's possible that she walked straight into it. They may have promised her something, money, enough for her to leave and go to Cairo with her boyfriend.'

'You mean she set the meeting up with you knowing they were going to kill you?'

Makana was not convinced. Rashida had seemed genuinely upset by Ayman's death.

'She wanted to tell me something. The problem is I don't think she trusted me.'

Doctor Medina nodded. 'That's possible. You're an outsider.

On the one hand you're the only person she can trust, and on the other she doesn't really know you well enough. This is going to hurt.'

Makana winced as the needle of the anaesthetic went into his hand.

'Who do you think did it? Her father?' Doctor Medina asked.

'Nagy? He's the obvious choice, but no, killing his own daughter? I don't think so.'

'Then who?'

'It's too early to say.' Makana didn't want to speculate or encourage the doctor to do so.

'Hold still.' Makana felt the cold sting of the disinfectant against his ear. 'You're going to need a couple of stitches. You're lucky you didn't lose it.'

'One thing is for certain, with Luqman still in prison, he couldn't have been the one who set the trap and killed Nasra.'

'Nasra?' Doctor Medina was looking at him strangely. 'Don't you mean Rashida?'

'Isn't that what I said?' Makana searched the doctor's face.

'No,' said the doctor thoughtfully. 'You said Nasra.'

'I meant Rashida.'

Makana stared at the table. It was made of mahogany, and like the doctor himself, implied a history that was once more promising and respectable than its present state. He couldn't feel his right hand but managed to light a cigarette using only his left.

'Perhaps you are working too hard. I can prescribe a mild sedative, or one of these . . .' Doctor Medina lifted his glass. 'Works miracles for the nervous system.'

'Why do you drink so much, Doctor?'

Doctor Medina looked up from the needle he was trying to thread.

'That's a personal question.'

'I mean, is there a specific reason?'

'We all have our reasons, and usually they are too complex and too petty to make sense to other people. You should take it easy, is what I am trying to say. The body reacts in strange ways when it experiences shock.' The doctor finished threading the needle with a remarkably steady hand. Either his powers of resistance to the effects of alcohol were remarkable, or he was a better actor than most. 'Have you experienced a loss of a personal nature recently?'

'Not recently.'

'Then who, may I ask, is Nasra?'

'My daughter.'

'Ah, and how old is she?'

The needle went into the back of Makana's ear and he managed to suppress a cry. Still, the pain left him gasping for breath.

'She died, or rather, I thought so until a few months ago.'

'Interesting.' Doctor Medina dragged the thread through and stuck the curved needle into Makana's skin again. 'When was this?'

'About ten years ago.'

'Don't talk while I do this.'

'You asked me a question.'

'That was just to keep your mind occupied.'

'My mind is plenty occupied, I don't need distraction.'

'I'm sure.' Doctor Medina carried on, finished sewing, tied off the thread and clipped it with a pair of scissors. After that he turned to the cut on Makana's right hand. The wire had sliced in at an awkward angle between middle and index fingers. It was deeper than he had realised.

'You are a troubled man,' murmured the doctor while he worked. 'Every society is filled with dread or hope when an outsider enters a little community. Dread that he might bring change, and hope that he will do just that. You brought murder. You can't expect people to love you.'

'It's not as if this place was the Garden of Eden before I arrived.'

'What do you think Rashida wanted to tell you?'

'She said Ayman had seen a ghost.'

'A ghost?' The doctor looked amused.

'The ghost of someone he had known a long time ago.'

'I'm going to give you something to prevent infection.' Makana gasped as the syringe was inserted into the raw wound. It felt as though a hot needle were being pushed into his bone. Makana felt his head swim with the pain. 'Sure you don't want that drink now?'

'Perhaps a small one,' confessed Makana.

'Excellent.'

Delighted, the doctor got up and went over to the refrigerator from which he produced a tray of ice from the freezer compartment and a bottle of clear liquid. He poured himself a good three fingers into his glass, dropped some ice and half a lime in and tasted it before preparing a more moderate version of the same which he set in front of Makana. 'Try it. It's very special. Only a special kind of date is used to make it.'

The dates may well have been special, but it was hard to tell why anyone would go to the trouble of turning them into alcohol. People went blind drinking this stuff. They lost the feeling in their limbs. Makana sipped cautiously at the icy spirit. It burned its way down his throat and lit a flame under his heart so that it started beating twice as fast.

'I think the ghost Ayman thought he saw was Musab Khayr,' Makana said, realising that the alcohol had induced a certain recklessness.

'I thought he was abroad.'

Makana bit his lip as the doctor pushed the curved needle into his hand. His skin felt numb but some of the nerve endings must still have been awake. A sense of invincibility had come over him, tempered by a touch of indifference so that it was almost like watching somebody else being stabbed repeatedly with a needle. As he watched the thread being pulled through he felt like a dead man watching his own carcass being sewn up from a great distance. Makana drained his glass.

'You may be right about this stuff, Doctor, it does help.'

'What did I tell you?' Doctor Medina held up his glass to the light in an admiring fashion.

When the doctor went back to work, however, he seemed distracted, operating with more impatience than caution. His hands were trembling. Perhaps there was a limit to the benefits of his potent wonder. When he had finished he tied off the thread and tossed the needle into the metal dish. Makana looked at the jagged line running along the palm of his hand. He managed to get hold of another cigarette and light it one handed. He looked over at the doctor who had moved around the table to the open window where he too was smoking.

'There is something that ties all of these deaths together. Ayman, the Qadi, Captain Mustafa and now Rashida. And it's all connected to what happened around the time Musab left here.'

'That was twenty years ago.' Beyond where Doctor Medina stood, glass in hand, the graceful fronds of the palm trees were visible as dark, slick waves, undulating slowly in the night air. 'What makes you think Musab would come back here?'

'So, tell me. What was he like?'

'He was a nobody, a small-time thug with big ambitions. He left here in disgrace. He couldn't come back even if he wanted to.'

'What happened?' Makana peered into the bloodshot eyes.

'A falling out between thieves. Musab had no choice but to leave.'

'Do you know why exactly, or who he fought with?'

'No, I'm sorry.' Doctor Medina gulped his drink.

'And Nagat, why did she go with him?'

'I suppose there was nothing left for her here.' The doctor shrugged. 'She had nothing to lose, and like so many young girls she dreamed only of the big city lights.'

Makana left the Norton parked in the doctor's driveway and walked back to the main square and the Desert Fox Hotel in about ten minutes. He had taken the key with him when he went out, a precaution that in the first instance had been pointless as someone obviously knew he was not in his room. The front door was locked. Was that the usual procedure, or was Nagy not expecting him back? As he stepped into the silent interior Makana was reminded of Rashida. The vision of her enshrouded body in the dark water floated before him. The lobby was already illuminated by the faint slivers of light that had begun to break open the sky outside. Exhausted, Makana climbed the stairs to his room where he dropped onto the bed fully clothed and fell instantly into a deep sleep which seemed to last all of five minutes.

Chapter Twenty-five

Someone was knocking at the door. Insistently. A pause, followed by another urgent rap.

'Makana, open up! I know you're in there.' Sadig was standing in the hallway. 'Let's go. The sergeant wants to see you.'

Without waiting for an answer he started off towards the staircase. Makana assumed they were going to the police station but when he got downstairs he found Sergeant Hamama outside, leaning against the side of his Chevrolet pickup with his arms folded and a matchstick in the corner of his mouth.

'Did I wake you? I apologise. No, actually, I don't.'

'What is this all about?' Makana asked.

'It's about time for you to be leaving us.'

'I don't understand,' Makana said. 'Did you find the girl?'

'Ah, yes, the girl. The reason you woke me and my wife up in the early hours of the morning and got me to drive out to Cleopatra's Eye?' Sergeant Hamama held Makana's gaze. 'Sadig, tell Mr Makana what we found out there.'

'Nothing,' sneered Sadig. 'There was nothing out there.'

'Nothing,' repeated Sergeant Hamama. 'We looked. We were

very careful about that. I had people inside the water, dragging it with chains.'

'Someone must have moved her,' said Makana.

'Naturally. They left the body there for you to see and then waited until you were gone to move her again.'

'It must be something like that. What does Nagy say?'

'Mr Nagy says his daughter is not missing.'

'Then where is she?'

'According to her father she is staying with her cousin in Mersa Matruh.'

'He's lying,' Makana said, turning to go back inside the hotel. Sadig put a hand out to restrain him. Makana shook him off. 'I haven't finished my work here.'

'Oh, yes. Believe me, your work here is done.' Sergeant Hamama straightened himself up from the side of the car. 'I gave you twenty-four hours and you came up with nothing except a lame story about a missing girl. I have guests coming from Mersa Matruh to see this case closed. I can't afford to have you running about like a mad man screaming about dead girls.' He tilted his head to one side. 'You can see that, can't you?'

'Whoever killed Ayman and the Qadi is still out there. Rashida is proof of that.'

'So you say,' Sergeant Hamama shrugged, reaching for his snuff pouch. 'But according to your own theory, the killer was putting his victims on display. Now, all of a sudden, he is hiding them. Does that make any sense?' He tucked a large pinch of tobacco under his lip. It gave him a dull, bovine look, but Makana was beginning to see that underneath those heavy-lidded eyes Hamama was anything but stupid.

'Fetch his things.'

'Key.' Sadig snapped his fingers in front of Makana's face. He was having a hard time hiding his amusement. Makana ignored him and instead addressed Sergeant Hamama.

'Luqman is innocent. He can't have killed them.'

'And what makes you so sure of that, eh? You see, that's the problem with you, Makana. You build all these little theories up, but you can't accept the truth when the facts refuse to line up.' The sergeant put his hands on his hips and ejected a long stream of tobacco into the dirt at his feet. 'Luqman has made a full confession.'

'I don't believe it.'

'Believe it.' Hamama's face was bloated and crumpled at the same time. As tough and weary as an old waterbag. He nodded over Makana's shoulder. 'See that fancy old house on the corner. Everyone thinks it's haunted, and in a way it is. Haunted by the old ghosts who used to rule this country like it was their own. Well, Gamal Abdel Nasser put an end to that and confiscated most of it. Since then they have been trying to get it back. Luqman is no different from the rest of them. If poverty is all you know you can manage, but if you are used to finery, why that's a different proposition.' The sergeant's mouth twisted. 'And there he is serving beer to tourists when he should be the lord of everything he surveys. A glorified waiter. That must be humiliation enough to kill a man, don't you think? The Qadi turned down his claim for a plot of land and that must have been the last straw.' Hamama took off his hat, examined the inside and then set it back in place, cocked at a jaunty angle on his head. 'Case solved. You can go home now with your conscience clear.'

'It still doesn't explain why he killed Ayman.'

'Once a man has turned that corner and killed, you can't reason why. You ought to know that.' Sergeant Hamama spat again. 'Ayman might have said something, or seen something.

We'll never know. Frankly, it doesn't matter. Now, either you can hand your key over to Sadig here or you can leave without your belongings. It's your choice.'

Makana handed his room key to Sadig and tried to recall if he had left anything of value among his meagre belongings.

'What happened to your hand?'

'I had an accident.'

'Lucky you weren't killed. That's the problem with riding around on a dangerous machine like that.' Sergeant Hamama grunted. 'You might have had a nasty accident.'

'What if I'm not finished here?'

'Take my word for it,' Sergeant Hamama opened the car door, 'you're finished. Sadig will put you on the bus. I have settled your bill. Consider it payment for your efforts in assisting us in our investigation. Have a pleasant journey.' A cloud of dust rose up around him as he sank into the driver's seat, the Chevrolet groaning in protest.

Makana looked back and saw Nagy standing by the window in the hotel lobby, careful to remain just out of sight. Sadig appeared carrying Makana's holdall, which he tossed into the back of his own pickup, parked behind the sergeant's.

'Get in the car, Makana. I'm not going to tell you again. That bus leaves in five minutes and you're going to be on it.'

Makana didn't see that he had much choice at this point. Sadig went round and started the engine. The pickup began moving almost before he had time to close the door. Without exchanging a word they rattled around the square and sped through town to reach the bus station where the driver greeted Sadig warily as he pulled up beside him.

'This is a special case,' Sadig said. 'Orders from the sergeant. You're to get moving right away.'

'But we still have ten minutes to go.' The driver tapped his wristwatch.

'I don't care. I want this man out of town as soon as possible. So unless you want to start causing trouble for yourself you'd better get a move on.'

The driver looked unconvinced. Leaving early would mean losing passengers. Nevertheless, he could see he had no choice. Dawdling as long as he could, he climbed aboard and sounded three long bursts on the horn to hurry people up. Along with his assistant they managed to bundle the last bits of luggage into the bay underneath the bus. Last-minute passengers appeared out of nowhere, hurrying along, weighed down with bags, or trundling up in taxis loaded up with astonishing numbers of suitcases and mountains of sacks trussed and bound to the roof. Makana stood aside to allow them to fuss over their things and get aboard, then he climbed up and sat just behind the driver with his holdall on the seat next to him. Through the front windscreen he saw Sadig leaning against the side of his pickup grinning to himself as the big engine growled and they swept away from the square.

As the old bus groaned and wheezed its way up the incline, Makana wondered just how deeply Sergeant Hamama was involved in everything. With a full confession Luqman would be sentenced to death in no time and the real killer would get away. Hamama would get his promotion and everything would carry on as before.

'Stop the bus.'

The driver, who was busy struggling to coax the old machine to the top of the escarpment, threw a worried glance over his shoulder.

'What's the matter with you?'

'You must stop. I have to get out.'

The driver waved him off. 'Forget it. Orders are orders. They could take my licence away, then where would I be?'

'Sadig told you to drive me out of town, which you have done. He didn't say anything about how far you were to take me.'

'No, no. He was pretty clear about it.'

'If he wants to get off the bus, then let him off,' an elderly couple sitting to Makana's right decided to get involved. The woman more vehement than her husband, who adopted a more statesmanlike demeanour, thumping the floor with the tip of his stick.

'I've never heard anything like it,' added the man for good measure.

'He's a customer like anyone else. He has a right to get on or off where he likes,' went on the woman.

'I don't know,' said the driver hesitantly.

'It's like the government. You put people in office to do a job and they end up thinking they can do what they like.' The husband was getting into his stride now.

'I am paid to drive the bus, nothing more.'

There were murmurs of dissent from further back. The driver studied his passengers in the big mirror over his head and decided he had a mutiny on his hands.

'All right, all right. Look, I'm stopping, *khalas*!'

The bus was already slowing down as the road levelled out. There was no other traffic in sight. The driver shifted down through the gears and hauled on the handbrake.

'Go on then, if that's what you want,' he said, pushing the button to open the door, letting in a gust of warm, dusty air. 'Only get on with it. I can't stay here all day.'

Makana caught a glimpse of curious faces. A row of passengers looking down at him in wonder as the bus started up again, growling away, grating its gears in haste. Then Makana was left alone with the wind and the sand. He breathed in deeply and once again felt that familiar tugging at his insides. Then he gazed down the long incline that led back towards the town and the canopy of palm trees through which a breeze passed like a wave, the fronds bobbed in the dusty air like a soft green ocean. It couldn't be more idyllic, he thought, as he picked up his bag and started walking.

Chapter Twenty-six

Madame Fawzia was not surprised to see him. News of his expulsion could not have reached her yet. She turned around to find him standing there on the school veranda.

'I thought you might be back,' she said, fiddling with her hijab. She cast a nervous glance at his holdall, wondering perhaps if he had come to stay.

'I needed to ask you about a couple of things.'

'Well, you'll have to be quick,' she said, unlocking the door she had just shut and ushering him into her office before closing the door behind him. 'I have a meeting in ten minutes.'

'It won't take long.'

'Very well.' Glancing at her wristwatch to remind him that she was taking note of the time, Madame Fawzia settled herself behind her desk in the same stiff upright position as on their first encounter, hands raised in front of her, fingers interlocked.

Makana produced the folded photograph from his jacket. Madame Fawzia looked dismayed at the tattered state of an object that had once been school property.

'Last time I was here you very kindly provided me with this picture.'

'Yes, I did,' she said, not without some regret. 'I was trying to be helpful.'

'And you were, indeed, most helpful. You remember the girl I was looking for, Nagat?'

'What about her?' Madame Fawzia's eyes darted left and right.

'You said there were three sisters. The eldest Butheyna went abroad early on. The second, Nagat, moved away around the time the third sister, Safira, disappeared.'

'It's all ancient history.'

'That's the problem with history, sometimes it just refuses to go away.'

Madame Fawzia inclined her head. 'So, what do you want from me?'

'Tell me about Safira.' Makana remained standing, close to the wall where the pictures of the schoolchildren were arranged in neat rows.

'What can this possibly achieve?'

'Three people have died so far and I believe their deaths are connected to what happened back then.'

'Three people?' Madame Fawzia looked mystified.

'Nagy's daughter, Rashida.'

'May Allah have mercy on her. Such an unlucky man. His wife left him, you know. He says she died, but I think that was just to hide his shame. I don't think he ever recovered from that.'

Underneath her generally rather taciturn appearance Madame Fawzia hid the avid dedication of an enthusiastic gossip.

'Tell me about Safira.'

'Safira was different. Everybody liked her. She was very pretty, more so than Nagat, and very popular. We were all devastated when she disappeared like that, with no explanation. It left a hole in the world.'

There was a knock at the door and Madame Fawzia jerked as if stung.

'Go away!' she shouted. 'I'm busy.'

There was a pause as the person outside the door considered how to respond to this, then a moment later there was another knock at the door, this time more insistent, and accompanied by a voice enquiring after the headmistress.

'Go away, I said! Leave me alone!' Another pause, then finally there came the sound of footsteps retreating as whoever was outside took themselves away. When Makana looked again, Madame Fawzia had tears streaming down her face.

'Why have you come here? All of this pain and suffering, what good can it bring?'

'It won't end by itself. You have to help. You have to tell me what you know.'

Madame Fawzia pressed her fists to her eyes and spoke between low sobs.

'The girls lived alone with their father. Their mother died while trying to give birth to a fourth child. The rumour was that it was a boy and the father never recovered from the shock. Three daughters, and just when she was about to bear him a son she died along with the baby.' Her voice settled into a low, monotone rhythm. 'He was a horrible man. Everyone was scared of him. Butheyna, the eldest daughter, left when her mother died. She married a man who took her abroad, to the Gulf. She never came back, not even when her father died. Some said . . .' Madame Fawzia broke off, her eyes fixed on her hands.

'What did they say?' Makana pressed gently.

'It was a rumour. Vicious tongues said that Abubakr would not be needing another wife because he already had two of them living under his roof.'

'Meaning what? His daughters, Nagat and Safira?'

Madame Fawzia cleared her throat and carried on. 'Nagat was a couple of years older. She was already friendly with Musab, who made himself out to be a big noise. Nagat told everyone he was going to marry her and take her away. I think she was jealous. Safira was always the pretty one. Nagat began spreading rumours about her.' She gave a loud sniff and blew her nose. 'We had a big argument around this time. I told her that she shouldn't treat her that way, that Safira was her sister. She called her a whore, said that she slept with her father.'

'Do you think it was true?'

'I don't know. Like I said, Safira was very pretty, much more so than Nagat, who was quite plain. And she was popular too. As I said, I think Nagat was jealous. But looking back, I suppose it was also to protect herself. By saying those things about her sister she cleansed her own name of the rumours that were circulating.'

'By sacrificing her sister?'

'Yes, exactly,' nodded Madame Fawzia, 'by sacrificing Safira.'

'What do you think happened to her?' Makana asked softly.

'What do I think?' Madame Fawzia raised her eyes to meet his. 'I think they left her in the desert for the jackals and the vultures. After they had used her.'

'Who had used her?'

'Men. Animals. A group of them. I don't know.' Her voice cracked. 'She was only fifteen.'

Madame Fawzia stared at him, imploring him to understand

what she was convinced he never could. 'We were never the same after that. We lost something.'

'The body was never recovered?'

'A few years later a body was found, or rather a few bones, some clothes. People said that it was her.'

There was another knock on the door. This time it sounded like a group of people were outside.

'Madame Fawzia, are you all right? Do you need help? Should we call for the police?'

'Yes, yes, I'm fine,' she called, 'I still don't see what all of this is to you?'

'I have one more question. Do you know who owns the Abubakr family land?'

'No, and I don't care. I can't bear to go over all of that again.' Madame Fawzia blew her nose and dried her eyes. 'In the days of my grandfather they were one of the leading families. It was all squandered though, over the years.' Getting to her feet, she said, 'I would prefer it if you didn't come back here. I don't want to see you again.'

Makana stood on the veranda and watched her go. The women in black who were waiting outside the door huddled around their headmistress like worried crows, herding her along. They cast anxious glances back at Makana, as if wondering what cruelties he had subjected her to.

Chapter Twenty-seven

The Norton was waiting where he had left it. The harsh white light off the buildings drove people into the shade so that no one saw him as he rumbled along the streets towards the road that led out between the lakes. He opened up the throttle so that the tepid air over the water provided some relief from the intense heat. In the far distance the landscape appeared to dissolve in the haze.

To his surprise he found Luqman's place was not boarded up. Makana surveyed the range of clutter scattered around the little shack, the nautical fragments, lengths of heavy Manila hawser, frayed rope, fishing nets, capstans, life rings, glass spheres that once served as net floats. It all served a purpose, adding to the nonchalant, laid-back mood of the place that Luqman had created. In amongst all of it sat an older man, heavy set and wearing a beard and gellabiya. He was painting the upturned hull of the old wooden rowing boat. Makana watched him dip the brush into the pot and began applying the paint in slow, lateral strokes along the wooden hull. It was a pale-blue colour; like everything here it seemed to be chosen to induce a sense of calm. The man stood up as Makana approached, brush in hand. His jaw was set and he frowned at Makana.

'What do you want?' he snapped.

'Nothing,' said Makana. 'I just thought I'd come out and see the place.'

'There's nothing here. I'm just sorting a few things out.' The man eyed the Norton warily. 'Isn't that the doctor's motorcycle?'

'Yes,' said Makana looking back at the machine. 'You know him?'

'I sold it to him.'

'I see.' Makana held out his hand. 'I'm Makana. Are you related to Luqman?'

'Muhammed. I'm his uncle.' The man nodded at the shack. 'On his mother's side.'

'You're painting the boat.'

'Yes.' The two men stared at the upside-down hull. 'I promised him I would fix it but I never got around to it. You know how it is. And now . . .' The man sniffed loudly. 'Well, the boy needs all the help he can get. I don't believe a word of what they say. He would never do those things.'

'They say they have a confession.'

'It's not worth the paper it's written on. We all know how they get confessions out of people.' The thought put him on his guard. 'Are you the one who's helping the police?'

'I was. They seem to not need my help any more.' Makana paused. 'I don't think your nephew committed those murders.'

'I know he didn't,' said Muhammed angrily. 'They're up to their usual tricks. They treat us like fools, but one day . . . well, anyway. We'll see.'

'He likes this place, doesn't he?' Makana gazed out at the lake.

'He loves it. There used to be a house here, but it fell into disrepair. Khalid was away for a few years. He went to study abroad. When he came back the house had collapsed. But he refused to let go of it. He built that little shack and started his own business. I think he still wants to rebuild the house when he has the time, and the money, of course.'

'Of course.' Makana offered his cigarettes and Muhammed took one. 'But I understood that he wanted to sell the land?'

'Sell?' Muhammed reared back from the lighter flame as if singed. 'He would never sell.'

'I thought that was the conflict he had with the Qadi. He wanted to sell and the Qadi said it wasn't his land to sell?'

'No, no. You've got it all backwards. The land is ours. It was left to him and we have the papers to prove it. The Qadi wanted to buy up the land cheaply. He was buying up everything he could once he heard about the gas reserves.'

'The gas reserves?' The flame from the lighter hovered in the air.

'Sure, this whole area,' Muhammed raised an arm and pointed east. 'Everything you can see along this strip. The surveyors say it's all sitting on one giant gas reservoir.'

Makana looked at the flat sandy landscape. 'So whoever owns this is going to be rich.'

'Sure. Of course, in the old days nobody had any idea about all that. But now . . .' Muhammed gave a philosophical sigh. 'Khalid is against it. Always has been. He knows that if they are allowed to do it they'll destroy this place. There are all kinds of birds that pass through here on their way down to Africa. Did you know that?' Makana shook his head. 'Well they do,' the other man went on. 'Khalid doesn't care about money. He has travelled the world you know, and he always said there was no other place like this anywhere. He's a good man and they should be ashamed, blaming this thing on him.'

'You don't have much faith in the law, then?'

'Which law? The one that keeps us poor, or the one that makes them rich? Khalid's mistake was going to them in the first place.'

'How do you mean?'

'I mean, he went to the captain and complained.'

'Captain Mustafa?'

'That's right. It's all down on paper. Then he went and got himself killed so nothing happened.'

Makana offered his cigarettes again and leaned in to light one for Muhammed. 'On the night the Qadi was killed some tourists said they saw a woman out here alone. Did Luqman ever mention a woman?'

Muhammed's eyes followed a crane winging its way low across the lake. 'There was only one woman he ever really cared for and she died a long time ago.'

'Who was she?'

'A girl when he was growing up. They lived on the farm next door to where Khalid grew up. Over there on the other side of the lake.'

'Is that the piece of land the Qadi wanted him to sell?'

'Yes, exactly. Like I said, nobody had lived there for years. The house had been quite handsome in its day, but the stuff we use for the walls contains too much salt, you know.'

'*Kharshif.* When it rains it washes away,' said Makana.

'You've been paying attention. Well, that's what happens. If you don't take care it falls down.'

'This girl who lived next door.' Makana turned back to the man. 'You don't remember the name of the family?'

'Sure I do, Abubakr, Safira Abubakr. She broke his heart twice, first when she turned down his advances and then later on . . .'

'When she died?'

'Yes, exactly.' Muhammed looked quizzically at him. 'How did you know?'

On the way back to town Makana felt the sting of sand grains against his face. He had to lean into the hard wind that cut across the lake as the Norton bumped its way through the ruts in the unsurfaced road. When the wind dropped, as it did from time to time, or gusted more strongly, it felt as if the ground were sliding away from under him.

The town's narrow streets were thick with traffic. Lorries swayed, donkeys stumbled along and a procession of battered cars struggled through the cloud of dust and heat. People were closing up their shops and offices and heading home. They wouldn't return until the cool of the evening. Reluctantly, Makana pulled up alongside the bicycle repair shop. Kamal was there, standing in the street looking worried.

'The headlight doesn't seem to be working. Do you think you could take a look at it?'

'Looks like you've had a bit of an accident,' said Kamal looking at a bent wing mirror and noticing Makana's wounds.

'It's just a scratch,' said Makana dismissing his bandaged hand with a wave. He followed Kamal inside the workshop.

'Not too bad. These old things can take a bit of battering.' Kamal stooped to try and repair the side mirror. For a time Makana watched him work.

'You're young,' he said finally. 'You still have time to make a life for yourself.'

'What are you talking about?' Kamal was smiling. An odd smile, a little uncertain of himself.

'It's about Rashida.' Makana watched the young man as he set down his tools and straightened up, wiping his hands with an oily rag.

'What about her?'

'She asked me to meet her last night. At Cleopatra's Eye.'

'Last night?' Kamal frowned.

'Yes. That's where I came off the bike.' Makana gestured and both of them looked at the Norton for a moment. 'She wasn't there. Or rather, I didn't see her at first.'

'What are you trying to say?' Kamal had grown very still. Makana took a deep breath. He had never been very good at this.

'She's dead, Kamal. Somebody drowned her.'

'Is this some kind of joke?' Kamal tried to laugh, but faltered. 'Are you trying to be funny?' He started to turn away, shaking his head. 'I saw her only yesterday afternoon.'

'They haven't found the body. Whoever did it must have removed her after I was gone.'

'You're lying.' He shoved Makana hard in the chest, sending him back against the wall.

'Why would I lie, Kamal?'

'Why?' Kamal cast around helplessly, hoping against hope for some reason that would make it not true. He walked away from Makana, to the doorway of the workshop where he stood for a moment, silhouetted against the light.

'I'm sorry. I had to tell you, but I can't prove it. I know you were close.'

'We were going to go away. I begged her to run away with me, but she kept putting it off. She said we needed more money.'

Kamal was talking to the open square, not looking at Makana as he came to stand beside him. 'I said we didn't need money, that we would make enough when we got to Cairo.'

'I know she wanted to leave with you.'

'She told you?' Kamal looked back at Makana. 'I can't believe it. It makes no sense. Who would want to kill her?'

'She wanted to tell me about what happened a long time ago. I think her father was involved.'

Kamal shook his head. 'I don't know anything about that. She never hurt anyone in her life. She was . . .'

'She was a good person, Kamal. She was brave, too. She was trying to help me,' Makana put out a hand to touch the boy's shoulder, but he pulled away.

Turning his back, Kamal bowed his head and a sob escaped him. After a while he said, 'I'll fix the bike for you and leave it round the back. You can pick it up later.'

There didn't seem to be much more to say, so Makana left him there.

If Madame Fawzia had shown no surprise at seeing Makana, the Qadi's assistant, Mutawali, was so taken aback he dropped the telephone he was holding and got to his feet.

'I understood you had been removed from this investigation.'

'There seems to be some disagreement on that issue,' Makana said, taking a seat without being asked. 'There are still a couple of points which need clearing up.'

'But I've told you everything I know,' Mutawali protested.

'And you were a great deal of help,' said Makana solemnly.

The Qadi's deputy sank down into his chair. 'I believe you misled me last time we spoke. I had the impression you were conducting some kind of investigation into the running of this office.'

'And what makes you think that I am not?'

'I . . . I don't know. I just assumed. Look, I told you before, I had nothing to do with the Qadi's private business deals.'

'I spoke to the survey company.'

'And?' Mutawali sat back.

'They tell me that they were ready to begin drilling when there was a problem with their land permits.'

'When was this?'

'A couple of months ago at the most. This office would have been in charge of issuing land permits. Can you think of a reason why there would have been a delay?'

Mutawali hesitated. He sniffed and then said, 'I believe there was an objection to the claims of one of the investment companies involved.'

'How does this relate to the land Luqman was claiming belonged to him?'

'Luqman disputed the ownership of the land. He said it belonged to him.' Mutawali sighed. 'Of course he was wrong. It's all legally documented. Luqman had no claim to that land whatsoever. It was just a pet obsession of his that he wouldn't let go of.'

'But Luqman was against the gas deal.'

'Oh, yes. He wanted to leave it as it was. He had some idea about tourists preferring things to be undeveloped. Like that absurd shack he has out there. Romantic nonsense.'

'Can you show me on a map exactly where this land is?'

Mutawali looked highly irritated. He glanced at his watch. 'I really shouldn't be speaking to you at all, especially after that business with the Qadi's wife. She's thinking of pressing charges, you know.'

'We both know she would never do that. She has too much to lose, as you well know.'

The deputy considered this for a moment and then got up and went over to a cupboard from which he produced a large-scale map that he spread out on the desk.

'Where is Luqman's land, the piece he was contesting?'

'That would be around here.' Mutawali drew an arc with his finger on the south-eastern side of the town.

'And where exactly is it in relation to the old Abubakrs' land?'

'They were adjoining. In fact, they used to be joined together. Luqman and the Abubakr family were related by blood. Look, if you are really looking for someone with a reason to do the Qadi harm why don't you talk to our respectable doctor?'

'Doctor Medina?' The day seemed to be full of surprises.

'The very one.' Mutawali nodded. 'I know for a fact that the Qadi was planning to expose him as a charlatan. It seems our friend has no more right to practise medicine than you or I. He was involved in some sordid business, practising abortions, which is an abomination not only in the eyes of the law but in the eyes of the Almighty.' His eyes seemed to glow with delight. 'Isn't that reason enough to take another man's life?'

'You'd have to take that up with the Almighty. Let's stick to the matter in hand. Now, the Qadi stood to gain a good commission if the deal went through, is that right?'

Mutawali shrugged. 'He was simply the middleman. He would gain a commission, but the main benefactors were a large investment company in Cairo.'

'How do I find them?'

'I'm sure I have it somewhere.' Mutawali rummaged through the heaps of paper. 'The lawyer was . . . ah, here it is.' He held up a business card with a name printed on it. 'Nadir Diyab.'

'May I keep this?'

'If it's of use to you, although I really can't see why.'

Makana pocketed the card. 'If the Qadi had an important meeting out there on the lake with investors, surely he would have driven there in one of his fancy cars?'

Mutawali gave a gesture of exasperation. 'How could I possibly know?'

'Well, let's say the Qadi didn't want to be seen. Those cars of his are pretty distinctive, aren't they?'

'I suppose so,' said Mutawali gloomily.

'So how could he have got out to the lake then, without his car?'

'I don't know. How should I know?'

'Just take a guess.'

'Well, I suppose he could have taken a karetta.'

'Very good, now, one last thing. Luqman went to Captain Mustafa shortly before he was killed and complained about what was going on. He was trying to raise a case against the Qadi, wasn't he?'

Mutawali's eyes roamed around the map as if searching for an object of great significance.

'I'm afraid you would have to ask Luqman about that.'

The sun was a soft, floundering ship, burning up on the distant horizon. At the telephone exchange the dull white strip lighting buzzed angrily, regardless of the hour. Magdy Ragab was surprised Makana was still in Siwa.

'I'm beginning to wonder at the wisdom of your being there. Do you really feel it is necessary? I don't wish to sound unappreciative, but it seems to me that you have played out this particular hand. There is no need to let it drag on if there is no progress to be made.'

It sounded as if he was beginning to get cold feet. His

commitment to the pursuit of justice appeared to be waning. Another reason for Makana to finish this case as soon as possible. Promising to keep him informed Makana hung up and dialled Sami's number but got no reply. He then tried Zahra and got a disconnected tone. All in all not a particularly successful session. He went back to Sami's number again and let it ring. As he waited, Makana lit another cigarette and slipped the photograph Madame Fawzia had given him from his pocket. Used to large classes, Makana had assumed he was looking at a single year of students. Now he realised that in a school that small what he was looking at was probably several forms in one picture. There had to be almost a hundred girls all arranged on the steps in front of the main entrance with the school's name on the sign overhead. They were lined up in rows with the eldest at the top and the youngest at the bottom. On one side of the group stood a tall, grey-haired man wearing tortoiseshell spectacles and a suit that was too big for him. This, Makana assumed, had to be one of Madame Fawzia's predecessors, back in the days when you needed a man as headmaster, even in a girls' school. On the other side were two teachers standing close together. The photograph had not been marked and there was no note or anything on the back or inside the envelope to tell him what to look for. With the receiver clamped between ear and shoulder he studied the faces of the girls one by one. Nagat was in the top right- hand corner of the picture. Her face ringed by a circle in ink. Now he wondered if her sister Safira might also be in the picture. He studied each face carefully, beginning in the lower left-hand side. It wasn't until his third sweep that he saw her.

'Hello?'

'Sami?' Makana set the picture down on the shelf in front of him.

'Ah, is that our emissary to the distant corners of the empire?'

'Have you any news?'

'The country is in a state of turmoil. The anti-Israeli protests are putting the government in an awkward position. They don't want to antagonise the Americans, but they are beginning to realise there is a limit to how much their own people will take. There is a lot of support for the Palestinians and this thing in Jenin is horrific. Whole families are being bulldozed in their homes. How about you, don't you miss Cairo?'

'Don't worry, I have a feeling I shan't be here much longer.' Makana tried to keep his voice down, as he recounted events, not wanting to share everything with the others in the place, but Sami appeared to be in a car and kept asking him to speak up.

'Where are you?'

'We're stuck in a taxi downtown. Rania is with me. She says hello. I'll bet you don't miss the traffic.'

In an odd way he did. The delights of this peaceful idyll were beginning to wear thin.

'Maybe it's time to call it a day. There are other cases, you know?' Sami sounded concerned.

'They've arrested the wrong person and have no intention of admitting it. The killer is still out there and unless I do something it's going to stay that way.'

'Sounds like you've got your work cut out. Was there something specific you wanted?'

'No,' said Makana. 'I just wanted to remind myself that there are people who know me not to be insane.'

'Well, don't count on me as your only witness,' Sami joked.

'There is one thing you could do for me. A lawyer named Nadir Diyab.' Makana read the telephone number off the business card Mutawali had given him.

'What do you want to know?'

'Anything and everything. He's connected to some kind of gas deal that's happening here.'

'I'll do what I can. Listen to me, Makana. You need to finish your business out there and get back to civilisation as soon as possible.'

'I'm not sure how easy that's going to be.'

The receiver dropped from his shoulder into his hand. He hung up and stared at the photograph again for a long time before tucking it away carefully. He paid the bearded man and had just stepped into the street when Bulbul went racing by, standing up in his karetta.

'Luqman's escaped and they've got him cornered. They say they are going to kill him.'

Chapter Twenty-eight

The mob had Luqman trapped inside Hamza's coffee shop. Even as Makana ran up he could see him climbing out onto the wall that ran around the veranda on the first floor. He looked weak and his clothes were dirty and torn. He was trying to edge around a corner pillar, clutching the brickwork with one arm while trying to fend off the hands that were reaching for him with the other. A small audience had gathered below waiting to see the outcome. Bulbul was stirring them up like a seasoned ringmaster.

'Come on! Come and see him jump!' He would have been selling tickets if he could have thought of a way of doing it. He worked the crowd into a frenzy. '*Yallah, yallah*, jump jump jump!' he chanted, hopping from one foot to the other, clapping his hands to a lively beat.

Makana pushed through the crowd until he reached Sergeant Hamama who was looking upwards.

'How could you let this happen?'

The sergeant turned slowly to look at Makana. He said nothing, but spat on the ground.

'You need to listen more carefully when people give you advice.'

'I told you I wasn't ready to leave.'

'It was for your own good. I was trying to help you.'

The barred gate that closed off the staircase leading up to the coffee shop appeared to have been ripped off its hinges. Nearby lay a chain that had been attached to a pickup. Luqman must have managed to lock himself in briefly.

'How did he get out?'

'A momentary lapse of security,' Sergeant Hamama shrugged. 'These things happen. You never know how desperate people can be.'

Upstairs, Luqman was pleading for his life. Makana saw a stick slam viciously into one of his hands. He let out a howl of pain and almost lost his grip.

'They're going to kill him. Aren't you going to intervene?'

Hamama pushed back his hat and scratched the top of his head. 'I can't risk the safety of my officers until I assess the situation. It would be irresponsible.'

Makana pushed past him and headed for the stairs. Nobody tried to stop him. Everyone assumed he just wanted to get in on the action. The staircase was crammed with men and boys who seemed undecided. To go up and join in the kill or to hang back and not get involved. Makana managed to get past them to find himself on the veranda. Two men had climbed up onto the balustrade and were closing in on Luqman from either side. Makana's way was blocked by a lean, bony face.

'You have to stop them.'

'Why?' laughed Wad Nubawi. 'What difference does it make?'

'It's wrong. He hasn't done anything.'

'How do you know that?' Wad Nubawi's smile faded, to be replaced by the blank look Makana had become familiar with.

'Killing him won't solve anything. This is something from a long time ago.' Makana thought he detected a flicker of response. He gestured. 'Luqman has nothing to do with it.'

A high-pitched scream announced that it was too late. There was a dull thud as Luqman hit the road below. There was a moment's silence, then a rush of men trying to get down the stairs and get away. A cheer went up from a couple of the men on the balustrade. An answering chorus rose up from the dusty street. As they pushed by a few glances flickered in Makana's direction. One or two of them stopped, forming a clot in the free flow of men past him. He had seen them before. They were young and hard looking and they clearly knew who he was.

'Why are you here?'

'What do you want with us?'

They pressed him back, clamouring in from all sides. It occurred to Makana that perhaps coming up here wasn't the wisest course of action. Wad Nubawi appeared to have retreated, melting away into the crowd like a bad rumour. The men pushed Makana back, bristling with tension. All talking at once.

'You killed him,' Makana said.

'We didn't touch him.'

'He fell. Just like that, he fell.' The speaker smiled the smile of the innocent.

Another leaned in. 'Just try and prove otherwise.'

'Leave him alone, boys,' called Wad Nubawi reappearing like a magician. They shoved Makana aside as they made their escape. He caught Wad Nubawi's eyes.

'Take yourself away from here while you can still walk.'

Makana remained there with his back to the wall listening as the clamour slowly diminished. He moved over and looked down at Luqman's broken, lifeless body lying in the street. Blood pooled from his head, already turning black in the sun. A donkey was braying hysterically in the distance. The crowd was breaking up as people went on their way. The mob moved away with Wad Nubawi at their centre. There was an air of celebration about them. They had done what they came here to do. Sergeant Hamama ignored them, concentrating instead on directing his men to clear the area and let the ambulance through. The whole town was in the hands of a group of thugs. Men who made a living driving out into the desert and ferrying contraband across the frontier. They had nothing to fear. They had the protection of the law, after all.

The sun was gently losing itself in the crowns of the palm trees on the western edge of the town as Makana turned into the narrow side street behind the hotel and stopped.

Coming towards him was a driverless karetta. Makana recognised the knock-kneed stagger and the flayed haunches. As it drew level he saw Bulbul stretched out in the back, his lumpy feet resting on the raised seat. With a click of his tongue the donkey drew to a halt and stood there twitching.

'Cigarette?'

Makana tossed him the packet. Delighted, the boy sat up and waited for a light.

'You look disappointed.'

Bulbul shrugged. 'I thought he would last longer.' He puffed away meditatively. 'What can you expect from someone like that?' He shrugged.

'I suppose this means you lose some business, if his place is closed.'

The boy's face scrunched up in pain. 'The girls . . . I'm going to miss the girls. They used to smell so nice.' He closed his eyes at the memory.

'Still, I suppose other people like to take trips out into the lake for romantic rides.'

The prospect didn't seem to cheer the boy. He gave another shrug.

'Like the Qadi, for example.'

This produced a sneer. 'You're still asking questions? It's all over. The Qadi and the man who killed him are dead.' He handed back the cigarettes.

'Keep them,' said Makana. 'You once asked me if I wanted to go to Abu Sharaf.'

'I didn't mean the place.' Bulbul rolled his eyes. 'It's a way of referring to certain girls who are willing to sweeten your time for a little money.'

'The Qadi used to know these girls.' Makana saw the frown on Bulbul's face. 'He's dead, remember? You told me yourself, the man who killed him is dead. I'm just curious.'

'I don't know what to make of you.' Bulbul shook his head. 'I'm just a little fish. I get by because of what the big fish leave for me, but that doesn't mean they don't respect me. Ask anyone. They all know Bulbul. Even the Qadi. I used to fix things for him.'

'You drove him when he didn't want to draw attention to himself with his big car.'

'Exactly. Everyone needs Bulbul sometime.'

'So you drove him out to the lake that evening, with a woman.'

'I didn't know the woman. He must have found her himself, don't ask me how.'

'So you drove them out there in the open?'

310

'Sometimes out in the open is safer.' Bulbul shrugged. 'There are quiet places in the dunes beyond the lake.'

'And you came back to fetch him?'

Bulbul nodded. 'One hour, he said. But when I got back and saw what I saw, I didn't hang around.'

'You didn't tell anyone either,' said Makana.

'That's how Bulbul is. He doesn't like to get involved in other people's business.'

As the karetta trotted away, Makana turned and slipped along the street, deep in thought. He climbed the hill into the old city. The fronds toiled like dark waves in motion. Crows, black against the deep red, twisted in the air like tightly knotted thoughts. Looking down over the back of the hill he could see that the Lada he had noticed the other day was gone now. He settled himself in the corner of a ruin that was reasonably comfortable and well concealed. With only half a pack of Cleopatras for company he decided to treat himself to one, which he cupped in his hand to shield the glow, and settled down to wait for dark. The edges of the buildings stretched themselves out as shadows flooded in beneath them, pushing the daylight before them. It was soon dark and Makana decided to give it another hour or so. His hand throbbed with pain. He fumbled for the bottle of painkillers the doctor had given him the night before. It reminded him that he had unfinished business with Doctor Medina.

Luqman's death would mean that officially the case could be sealed up. The question of what had been done with Rashida's body still bothered Makana but he knew that it was bound up with everything else that was happening here. Whoever killed her had set the wire across the road to decapitate him. They wanted him out of the way. And since Rashida's death was quite different in style than the other two, there was a strong possibility that it was done by somebody else.

Shadows rose up about him as he stirred. The walls were dark echoes of the homes they had once been. Down below he could see the back of the hotel and the watery green glow of the light at the end of the street. The entrance to the old abandoned mosque was guarded by two grey cats playing in the shadows. They observed him curiously as he moved past them into the interior. Makana drifted through the rooms with the aid of his flashlight. There was a chamber to one side of the entrance which contained a narrow bathroom. Taps stuck out of the wall. Broken tiles were scattered around the floor in little heaps, like shells on a beach. The main area of the mosque had become a storeroom at some stage. A stack of old chairs that nobody had any use for leaned against one wall. The floor was bare, as were the walls. The mihrab was cracked and chipped. The wooden pulpit or minbar rising from the floor resembled the prow of an abandoned ship. There was no sign of anyone having been in here for months.

Disappointed, Makana followed the corridor round past the bathroom. He was forced to climb over another pile of broken furniture to reach a staircase that wound its way up into the minaret. Pigeons scattered wildly as he stepped into narrow space, barely high enough to stand up in. A tiny window looked down onto the street behind the hotel.

The shadow moving down the street was little more than a line that traced itself along the far wall. With great care not to make any noise, Makana moved closer to the window to get a better look. Light entered the narrow street only through a couple of gaps along its course. At the far end was a street lamp that washed the darkness with a pale-green glow. With some difficulty, Makana followed the progress of this curious shape as it slid along the walls. He could just barely make it out. The long garment swayed, and it was this movement more than anything which allowed him to see her. Luqman and the German girl had spoken of a woman out by the lake that fateful evening. He himself had spied a lone figure from his hotel room window. Could this be the person he was looking for? As the figure passed by beneath him Makana moved, without using the flashlight, feeling his way with his feet until he reached the stairs. He edged his way down, making slow progress. He was just beginning to think he was doing well, congratulating himself on not having broken any bones, when one of his feet caught on the leg of a chair at the bottom of the stairwell. It triggered an avalanche, with chairs tumbling over one another. By the time he reached the entrance to the mosque, whoever had been out there would have fled to the distant hills. He stood for a moment. A minute went by, then another, then a third. Five full minutes by his rough estimation went by before he saw it. A faint change in the nature of the darkness at the far end of the street. He moved out and began to follow, staying close to the wall, keeping one eye on the darkness ahead of him and one eye on the uneven ground. Gradually, his eyes adjusted to the gloom and he could make out a faint darkening against a white wall in the distance. As the figure disappeared around the corner up ahead, he allowed himself to move more quickly, breaking into a jog. When he reached the corner he thought for a minute that he had lost her. Then he spotted her again, as she crossed another street. Light from the main square sketched her outline as clearly as a cut-out against a screen. Makana moved again, keeping close to the wall.

Ahead of him the tall palm trees protruded high over the walls of the old Ottoman house like sentinels. Trees threshed high above. Makana watched the shadow slip into the next street. When he reached the corner she had disappeared. It was also fairly unlikely that she would have been able to cross the street or get away by some other route. He reached the next corner. Nothing. Retracing his steps, Makana examined the rear door of the big house. It was made of sheet metal, wide enough for a single person at a time. It was locked. He pressed it and got nothing in return. He stepped back to look up and down the street. It was impossible. Nobody could disappear into thin air. She had to have gone through this door. There was no other option. Turning back to the metal door he examined it again, this time more carefully. There was an old-fashioned keyhole for which either the woman had a key or some way of making it open. Makana began to probe around the sides of the door until his fingers encountered a loop of wire. It was set on the inside of the door and you needed slim fingers to reach that far. Makana could barely reach it but eventually he managed to hook the tip of his middle finger over it and push outwards until he was rewarded with a click. The door swung open before him.

The garden was extensive, overgrown in places, bare and ragged in others. An old Mercedes resting on its wheel rims added to the sense of abandonment. The whole setting seemed to have been forgotten for decades. Makana approached the house. The veranda steps and the balustrade were made of wood in some kind of elaborate style that he assumed was Turkish.

A short, narrow flight of steps led upwards from the path to a veranda that ran along the back of the house. Beyond this an archway led through to a central courtyard. A gallery ran around the first floor above. He stood for a moment, listening for the sound of anything that moved, but heard nothing save for the hiss of the palm-tree blades sharpening themselves against one another. He moved carefully, going through the house opening doors quietly and closing them again. It was clear from a glance, from the cobwebs and the layer of undisturbed dust on the floor, that nobody had been through them. On the far side of the yard he found a kitchen with a window facing onto the rear garden. It had been stripped of everything including lights and stove. A fireplace in one corner had painted black streaks of soot up the wall. A stone counter ran along under the window. On top of this were signs of more recent habitation. A small primus stove half full of kerosene, ringed by spent matches like a scattering of petals. Also, a tin teapot, some tea, a bunch of withered mint. High up on one of the shelves he found several plastic bags, carefully closed and tied, the cupboard tightly wedged shut to put paid to any inquisitive mice. The bags contained bread, biscuits, a tin of processed cheese from Holland, some soft tomatoes, dates, a couple of gently rotting bananas and a red onion. Makana left the items as he had found them and closed the cupboard quietly. He walked out of the kitchen and along around the ground floor until he came to a bathroom. It must once have been grand. Lined with marble and big enough to park a bus in. A bath was sunk into the floor, deep enough to stand waist deep in and a huge brazier, presumably for creating steam. The walls were decorated with carvings of animals and forests, palm trees and elephants, remainders of a brief flare of decadence that had been quenched by time.

He climbed the stairs, testing each one with his weight as he went, listening for signs of movement but hearing nothing. On the first floor he followed the gallery around trying each door he came to. The rooms were deserted with no sign of anyone having inhabited the place for years. At the rear of the house, however, the dusty, abandoned odour was replaced by a vaguely familiar scent that disturbed him even as it played tricks on his memory. Uneasily, he stepped inside a large room with a high ceiling and big wooden beams overhead. This would once have been the master bedroom. It had a raised dais on one side where presumably the bed would have stood. Now this area was littered with the personal objects of whoever was staying here. There were blankets and a few personal items. A nylon bag half filled with women's clothes. There were candles and matches. Makana went through the bag finding a number of medical items in a side pocket. Disposable syringes. Swabs, bandages, surgical blades still sealed in their wrapping along with a startling array of drugs. Makana left all these things as he had found them.

As he turned, Makana glimpsed a shadow crossing the doorway to the gallery. He ran out and reached the balustrade in time to look down and see the figure disappearing under the staircase below. Moving quickly, Makana took the stairs two at a time. At the back of his mind a warning note told him he was being reckless and in that instant he felt the wood crack beneath him. His foot went through the splintered stair, the sharp edges digging into his ankle painfully and for a moment he was trapped. When he finally tugged his foot free he hobbled down to the bottom. He plunged out onto the veranda and down the steps. The door to the street stood open and when he reached it he looked both ways but there was nobody to be seen.

Makana limped back into the house and sank onto the veranda steps to examine his ankle. He sat there for a time smoking a cigarette while looking at the garden, thinking about the faint scent he had picked up inside the house. He tried to imagine the place in the old days, inhabited by pashas and Ottomans. Luqman's old family. Glorious women and pompous men circulating through garden soirées where sumptuous feasts were served by lamps glowing on the backs of tortoises.

Rubbing his ankle, Makana made to stand up. As he turned to walk down he noticed something. He moved along until he came to a gap in the railing. Using his flashlight he examined the spot where a post appeared to have been broken off roughly and removed. It probably hadn't been too difficult because the wood was fairly old, but that was what made the break interesting. It was recent. He played the light over the wood of the next post in line to see what colour it was. Green. The same colour as the object that had killed Ayman.

Chapter Twenty-nine

Doctor Medina was in his clinic doing tests of some kind. He looked like a mad scientist in his lab coat and protective goggles, bowed over a counter cluttered with all manner of instruments, plastic hoses, old Bunsen burners and test tubes.

'I thought you had been expelled from our fair community?'

'Not quite,' said Makana. The doctor appeared to be sober, which made a change.

'I could have guessed as much. And now you've come to haunt me.'

'I caught a glimpse of our mysterious lady this evening.'

'Oh, yes?' Doctor Medina lifted his goggles and gestured towards the table in the middle of the room. Last time Makana had been down here a dead body had been stretched out on it. Now it was laden with what looked like the remains of a small feast.

'I usually eat down here when I'm working,' explained the doctor. 'Help yourself. I'm glad you came back. I wanted to tell you about my discoveries.'

Makana declined the offer of food but he took a seat while the doctor busied himself with a brass coffee pot.

'What discoveries?'

'About the Qadi. Remember I told you that I thought he had been drugged?'

'Some kind of tranquilliser.'

'That's what we assumed.' The doctor nodded as he lit the gas burner. The brass coffee pot rested on a rusted iron tripod. 'The real question was how it was administered.'

'I get the feeling you know the answer.'

'I'll come to that in a moment.' The doctor couldn't help but grin with delight. It took about ten years off his age. 'Have you ever heard of Ketamine? It is often used for animals, but has the advantage of being odourless. It has no colour and it is tasteless.'

'So it could have been put into a drink?'

'Even more ingenious.' Doctor Medina, still beaming, placed a bowl of what looked like roasted melon seeds on the table. 'It is a national vice. We eat these things all the time. It's the salt.'

'You mean someone coated these seeds in Ketamine?' Makana asked.

'Mixed into the salt. Our killer is smart. He, or she, studies the habits of their victims. I took those seeds from a packet in the Qadi's pockets. Now, when it came to Ayman, the killer chose something different.' The doctor bent to the refrigerator and produced a transparent plastic bag containing a tiny flake of some kind of brown substance, no bigger than a grain of rice. He set it on the table like a conjurer about to produce a flock of doves.

'And this?' Makana asked.

'A piece of caramel. I found it in Ayman's mouth. It was trapped between his upper molars. I analysed it and guess what?'

'Ketamine?'

'Even better.' The doctor was having a field day. 'Ever hear of

Atropine? It's a parasympatholytic. Popularly known as Belladonna. Cleopatra used drops of it to dilate her pupils and make her look more beautiful.'

Makana searched through his pockets and located the wrapper he had found on the hill where Ayman was killed. He placed it on the table next to the scrap of caramel.

'That would have been a small dosage, enough to make him woozy, even knock him out briefly. I found a puncture mark on Ayman's neck. He was a big man, so my guess is that the killer injected him with more, just to make sure.'

'How sure are you that the mutilation took place after death?'

'It's fairly simple.' Doctor Medina looked offended. 'You have lost faith in my skills?'

'I need to know if it's possible they were tortured before death.'

'How would that change things?'

'It might provide us with a motive.'

'I see.' Doctor Medina regarded Makana for a time before shaking his head. 'It's not possible. They were sedated before the mutilation, and in this particular case he was actually dead. Atropine was a popular poison in ancient Rome. The Emperor Augustus was murdered by his wife. She injected it into figs.'

'Does that mean it's easy to come by?'

'It occurs naturally. *Atropa Belladonna* is part of the Deadly Nightshade family. It's related to tomatoes and aubergines.'

'Our killer didn't have to search for it.' Makana described the supply of drugs he had found in the old house.

'So we have our killer?'

'I think we can assume they won't be foolish enough to go back there now.'

Doctor Medina held the coffee pot over the blue finger of the Bunsen burner and waited for it to boil.

'Sergeant Hamama means to close down the case. I've already been told to prepare the bodies for collection. They will be buried tomorrow.'

'No loose ends.'

'Exactly.'

Makana studied the toxic blue colour of the filter on the Cleopatra he was holding and considered the wisdom of lighting it.

'You've done a good job, Doctor, but if there is an investigating committee from Mersa Matruh they are going to ask questions.'

'What do you mean?' Doctor Medina seemed puzzled.

'They might want to check your credentials as a medical practitioner.' Makana nodded at the coffee pot which was bubbling madly. 'Maybe you ought to turn that off?'

The doctor didn't appear to have heard so Makana reached across for the gas valve and switched off the flame under the coffee pot.

Doctor Medina remained staring at the bubbling brown liquid as it settled in the pot.

'I made a mistake, once. A long time ago.'

'Is that why you came here?'

The doctor nodded.

'I was a fairly idealistic young man. Who isn't? When I first graduated I went to Palestine, to Gaza, and later to the camps in Lebanon to serve the refugees there. They had nothing. No medicines, no doctors or nurses. They were desperate and they greeted me as a hero. It was a good time, despite the hardship and the suffering. It felt good.' His voice trailed off. 'I thought I would change the world. Instead it changed me.' His mouth glistened with spit and he wiped it with the back of his hand. 'I need a drink.' He turned to the small refrigerator tucked underneath his workbench. Producing a rounded chemical flask and a dirty glass from the sink he gulped greedily. 'How did that happen? Where did doing good turn into something bad?' He stared through Makana, as if he wasn't sure he was really there, as though he were addressing a ghost. 'I came home. I tried to help young women. Do you know how many illegal terminations there are every year in this country? It's horrible. Most of them are carried out in grubby backstreets by old hags with no formal medical training. The same women who perform the circumcisions. We are hypocrites. We like to pretend we are above all that, that we are good observant Muslims.'

'You tried to change that?'

'Women were dying of septicaemia, bleeding to death on filthy kitchen floors. I helped where I could.' Doctor Medina paused, staring into space. 'Until one day I made a mistake. A simple error that comes from working two jobs, sleeping only when I could no longer keep my eyes open. I was so tired I couldn't see straight. I'm not making excuses for myself, you understand? I'm just telling you how it happened.'

'You lost a patient?'

'A young girl whose family lived in misery. She worked as a maid in the home of a nice, respectable judge who was in the habit of abusing her on a regular basis. She couldn't afford the scandal, nor the child. Her whole family depended on her income. There were complications. By the time they called me I was too tired to go all the way back across town to see her. It was a momentary decision. I had to sleep. I told them to give her some pain killers and if the fever got worse they should call a doctor. But they were afraid of taking her to a doctor, afraid of the consequences, and so they did nothing and the girl died. She was nineteen.'

'But you don't know for certain that you killed her.'

'I should have gone!' Doctor Medina thumped his fist on the table so hard it made his glass jump. 'If I had gone I could have saved her life . . . and mine.'

'Instead you ran away.'

'I had no choice. Shortly after that I was denounced. I wasn't surprised. I half expected it. Luckily someone warned me and I managed to get out. I had to flee overnight. I left my belongings behind. I left everything.' Doctor Medina poured himself another drink. 'I thought if I went far enough I could get away from myself. But there is nowhere that far in the world. You can't do it. I tried, Allah knows I tried. But I didn't make it. I wound up here and for a time everything was good. Nobody asked any questions. I did my work and gradually I built up people's confidence in me. It's not easy. It took time.' The doctor's eyes were haunted. 'Then one day a young girl walked into my clinic.'

'One of the Abubakr sisters?'

'Safira. They both came actually. I mean, Nagat brought her. They were both very nervous. They didn't want their father to find out.' An absent smile played around Doctor Medina's face as he recalled that first encounter. 'I promised them their secret was safe with me. Doctor–patient confidentiality is sacred, I said. They liked that, and then they showed me what he had done.'

'The girls' father was abusing them?'

'He had broken her arm. It wasn't the first time. There was evidence of other breaks which had healed badly. Fingers. Toes.' Doctor Medina paused to take a deep breath. 'And in the process of examination I discovered she was pregnant.'

'He was using them sexually?'

Doctor Medina snorted. 'It's more common than you might think. People live isolated lives. This man's wife had died years

323

ago. I suppose there are a million ways to explain it. Nobody talks about it because of the shame.'

'Was it only the younger daughter who was being abused?'

'There were indications that another daughter had also been abused.'

'Butheyna.'

'She left early on and never came back. Nagat was tougher, in a way. Safira was more vulnerable. Do you think I could have one of those?' The doctor pointed at Makana's Cleopatras. Without waiting for an answer he reached out. Makana lit it for him. 'I could show you a thousand reports on the dangers of tobacco,' Doctor Medina said as he exhaled, 'but none of them address the question of how to substitute the comfort these bring.'

'Go on with your story, Doctor.'

'It's the oldest story in the world. A sad old man falls in love with an innocent young girl. I don't know when or how it happened, all I know is that it did. I did the termination and I set her arm. There was a certain amount of physiotherapy involved to help her recover mobility. In the course of those meetings naturally we talked. We had the most enchanting conversations, right here in this room.' The doctor glanced around them at the lifeless space they sat in as if wondering how such a dismal place could ever be infused with magic. Makana wondered too how much of this was in the doctor's head. 'Such vitality, such imagination. We talked about every-thing. She wanted to know about the world. Circumstances. What opportunities are there for a girl like that in a place like this? People demand that you conform. It's what is expected. As a woman your duty is to obey your father, then your husband and finally your sons.'

'It must have hurt you to know that she was being abused by her father.'

'Naturally, it hurt.' The doctor paused. 'I'm not a brave man, Makana,' he said. 'It pained me to know what that man did to her. I wished there was a way of saving her, of getting her away from that house. But what could I do?' He rubbed his eyes. 'She asked so many questions. About the world in general. About Cairo. What was life like in the big city? Were people really free? Could a woman marry a man out of love rather than out of family obligations?' Doctor Medina raised his eyebrows in wonder at the memory. 'But it was more than that. I marvelled that her mind could be so unsullied by the life she lived. All day working the land, which is hard, back-breaking toil. Even the way her father used her; she seemed to be able to shrug all that off.'

'How do you explain that?'

'I don't. I can't, not really. Looking back now, I suppose it was almost as if she had created a space in her head where she was free. And somehow . . . somehow I was allowed in.' The doctor's courage seemed to falter then. 'It felt like a privilege.'

'Who killed her, Doctor?' Makana asked softly.

Doctor Medina hung his head, suddenly very tired. 'Musab got greedy. He was always hot-headed and arrogant, but at a certain point he became ambitious. Wad Nubawi had treated him like a son. He didn't like being on the road for days at a time, which left Musab to his own devices. The inevitable happened. It occurred to Musab that he didn't need Wad Nubawi, so he plotted a little coup d'état. He managed to rally a few other discontented souls and they dragged Wad Nubawi off to teach him a lesson. They turned up here in the middle of the night. I was asleep. I could barely recognise him, he was so badly beaten. Musab wanted me to amputate the fingers of his left hand.' The doctor splayed out his own hand on the table. 'One by one. He wanted it to be done properly, didn't want him to die, you understand, just to suffer until he surrendered command. That was important to him.'

'And you refused.'

'I couldn't do it.' Doctor Medina held Makana's gaze steadily. 'I know it sounds foolish, but everything had changed for me. She changed me. Before, when I first came here, I was a mess. Musab helped me to set myself up. He brought me patients. I patched up his men when they were hurt, got them drugs, amphetamines to keep them awake when they drove long distances. Small things. In return he would pay me in good Scotch whisky. It was a weakness. But this was different. Removing a man's fingers. I couldn't do that. I wouldn't be able to look her in the eyes after that. I decided I couldn't bear that. I wanted to change for her. I wanted to be a better man.'

Doctor Medina was looking at Makana as if he expected him to somehow express his understanding, or even his tacit approval.

'You turned Musab down. That took courage.'

'Well, it made no difference. Musab did it himself. He took off two fingers with a cleaver. It was lucky Wad Nubawi didn't lose his whole hand.' Makana offered the cigarettes, but they were brushed aside as Doctor Medina reached for the flask again. 'Drink with me. I don't trust a man who won't drink.'

Makana watched him fill another glass and set it before him. The raw spirit burnt a hot trail down through Makana's insides. He put the glass down. The doctor was pouring it down his own throat so fast tears sprang from the corners of his eyes. It looked like a form of punishment.

'I was a fool. I should have known that Musab would never

326

forgive me. I had stood up to him in front of his men. Nobody did that. You did what he asked without question. He had to teach me a lesson. Something I would never forget.'

'What happened next?' Makana asked quietly.

A sob escaped Doctor Medina as he choked back his tears. 'Some men took her out into the desert and did terrible things to her. They raped her and left her out there for the scavengers.' He sighed heavily and pressed his hands to his eyes. 'I don't know how many of them there were. They took everyone along, even poor Ayman. They made him watch.'

'How many people knew about this?'

'It's a small town, nothing stays secret for very long.'

'So Safira's disapearance was simply a convenient story.'

'Musab encouraged his men to behave like animals.'

'And Nagat? Did she know that the man she was to marry had arranged the rape and murder of her sister?'

'I don't know.' A shudder went through the doctor. 'There was a complex relationship between them. Nagat was jealous of Safira. Once the news got round, Nagat was shunned. People avoided her. They would spit on her in the street. She had no choice but to flee. And when Wad Nubawi turned the tables on Musab he had to run as well.'

'This matter never came to the courts?'

'Of course not,' Doctor Medina laughed bitterly. 'People disappear. The Qadi wouldn't order an investigation. The police did nothing. Nobody wanted any trouble.'

'The body was never found.'

'Well, that's not completely true,' sighed Doctor Medina. 'A few years later a herdsman was travelling through the area and he came across some human bones and clothes. When he brought them back to town it woke up the whole business again.

People had looked for Safira when she went missing. A young, innocent girl. There was a lot of concern.'

'But they never found anything?'

'Not until that herdsman appeared with his sack of bones.'

'Did you ever examine them?'

'No.' The doctor shuddered. 'I couldn't. I didn't need to anyway. There were other things. Items of clothing. A ring. They were identified as belonging to Safira.'

Makana watched the doctor pouring himself another drink. The room was silent for a time. In the distance the sound of a motor scooter died into the night.

'The funny thing is I would give anything to go back to those days. Before it happened. I felt alive. Just thinking about her now, remembering her eyes, makes me feel capable of anything.'

Doctor Medina seemed an unlikely advocate for love but then again, why not? He was no different from anyone else in the world. Love was by nature absurd. How could you go from living your life quite happily to being unable to imagine your existence without the presence of one single person? Makana had to concede that he himself was not exactly an expert on the subject. But he did have a better understanding of why people were convinced that Musab would never come back here.

'Where are you staying, by the way?' Doctor Medina asked. Makana shrugged. He hadn't thought that far ahead. 'Well, you can sleep on the sofa upstairs if you want.' He rose slowly to his feet. 'How's the hand by the way?'

'Right now I can hardly feel it.'

'It does the trick every time.' The doctor raised his glass in salute before draining it. With that he staggered off into the darkness, the sound of his steps gently scuffling their way up the stairs, flask still in hand. Makana switched off the lights and made sure that the taps on the gas burners were closed. The door to the storeroom that had once served as a garage stood open. The blue glow emanated from the freezer compartment where the Qadi lay. Not so much a beloved leader lying in state as the dark lord of an underworld into which Makana had unwittingly stumbled. The question was, how was he going to find his way out? Wisps of condensation leaked gently into the air between the sheets of styrofoam.

Chapter Thirty

Makana slept uneasily that night. The struts of Doctor Medina's rather battered sofa dug through the skinny mattreess and into his side like sharpened bones. It was also far too short. His feet hung over the end. The doctor though appeared to have an even worse night. Makana was woken several times by the sound of his shouts. He lay there in the dark wondering at the demons that were plaguing the man. In the morning, however, when Makana woke up, he found him fully restored. Seated at the big dining table, Doctor Medina appeared to have washed and shaved. He wore a clean set of clothes and was tucking into a large breakfast spread before him while reading the newspaper. The window behind him was open to reveal the palm trees in all their splendour. The birds were singing.

'Ah, there you are,' said the doctor as he looked up. 'I'm sure you are hungry. I was famished. Sit down and help yourself.'

A small, familiar figure appeared in the kitchen doorway.

'We have guests, Umm Hamida,' said the doctor.

'He knows my cooking,' said the little woman whom Makana recalled from her restaurant.

'Umm Hamida comes in to cook for me once a week,' said Doctor Medina. 'Without her I would have withered away years ago. She is undoubtedly the best cook in this miserable town.'

She gave a little bow. 'We are honoured by your presence. Will our guest be wanting breakfast?'

'Certainly. Please bring another cup for him.' Doctor Medina was transformed into the perfect host. 'How would you like your eggs? Fried or scrambled? Umm Hamida does them with basturma. You can't resist.'

While Umm Hamida went back to the kitchen to see about eggs Makana marvelled at the change in Medina. It suggested a previous life, affording a glimpse of the doctor as he was perhaps years ago.

'I'd like to thank you,' smiled the doctor. 'I haven't talked so much for years. I feel the better for it. Did you sleep well? That sofa is worse than lying on a dead donkey.' Doctor Medina smiled and tapped his newspaper. 'The Americans have discovered a new life as the policemen of the world. This business in Palestine threatens to tip everything in the region into a crisis.'

'The war on terror,' said Makana, thinking of Musab.

'Exactly. War on terror,' snorted the doctor. 'We've been fighting against terrorists for years. Nobody ever thought of paying attention. What could they possibly learn from a bunch of stupid Arabs, eh? And now look, they all need our help.'

Umm Hamida appeared at Makana's elbow and set a glass of tea in front of him.

'You can stay here as long as you like,' said Doctor Medina, folding the newspaper and putting it aside.

'That's generous of you, but you need to consider your own situation.'

Doctor Medina smiled. 'You don't understand. Last night, I

331

felt I was being honest for the first time in longer than I care to remember. I like this feeling. I want to keep it. I'm not going back to hiding under a stone.'

'I understand,' said Makana.

'Dignity. You gave me back my dignity, or what's left of it. I thank you for that.' Doctor Medina sat back and splayed his hands out. 'Now, what is the plan for today?'

'I'd like to talk to a couple of people, but before that I need to make a few calls.'

The first was to Zahra. He wasn't sure why this was his first priority. It would be the quickest call to make, he decided, since he had no wish to spend too long with the doctor and whoever else might be eavesdropping on the conversation. He was spared in that the call went straight to voicemail. Makana tried to think of something to say and then, at something of a loss, he hung up without uttering a word. He would try again later, he told himself. The next person he called was Sami. The line was bad. Sami might have been on the other side of the moon.

'The lawyer you asked about.'

'Nadir Diyab. What did you find out?'

Sami said something that dissolved into scratching and buzzing.

'Say that again. I didn't hear.'

Again more interference on the line and then, '. . . interesting background. The man is very well connected.' Once more the voice was drowned in static noise.

'What?'

'Arousa Resources is the name of the investment company. I'm trying to find out who is behind it.' Sami's voice rose and fell as if he were bobbing on the waves on a distant ocean. 'There is one connection you might be interested in.' Again he sank from sight, only to rise briefly. Makana caught the word 'Ragab' and then he was gone for good. Makana replaced the telephone on the hook and it buzzed again as though alive. He lifted it and heard a timid male voice.

'Could I speak to Umm Hamida?'

Makana called the tiny woman from the kitchen. She wiped her hands carefully before touching the receiver. She listened for a moment and then hung up before turning to Makana.

'That was my husband. He overheard some of them talking in the restaurant. They are out looking for you and apparently some of them are coming here.'

'When?'

'They're on their way now.'

'There's no time to waste,' said Doctor Medina. 'Leave by the back. There is a path that leads through the trees and brings you out near the main square. Come back later. If I know these people they will take one look and then move on. They don't have the patience to wait here.'

Behind the house Makana found a narrow path leading away from town. In a few metres he was completely hidden from view. It proved to be a pleasant walk. The ground was soft underfoot and there was an idyllic silence broken only by the sound of the birds. Twice he stopped, thinking he heard voices, only to realise it was the sound of men singing as they worked in the trees. It sounded as though they were performing some ancient rite.

The path delivered him to a spot just off the main square. Keeping close to the wall, Makana walked swiftly along and crossed the road without looking left or right. Another corner brought him to the rear entrance of the hotel.

When Nagy looked up to find Makana standing there his first instinct was to reach for the telephone, but Makana beat him to it, lifting the receiver and rapping Nagy sharply over the knuckles with it. With a cry of pain, Nagy pulled his hand back and staggered away from the counter.

'I don't think you should call anyone until we have a little talk.'

'What do you want with me?'

'How could you do that, sacrifice your own daughter?'

'No,' Nagy shook his head. 'You're crazy.'

'Where is she, then? Where is Rashida?'

'What does that have to do with you?'

'How much did they pay you?' Nagy backed away as Makana came round behind the reception desk.

'Who? I don't know what you are talking about.'

'She's dead, Nagy.'

'She's not dead. She's visiting her cousin.'

'She's dead. I saw her in the water.'

'You're wrong.' Nagy was angry. He clearly did believe his daughter was still alive.

'What did they tell you?'

'They didn't tell me anything.' Nagy was wild-eyed and staring, as if afraid that his world was about to cave in.

'Who was it? Was it Sadig? Did he ask Rashida to arrange a meeting with me?'

'What are you talking about?' Nagy scuttled back, further into the shadows, but his eyes gleamed with fear, and finally, doubt. 'Why would she lie to me?'

'Maybe because they promised her enough money to leave, this town, this life, this place, to get away from you.' Makana glanced around the dark and gloomy interior. 'You can't blame her for that, can you?'

'She would never go behind my back,' Nagy faltered, seeing

the flaw in his argument even as he spoke. His face crumpled. 'Why would they kill her?'

'Because she's not afraid to talk. If she and Kamal ran away this story might get out.' Makana stepped back from Nagy, suddenly unable to bear the smell of the man. 'She knows what happened all those years ago. She knows why her mother ran away. She knows what you did.'

'No, she can't.'

'On the other hand, maybe they just hold women in contempt.'

Nagy shook his head from side to side. 'She's staying with her cousin.'

Makana regarded him for a time. When you looked beyond the bad temper there wasn't much more than a small, frightened man.

'You were the one who took Ayman along, weren't you? You thought it would be funny to see his reaction.'

Nagy licked his lips. 'I don't have to talk to you,' he said, making to move, but Makana blocked his way. Nagy reeled back against the counter. 'What is it you want from me?'

'The truth. I want to know what happened.'

'Why? What difference does it make? Why should you care about something that ended so long ago?'

'Because it hasn't ended yet. Ayman thought he saw a ghost. Someone he remembered from a long time ago.'

'Ayman's head was not right.'

'Is that why he came to stay with you, or did his parents disown him?'

'You're making no sense.'

'Whatever happened back then is the reason Ayman was killed, and the Qadi, and now it has cost the life of your daughter.'

'She's not dead!' Nagy wept. He buried his face in his hands, repeating the words, only this time quietly, almost to himself. 'She's not . . . We were supposed to teach the doctor a lesson. He was fond of the girl and he was an arrogant little shit from the city who thought he could come here and tell us what to do, just because he was educated.' Nagy fell silent. Each word seemed to be dragging him down. 'We took her out into the desert.'

'You killed her.'

Nagy nodded his head. 'We got a little carried away. Some of the boys had been drinking. I took Ayman along. He was just a kid. He didn't understand.' He broke off again. 'Give me a cigarette.'

Makana tossed a cigarette over. 'You raped her.'

'It just got out of hand.'

'You raped and murdered her and then left her out in the desert.'

'I swear, not a day has gone by since I haven't thought about it. What we did was wrong.' Nagy rocked from side to side as if trying to get away from himself.

'Is that why your wife left you?'

'She found out. A few years later someone came across some bones out in the desert. Everyone had been looking for the girl. When they found these bones they thought it was her. One of the boys in the group talked and in no time at all everyone knew.' Nagy rubbed a hand across his eyes. 'The whole town could speak of nothing else. Soon the story would be in the papers, on the radio. Can you imagine if the whole country heard about it? People said it would bring shame on us all.'

'That's why there was no trial?'

'The case was brought before the Qadi but he dismissed it, of course.'

'He was paid off?' Nagy gave another nod. 'And your wife?'

'My wife said she could not live with a person who had done something like that. So she left. She went to Port Said to live with her sister.'

'Why didn't she take Rashida with her?'

'She said that every time she looked at the child she saw me.' Nagy coughed and spluttered. He wept into his hands.

'Who arranged it? Who asked Rashida to set up the meeting with me?'

'I don't know. I swear.'

Makana straightened up with a sigh. He wanted to get out of here, away from this pathetic figure of a man.

'What did they do with her, the bones I mean?'

Nagy looked lost. 'They buried her, in the cemetery.'

As he turned to go, Makana said, 'You should bear in mind that whoever killed Ayman and the Qadi will not stop there. If they are looking for revenge then they will be after all of those involved. And that includes you.'

Makana saw the fear in Nagy's face turn to despair.

'What does it matter? What do I have left to live for?'

Makana found the Norton where Kamal had left it. The workshop was closed. The motorcycle started instantly and once more the steady hum of the engine had a reassuring effect on him as he rode through the backstreets. Skirting around the square, Makana picked up the road out of town towards the north-west.

The cemetery wasn't much to look at. In contrast to the ancient world, contemporary graveyards were simple, unadorned. In this case most of the mounds of earth were unmarked. Here and there a simple piece of wood or metal

337

bearing the name of the deceased. Most of the time there was nothing to mark the passing of a life through this world, and perhaps that was the way things ought to be. Makana parked the Norton and wandered along between the rows. He wasn't really sure why he wanted to do this. He didn't expect to find anything, but he felt somehow that he owed it to Safira to at least try. A dog the colour of sand leapt up out of a hollow, startled. It stared mournfully at Makana before turning and loping away through the graves.

'You won't find any answers here.'

Makana turned to see an old, frail figure standing behind him. He recognised him as Amm Ahmed, the living record book that Sergeant Hamama had taken him to visit on his first day here.

'How do you know what I'm looking for?'

'Because everyone wants the same thing.'

'And what might that be?'

'The answers that will explain everything, once and for all.' The old man's lips flapped around toothless gums.

'There was a girl buried here. They found her remains out in the desert.'

'I know the girl you mean. Her spirit hangs heavily over this town.'

'Maybe if someone had tried to bring her killers to justice . . .'

Amm Ahmed smiled. 'You are young. You still think the law can bring justice.'

'Then what?'

'An eye for an eye. That is the law according to Allah.'

Makana turned to survey the cemetery once more. 'I thought I might find her here.'

'You won't find her.'

'Maybe that's just the way of things,' said Makana.

'Is that the reason you came here, because of something that happened long ago?'

Makana thought about the question. 'In a way, yes.'

'You can't find your way back into the past.'

'Because it's gone?'

'Because it's always there with us.' The toothless smile broadened. 'You won't find any answers here. Take the advice of an old man and leave while you can.' With that he turned and began walking away.

'What about Musab Khayr?' Makana called out. 'Is he back?'

The old man turned and smiled again. 'You know the answer to that one too.'

Then a gust of wind swept across the graveyard, enshrouding the figure in dust. The white cotton flapped in the breeze and he was gone.

Chapter Thirty-one

By sunset Makana decided that it was safe enough to return to Doctor Medina's house. He was disappointed to discover Sadig's police Chevrolet parked across the entrance. Killing the engine, Makana pushed the Norton in through the gate and round to the back of the house. Setting the bike on its stand Makana went over to take a look at the pickup. Coiled in the back lay a collection of tools. A shovel, an axe, an old canvas tarpaulin and a length of steel cable.

The lights were already on in the clinic downstairs and the door was open. Makana walked through the waiting area and into the back to find the place crowded with people. Sadig was there, as well as what looked as close to a lynch mob as he would like to get, except that they didn't seem too interested in Makana. In fact, as he pushed his way through the crowd, Makana found himself largely ignored. Doctor Medina was at the centre of the tumult and appeared to be working on a patient. When he saw Makana he threw up his hands in exasperation.

'I need room to work here! Get them out, all of them.'

Sadig hustled the men in the direction of the door. He seized Makana by the arm.

'I'll deal with you later.'

'Leave him alone.' Doctor Medina tugged Makana firmly into the clinc and shut the door behind him, taking care to lock it. 'You shouldn't have come back so soon.'

'I'm not very good at hiding. What happened here?'

At the centre of the room, laid out on the examination table, was Wad Nubawi. He was unconscious and bleeding from an open wound in his neck. His shirt was clotted with blood.

'Half a centimetre to the right and he would have sliced through the carotid artery.'

'How did it happen?' Makana asked.

'Nobody seems to know.' Doctor Medina mumbled as he leaned over to tie off a thread he had just used to sew up Wad Nubawi's chest. Aside from the wound to the neck there were three cuts to his upper body. There were also lacerations on both hands and forearms.

'What does that look like to you?' Doctor Medina asked.

'He was involved in a fight?'

'Exactly.' The doctor lifted one of Wad Nubawi's hands and turned it over. 'He was trying to fend off an attacker armed with a knife. A short blade, very sharp.'

'Like a scalpel?'

'Possibly.'

'Where did this happen?'

'In his supermarket. He's lucky he didn't bleed to death. Apparently they were out looking for you when they found him.'

'I'm honoured.' While the doctor was cleaning up the mess in the clinic, Makana went out to talk to the men who were ranged around the waiting room.

341

'How is he?' one asked.

'It's too early to say,' Makana replied. 'The doctor has finished sewing him up but he's asleep for now. Who found him?'

'Who put you in charge of this?' Sadig asked. He was standing by the entrance, smoking a cigarette which he now dropped to the ground before stepping inside. The screen door slapped closed behind him.

'Where's Sergeant Hamama?'

'He's busy talking to his superiors about his promotion. That's about all he cares about these days.'

There were a few sniggers around the room. Makana wondered if Sadig was making his own bid for promotion.

'Because I don't see anyone else asking questions,' said Makana.

'Let him ask,' said the first one. 'He might help us to find the person who did this.'

Sadig stared sullenly for a moment and then nodded his consent.

'Who found him?' repeated Makana, looking around the group.

'I did,' said a short man with a large mole on his cheek. 'I came to do a delivery. The door was open so I walked in. I saw a trail of blood leading through to the back room. There's another door there that leads into the street behind the supermarket. I followed it out and there he was, lying on the ground.'

'You didn't see anyone? Nobody at all?'

'No.'

'Then you probably saved his life. The killer heard you and ran away.'

Sadig said, 'Is that it? Is that all you can tell us? Maybe I have a question.'

'All right,' said Makana. 'Let's hear it.'

'Where were you when he was attacked?'

'Why would I want to kill Wad Nubawi?' asked Makana.

Sadig began to pace around the room, circling Makana. 'Who knows what sick thoughts go through your head. All I know is that ever since you arrived here people have been dying.'

'People began dying long before I arrived.'

Sadig swivelled to face Makana. 'What is that supposed to mean?'

'I don't know. You're the policeman, you work it out.'

There was some laughter, some shifting of weight around the group.

'Why did you come here?'

'We've been through all that.'

'No, I mean why are you really here? Are you with State Security?'

'Is that what you're worried about?' Makana glanced at the men gathered around them. 'Are you afraid State Security is going to come here and start asking questions?'

'We do things our own way around here. We take care of things our way.'

'Sure, like Rashida and Captain Mustafa.'

'Captain Mustafa had a bad accident. A faulty fuel line. The car just . . . exploded.' Sadig snapped his fingers. 'You see that's the thing about police work, and you ought to know this.' Sadig smiled. 'You need evidence. And what you don't have, my friend, is evidence.' He jabbed Makana in the chest with his forefinger. 'You're a long way from home, and bad things happen to people sometimes when they are far from home. You should be very careful.' Then Sadig turned around and signalled his men.

As they filed out past him behind their leader, Makana had

the sense that he was watching a master perform an act of sleight of hand. He couldn't put his finger on it, but it was happening right in front of him. He watched the men walk out and hop up into the pickup. As it bounced away he recalled the shovels and the rolled-up canvas he had seen in the back. A tarpaulin big enough to hide a girl's body in.

Back inside the clinic, Doctor Medina had finished his work and was sitting on a battered wooden stool smoking. His face was slick with sweat and he was staring vacantly. Wad Nubawi seemed to be sleeping peacefully. The doctor looked up when Makana came in.

'He's a monster,' he murmured quietly. 'They all are. Brutes who use force to take what they want. The world is full of people like him.'

'He'd be dead now if not for you.'

Doctor Medina stirred at that, getting to his feet. 'I've been saving them all for years. Patching them up so they can go out and hurt more people.' Throwing out a hand, the doctor swept the counter clear, sending glasses, flasks, metal trays and bloody dressings, test tubes, vials, all flying. They crashed into splinters and spun around the floor. The doctor bowed over. 'I've never had the courage to stand up to them.'

'They wouldn't hesitate to kill you, then or now. You know that.'

'Well, at least I would have died with some remnant of dignity.'

Doctor Medina peered down at his patient. 'He has a family, you know. A wife who has stood by him for thirty years and about five children. He's a local hero, like the warlords of old. He has his own army of helpers, mostly young men who are tired of tilling fields and harvesting dates. They look at the world out there on their television sets and wonder why they don't have that kind of life instead of this.'

'And he gives them what?'

'He gives them more money than they could dream of, and refrigerators and televisions, and expensive toys for their children. All of it comes out of that great sea of sand out there. He's the grand magician, the sorcerer, the genie in the lamp. He conjures it all up out of nothing.'

'The killer was surprised by the delivery man.' Makana lit a cigarette. 'Did you check his blood for any signs of a sedative?'

'You think that's possible?'

'Supposing he didn't consume enough of whatever it was put in to. Enough to make him a little groggy but not enough to knock him out. He's a tough man.'

Doctor Medina nodded. 'That would explain the cuts. He was still alert enough to try and fight off his attacker, and then the man with the delivery arrived. I'll take a blood sample.' As he drew the blood into a syringe, the doctor stopped.

'What is it?' Makana asked.

'Why am I trying to help him?' Doctor Medina set down the syringe. He gazed down at Wad Nubawi, the gentle rising and falling of his chest. His hand reached out and picked up a pair of sharp scissors lying on the counter. Makana put out a hand to grasp his wrist.

'Maybe it's time for a break, Doctor?'

Doctor Medina stared at him and then, very slowly, he released his grip on the scissors. They clattered to the floor as he stepped back from the examination table. Then he began to laugh. It started out as a kind of cough deep down in his throat, but it went on, gathering intensity. Wiping tears from his eyes, he staggered sideways. Makana watched him lean over and pull open the refrigerator to extract the flask containing the clear spirit set among ampoules and tubes, vaccines and syringes. He located a grimy glass that was still intact, filled it to the rim and drank greedily.

'What would be the point, anyway? I mean, me? When have I not made things worse?'

'Maybe you should take it easy with the drink. Sadig and his men will be back in a while.'

'So what?' Doctor Medina poured another liberal dose into his glass. 'What would be the point of ending his life? Would that bring her back? No, of course not. And as for guilt, well, I might as well take my own life.' He raised his glass in salute before draining it.

'You're not making much sense, Doctor.'

The doctor's eyes were bloodshot and weary. 'I feel so tired. All of this . . .' He swayed for a moment and looked as though he might fall to the ground.

'Maybe you should sit down.'

As Doctor Medina sank down onto the stool he shot Makana a wary look.

'You're a sly one, you know. You don't appear that way at first, but you are. Always there, one step ahead.' He poured himself another drink. 'Do you never give up and go home? Maybe you don't have a home to go to. Is that it? You're like me, lost in this ridiculous mess we try to make sense of. I was a doctor. You understand? I believed in what I did, but look at me now . . .' He rolled his hand at their surroundings. 'I'm an actor in a play who no longer believes his own lines.' He held up his glass to examine the cool, clear liquid in the light. 'I need to keep a clear head,' he said, almost to himself. 'Those animals will be back and they will rip me limb from limb if they think I'm drunk.'

'He's back, isn't he?' Makana said quietly. 'Musab.'

Without looking up, Doctor Medina nodded his head. He was

staring at his glass. 'He came to see me today while you were . . .' He waved a hand absently at the outside world, then he raised his eyes. 'You knew that already.'

'I thought he would be busy running for the border.'

'He doesn't need to.' The spirit vanished down Doctor Medina's throat in one gulp leaving him staring at the empty glass wondering what had happened to it. 'He's made a deal.'

'With State Security?' The image of Sharqi and his men camped out on Jebel Mawtah resurfaced in Makana's mind.

'I suppose so. They agreed to let him have his old life back.'

'In return for what?'

'I don't know.' The doctor shrugged his shoulders and licked his lips. 'He's come back for what belongs to him. He still thinks he should be ruling this part of the country like some emperor of old, like Alexander.'

A tremor went through Wad Nubawi's body, as though he was shuddering at what the doctor had just said. To explain the presence of Sharqi and his men would have to mean that State Security had allowed Musab to escape. But why? What was the purpose of bringing him back here?

'If Musab did this, why the Qadi? Why Ayman?'

The doctor didn't seem to hear. He was busy measuring out another glassful with all the care of a man handling nitroglycerin. 'He knows all about you,' he said, never taking his eyes off his task. 'Everything. Where you come from, what you are doing here. He knows things about your past.'

'How could he know that?' Makana was mystified. It had to be connected to Sharqi.

'He's older, and heavier than he was, but he's just the same as always. People like Musab know that the rest of us are weak because we have a conscience to struggle with. We think we can

347

rise above being mere beasts, but we are wrong and he knows we are wrong. We're all capable of evil,' growled the doctor, spittle hanging from his lower lip. He seemed to be reaching the point of no return. The little round flask was emptied as he drained the last drop into his glass.

'I have more upstairs.' A wave of weariness passed over him and he leaned his head against the high cupboard in front of him. Then he turned and lurched from the room. Makana, with a brief backward glance at the still unconscious Wad Nubawi, followed. When he got up to the apartment the doctor was nowhere to be seen. A sound brought Makana's attention round to the kitchen doorway, where Doctor Medina was leaning. In his left hand he carried an automatic pistol which he levelled at Makana.

'Why did you have to come back?'

'My work here isn't over yet.'

'Your work? You think anyone cares about your work?'

'I care.'

'Of course you do,' nodded the doctor. 'You're the old-fashioned type they talk about in legends. The last noble warrior.'

'A girl was killed, burned alive while she slept. Isn't that supposed to mean something?'

'And then what? You bring the killer to justice?' Doctor Medina laughed. 'You talk as if it's so easy to separate good from evil. Nobody believes in justice and righteousness any more. It's all about you. Giving yourself the best you can because nobody deserves it more than you do.' The doctor had reached the refrigerator and was now hanging onto the handle as if it was a safety bar on a high trapeze. 'So many damn questions. A man could die of thirst from so many questions.'

'Maybe you shouldn't have another drink. The others will be back soon.'

'It's all right for you. People like you always find a way. You move on, you settle somewhere new. Well, I don't have that option.' The doctor poured himself another drink, reached for half a lime that lay on the table, tried squeezing it and then tossed it aside. 'This is all I have. I'm too old to start again. Too old, and too tired.' He emptied the glass and seemed to be about to say something else, but instead he lurched towards the kitchen, dropping his glass in his haste. It shattered on the tiled floor. He almost made it. Instead he threw up mostly over his shoes and the floor. He hung there in the doorway, heaving, his back to Makana. A sour smell filling the air. The automatic pistol still dangled in his hand. After a time he straightened up and wiped a hand across his mouth. The gun lifted to point at Makana once more.

'I don't have to kill you. All I have to do is hold you until they get here.'

'Why do they want me?'

'Who knows? You're the bonus. They weren't expecting to find you here, but you seem to have some value to them. I don't have to kill you, but if you force me to shoot you, I will.'

Doctor Medina sank down onto the sofa and stared morosely at Makana. The doctor weighed the gun in his hand and then tightened his grip.

'Do you have any experience of using firearms?'

'How difficult can it be? You know how stupid most people in the army are?' The gun came up until it was pointed squarely at Makana's chest. To prove his point the doctor pulled back the slide and slipped off the safety catch. 'Is that better?'

A good lesson in how to keep your mouth shut. You could pick worse opponents than a drunk with little experience of using firearms, but not many that were more unpredictable.

'How did Musab ever learn about me? I've never met him.'

'Not Musab, the people with him. Very important people. The point is they know all about you. About your daughter, for example.'

Makana stiffened. 'What about my daughter?'

'I'm telling you. He knows all about you. It's all part of the deal he's made to save his skin. Don't worry, it'll all be fine.'

The doctor's hand was swaying from the weight of the pistol. The barrel waved up and down like a palm frond in a stiff breeze. If the gun went off now it would fire somewhere in the region of Makana's midriff, which would be as good as a death sentence in this part of the world, with the only available doctor being the inebriated person whose finger was on the trigger.

'You need to think about yourself.'

'What?' Doctor Medina squinted, chest heaving.

'Think about everything you've uncovered these last few days. All that brilliant work.' Makana's efforts were rewarded by a fractional wavering in the gun barrel. 'The killer is motivated by revenge. It's not Musab. We know that. No matter how mad he is. It makes no sense for him to kill the Qadi and Ayman.'

'What are you saying?' slurred the doctor, his eyes batting heavily.

'I'm saying that if there is one man in this town who needs to be very careful at this time, it is you.'

'Me? But I . . . I mean, who? Who would go to such lengths?'

'Somebody from a long time ago. The ghost that Ayman saw.'

'Musab. We agreed that it had to be Musab, and we were right. I saw him.'

'Not Musab.' Makana shook his head. 'Someone else.'

'Who?' Doctor Medina blinked. Already the gun barrel was beginning to sag, as if the weight of conviction were tugging it down. The butt of the gun touched the doctor's thigh gently, as if sinking through water to land on a sandy bottom.

'You said it yourself,' said Makana softly. 'You never verified her remains.'

'Safira? No . . .' Doctor Medina was staring off sightlessly into the distance. Reaching out in a steady, slow movement, Makana clamped his hand gently over the barrel of the gun and pushed his finger through the guard to block the trigger. When he twisted it from the doctor's grip it was like taking a toy from a child who had forgotten it even existed. He was just straightening up when a voice behind him spoke.

'Looks like I came back just in time.'

Chapter Thirty-two

Sadig was standing in the open doorway. He was holding not a pistol but an AK47, and it was aimed in their general direction. In that confined space one squeeze of the trigger would have sprayed the room with bullets, killing both Makana and Doctor Medina, without even troubling to aim. He edged forward carefully, never taking his eyes off Makana. The doctor he seemed less concerned about. When he reached the table he lifted the automatic out of Makana's hand and waved the barrel towards the door.

'Well, the captain is going to be pleased with this.'

'You mean his promotion came through?' asked Makana.

'That's right,' smiled Sadig. 'That means I get to be sergeant, and everyone's happy.'

'*Mabrouk*,' said Makana.

'Thank you,' said Sadig, waving the gun at Doctor Medina. 'Up.'

'He says she might be alive,' the doctor groaned.

'Shut up, you old fool,' muttered Sadig, his eyes on Makana.

'But it is possible. I mean, I never did examine the remains.'

'Think what you are saying. How could she be, after all these years?'

'We buried someone else.'

Sadig stepped forward and slapped Doctor Medina hard across the face. 'Snap out of it. It's just him playing with your head. Can't you see that? Now shut up and let me finish your work for you. I'll have to take him to Musab. Why are you so worried about that woman? She was a slut. Everyone said so.'

'How can you talk like that?' Doctor Medina lurched to his feet. 'You murdered her!'

Sadig had no choice but to bear the brunt of the doctor's considerable weight. As Sadig turned to fend him off, Makana took his chance and threw himself across the room, heading for the open doorway. There was a second's delay, but he heard the rip of the gun and bullets slamming into the wall alongside the door as he went through it. He didn't bother with the steps, hopping instead straight over the railing, counting on the sand below to break his fall. Sadig's pickup blocked the entrance to the road, but Makana's first concern was starting the Norton. He swung his leg over the seat and switched on the ignition before kicking down on the starter. He silently thanked Kamal for taking such good care of the machine as he tipped the lever down into first gear. By then he could hear Sadig shouting from the top of the stairs. Without turning around to look, Makana aimed the Norton for the narrow gap between the pick-up and the gatepost, hoping that Sadig would think twice about shooting his own car up. He heard the rattle of shots and felt the sand kicking up to his right. The shots stopped then. Makana's knee scraped against the gatepost and then he was through.

There wasn't much choice about which way to go, right would

take him back to town where he knew he would be trapped like a rat in a maze. Left led out into the open desert. He had no idea where exactly, but it seemed like the best option. Perhaps it was some kind of primitive instinct that guided him. In either case, he drove faster than he ever had. The motorcycle was rattling so hard he had to use all his strength just to hold on to the handlebars and not be thrown off.

The road ahead was as dark as pitch. He turned again, onto a narrow track that cut through a grove of palm trees. The fronds overhead blotted out any light that might have filtered down from the heavens. He rode with barely an idea of which way the track led. It wasn't long before flashes of light began to bounce off tree trunks around him and he knew that Sadig wasn't far behind in the pickup. He could hear the grind of the engine punctuated by the occasional thump as the car scraped past tree trunks along the way. Then the trees were gone and Makana was out into the open. With only the stars ahead of him, he screwed the throttle over as far as it would go. The Norton was an old bike and unlike modern machines it weighed a lot. Makana was struggling to keep it upright on the uneven surface. He knew that it was only a matter of time before he either fell off or Sadig caught up with him. The high-pitched whine of the strained engine told him the lightweight pickup was drawing closer. The headlights were on full beam and seemed to light up the world. Makana saw his shadow stretching ahead of him in the hot blaze. Beyond that he could see nothing but the long straight road.

The engine was at full throttle and Makana knew it wouldn't be able to maintain that pace for much longer. Sadig would catch up and when he did he would not hesitate in running him down. Makana slowed slightly and leaned over to send the Norton rearing out over the low ridge of sand that lined the track and cast himself into the unknown. Luckily it felt firm underneath. He heard the screech of the Chevrolet's brakes and knew that the pickup had in fact been closer than he had realised. There was a grinding of gears and then the big engine was careering after him again. What was the point of trying to run, Makana wondered? If he couldn't outrun the car on the road, what chance did he have out here? At any moment, he knew he might hit a trough of soft ground and be sent flying over the handlebars. He was riding without his headlights on. In other words blind, save for the light from the stars. Was it possible Sadig might grow tired of the chase? It seemed unlikely, but Makana was having trouble imagining safe ways out of his predicament. At the present time anything sounded reasonable so long as it did not involve him being maimed or killed.

From the sound of the engine he knew the pickup was gaining again. The full beams came on and suddenly he was trapped in the funnel of bright light. Makana swung left in a looping arc and then back right again in a tactic he hoped would gain him time. It wasn't helping though. The Norton careered unsteadily left and right, weaving an insane pattern in the sand and Makana could feel that with every sweep Sadig was closing the gap. It was as if Sadig was anticipating his actions before he moved. Despite himself, he began to feel a grudging respect for his pursuer. Perhaps he had misjudged him? Makana had to keep raising the level of risk he was taking with each manoeuvre. He waited until the last second before twisting the handlebars and hearing the rush of the Chevrolet go by so close he could feel the heat of its engine. He varied his turns like a musician learning to improvise, left, left, then right, then left again. Never the same manoeuvre twice in a row, and then three times. He was running out of ideas. It was only a matter of time before he made a mistake and wound up under the pickup's wheels. And then the obvious happened. He hit a rock. The front wheel vibrated out of his hands and then slid from under him. The fall must have saved him because the pickup shot by so close to his face he could have touched it. Makana tumbled over and came to rest on his back. He picked himself up slowly. The Norton was lying on its side. He limped over to it, his ankle in pain. As he leaned his weight down to try and right the motorcycle he felt a searing pain in his left shoulder. In the distance he watched the police pickup skid round as Sadig stepped on the brakes. Through the cracked, grimy windscreen Makana could see his face. The dashboard glow revealed Sadig with the intense stare of a predatory hunter who senses that the kill is close. He paused, as if to savour the moment, and then he put the car in gear and pressed the accelerator to the floor. The engine roared, the rear wheels spun and the pickup fishtailed from side to side. Then something else happened. There was a flash followed by a light popping sound. It didn't even seem that loud. Black smoke and sand erupted in a thick plume as the car lifted off the ground to hover in the air for a second before dropping again into its tracks. Flame billowed out from underneath the chassis, soon enveloping the cab and Sadig. Thick black smoke tried to engulf the flame. Makana could hear Sadig screaming in anguish and pain. He got to his feet and took a step forward. He could feel the heat against his upraised hand even from where he stood. The car was an incandescent beacon against the dark horizon beyond. The screams grew fainter and died away. It didn't take long. Flakes of burning paint lifted off the bodywork and sailed towards the sky like fireflies. After a time a smell like roasting meat reached Makana's nostrils. He recalled Doctor Medina's warning. About not leaving the roads because of the danger from millions of unexploded mines that were still scattered out there. Meticulously buried by the Germans to halt the British advance. A war that people could barely remember and yet it was still capable of killing. Surely there was a message in that?

As he watched the fire burn down, Makana wondered if anyone would bother coming out here to investigate. By now the pickup was blazing out of control. Inside the cab Makana could make out the charred remains of what had been Sadig a few minutes ago. The body garishly still grinning, although twisted now and shrunken through the windscreen that had popped out of place. The fire still raged. The acrid smell of burnt rubber came from the black smoke that still poured from the vehicle.

Makana looked back in the direction of the town. It was impossible that the fire had not been seen. He lifted the Norton to a standing position and checked that it was all right. He thought he might have broken a bone in his foot. He leaned his weight on his leg carefully and it held. He could move, slowly. His shoulder was sore, but apart from scrapes and tears he seemed all right. With some effort he managed to get the bike started. He puttered cautiously forward, headlight angled down-wards, tracing his own tracks back in the direction of the road. It was absorbing work. He found himself so acutely aware of the danger he was in that he had to stop twice to calm his nerves before carrying on again. Most of the old landmines must surely have decayed to the point where they were unlikely to detonate if triggered, but he had just seen the evidence against this argument, so he watched the sand ahead of the front wheel for anything out of the ordinary. A needle sticking up, an odd, unnatural shape protruding. The task was hypnotic, which he found comforting, though he knew he could easily be lulled into missing a vital clue. When he finally eased the bike over the ridge of sand and back onto the road he heaved a sigh of relief.

Chapter Thirty-three

A t the top of the stairs the door to Doctor Medina's apartment stood open. The lights were on. The fan turned
slowly overhead. Papers fluttered gently on the cluttered dining
table. The place was a wreck. Pictures hung shattered and
askew on the wall joined by an uneven ribbon of pockmarks
that traced a line of bullet holes. Glass from broken windowpanes crunched underfoot as Makana moved into the centre of
the room. He crossed the room to shut the refrigerator door
which hung open, the machine whirring madly to fight the
evening heat. The doctor lay slumped on the floor, jammed
between refrigerator and wall. It looked as though he had just
sat down for a rest. His glasses were missing and he was out
cold, the empty flask beside his outstretched hand. Makana
bent down to feel for a pulse and found one. There was no sign
of the gun he had been waving about which suggested that
Sadig must have taken it with him. As he stood up Makana
heard a sound from down below. He descended the stairs as
quietly as he could. The door to the clinic stood open. A low
desk lamp on the front counter was his only guide. He was

almost through the outer waiting room when a shadow crossed his line of sight. Someone was inside the clinic, moving about in the dark. Makana remained motionless, listening to his heartbeat. Whoever was inside was in a hurry, they seemed to be looking for something. The only light within came from the glow coming from the freezer container in the next room. Wad Nubawi lay stretched out on the examination table, still under the influence of the sedatives the doctor had given him earlier. The figure in black had her back to him. She held something up to the faint light and Makana caught the glint of what he took to be liquid in a syringe, before bending to her work.

'Hello Zahra,' said Makana.

The figure started, turning and thumping into the examination table as she did so. The syringe tumbled from her hand to the floor where it winked in the poor light. She backed away towards the wall. A veil covered the lower half of her face. Only her eyes showed, darting left and right in desperation. With a moan of despair she turned away and buried her face in her arm. A shudder seemed to go through her body and she went very still.

'It's okay,' he said. 'I'm not going to hurt you.'

Very slowly, the figure turned to face him. Then she reached up and pulled away the scarf covering her head and removed the black veil. Zahra's face was damp with sweat. Hair was plastered across her forehead. She slumped back against the wall and stared at him for a long time before she spoke.

'How did you know?'

'I didn't, not for certain. But I've had a feeling for some time. It's funny how you can identify someone just by a certain way in which they move.'

'You saw me?'

'A couple of times, in the street behind the hotel.'

Her head bowed. 'You are very attentive to detail.'

'It doesn't work with everybody.' Makana was aware of trying to fight off the weight of sadness that was rolling over him in a wave. The truth was he had not been certain. Right up to that final moment he had clung to the slim hope that he might be wrong. He could always be wrong. He had never wanted more to be wrong.

'You came to finish the job.'

She glanced at Wad Nubawi. 'I messed up the dose. I wanted him to lead me to Musab. I was in too much of a hurry. I knew you would catch on to me if I stayed here too long.'

She made to retrieve the hypodermic from the floor and stopped, wincing with pain and clutched at the side of the table. Makana put out an arm to support her. The side of her garment was slick. When Makana looked at his hand he saw blood.

'You've been hurt.'

'He fought back. I wasn't expecting that. I thought of him as an old man.'

'How did you administer the sedative?'

'It was easy enough. He keeps a bag of dates by the counter, which he eats all day. I poured a liquid solution over them when he wasn't looking.'

'You planned this well.'

'Not well enough,' she replied. With a heavy sigh she lowered herself to sit on the floor by the medicine counter. She loosened the scarf from around her neck and shook her hair free. 'Do you have a cigarette?' Makana held them out and lit one for each of them. Zahra leaned back and blew smoke at the ceiling. 'I thought I was over it. I told myself it was behind me, forgotten. I had to get on with my life and to do that I had to shake off the past once and for all.'

'Something brought it back.'

'Karima,' she said.

Makana stepped closer to Wad Nubawi and pressed his fingers to the man's neck to check he still had a pulse. Zahra looked up at him.

'Why do you care about someone like that?'

'I don't,' said Makana. 'But that doesn't mean I think he should be executed without a trial.'

'The law?' She gave a snort of derision. 'How can you still believe in the law?'

'There's a difference between the law and the people who exercise it, like the Qadi.' He sank down to sit beside her.

'I told you not to come,' she said quietly.

'I should have listened more carefully,' Makana sighed. He watched the smoke curling out between her lips. 'I'm listening now.'

Zahra was quiet for a time, then she said, 'When my mother died, my eldest sister left us. My father found himself alone with two daughters. One was contrary and angry. Nagat and my father fought all the time, but I was younger and more forgiving. I just wanted to make everything right. I hated conflict and dreamed only of the time when I was small, when my mother was still alive. I wanted to make things like they were.' Zahra's voice hardened. 'But I couldn't, no matter how hard I tried.'

'Your father forced you.'

Zahra took a deep breath. 'When you are that young you don't know what is wrong or right. It's confusing. I don't know how it happened. Either way, I couldn't stop it. Then one day the inevitable happened and I became pregnant.'

In the faint light Makana could discern the outline of her face. He was aware of everything in the room having come to a halt.

Even breathing seemed to require great effort. Her hair was damp with perspiration. He wanted to brush the strands away from her forehead.

'It was as if a light went on. I realised that I had known all along what we had done was wrong. I didn't want a baby. I had to get rid of it. I went to Doctor Medina. At first he was so kind and understanding. He didn't want to do it at first. He said that part of his life was over. I told him I would kill myself and I meant it. Finally he agreed to do it. It was to be our secret, and after that we became friends. I didn't realise that it was more than that to him.'

'He was in love with you,' said Makana. 'Is that so strange?'

Zahra shifted her position in the dark and stubbed out her cigarette on the floor. 'Why do men need to have everything they see?'

'Maybe because they are afraid.'

'Afraid of what?'

'I don't know. Perhaps of losing something they have never had?'

'They took me in order to teach him a lesson. I find that tragic. Don't you?' She laughed softly to herself in the gloom.

'What is it?'

'There's something about you. The first time we met I thought you were different. I said to myself, he's like me. He doesn't need anything or anyone. I thought that we . . . well, what does it matter now?'

'It's not too late, Zahra.'

'Aren't you going to arrest me?'

'I don't have the authority to arrest anyone and besides, the next time Hamama sees me he is as likely to lock me up as you.'

'Then let's run away, together. We could go now, tonight.'

For a brief moment they floated on a cloud of her own making. 'Couldn't we do that?'

Why couldn't they? Why not run away and start a new life together? What was to stop them? There was no real evidence against her. On the contrary, Hamama would soon have enough of his own problems, and besides, he had already pinned the murders on Luqman. He wasn't interested in reopening the case.

'Don't you want to know?' she asked as she took another cigarette from him.

'Know what?'

'What they did to me?' The tiny flutter of hope had gone from her voice. Now she sounded flat and lifeless, as if nothing in the world would be able to restore her. There was a hard edge to her voice now, as if the child she had recalled earlier had been erased. Makana was silent. He wished there was something he could say that could make all of this go away, to alleviate her pain, but there was nothing, only darkness.

'They came for me one night,' she began. 'I was alone at home. I heard them talking about teaching the doctor a lesson he would never forget. I had no idea what they were talking about.' She spoke matter of factly, as if describing something that had happened to someone else.

'Did Nagat know about the attack?'

'I don't think so. I think she believed that it was nothing to do with her, or Musab. People turned against her. They had to flee, both of them. Wad Nubawi gathered his men and regained control. Everyone knew Musab had ordered the attack on me.' The sound of a car outside in the street caused her to break off her story. When it had passed by she carried on.

'They left you for dead. How did you manage to survive?'

'When they came for me that evening, I ran. They chased me through the fields. I remember running and running until I was too tired to run any more. They caught me and threw me into the back of the car. Then they drove me out into the desert where no one would see their filthy deeds.'

In the dark Makana could only hear her breath coming in short stabs as she fought to control her emotions. He lit their cigarettes and thought the acrid smoke would make him vomit.

'I thought I would die out there. I wanted to die. I lay there and watched the sun go down and it felt like the last night on earth. Then the stars came out and I was cold, so cold. My whole body was shaking. More than the physical pain I felt dirty, worthless. I felt lower than any other creature in the world. I simply wanted to die. So I lay there and looked at the stars and waited for them to seize me. That's how I felt. If I just closed my eyes for the last time I would float up into the stars and disappear for ever.'

'But you didn't die.' He felt as though she might just melt into the darkness.

'I opened my eyes and found that I was still alive. I must have been in shock. I stripped off what was left of my clothes. Everything, rings and all, and I walked into the desert. I just wanted it to swallow me up for ever. It didn't. A family of Bedouin found me. I don't know what they must have thought. A half-dead girl lying naked in the sand in the middle of nowhere. The man carried me back to the camp and they nursed me back to health. They were the kindest people I have ever met. They never asked me questions. They gave me clothes and food. I was so weak I couldn't stand. I must have lost a lot of blood. They took me across the desert with them. For three months I didn't say a word. I had no will to go on. Gradually, though, I learned how to live like them, to take care of the camels, to help gather firewood, pack and unpack the camp. It was as if I had really died and been born again. That was when I became Zahra. My old self as Safira was left behind. I never wanted to go back there. Never.' Her voice swam towards him like a distant echo. 'I knew I would have to leave them one day and eventually I did. I made it to Cairo. I began studying again. I trained to be a nurse. I wanted to help women. I joined an organisation.'

'And one day you found your sister.'

'It was quite by accident. I didn't know she was in Cairo. By then I was working for an organisation that gave assistance to women who lacked family support. One day there she was. Musab had gone, and she was dying of liver failure. I can't tell you what I felt. On the one hand I wanted to kill her for what she did to me. On the other hand she was the only family I had in the world. She told me that she hadn't known about it, that she didn't realise until years later what he had done and that since then she had refused to have anything to do with him.' Zahra covered her eyes with a hand. 'I had built up so much hate for her over the years, and now it no longer seemed worth it. Karima made all the difference. Nagat had a young daughter. She begged me to take care of her when she was gone.'

Somewhere in the distance an owl gave a long, plaintive cry that sounded almost human. On the examination table above them Wad Nubawi stirred. Zahra waited until all was still and calm again before carrying on.

'I felt as though I was finally reconciled with my life. Finally, I could put it all behind me. I was living in a hostel and Karima was running the shop, but as soon as we found a place we could afford we were going to live together. Then one night Karima called me in a terrible state. She was terrified. Musab had just appeared out of nowhere. When he left she had been a small child, and before that he was in prison. She could barely remember him. Now he was back. He told the craziest story, about being kidnapped in the middle of the night and blindfolded and carried in an aeroplane from Europe to a prison somewhere. He seemed delirious. He wanted money. I went there to try and help Karima. When he saw me he thought he had lost his mind, that he was being persecuted in some strange way. He accused me of being a witch. Karima knew some of the story, but not all of it. Now he started to bring out all the details, insulting me at the same time. He laughed and said we were all whores. Not just me, but Nagat too, that Karima wasn't his daughter and no doubt she would turn out to be a whore too. He had some idea Nagat had betrayed him while he was in prison.'

'With Ragab.'

'Exactly. His lawyer, your client,' Zahra managed a weak smile. 'You remember that afternoon in the market? When we sat and talked? All you wanted to talk about was Karima and who had killed her, and I could hardly speak. I wanted to tell you everything, but I couldn't. Everything was turning around in my head. It was as if the past had leapt out of the ground to swallow me up.'

Zahra paused once again as if she had lost the thread. Her head kept dropping as though she was nodding off.

Makana started to rise. 'Let me see if Doctor Medina is awake. He should take a look at your wound.'

'No.' She reached out and clutched his hand. 'Please, just stay with me.'

Reluctantly, Makana sank back to the floor and she went on with her story.

'Karima was scared. She didn't want to be alone with Musab

and insisted I stay the night with her. I couldn't. I was on night shift at the hospital and they are always looking for an excuse to fire you. And besides, seeing Musab had brought back too many memories. I couldn't deal with it. I needed time myself. I needed to remember who I had become, not the victim I had once been. So I left her there alone with him. The next day when I came back the place had burnt down and Karima was in intensive care.'

'Why didn't you tell anyone all this?'

'The truth? Who would believe me? That a man who has been out of the country for years had appeared out of nowhere to set fire to the place and then vanish? And besides, if the police took an interest and started investigating me they would find I was living under another name. No. There were too many risks. Nobody would ever believe me.'

'And you're sure it was Musab who set fire to the place?'

'Who else? He was terrified out of his mind, completely paranoid. He kept saying he had been tortured. He thought we were witches.' She sighed and her head dropped.

'Let me get the doctor,' Makana urged. 'You can't go on like this.'

'Please, I need you to understand this. All of it. It's important.' She leaned towards him, until her head rested on his shoulder. 'I wish I could take it all back. The poison. The anger. I told myself that it had to be done. I had to rid the world of these monsters and I had to show them why.'

'Which is why you mutilated the bodies?'

'It had to be done.' She pulled away from him, straightening up. 'Don't you see? It's not just about me, it's about Karima, too. It's about all the women whose cases I dealt with over the years.' She broke off and he sensed that she was shaking. 'I wanted people

368

to see, to understand what they had done and why they had to die. It's what has been done to women for years.' She stared into the darkness ahead of her. 'That's why I had to stop. I realised it would never be enough, that there was no end to it. That I would never get back what they had taken from me, and even worse . . . that I was turning into one of them. I was becoming the monster.'

A groan from the examination table made her break off. Wad Nubawi was stirring.

'Revenge is not as simple as you think. I wanted to get all of them, but I picked off the weakest first. A retarded boy and a fat old man. After that I couldn't go on. This was to be the last.'

'Makana, is that you in there?'

'Doctor. Come through.' Makana got to his feet. I was just going to come and find you.'

'I have a terrible headache.' Doctor Medina hung in the doorway like a sorrowful bear. 'What happened to you, anyway? I thought Sadig—'

'Sadig ran into troubles of his own. Can you take a look at someone? She's been stabbed. I don't think it's too bad but there's a lot of blood.'

'Another patient? My, we are busy tonight.' Doctor Medina rubbed his eyes. 'This place looks like a storm hit it. I need to tidy up. Where is this patient of yours?' As he spoke Zahra rose to her feet, leaning on Makana's arm. The doctor stared at her for a long time.

'Hello, Doctor.'

'I . . . Have we met before?' Doctor Medina squinted, then he moved over and switched on the overhead lights. For a long moment his face seemed to register nothing and then shock mixed with disbelief and a dozen other emotions all contorted his expression. 'You're supposed to be dead.'

'She will be if you don't do something about this wound,' said Makana.

'Yes, of course. Right away. I don't understand. How . . . ?' He glanced back and forth between the woman and Makana as he turned to begin scrubbing his hands in the sink.

'There will be time to talk later, Doctor,' said Makana.

'Yes, naturally. I just . . . I'm sorry, I wasn't expecting . . .'

Whatever the doctor had been about to say was cut off as Wad Nubawi came awake with a loud gasp. He groaned and rolled away to begin throwing up over the side of the metal examination table. Makana handed Zahra to Doctor Medina and went over.

'Who's there?' Wad Nubawi fumbled blindly. 'Who is it?'

'It's me, Makana.'

'Where am I? What am I doing here?'

'You're in the doctor's clinic. Do you remember being attacked?'

'Of course I remember,' Wad Nubawi pushed Makana away from him. 'You think I'm a fool or something?' He struggled to his feet. As he rose up he saw Zahra. He squinted at her. Puzzlement turned to anger and he stepped forward and slapped her across the face. 'You're the one? *Sharmuta!*'

'Don't call her that.'

It took a moment for Makana to realise that Doctor Medina had backed away and was holding the same automatic he had had earlier. Sadig must have missed it, or in his haste to chase Makana had dropped it. A smile, more of pity than amusement, spread across Wad Nubawi's face.

'Come on, Doctor. Who are you trying to fool here? It's me, remember? I know what a pathetic little man you are. You hide away in the dark and drown yourself in drink.'

As he spoke he turned towards the doctor, steadily, without hesitation, and when he was within reach he slapped him, hard across the side of his head. Doctor Medina staggered back. A second, backhanded blow followed, sending him reeling against the wall. Somehow he managed to retain his grip on the automatic. He straightened up and fired, without even pausing to aim. Then the two men were struggling for the gun which Doctor Medina refused to relinquish. It didn't take long for Wad Nubawi to subdue the doctor but by then Makana's attention was elsewhere.

Zahra had slumped back against the counter and Makana realised that at least one of the stray shots must have hit her. As she slid to the floor, Makana knelt beside her. He could see the tear in the front of her garment and blood pulsing out.

'I'll get the doctor.'

'No, no.' She clutched his hand tightly to stop him rising. 'Just stay with me a while.' She smiled and then gave a sigh and sank back. Her eyes closed and she was silent for a long time. Then, just when he had given up hope, they opened again.

'Can you forgive me?' Her nails dug into his skin. 'It's important to me. I'd like to know.' Makana tried to speak but found his throat dry. 'There was something, wasn't there?' she whispered. 'It wasn't just me. You felt it too, didn't you?' Her lips were flecked with blood. He saw the beginnings of a smile that went on and on before slowly fading and he knew that she was gone. Getting to his feet unsteadily, Makana slumped against the wall looking down at the slight figure.

'She deserved to die.'

Makana turned and Wad Nubawi raised the pistol. At his feet Doctor Medina lay motionless, his head twisted awkwardly to one side, his eyes staring at the ceiling.

'You'd better run,' said Makana. In the distance he could hear a siren approaching. 'You'd better run long and hard.'

Wad Nubawi sneered. 'Why? You think I have anything to fear from you?'

The sirens had arrived. The flashing blue and white strobes pulsed through the darkness at them.

'Just stay where I can see you,' said Sergeant Hamama, as he came in through the waiting room. He was holding a revolver at arm's length with both hands as if afraid it might bite him. 'Put your hands in the air or I'll shoot.'

Makana raised his hands as two officers ran forward to secure him.

Chapter Thirty-four

Makana was vaguely aware of the commotion around him. His mind was elsewhere. He had the unshakeable feeling that a door had just closed on him. An opportunity he had barely caught a glimpse of had been snatched away along with Zahra's life. Her body, covered by a bloodstained sheet on an ancient stretcher, was being ferried through the crowd of onlookers that had emerged out of the shadows and now thronged the gate to Doctor Medina's house. Wad Nubawi, who was being patched up in the back of the ambulance, was asked to stand up and make way for her. Meanwhile, the police were searching the house under Sergeant Hamama's orders while Makana was made to sit in the back of Hamama's pickup with his hands cuffed.

'You should have stayed on that bus,' the sergeant was saying. 'Though I have to say I really would not have expected this of you. Doctor Medina, I understand. You had some kind of relationship with him.' His face screwed up in distaste at the thought. 'I don't want to speculate on such matters, but the man gave you his motorcycle and his home. In return you killed him. Who can understand the mind of a madman, eh?'

Makana said nothing. None of it seemed to matter any more. Sergeant Hamama, warming to his task, carried on.

'But why the girl? I mean, who was she? How did you know her? Let me tell you what I think.' He rested one dusty and shapeless boot on the rear wheel of the pickup. 'You were in this together. You and her. What was your motive? Maybe it was one of those strange sexual relationships we hear about.' The sergeant shrugged and hitched up his trousers as he stepped back. 'What do I know? I'm just a simple police officer trying to do my job, but that's what I think.'

'Maybe thinking just isn't your strong point.'

'You're not winning yourself any friends, Makana. Maybe that's why people like you end up in places like this, far away from home, far from anything that you know. You're better off that way, always on the move, because that way nothing ever sticks.'

Hamama waved Wad Nubawi over. He looked weak and unhappy, as well as about ten years older, as if age had sneaked up on him unannounced.

'That bitch almost had me. And you were helping her.' He made a clumsy grab for Makana, but Sergeant Hamama intervened, restraining him easily with a hand on his shoulder.

'Easy now, this is almost over,' he said softly, glancing around him to see if anyone was standing within earshot. 'Now we're going to end this.'

'What do you need me for?' demanded Wad Nubawi.

'You know why.' Hamama nodded at Makana. 'He's a slippery one. I don't want to take any risks and besides,' he smiled, 'I thought you might like to take care of this yourself.'

Wad Nubawi looked at Makana and nodded. Sergeant Hamama produced Doctor Medina's pistol out of his waistband and passed it discreetly over to him.

'Go on,' Hamama nodded for Makana to climb onto the back of the pickup. Makana did as he was told and Wad Nubawi followed. He climbed up and sat with his back to the driving cab. The relationship between these two men had been turned completely around. Up until now Makana had assumed it was Wad Nubawi who was running things, but now he saw that perhaps he had underestimated the bumbling, overweight sergeant.

'By the way, you haven't seen Sadig recently, have you?'

'Why, the pressures of your rank getting to you already, Captain?'

'Hah, you heard about that, eh? Well, it's not official yet, so I'm still just a sergeant until confirmation comes through.' Hamama tapped triumphantly on the roof of the cab. 'Keep a close eye on him,' he said to Wad Nubawi. 'If he moves, shoot him.' Raising his voice he yelled a few orders to his men before climbing in behind the wheel. Over the bouncing tailgate and the flurry of dust in their wake Makana watched as the scene behind the doctor's house began to shrink. As the lights dwindled he thought about Zahra and what might have been, and then the darkness closed in until it all seemed as distant and unattainable as a dream.

The back of the pickup was noisy and dusty and sitting on unlined metal was not the most comfortable of rides. In addition, Makana had both Wad Nubawi's sullen stare to contend with and a loaded gun pointed at him.

'Maybe you could aim it away from me. I don't want to be killed by a bump in the road.'

'What difference does it make which way it comes?' smiled Wad Nubawi. There was a bruise on his forehead and blood trickled from the corner of his mouth, so Doctor Medina had managed to get a few blows in. Even in the fraction of light afforded by the backglow from the headlights, it was plain that Wad Nubawi was no longer the strong man he had once been. Musab had challenged his authority years ago and failed, but it looked as though Hamama had been more successful. Or maybe Wad Nubawi had been just that much older and more frail. All he wanted to do was stand in his shop all day. He was a useful front man, but that was about it.

By now the last of the lights had all but faded behind them, the town dissolving into the vast bowl of the heavens like a pearl sinking into a fathomless ocean.

'You're not worried about Musab coming back after all these years?'

'I told you, he'd never come back here.'

'What if I told you he was already here, and that he's working with State Security?'

Wad Nubawi grinned. 'I'd say you tell a good story but you can keep all that for the birds.'

Makana had to assume that Hamama knew about Musab being in the area, which begged the question of why Wad Nubawi didn't. Perhaps Musab planned to surprise them all.

The sky was wide above them now and crammed so full of stars it was impossible to even imagine a number let alone count them.

'Out here,' mused Wad Nubawi almost in wonder, 'you can lose an army.'

'So I am told.'

Through the bars and the windscreen of the cab Makana saw more nothingness rushing up to meet the headlight beams. An army was one thing, but a single man would vanish as easily as a speck of sand. Or maybe not. The pickup was slowing to a halt. Sergeant Hamama leaned out of his window. He was staring off the road at something in the distance.

'Does that look like a fire out there?'

Wad Nubawi squinted out into the darkness. 'I can't see. My eyes are no good any more.'

'It's faint, but it looks like something burning out there,' said Sergeant Hamama slowly. 'A fire burning down. Could be a car.'

'There's nothing out there,' said Wad Nubawi dismissively. 'You'd have to be a fool to drive off in that direction. That area is still mined.'

Sergeant Hamama mused over this for a while and then engaged gear again. Slowly they rolled out into the open land. Wad Nubawi settled down with his head resting against the cab. From time to time his eyes would close and Makana was tempted to try and take the gun from him. As if reading his thoughts, Sergeant Hamama glanced back and thumped his fist against the rear of the cab from his side.

'Don't fall asleep on me, old man. I told you, he's a tricky one. You keep your eye on him.'

'Don't worry,' said Wad Nubawi. 'If he makes a move it'll be the last thing he ever does.'

They drove for over an hour. In that time the threat of being shot retreated, but so too did the idea of escape. Out here in the dark what chance did he have of getting away? Makana had respect for the desert. As he stared at the cloud of dust billowing out behind them and listened to the creak of the pickup he recalled crossing the border when he first came north to Egypt. It seemed all the more ironic that it should all end here, in the same desert from which he had emerged.

Ten years ago he had stumbled off the bridge in Khartoum into the dark, deserted streets. He carried nothing. No baggage, no clothes other than what he wore and no weapon. He also had no real idea of where he was going. All he had was the memory of his daughter Nasra's face as the car holding her and her mother, Muna, went over the edge of the bridge and fell into the river below. Death at this point might even be fitting, considering that a part of him had died with them that night on the bridge.

His journey across the desert had been arranged by one of the few old friends he could still call upon in those days, his old boss, Chief Inspector Haroun, the man who had guided his course ever since he joined the police force twelve years earlier. It was Haroun who had seen the promise in Makana as a young officer and had promoted him, offering him command of complex cases as a kind of test. At the time Makana had not been aware of it, but he later realised that Haroun had been grooming him, preparing him to one day take over his position as head of the CID. Events took their own course, however, and with regime change in Sudan in 1989, Haroun had reluctantly bowed to the new order of the day, taking early retirement and allowing his precious team of criminal investigators to be dismantled. The regular police were set aside, gradually ceding their authority to a series of new militia groups whose purpose was not so much to enforce the law as to introduce terror into the lives of innocent people. Loyalty was what counted and that was where Makana found himself overtaken by his former NCO, Mek Nimr.

That night on the bridge, Makana realised that his life as he knew it was over. His wife and child were gone. His home was gone. If he tried to go back he would almost certainly be killed. The only way forward was ahead, into the unknown. First to

Haroun's house, where the old, white-haired man stared him in the eye as if seeing a long dead friend before him. Then he drew him in from the street and set about making the arrangements for his onward journey. There was no chance of him staying. Mek Nimr would hunt him down, no matter how long it took. As to where he would go, Egypt was the only real option. It was true he could disappear south into central Africa and beyond, losing himself in the interior of the continent just as he had once read the mad Englishman General Gordon had once dreamed of doing. But in Cairo he could join the ranks of the exiled and could keep in touch with news from home. Makana was not in a clear state of mind and Haroun made the decisions for him. A cousin of his had business in Port Sudan and would arrange for him to travel up to the Red Sea coast in one of his lorries. An old Bedford with a metal-sided flatbed loaded with bales of cotton and a driver who was missing an ear. The doors of the driving cab were simple latched squares of beaten iron decorated with painted motifs, the eye of fate and words of faith. The windscreen was cluttered with lucky charms, leather *hijabs* stuffed like pockets with scraps of holy scripture, bird feathers, the toenails of a saintly man and heaven knows what else. The whole cab rattled and shook like an orchestra of tin drums and amber beads, chains, polished bones, along with the obligatory acrylic zebra-skin fur on the dashboard. The lorry was a rolling tableau of inscriptions, a moving graffiti wall pleading for mercy, compassion and speed.

When they reached the Red Sea, the driver turned north and they drove with increasing difficulty towards the Egyptian frontier, along roads that seemed at times more like goat tracks than anything a manufacturer of four-wheeled vehicles might have taken into consideration in their design. Somehow they made it, without major mechanical problems or run-ins with the law, and Makana climbed down from the cab and contemplated the emptiness that would lead him to safety. When he turned around the lorry was already almost out of sight.

Sergeant Hamama's pickup had begun to slow. Wad Nubawi yawned and stretched, careful not to take his eye off Makana. Ahead of them the headlights raked over the striations of a rock formation and beyond that a deep gully appeared to beckon. Makana imagined he saw lights in the distance, the warm flicker of fire against rock. The pickup rolled to a halt and Sergeant Hamama climbed from the cab and stretched. It seemed rehearsed somehow. The nonchalance, the casual, informal nature of the stop being emphasised.

'If you want to stretch your legs, now is the time,' said Sergeant Hamama.

'Are you sure about this?' Wad Nubawi seemed uncertain of his role. Makana needed no prompting. On your feet was better than being trapped in a vehicle. He swung his legs over the side and dropped to the ground.

'Of course I'm sure. Where is he going to go?' Sergeant Hamama gestured at the blackness beyond the furrow made by the vehicle's headlights. Where indeed? Makana contemplated the odds of running straight into the blackness. How far would he get before they shot him?

'I need to take a leak,' said Wad Nubawi. As he walked past, Hamama held out his hand.

'Leave the gun with me,' he said helpfully.

While Wad Nubawi walked back a few paces into the shadows behind the pickup to find a quiet spot, the sergeant gestured for Makana to move further forward until he was in the full glare of the headlights. Makana backed away from him, never taking his eyes off Hamama who in turn watched him closely as they waited in silence. When Wad Nubawi had finished he walked back up along the side of the vehicle until he was standing next to the sergeant.

'Why not let me do it?'

'You think you're up to it?' Sergeant Hamama asked, his gaze still fixed on Makana.

'Sure,' nodded Wad Nubawi. 'I never liked this one since I first set eyes on him.'

'Okay, if you think so.' Without further preamble, Sergeant Hamama turned and lifted the gun. He shot Wad Nubawi through the temple at point-blank range. The shot sounded strangely muted out there in the open. Wad Nubawi dropped without a sound. His head and torso beyond the edge of the road, leaving only his legs and scuffed shoes in the cone of light. They twitched once and then went still.

'Help me roll him off the side,' said Sergeant Hamama, tucking the pistol into his belt. When Makana hesitated the sergeant looked up. 'If I'd have wanted to kill you, you'd be dead by now.'

There was no arguing with that. Makana stepped forward.

'Take the legs,' said Hamama. Together they rolled the body over the side of the road and watched it slide down the gentle incline to come to rest on the sand some three metres away.

'Aren't you going to bury him?'

'It goes faster like this,' said the sergeant. 'In a couple of days there'll be nothing left.'

'Why now? Why here?'

'I don't know. Sometimes things just feel right. Don't you ever get that?' Hamama squinted at Makana. Hands on his hips, Hamama craned his neck back to look at the stars. 'It's not a bad place to die, though, you have to admit.' With that the sergeant walked around and climbed in behind the wheel. He waited a minute, staring ahead through the windscreen, before leaning over. 'Are you coming?'

Makana, still handcuffed, got in on the passenger side as Hamama started up. They rolled along, small stones crunching under the wheels. Ahead of them to the south the desert rose up in two high walls separated by a cleft. As they drew closer the glow of the headlights revealed recesses in the rock, old burial chambers, pockmarking the left-hand wall.

'Where are you taking me?' Makana asked.

'Don't start getting any ideas. If it was up to me you would have stayed behind with our friend back there. It seems that you are of value to somebody. Any idea who that might be?'

'Only one person. Someone who used to work for me, my old NCO, Mek Nimr.' Even as he spoke, Makana was reminded of Zahra and how long she had waited for her revenge. Eleven years didn't seem all that long to end what had begun that night on the bridge.

'Your NCO?' Sergeant Hamama tipped his head. 'How the world turns. Well, I have responsibilities. It's the same every-where. Show me someone who has complete independence and I'll show you a liar, or a fool. Take your pick. Even the president of the most powerful country on earth can't do anything without the support of congress, and that's how it is.'

'That's the deal. You hand me to Musab and Musab hands me to Mek Nimr?'

'Something like that.'

'In return for what?'

'Oh, I don't know, and frankly, I don't care. All of that stuff goes on above my head. All I do is take care of my little plot of land. They ask me a favour and at some stage I get one in return. That's a lesson that might have benefitted you, if I may say so.'

'What lesson is that?'

'Knowing your limitations. Everyone has a station in life. You go beyond that and you are just asking for trouble.'

Up ahead a strange glow appeared to emerge from the desert floor. Makana peered into the darkness, trying to make sense of the way light seemed to be coming up from below the ground.

'What is that?' he asked.

'That is Kalonsha.'

Chapter Thirty-five

Kalonsha emerged from the darkness like a scene from a phantasmagorical dream. A nightmare inhabited by spirits left behind in this desert over the centuries. The men walking could conceivably have been modern-day counterparts to the warriors of the army of Cambyses that was swallowed up by the sand. They wore a mixture of traditional cotton robes and head-dresses, military fatigues, camouflage trousers, army boots, sandals. Some had shaved heads while others sported the woolly afro of Hadendowa tribesmen. There was a range of racial typologies, reflecting the span of countries around the Sahara, north and south, east and west; from the green hills of Rwanda to the arid coastline of Mauritania, from Igbo to Bambara and back again. All of Africa was here and a handful of white faces testified to links further afield. A Toureg in a cowboy hat of fletted nylon strode by, his face masked by huge retro sunglasses with metal rims that looked like something from the 1970s. Other faces looked Cuban, or Latin American perhaps. Most of the men were armed. AK47s of various types were slung from shoulders as casually as waterbags along with other weapons from a range of sources. Around the sheltered bays were arrayed a startling display of vehicles along with military hardware including an old jeep with Wermacht markings on the side. It was being admired by a group of youths chewing qat in a scene that could have taken place in a museum painting. The man who leapt out from underneath was clearly white. A modern-day Robinson Crusoe, his skin so harshly burned by the sun it looked like leather. He mistook the curious onlookers for interested buyers. 'Type 82 Kubelwagen, one of the most reliable cars ever made. I'll take any offers.' Clearly a labour of love, although it would never be of more than passing interest to these kids, for whom the history of cars was as dead as the pharaohs. Further over was a converted Nissan pickup with an anti-aircraft gun mounted in the back. The chassis was probably shot to pieces from the recoil but it drew the kind of admiring looks a decent camel used to get, or a beautiful woman. Even thinking in those terms was redundant.

Everywhere was the smell of food. Kebabs sizzled over hot coals, beans bubbled away in fat cauldrons. A plump man broke off from stirring a mountain of pasta to ladle steaming hot sauce over pots of the stuff. Fires flickered here and there. The moving flame throwing a montage of dark shapes over the sheer cliffs surrounding them. The depression they were in was roughly divided up between the various items on offer. There were large sections for vehicles and arms – stalls selling every make of weapon and ammunition available in the world. Evidence, if it was ever needed, that the one thing man had perfected in thousands of years of evolution was the weapons he used to kill his fellow man with. If that wasn't a sign of progress, thought Makana, what was? Potential customers pored over shiny automatic pistols and high-calibre rifles like connoisseurs. They were in the middle of the African continent. As far from the coast in any direction you cared to choose. Transport and portability were the keys to survival. Further over were white goods: refrigerators and washing machines, which seemed almost surreal in their domesticity. Beyond that were television sets as big as doors, air-conditioners, stereo systems, towers of loudspeakers blasting nomad rhythms to the stars. Were there homes that still dreamed of power supplies and happy families in clean clothes? Perhaps they represented a kind of ideal for these warriors. A market of utopian dreams? One day they would put down their weapons and plug in their appliances and life would be good. Whatever it was, Kalonsha was clearly beyond the reach of any kind of law and order. Beyond any known logic, thought Makana as he passed an aircraft jet engine with Chinese characters on it. Were they still in Egypt? He wasn't sure. Sergeant Hamama's presence seemed to provoke no signs of nervousness. Here his uniform was really just a variation on a theme. Everyone was wearing the clothes of one army or another. Gaddafi's African Legion, the Interahamwe, along with a dozen other militias and scraps from the national armies of about ten countries.

Sergeant Hamama decided to remove the handcuffs. In a place devoted to liberty, market and otherwise, and ruled by lawlessness, restraints might be considered a provocation. As he wandered along behind the sergeant, Makana could hear the enterprising salesmen promising delivery in any of a dozen cities on the edge of the Great Sand Sea.

It was all so much like a dream that when Makana caught a glimpse of Daud Bulatt he was sure it was simply the product of his over-stimulated imagination. A half-seen silhouette. The distinctive shape of a man whose right arm was missing. Shadow and light swimming in and out of one another like two halves of a menacing dance, like snakes mating. His quarry disappeared,

386

ducking into a crowd of men gathered around the skeleton of a vehicle of some kind. All that remained was the chassis, a gearstick poking upwards like a flower in a graveyard. When the men shifted position the one-armed man was gone.

A hurricane lamp hissed by his ear as they passed a stall with a glass-sided cupboard crammed with trays of sticky baklawa. Crushed flies adorned the grubby panes. Behind it a string of coloured lightbulbs hung like incandescent fruit over another counter where a young boy was twirling strings of dough into cheese pastries.

'The first time I came here was twenty years ago.' Hamama was talking over his shoulder. 'It's been here all this time. Every now and then someone sends his army in to try and break it up, but there's nothing they can do. The people drift away and after a time they come back. New faces, new markets, new conflicts. That's flexibility. People just melt into the sand and reappear somewhere else. There is a demand and there is supply. It's been like this for centuries probably. Captain Mustafa never understood that.'

'That's why you killed him?'

'Among other things.' Sergeant Hamama shrugged. 'He objected to certain plans.'

'You mean the Qadi's business with the gas company?'

'He didn't understand. He thought he could change things. But this . . .' Hamama shook his head. 'You can't change this.'

Makana moved as the sergeant spoke. Hamama's hand was raised which blinded him on one side, and his focus was elsewhere. Makana knew there would be no better chance than this. He threw himself sideways so that he struck the sergeant with his shoulder. It was difficult to put much force into it from so close, but it was enough to knock Hamama off balance. The uneven ground helped and Sergeant Hamama stumbled into the nearest counter which subsequently collapsed, sending pots and pans, trays of food flying along with a vat of boiling oil that tipped over with a hiss. Hamama went down on one knee giving a howl when his hand came to rest on the scalding oil. By then Makana was already running, back through the crowd hoping to lose himself. Moving left and right, randomly changing direction. At first he tried to seek out large gatherings. The more people the better. He twisted and turned, suddenly finding himself trapped within a circle of men arguing over something. He could not understand what language they were speaking, but the way they were brandishing their weapons it was all about to turn nasty. Makana began slipping through looking for a way out when he bumped into someone. Apologising, he tried again, only to have the same thing happen. This time the response was a hard shove which sent him sprawling. As Makana started to pick himself up a pair of shiny military boots appeared in front of his face. They were on the end of a pair of fancy army trousers with lots of patches and pockets on them. Not standard military issue. The man wearing them was shaven-headed and muscular.

'Hello Makana,' he said.

'Lieutenant Sharqi.' Makana struggled to sit up. 'What a surprise.'

'I'd say the same, but nothing about you surprises me any more.'

'I didn't know you took an interest in smuggling.'

Sharqi's hard face betrayed little emotion. He was an ex-paratrooper, then a member of Egyptian Special Services. Specifically, Task Force 777, a counterterrorism unit founded in the wake of President Sadat's assassination. More recently, Sharqi had been promoted to running his own elite and rather shadowy unit within State Security. He gave the signal and two of his men hauled Makana to his feet and held him in check.

'Bring him along. We need to talk.'

'What's wrong with here?' Makana was reluctant to be led off into the dark. Sharqi smiled.

'I'm not going to lose you that easily. Watch your step, it's quite tricky.'

Sergeant Hamama burst breathlessly into sight, provoking a scuffle and some shoving among the other men who had been arguing earlier. They noticed his uniform and drifted away.

'There you are,' Hamama addressed Makana as he closed in. 'Now I'm going to teach you a lesson.' He clapped the handcuffs back onto his wrists.

'Nobody is teaching anyone anything here without my permission,' said Sharqi.

'Lieutenant Sharqi,' said Makana. 'This is the man you want. Sergeant Hamama has been running a smuggling ring in this area. He and his men are bringing in illicit alcohol, cigarettes, along with a range of electical appliances.'

'Nice try, Makana,' grunted Sharqi, turning to Hamama. 'You were told to bring him to us down in the gully on the other side. What happened?'

'That's what I was doing,' protested the sergeant. 'He's devious, this one. You want to keep a close eye on him.'

'Don't worry, he's not going to try anything with me.' Sharqi gave the signal for them to move on.

Murky shadows swelled up from beyond, dancing on the walls in the moving flame from scattered fires, writhing hypnotically. Then the light and noise faded, giving way to the silence of the vast landscape as the cliffs rose on either side of them. A few pockets of men still congregated here and there, consulting in low voices, away from the lighted spaces. The sound of banknotes being counted deciding the fate of far-off places. Conversations snaked over the sand with barely a whisper. Ahead of them a gap opened up in the wall of rock as the land dipped and a stony path dropped into the unbroken darkness that stretched out below. Makana concentrated on not stumbling. The sound of stones rolling underfoot carried on, echoing back from the walls. There was so little light that he could barely see where he was going. There were voices coming from below. As his eyes adjusted he could make out the small convoy of SUVs he had seen on Jebel Mawtah. Around them a group of shadows stood loosely placed. They looked up as the new arrivals stepped onto the track. Sharqi strode ahead.

'We've got our liaison man,' he said in English. Makana recognised the woman and man he had seen previously. The Americans.

'Well good for you, Sharqi,' laughed the woman.

'You might just pull this one off, buddy,' said the man.

'Just you wait and see.'

Another newcomer was waiting for them, seated inside an old Lada that Makana recognised. A sullen, puffy-faced man. Makana guessed this was Musab Khayr. As he opened the car door the interior light came on summoning a curse from Sharqi.

'Get that light off, you idiot. I told you, no lights showing!'

The light went off. There were no doubts who was running this show.

Sharqi turned to Makana and smiled. 'We've been keeping tabs on you since Cairo.'

Makana recalled the two men he thought had been following him in the Ghuriyya market. It seemed like a lifetime ago but was barely a week.

'Since you are now an integral part of this operation, I shall explain.' Sharqi put his hand on Makana's shoulder and led him to one side. He waved back the men who had escorted him. It was a formality. There was nowhere to run and Makana was in no doubt that Sharqi would shoot him dead on the spot before he had gone ten paces.

'A few months ago Musab came up on some list of possible terror suspects. You understand, our American friends are all a bit jumpy since 9/11. They started pulling in anyone with the slightest smudge against their name. So, Musab gets pulled off the streets of his comfortable European home and flown back here. You know how it is. They always want us to do their dirty work for them. In this case, to torture Musab and get the information from him. It's a legality issue. And besides, this is Egypt. We have our ways.' He might have been talking about the Olympic swimming team, or the triumphs of the national soccer side. Pride ran deep regardless. 'Makes no difference anyway,' Sharqi went on. 'The point is that the information Musab had was low grade and out of date. He was always small-time, never seriously involved in the jihadist movement. He saw it as a way out, as lots of them did. Now the problem is what to do with him. He doesn't have anything for us. Musab, of course, is terrified. He's been flown halfway around the world and this is not where he wants to be. So he offers to make a deal. It turns out he was in prison, near here in fact, in Al Wahat, with a certain Daud Bulatt.'

It was four years since Makana had come face-to-face with Bulatt for the first time. Bulatt had a history. Before he turned himself into a jihadi, he had been running a violent gang in Cairo. He was tied in to a case Makana was working on and when he caught up with him Bulatt had just blown up a holiday resort on the Red Sea.

'The last I heard Bulatt had fled across the border into Sudan.'

'Exactly, under the protective wing of your old friend, Mek Nimr.'

Bulatt had been hiding in Sudan for years and he knew he would find shelter there again. Mek Nimr had asked Bulatt to kill Makana and on that occasion he could have done so easily. For his own reasons he had chosen not to.

There was one piece that still puzzled Makana, but for the moment he would have to let that go. Sharqi was calling the tune.

'So Musab offers to bring Bulatt to you?'

'You catch on quickly,' Sharqi smiled. He was overdoing the friendliness. Trying too hard to put Makana at ease, which made him worried all over again. 'It seems that our friend Bulatt has become something of an embarrassment. In the post 9/11 world everyone wants to wash their hands of the Islamist threat. It's too dangerous. Someone has stirred the sleeping giant and everyone knows somebody is going to get hurt. Today Afghanistan, tomorrow, who knows? Maybe the Americans decide you've killed enough Southerners and intervene in your civil war?'

'So Mek Nimr is eager to play along.'

'Your friend Mek Nimr has come a long way. He's a big fish now. Years of rubbing shoulders with terrorists have turned him into a valuable asset. So he's co-operating. He will give us what we want.'

'What has any of this to do with me?'

'In return for helping us so generously, Mek Nimr has asked for a certain amount of money to be placed in a bank account of his own choosing, and for you to be returned to him.' Sharqi went on quietly. 'He must miss you.'

'Why me?'

'You'll have a chance to ask him that yourself before too long. He's just across the border waiting for you.'

Makana glanced over his shoulder at the darkness. 'How is the exchange to take place?'

'Musab has the details. Between the two of us he's a pompous pain in the ass, insists that he is in charge. I suppose he wants to impress the Americans.'

'What happens once I'm handed over?'

'Nothing. We wish you a safe life and good prospects, or whatever. I don't think we'll be seeing you again anytime soon.'

'You know that he'll kill me.'

'We don't know that. Not for certain.' Sharqi paused. 'Maybe he's had a change of heart now that he's such a big star.'

'Is he really that big?'

'They fly him to Washington DC on their Gulfstream jets.'

'That's good is it?' Makana managed to reach into his pocket for his cigarettes. Almost a whole packet. He wondered if he would get a chance to smoke them.

'A private jet from here to Washington? I don't get treated like that.'

'It'll come,' nodded Makana. 'You obviously know how to make an impression.' He tilted his head towards the American couple who stood off to one side talking in low voices.

'To be honest with you, I don't know what all the fuss is about. Daud Bulatt was our problem. He's not a terrorist mastermind.'

'Maybe you're underestimating him.'

'Yeah, and maybe you have too much time on your hands.' Sharqi snatched the cigarette from Makana's mouth and ground it out under his heel. Then he whistled and made a signal with his hand in the air. The men began moving towards the vehicles. 'You ride with our friend and the fat policeman.'

Sergeant Hamama and Musab were waiting by the Lada.

'We will be three minutes behind you. When you reach the meeting point don't hang around. Make the exchange and move on.'

'Are you sure they won't see you?' asked Musab.

'Don't worry about it. We're professionals.'

Just the kind of reassurance that made you feel worse, thought Makana as he climbed into the back seat of the Lada. Sergeant Hamama leaned in and clipped the handcuffs through the hand-rail over the door.

'That'll keep you from getting any ideas,' he said. Then he went round and climbed into the passenger seat. 'Are you sure you remember the way?' he asked.

'I remember,' muttered Musab as he turned the ignition. They rolled up the stony track and came up into the open plain. It was pitch black. Musab must have meant what he said. He paused and leaned forward from time to time to look at the sky. He was navigating by the stars. Small-time crook he may have been but someone had taught him about travelling in the desert. Makana had seen guides like this before. It was impressive to see them work, especially at the speed of a moving vehicle.

'What exactly are you getting in return for me?'

Musab's eyes never left the road. 'Weapons, for the Palestinian people.'

'The Palestinians?' Even Sergeant Hamama thought that was a little far out. Makana was silent. Something felt very wrong here. Sharqi could not be making a deal allowing weapons for the Palestinians into the country. That could set off a war between Egypt and Israel faster than you could strike a match.

'It's all a set-up,' Musab went on, stifling a yawn. 'The Israelis kill a few militants in Gaza. The Egyptians arrest a few people on this side of the border and everyone looks like they are doing their bit in this stupid war on terror.' Musab chuckled to himself. He seemed to have it all worked out. Makana craned his neck to look back to see if he could catch sight of the three Jeeps. Strangely, it would have been a comfort to know that Sharqi was close by. All he saw was blackness. If Sharqi and his team were following close behind they were doing a good job of concealing themselves. He grasped the handrail and used all his weight on it. To his satisfaction he felt it give slightly.

'One thing I don't understand,' said Makana, leaning forward. 'Why did you kill your own daughter?'

Musab grunted. 'I didn't.'

Sergeant Hamama chuckled. 'Some investigator.'

'But you went to see Karima, just after you escaped,' Makana persisted.

'I had nowhere else to go. I thought it would be a good place to hide.'

'You set fire to the place. Was it because she wasn't your daughter?'

'You seem to know a lot about it.' Musab looked at Makana in the rear-view mirror. 'Why so much interest?'

'He's working for some rich lawyer in Cairo.'

'Ragab?' Musab sneered. 'Well you can tell him from me I wouldn't stoop that low, either for her, or that whore of a mother of hers.'

They drove on for half an hour before Musab murmured, 'There they are.'

Makana followed his finger and could make out two heavy

shapes that stood out against the sand. Rigid, square shapes that looked like lorries. The Lada pulled up alongside and Musab got out. 'You'll do the driving from here,' he said to Sergeant Hamama. 'I'll direct you.'

Makana thought they looked like the Magirus-Deutz lorries he had seen at the depot on the road out of town. They looked empty. A couple of figures broke away from the shadows to meet Musab as he approached.

Sergeant Hamama climbed in behind the wheel. 'I don't like this,' he murmured.

'A little out of your depth here, are you, Sergeant?'

'I don't know who these people are. This wasn't what I understood at all.'

'What were you told?'

'Like with any shipment, I would guide them into the depot and then check the goods and that would be the end of it. I get my share and the goods go out according to supply.'

'So you had no idea what they were bringing in?'

'Certainly not weapons for the Palestinians.' Sergeant Hamama was chewing gum fiercely. 'You don't get involved in politics. That's the rule. This is a business deal.'

'That's what Musab told you.'

'Between you and me I wasn't that keen on letting him back in, but he made out that he had money to invest. I figured we do one deal together and see how it goes.'

'So he played you.'

Sergeant Hamama twisted in his seat. 'Can you see anything out there?'

Makana looked. 'Probably Sharqi and his men.'

'No, they would be coming from over there.' Hamama pointed a little further to the left. 'And I can't see any sign of them either.'

Musab returned and climbed into the passenger seat. 'All set,' he said

'The sooner the better,' said Hamama, as he started the engine. 'You lied to me.'

'Take it easy. This is a good deal. It pays well and it puts the security forces in our debt. We will have a friend to call on if we ever have trouble in the future. So just relax.'

The big diesel engines broke into life with a sharp series of coughs. They grumbled as the drivers revved them up. Each of them flashed their lights to signal they were ready.

The Lada took off with an awkward lurch and Musab pointed them south again, further into the desert.

'Did you take care of Wad Nubawi?' Musab murmured.

'Yes.' Hamama had other things on his mind. 'How do you know we can trust them? They're State Security. They could turn us in at any moment.'

'Why would they do that?' Musab asked. 'Look, trust me, it's almost done. All we have to do now is transfer the weapons to our lorries and hand the shipment to Sharqi. He's probably expecting a medal or something.'

'And then you're free?' Even Hamama seemed incredulous.

'Oh, well, you know how it is.' Musab gave a dismissive wave. 'I promised to keep passing them information.' He glanced over at Hamama. 'What's the matter? Not happy?'

'I just don't trust them, that's all.'

'Well, you don't have to trust them, I do. If you had any idea what they did to me in that place . . .' Musab stared straight ahead of him, at the unbroken darkness. 'You wouldn't believe it.'

'*Hamdilay salamah*,' muttered Sergeant Hamama.

'The point is that I'm back. We're partners now. Things have changed.'

Sergeant Hamama tossed his gum out of the open window and reached for his tobacco. They changed direction. The wind threw sand grains at them that screeched softly along the side of the Lada like the scrape of tiny fingernails. Out through the windscreen a pair of yellow eyes glowed briefly in the headlights before vanishing. A desert fox? A nocturnal creature of some kind? What appeared silent and empty was in fact no more than a soft veil drawn over teeming life. The Lada was old and held together now more by habit than by sound mechanics. Although the handrail was not entirely solid it was still firmly attached. Makana worked it back and forth to loosen it.

'I thought I saw Daud Bulatt back there.'

'Who?' Sergeant Hamama asked, tucking snuff into his cheek.

Musab glanced back at Makana. 'What do you know about Bulatt?'

'Only that he's a fairly dangerous character to mess with.'

'In Kalonsha? You can't have seen him there.' Musab sought out Makana's eyes in the mirror.

'Maybe I did, and maybe you don't know who you are dealing with.'

'It's not your concern.'

'I think it is, since you've decided to hand me over in exchange for him.'

'Who is this Bulatt you're talking about?' growled Hamama.

'He's a jihadist,' Makana said. 'The serious kind, not like our friend here. He lost an arm to Soviet special forces in Chechnya.'

'And where does he come into this?' Sergeant Hamama spat carefully out of the window.

'He's what this is all about,' said Makana.

'I like this less and less.' Sergeant Hamama cursed and spat again, this time getting most of it on his uniform.

'It'll be fine. He's trying to make you nervous.' Musab gave Makana a wary glance.

Through the rear window Makana saw the two lorries moving quickly behind them. Beyond that he caught a brief glimpse of something glinting in the starlight. Sharqi and his boys following along at a distance.

'What is that?' Sergeant Hamama was squinting out through the side window.

'What?' asked Musab.

'There. To the right. I thought I saw something.' Hamama had slowed down and was squinting out of the window. Makana saw nothing. 'Where are they supposed to be meeting us?'

'We're not there yet,' said Musab, glancing at his wristwatch. 'They should be waiting for us up ahead at the well.'

Almost before he had finished speaking five sets of powerful headlights came on to their right, illuminating everything. The inside of the Lada was lit up as if the sun had suddenly appeared over the horizon. Hamama cursed and slammed on the brakes.

'What is this?' Musab asked.

There was a long silence, broken only by the hum of engines. In the distance behind them the hiss of hydraulic brakes could be heard and the lorries came to a halt.

'What *is* this?' Musab repeated, opening the door.

'Don't get out,' Hamama warned. He sounded nervous.

'Don't stop here, keep moving.' Makana felt the handrail give.

'Don't be stupid. We have to stop. But this is not where we agreed. Let me see what's wrong.' Musab slipped out and began walking towards the lights, one hand held up to shield his eyes from the glare.

'Drive on,' Makana urged Hamama. 'There's still a chance, but you have to move now.'

It was too late, though, much too late. Heavy-calibre machine guns mounted in the back of the vehicles fired with a dull, regular thump. Musab disintegrated in the blast. His upper body came apart. Bullets slammed into the Lada. The wheels sank onto their rims as the tyres burst. The windows cracked, smashed, flew into shards, the engine expired. The whole car rattled and shook as if in the grip of a fever. Makana flung himself out through the door. He heard Hamama give a terrible cry. Shells slammed into the uphol-stery, the framework. Makana crawled behind the rear wheel and drew his knees up, squeezing himself into the smallest possible size. He heard Hamama groaning in the front seat. Further away the roar of diesel engines as the lorry drivers turned and fled. The shooting stopped. The Lada was still making noises. Steam hissed from the front and hot metal was clicking somewhere. The lights went off and the world was plunged back into darkness.

'Help,' Hamama groaned. 'Help me, please.'

Makana waited until he heard the whine of the Land Cruisers racing away, then he slowly straightened up. There was blood on his face and arm where he'd been hit by flying glass or metal. His legs were shaking so hard he could barely stand. The Lada was riddled with holes. A blue flame flickered beneath the engine. When he pulled open the driver's door Sergeant Hamama fell heavily into his arms. As he lowered him to the sand he screamed in pain. Both his legs had been shattered.

'You have to help me,' he pleaded, clutching Makana to him.

'A moment ago you were happy to hand me over to certain death.' Makana found the key in the sergeant's pocket and freed himself of the handcuffs.

'Come on, I had no choice. Those were the terms.' Hamama's voice was hoarse, his face twisted in agony. 'You've got to help me. I need a doctor.'

'There are no doctors out here, and I can't carry you.'

No sign of Sharqi and his boys either. Maybe that was part of the plan too. Or maybe they just ran for cover. Makana surveyed the darkness around him. The thick mass of stars overhead. The silence that had absorbed the noise and fury.

'Hey! Where are you going? Come back! Help me!'

Makana considered the idea. Then he thought about Rashida and Luqman and finally about Zahra. He didn't look back. He simply turned and began walking, straight into the darkness.

Chapter Thirty-six

After the immense silence and open space of the desert, the city fell over him like a cloak. And while the congestion felt oddly alien, it also came as a relief. The traffic surged with the same feral intensity, lights flashed in quick succesion like a series of silent detonations, people hurried through the shadows as if seeking shelter from the onslaught. Sindbad was waiting by the battered old black and white Datsun, a sorrier and more welcome sight Makana could not imagine.

'*Ahlan wasahlan, hamdilay salamah, ya basha.*'

Sindbad looked in vain for a bag to carry and, loyal as he was, concealed his dismay at the lamentable state of Makana's clothes.

'The journey was fruitful, I hope?'

Makana sighed as he climbed into the car, removing a damp package of what appeared to be a large fish wrapped in newspaper.

'My wife,' muttered Sindbad in a tone of despair as he chucked the offensive passenger into the back. 'She insists we eat fish twice a week. I tell her if Allah had intended for us to eat that much fish he would have given us whiskers and a tail. A man needs meat, wouldn't you agree?' He broke off when he realised that Makana was not in the mood for idle banter. 'A thousand apologies, *ya basha*, and a thousand blessings for arriving safely.'

Makana sat quietly. For a moment he felt as though he was still detached from this place, still in that bus rolling through the desert. In time the memory would fade from his body like a fever, leaving only a distant trace of its having passed through him, but for now he felt like a man who hovered somewhere between this world and the next. A time that now seemed like a long dream. For two days he had slept and walked and shivered and sweated. He lay on the ground and listened for the approach of scavangers. Two days was the time it had taken him to walk back to the main road and find a lift back into Siwa. Two days during which he was no less than a step away from dropping to the ground and letting the sun do its work.

They sat there in the car for a time. Makana smoked a cigarette and Sindbad said nothing; he knew better than to disturb the great man while he was thinking. After a time Makana stirred and turned to look at Sindbad as if wondering how he had got to this place.

'There are a couple of stops we have to make before you take me home.'

'I am at your command, *ya basha*.'

Sami Barakat was expecting Makana. They had already spoken on the phone and so he was somewhat prepared, although his friend's gaunt appearance shocked him more than he cared to admit. Rania let out a cry of alarm when she set eyes on him and the two of them stood there staring at Makana as if he was, indeed, the ghost of the person they had formerly known. When their business was concluded they agreed to meet again the next day to talk things over at length.

It would be safe to say that Magdy Ragab on the other hand

was not expecting Makana, who had chosen not to announce his arrival by telephoning ahead. Being familiar with his client's habits, Makana had a fairly good idea that the lawyer would be home on a Friday evening at this time. A maid showed him into an elaborate salon for receiving visitors. The room was weighed down with a heavy assembly of furniture in the ornate Louis XIV style so popular among the middle classes. Chairs and divans with clumsy feet and tightly buttoned upholstery, the arms and back adorned with elaborate carvings. A large green marble mantelpiece framed a fireplace over which a stained, gilt-edged mirror revealed the sorry state Makana was in. His hair was full of sand, his face blasted by wind and sun and his clothes tattered and torn. Makana turned his back on his own image, thinking that this probably explained the maid's look of disapproval. It may also have applied to the acute concern in the expressions of Ragab when he entered the room, and his wife who arrived close on his heels.

The couple were dressed informally. He wore slippers and a paisley dressing gown over a white shirt and dark trousers. He was smoking a pipe and looked for all the world like a character who had stepped out of a French period drama. His wife was dressed somewhat less stylishly: a dull-brown tracksuit whose shapelessness did little to complement her dumpy figure. They sat together on the divan, while Makana preferred to remain standing, his back to the mirror.

'I wasn't expecting to see you, having not heard . . .' Ragab began. Right from the outset there was an air of disappointment, as if nothing Makana could say or do would rectify this breach of protocol. He reached into the pocket of his gown to produce an envelope which he placed on the low white coffee table. 'I suppose this is what you came for.'

Makana picked up the envelope and peeked inside at the bundle of banknotes. He set it quietly back on the table.

'I think perhaps you'd better hear what I have to say first.'

'Very well,' nodded Ragab, folding his arms and sitting back. 'First of all, I am assuming that you have not managed to solve the case. You didn't find the man who killed Karima?'

'I'll come to that in a moment. But to begin with I'd like to take you back to the beginning,' Makana said. 'Mrs Ragab, you were worried that your husband was involved with another woman, which is why you originally contracted my services.'

'I know,' she twittered coyly. 'I can't think why I ever got such a foolish thought into my head.' She glanced at her husband. Clearly the matrimonial rift had been healed, if it had ever existed. There was no gesture of physical affection, which would have been unseemly, but the degree of intimacy and trust between them was plain. For his part, however, Ragab looked uncomfortable at such displays in front of a stranger. He scowled at the bowl of his pipe as he tamped down the tobacco with his finger and bent the flame of an expensive gold lighter to it.

'In a way,' he puffed magnanimously, 'we could say that we owe you a debt, Mr Makana. You have brought our marriage back to life after all these years.' He gestured at the envelope. 'That is the reason you will find I have been a little more generous than necessary in calculating your fee.'

'I'm very grateful, I'm sure. But if you will bear with me,' Makana said. 'I need to just lay things out in the right order. Now, as you know, I followed you for several days and discovered nothing that justified any of Madame's suspicions. Until the final day, that is, when I followed you to the Garnata Clinic and Karima.'

'Yes,' Ragab shook his head to himself. 'Such a tragedy.'

'Yes, indeed. And unnecessary.'

'Unnecessary?' Ragab queried. 'How can you say that?'

'The fire was started by someone. We are agreed on that. That is what you asked me to investigate. I believed it was connected to Musab. He was on the run. He had returned home and something had gone wrong. I learned that he had been recently tortured and that can turn a man's head. He was terrified of being caught again and sent back. He was also suspicious of Karima. He never really believed she was his daughter. He had been convinced that Nagat had been unfaithful to him while he was in prison. In short, Mr Ragab, he believed Karima to be your daughter.'

Ragab champed his teeth down on the stem of his pipe. 'It's true that he was paranoid, even in the old days. He trusted no one, including myself. I assured him many times that I would never have committed such a dishonourable act. But I told you all of this before.'

'Yes, of course.' Makana tilted his head in concession. 'I just need to clarify things.'

'I understand, for the record. Very well, please go on.'

'Well,' said Makana. 'I began to wonder if perhaps Musab was not the only person to suspect Karima of being your daughter.'

Mrs Ragab had appeared to have lost interest in the conversation. She not only did not speak, she barely seemed to be breathing. When Makana's eyes came to rest on her she shifted in her seat.

'Who else might have suspected that all those years ago her husband had been unfaithful? Even more, that he had maintained the outcome of that brief liaison secret all these years? Wouldn't that be enough to provoke a fit of jealous rage?'

Makana paused for long enough to light a cigarette. He tossed the matchstick into the fireplace before realising that it was meant as mere decoration. 'Somebody started that fire with the deliberate intention of trying to kill Karima, regardless of who else was in the house.'

Neither of the Ragabs said a word. Makana went on. 'For a long time I struggled to try and make the facts fit into this picture. I couldn't. The problem was that I assumed Karima's death was the result of jealousy, or some twisted sense of honour. Either on the part of Musab, or . . . someone else.' Makana glanced at Mrs Ragab but left the rest unsaid. He reached in his pocket for the sheet of paper Sami had given him. 'I took a chance in going to Siwa, but I was angry about Karima. I wasn't thinking clearly. All I could think was that she had been young and she had died a painful and unjust death. I was convinced Musab was the key and that I would find him in Siwa. It was a risk, but in this business sometimes you have to take risks to make progress.'

Magdy Ragab shifted his weight and crossed his legs. His pipe had gone out and after a time he gave up trying to puff it back into life and took it out of his mouth and just stared at it.

'I learned a lot in Siwa,' Makana went on. 'It's surprising how much goes on in such a quiet place. You'd be amazed.'

'I've never been,' said Mrs Ragab. She was picking at a loose thread on her sleeve.

'No, but your husband has.'

'For business,' Ragab shrugged indifferently.

'Yes, exactly. And that's what began to interest me.' Makana unfolded the sheet of paper. 'Do you know a man named Nadir Diyab? You should. He's a lawyer who used to work for your company.'

'Yes, I recall him, vaguely.' Ragab was irritated.

407

'Mr Diyab was in charge of taking care of some important business in Siwa. He was buying up land, very valuable land it turns out for an investment company he set up called Arousa Resources. A survey company named LandTech believes there are substantial gas deposits just to the east of the town.' Makana shrugged. 'I really don't know a great deal about the subject, but Mr Diyab was very helpful when a colleague of mine contacted him posing as a potential investor. The land is private. Whoever owns that land stands to make a small fortune. LandTech say it's not worth mounting the extraction operation unless they have access to the entire area. As it happens, Arousa Resources has been busy doing just that, buying up plots of land over the years with the idea of creating a package to sell to the developers. In this they were helped by the local Qadi who had a substantial stake in Arousa. They had almost achieved their goal, but there was only one outstanding plot left and it belonged to an old Siwan family who had fallen on hard times, the Abubakrs.'

Ragab flapped a hand through his pipesmoke in protest. 'I understand your need to clarify the details, Mr Makana, but I really can't see where this is leading.'

'I assure you, I am doing this as fast as I can.' Makana smiled as graciously as he could. Mrs Ragab looked as though she might be sick. 'Musab had signed over his legal rights to you years ago and so it wouldn't have been difficult for you to take care of his side of the ownership. Karima was the problem. You could have offered to buy the land but she might have become suspicious. Why would you want a worthless piece of farmland on the other side of the country? You would have had to explain your interest but then she might have demanded a substantial share, or even worse, decide to hold onto the land and sell it herself.'

'This is preposterous. Pure speculation. I have never been so insulted in my life.'

Makana ignored Ragab. He felt suddenly tired, weary of a world driven by material gain. Weary of greed, weary of stupidity. 'You took care of Karima's affairs. She was a simple girl. She knew nothing about gas or land. She ran a small shop in the market selling foam mattresses and pillows. But she had known you since she was a baby and she trusted you, but when you asked her to sign a document making you her legal executor, she grew suspicious and refused. What happened then? Did she accuse you of taking advantage of her, of trying to profit from her?'

'I protest!' Magdy Ragab got to his feet.

His wife put a hand on his arm and said quietly, 'Sit down.'

'I imagine that must have annoyed you. A mere peasant of a girl getting in the way of your plans? Who was she anyway? Still, she posed a problem and getting rid of her wasn't going to be easy. You needed a witness to prove that you had nothing to do with it. That was where I came in. Mrs Ragab gave me the story about her fears you were seeing another woman behind her back and so I followed you. For that whole week I provided the alibi you needed to prove you not only had nothing to do with Karima's death, but that you were heartbroken, devastated and spared no expense to try and save her. I was the perfect witness.'

'You have not a shred of evidence for this fairy tale you are spinning. It belongs in the *Thousand and One Nights*!' Ragab puffed himself up.

'Then Musab turned up, quite by coincidence, to provide the perfect scapegoat. Nobody was supposed to know that he was in the country, but a man like yourself, with connections high up inside the Ministry of the Interior, would have a friend somewhere who might just warn him that his old client had turned up. You knew that I would pursue Musab if I found out, and so you leaked it to a certain member of the press. Remember that evening when you visited me and you were studying the newspaper cuttings on the wall of my office? That was where you got Sami Barakat's name.'

Ragab sank back down in his chair as Makana continued. The fight seemed to have gone out of him, or perhaps he was gathering his thoughts.

'You knew that I would in all likelihood not find anything in Siwa. You knew why Musab could never go back there. Your friend the Qadi would have confirmed that for you. Your efforts to find the killer no matter the expense would only add to your innocence.'

'You have no evidence,' Ragab spoke in a low voice. 'Nothing to back up your claims.'

'Perhaps, but the same member of the press who was so useful to you will be happy to make the whole story public and I imagine that will not help your reputation. Then there is the matter of the fire itself. I can't imagine you would dirty your hands yourself, so someone in your employ would have set the fire. Let's see how they respond to police questioning.'

Downstairs in the street, Makana stood for a moment and waited as Okasha climbed out of his car and came towards him. A dozen policemen ran past and into the building.

'I've softened him up for you, but you'll have your work cut out.'

'I have a feeling I'm going to enjoy this. Aren't you going to stick around?' Okasha asked.

But Makana was already gone, walking with purpose.

Chapter Thirty-seven

The late afternoon sun played its golden light on the water bringing a timelessness to the scene. The sound of children's laughter drifted across the river from the playground on the Zamalek side as the chatter slowed down and everyone sank back into their own thoughts. Okasha was settled back in the big chair talking into his telephone. Sami and Rania were sprawled on the sofa talking in low voices, while Sindbad was gathering up plates to go downstairs and take care of the kitchen. He had produced rather a splendid feast, proving himself to be a man of many talents. The party was partly to welcome Makana back to town after his excursion to Siwa, and also to give them all a chance to catch up.

Makana stepped out to lean on the railings. In the thickening twilight a single heron floated by on a raft of papyrus, looking for all the world like a hieroglyphic that had come to life. He was tired of talking. It seemed he had done nothing but talk for the last three hours. Now, as night was falling, he felt the exhaustion of his long walk through the desert sinking into his bones. He would be asleep in seconds if he closed his eyes. Instead he lit a cigarette and watched the pale ghost of a moon rising over the city's lights. The sound of the others chatting was a welcome background. It felt as though perhaps this was the closest he was ever going to get to the idea of home.

'Were you scared?'

He turned to find Aziza standing behind him. She had been given special permission to attend the meal by Umm Ali who made her promise not to bother the *bash muhandis* and his guests. She was an odd little girl with her hair sticking out in all directions and her eye that wasn't quite straight. For the occasion she was wearing her best dress, a dark-green outfit that looked as though it had been handed down once too often.

'In the desert, you mean?'

Aziza nodded.

'Sometimes,' said Makana. He wasn't thinking so much about the ambush, but about the long game Sharqi had tried to play. Exchanging one terrorist for another. No mention had appeared in the paper of Daud Bulatt which described a plot that had been foiled by State Security and Investigations. Jihadists, planning to exploit public anger about the Israeli incursion into the West Bank by creating an armed uprising in this country, had been stopped. Musab Khayr, a key terrorist on the world's list of wanted men, had been killed.

'Are there scary animals out there?'

'A few,' said Makana. 'But most of them are more scared of us than we are of them. They keep away.'

'What did you think about when you were out there alone at night?'

What did he think about? Out there everything seemed jumbled up in the mind, the way the stars seemed to turn in a confusion that was impossible to comprehend.

'I thought about my daughter, Nasra.'

It was Aziza's turn to nod. 'I'll bet she knows you're thinking about her.'

'I hope she does,' said Makana.

A NOTE ON THE AUTHOR

Parker Bilal is the pseudonym of Jamal Mahjoub. Mahjoub has
published several critically acclaimed literary novels, which have been
widely translated. *The Ghost Runner* is his third Makana Mystery. Born
in London, Mahjoub has lived at various times in the UK, Sudan,
Cairo and Denmark. He currently lives in Barcelona.

A NOTE ON THE TYPE

The text of this book is set in Baskerville, named after John Baskerville
of Birmingham (1706–1775). The original punches cut by him still
survive. His widow sold them to Beaumarchais, from where they passed
through several French foundries to Deberney & Peignot in Paris,
before finding their way to Cambridge University Press.

DON'T MISS OUT ON THE COMPLETE
MAKANA MYSTERY SERIES

"Shows modern Cairo as a superbly exciting, edgy and dangerous setting for crime fiction."
—The Times

THE GOLDEN SCALES

ISBN: 978-1-60819-796-5
eISBN: 978-1-60819-795-8

The first Makana Mystery takes place in 1998. Makana accepts a case for the corrupt owner of a soccer team, setting him on a treacherous course toward an encounter with an enemy from his past.

"An enthralling read."
—The Guardian

DOGSTAR RISING

ISBN: 978-1-62040-531-4
eISBN: 978-1-62040-130-9

Set in summer 2001 against a backdrop of religious mistrust. Makana's case seems like no more than a family feud, until he discovers links to a series of murders—and becomes the sole witness to another.

"Bilal's story has a depth and resonance which stretches far beyond its cast of characters."
—The Independent

Available now wherever books are sold
www.bloomsbury.com